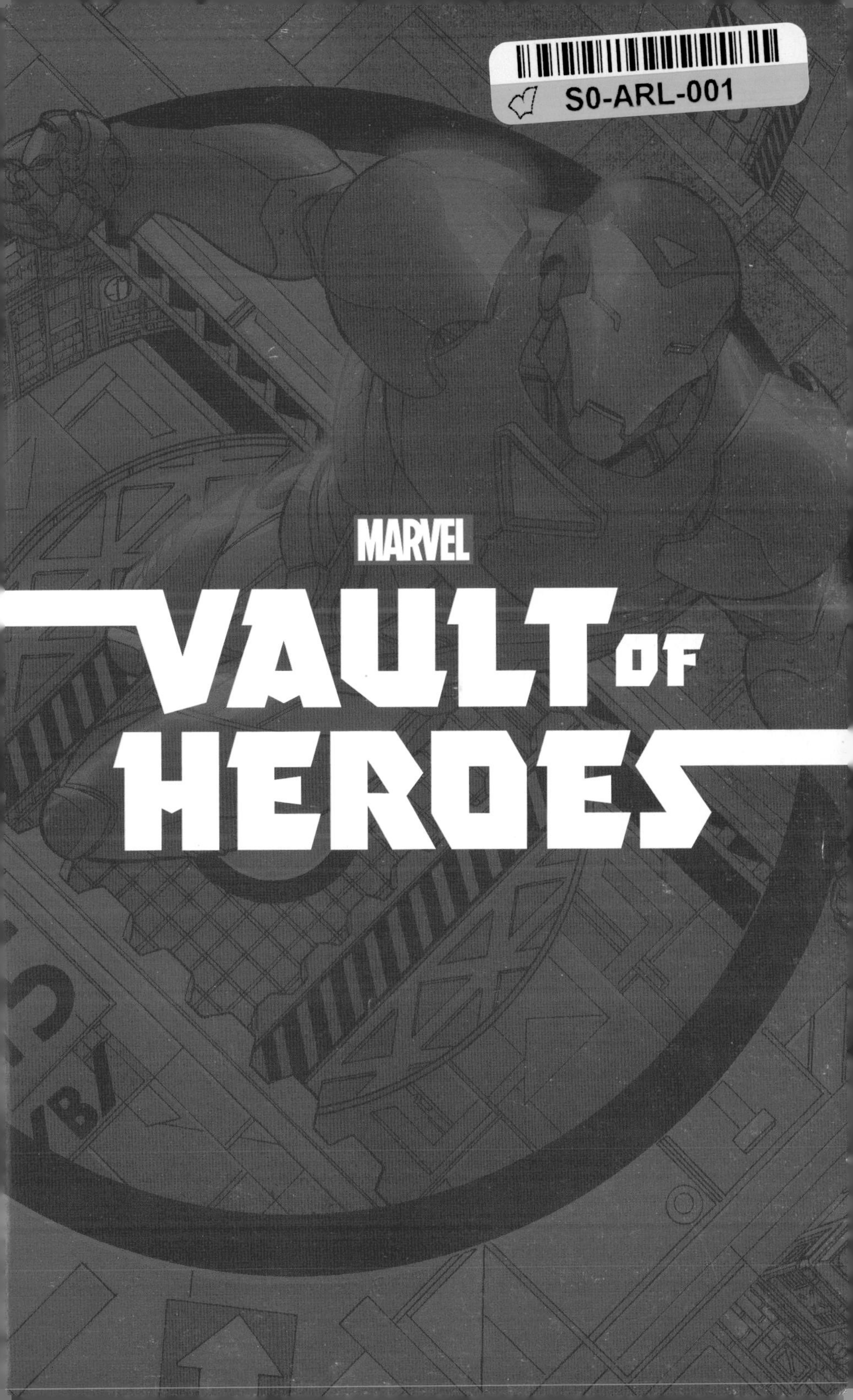

MARVEL

VAULT OF HEROES

ISBN: 978-1-68405-734-4   23 22 21 20   1 2 3 4

Cover Art by
Michael Golden

Collection Edits by
Alonzo Simon and
Zac Boone

Collection Design by
Jeff Powell

Originally published by MARVEL as MARVEL ADVENTURES: IRON MAN issues #1, 3–9, and MARVEL ADVENTURES: IRON MAN & HULK 2007 FREE COMIC BOOK DAY.

Jerry Bennington, President
Nachie Marshum, Publisher
Cara Morrison, Chief Financial Officer
Matthew Ruzicka, Chief Accounting Officer
Rebekah Cahalin, EVP of Operations
John Barber, Editor-in-Chief
Justin Eisinger, Editorial Director, Graphic Novels & Collections
Scott Dunbier, Director, Special Projects
Blake Kobashigawa, VP of Sales
Lorelei Bunjes, VP of Technology & Information Services
Anna Morrow, Sr Marketing Director
Tara McCrillis, Director of Design & Production
Mike Ford, Director of Operations
Shauna Monteforte, Manufacturing Operations Director

Ted Adams and Robbie Robbins, IDW Founders

Marvel Publishing:

VP Production & Special Projects: Jeff Youngquist

Editor, Juvenile Publishing: Lauren Bisom

Assistant Editor, Special Projects: Caitlin O'Connell

VP Licensed Publishing: Sven Larsen

SVP Print, Sales & Marketing: David Gabriel

Editor In Chief: C.B. Cebulski

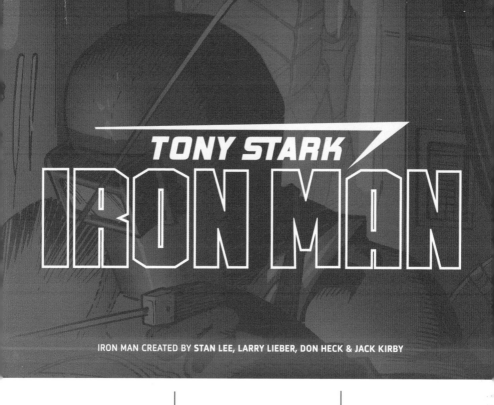

TONY STARK
IRON MAN

IRON MAN CREATED BY **STAN LEE, LARRY LIEBER, DON HECK & JACK KIRBY**

• ISSUE 01
The Titanium Trap
WRITTEN BY **FRED VAN LENTE**
PENCILS BY **JAMES CORDEIRO**
INKS BY **SCOTT KOBLISH**
COLORS BY **MARTE GRACIA**
LETTERS BY **NATE PIEKOS**

• ISSUE 02
Heart of Steel
WRITTEN BY **FRED VAN LENTE**
PENCILS BY **JAMES CORDEIRO**
INKS BY **SCOTT KOBLISH**
COLORS BY **MARTE GRACIA**
LETTERS BY **NATE PIEKOS**

• ISSUE 03
The Creeping Doom
WRITTEN BY **FRED VAN LENTE**
PENCILS BY **RONAN CLIQUET**
INKS BY **AMILTON SANTOS**
COLORS BY **MARTE GRACIA**
LETTERS BY **NATE PIEKOS**

• ISSUE 04
Hostile Takeover
WRITTEN BY **FRED VAN LENTE**
PENCILS BY **JAMES CORDEIRO**
INKS BY **GARY ERSKINE**
COLORS BY **MARTE GRACIA**
LETTERS BY **NATE PIEKOS**

• ISSUE 05
Pirated!
WRITTEN BY **FRED VAN LENTE**
PENCILS BY **RAFA SANDOVAL**
INKS BY **ROGER BONET**
COLORS BY **MARTE GRACIA**
LETTERS BY **DAVE SHARPE**

• ISSUE 06
Destructive Reentry
WRITTEN BY **FRED VAN LENTE**
PENCILS BY **JAMES CORDEIRO**
INKS BY **GARY ERSKINE**
COLORS BY **MARTE GRACIA**
LETTERS BY **DAVE SHARPE**

• ISSUE 07
Ghost of a Chance
WRITTEN BY **FRED VAN LENTE**
PENCILS BY **GRAHAM NOLAN**
INKS BY **VICTOR OLAZABA**
COLORS BY **MARTE GRACIA**
LETTERS BY **DAVE SHARPE**

• ISSUE 08
The Simple Life
WRITTEN BY **FRED VAN LENTE**
PENCILS BY **RAFA SANDOVAL**
INKS BY **ROGER BONET**
COLORS BY **ULISES ARREOLA**
LETTERS BY **DAVE SHARPE**

• ISSUE 09
The Bunker
WRITTEN BY **FRED VAN LENTE**
PENCILS BY **GRAHAM NOLAN**
INKS BY **VICTOR OLAZABA**
COLORS BY **MARTE GRACIA**
LETTERS BY **DAVE SHARPE**

01

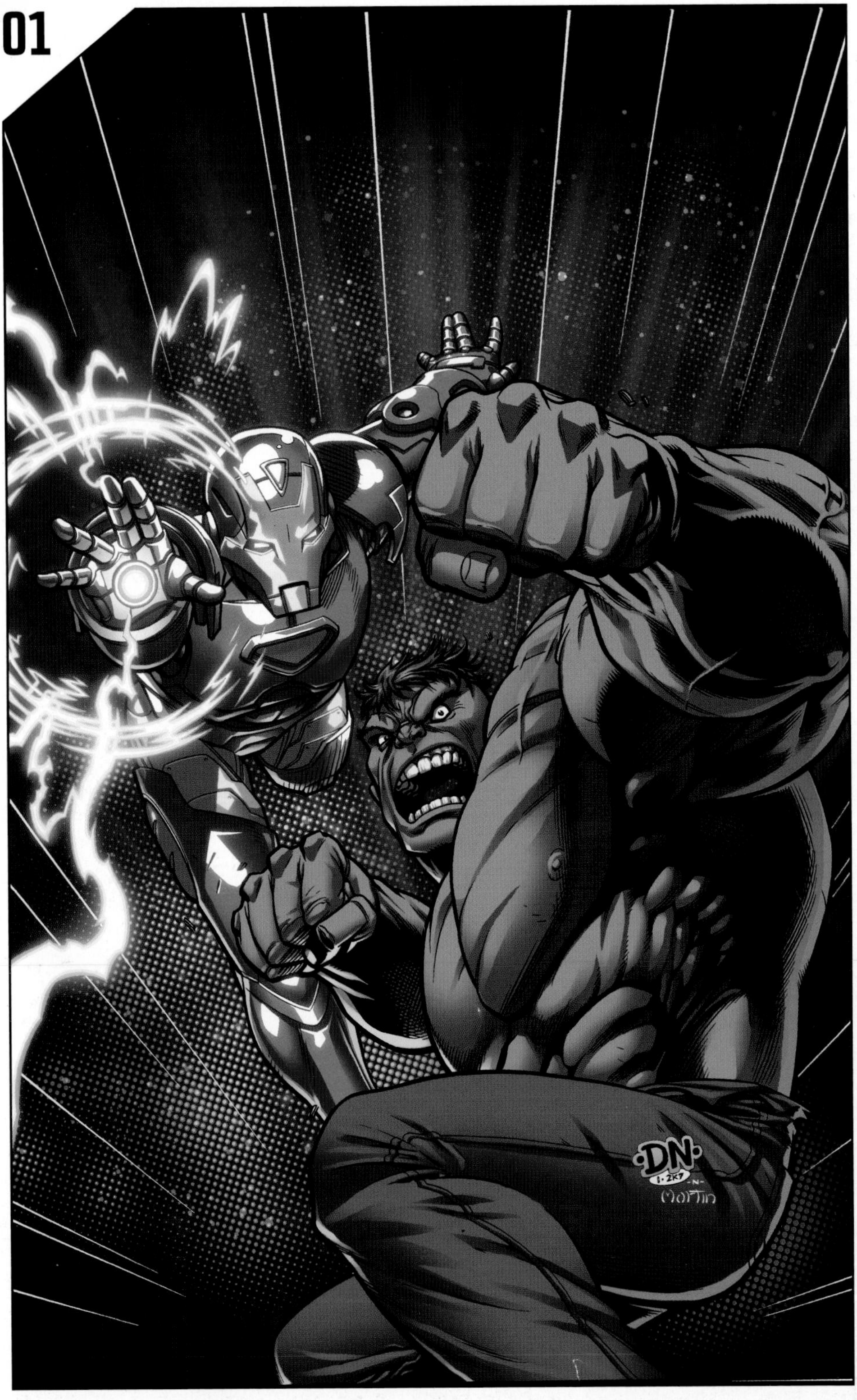

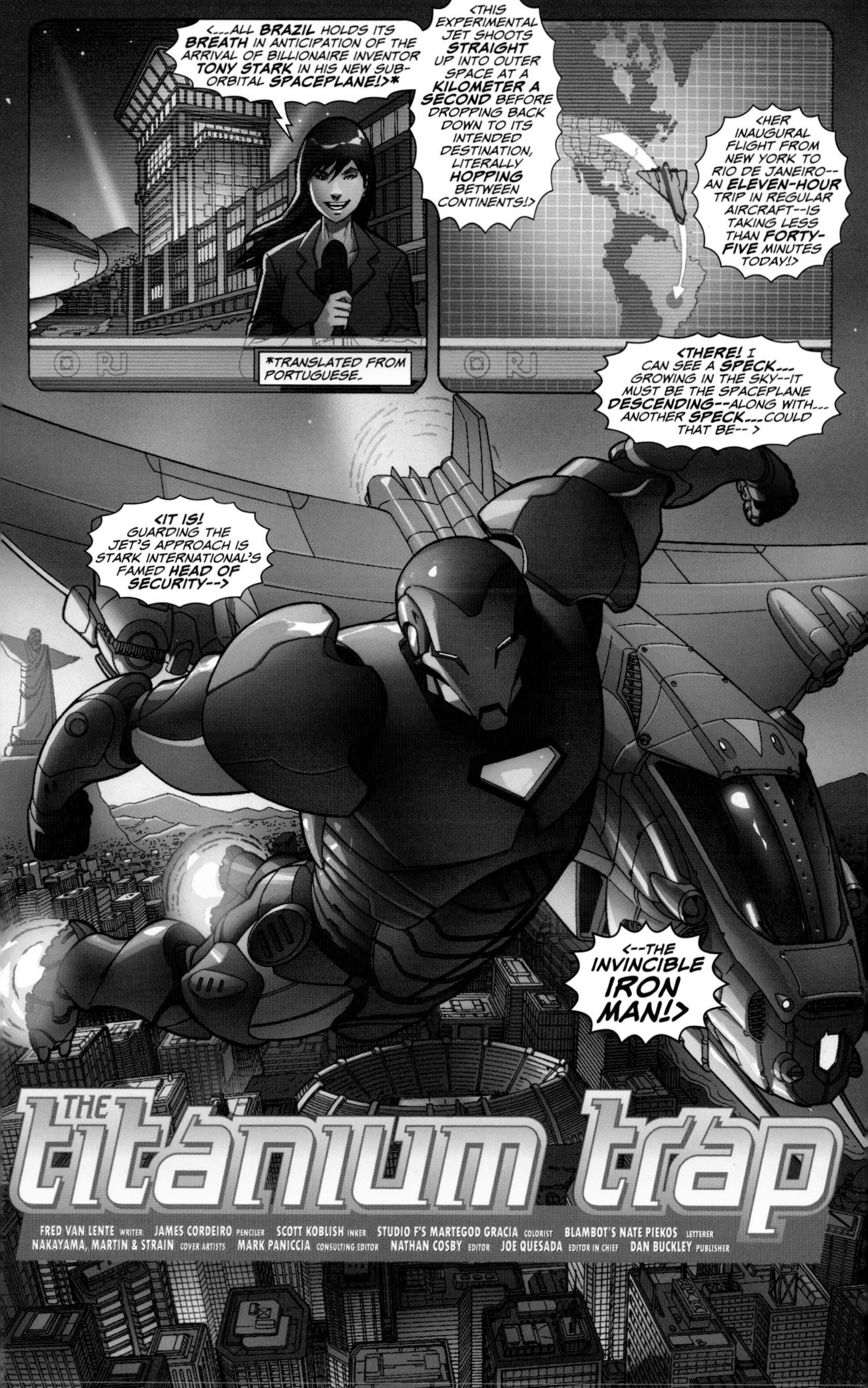
<...ALL BRAZIL HOLDS ITS BREATH IN ANTICIPATION OF THE ARRIVAL OF BILLIONAIRE INVENTOR TONY STARK IN HIS NEW SUB-ORBITAL SPACEPLANE!>*
<THIS EXPERIMENTAL JET SHOOTS STRAIGHT UP INTO OUTER SPACE AT A KILOMETER A SECOND BEFORE DROPPING BACK DOWN TO ITS INTENDED DESTINATION, LITERALLY HOPPING BETWEEN CONTINENTS!>
<HER INAUGURAL FLIGHT FROM NEW YORK TO RIO DE JANEIRO--AN ELEVEN-HOUR TRIP IN REGULAR AIRCRAFT--IS TAKING LESS THAN FORTY-FIVE MINUTES TODAY!>
*TRANSLATED FROM PORTUGUESE.
<THERE! I CAN SEE A SPECK...GROWING IN THE SKY--IT MUST BE THE SPACEPLANE DESCENDING--ALONG WITH...ANOTHER SPECK...COULD THAT BE-- >
<IT IS! GUARDING THE JET'S APPROACH IS STARK INTERNATIONAL'S FAMED HEAD OF SECURITY-->
<--THE INVINCIBLE IRON MAN!>
THE TITANIUM TRAP
FRED VAN LENTE WRITER JAMES CORDEIRO PENCILER SCOTT KOBLISH INKER STUDIO F'S MARTEGOD GRACIA COLORIST BLAMBOT'S NATE PIEKOS LETTERER
NAKAYAMA, MARTIN & STRAIN COVER ARTISTS MARK PANICCIA CONSULTING EDITOR NATHAN COSBY EDITOR JOE QUESADA EDITOR IN CHIEF DAN BUCKLEY PUBLISHER

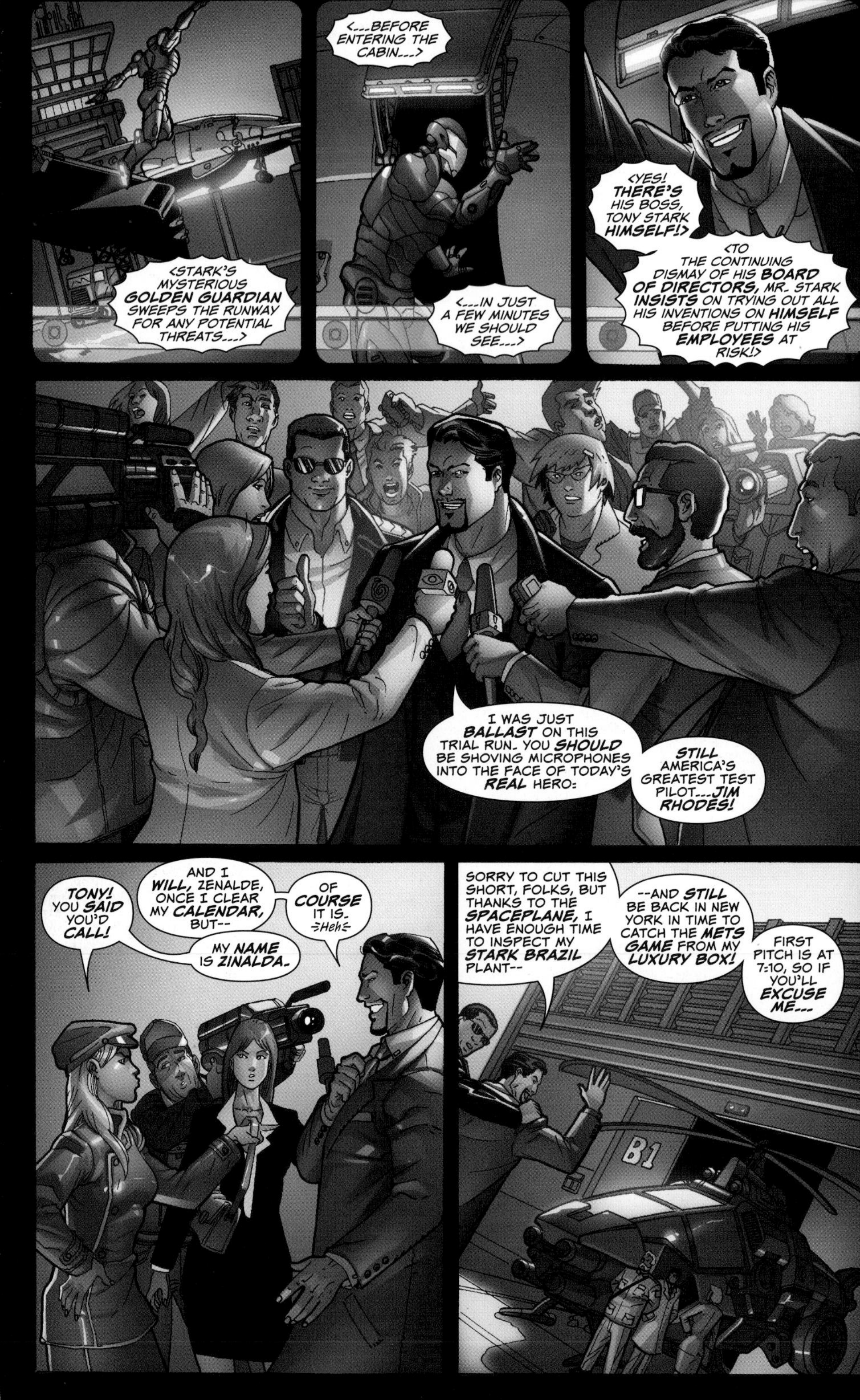

<STARK'S MYSTERIOUS GOLDEN GUARDIAN SWEEPS THE RUNWAY FOR ANY POTENTIAL THREATS...>
<...BEFORE ENTERING THE CABIN...>
<...IN JUST A FEW MINUTES WE SHOULD SEE...>
<YES! THERE'S HIS BOSS, TONY STARK HIMSELF!>
<TO THE CONTINUING DISMAY OF HIS BOARD OF DIRECTORS, MR. STARK INSISTS ON TRYING OUT ALL HIS INVENTIONS ON HIMSELF BEFORE PUTTING HIS EMPLOYEES AT RISK!>
I WAS JUST BALLAST ON THIS TRIAL RUN. YOU SHOULD BE SHOVING MICROPHONES INTO THE FACE OF TODAY'S REAL HERO:
STILL AMERICA'S GREATEST TEST PILOT...JIM RHODES!
TONY! YOU SAID YOU'D CALL!
AND I WILL, ZENALDE, ONCE I CLEAR MY CALENDAR, BUT--
MY NAME IS ZINALDA.
OF COURSE IT IS. *Heh*
SORRY TO CUT THIS SHORT, FOLKS, BUT THANKS TO THE SPACEPLANE, I HAVE ENOUGH TIME TO INSPECT MY STARK BRAZIL PLANT--
--AND STILL BE BACK IN NEW YORK IN TIME TO CATCH THE METS GAME FROM MY LUXURY BOX!
FIRST PITCH IS AT 7:10, SO IF YOU'LL EXCUSE ME...
B1

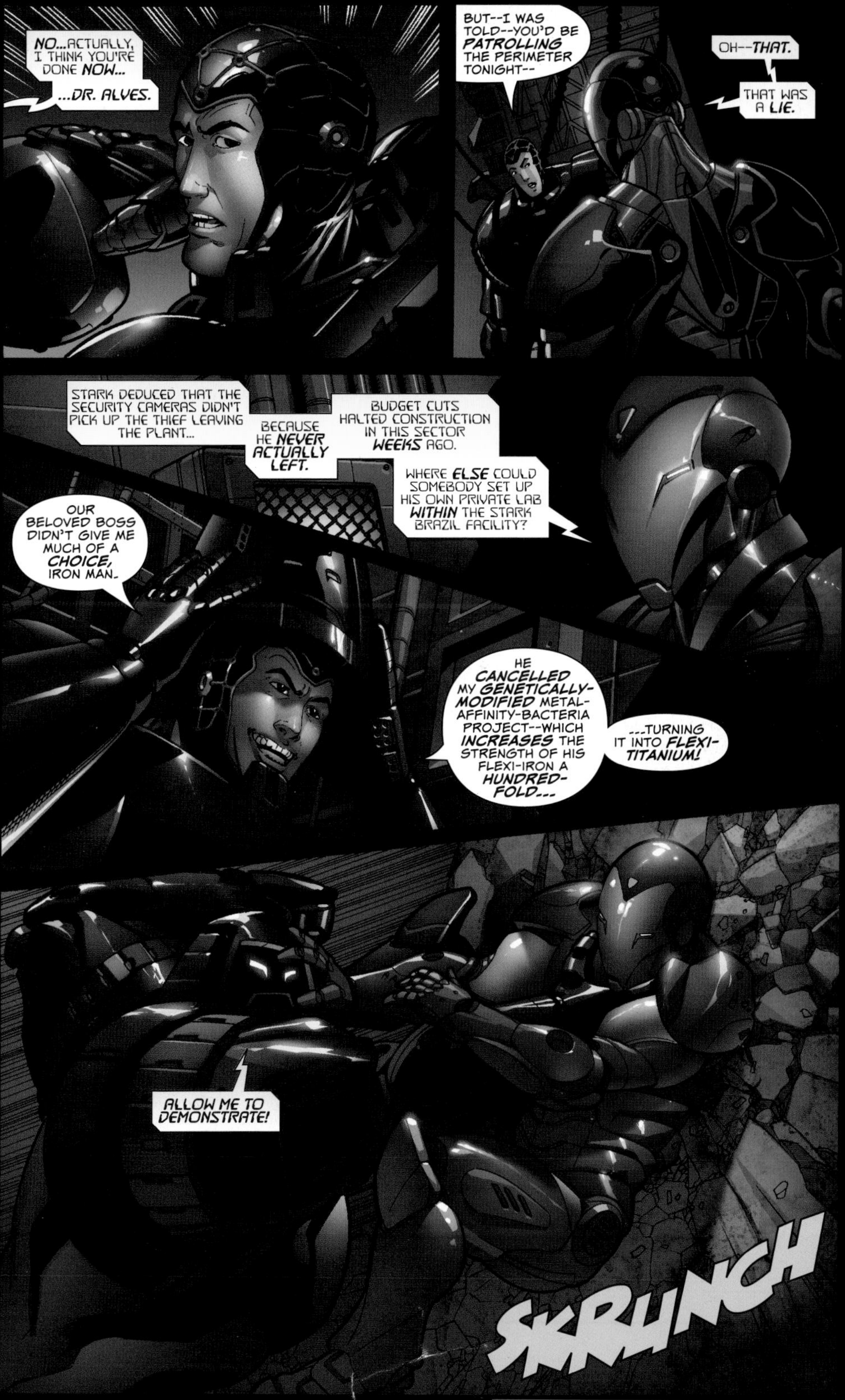
NO...ACTUALLY, I THINK YOU'RE DONE NOW...
...DR. ALVES.
BUT--I WAS TOLD--YOU'D BE PATROLLING THE PERIMETER TONIGHT--
OH--THAT.
THAT WAS A LIE.
STARK DEDUCED THAT THE SECURITY CAMERAS DIDN'T PICK UP THE THIEF LEAVING THE PLANT...
BECAUSE HE NEVER ACTUALLY LEFT.
BUDGET CUTS HALTED CONSTRUCTION IN THIS SECTOR WEEKS AGO.
WHERE ELSE COULD SOMEBODY SET UP HIS OWN PRIVATE LAB WITHIN THE STARK BRAZIL FACILITY?
OUR BELOVED BOSS DIDN'T GIVE ME MUCH OF A CHOICE, IRON MAN.
HE CANCELLED MY GENETICALLY-MODIFIED METAL-AFFINITY-BACTERIA PROJECT--WHICH INCREASES THE STRENGTH OF HIS FLEXI-IRON A HUNDRED-FOLD...
...TURNING IT INTO FLEXI-TITANIUM!
ALLOW ME TO DEMONSTRATE!
SKRUNCH

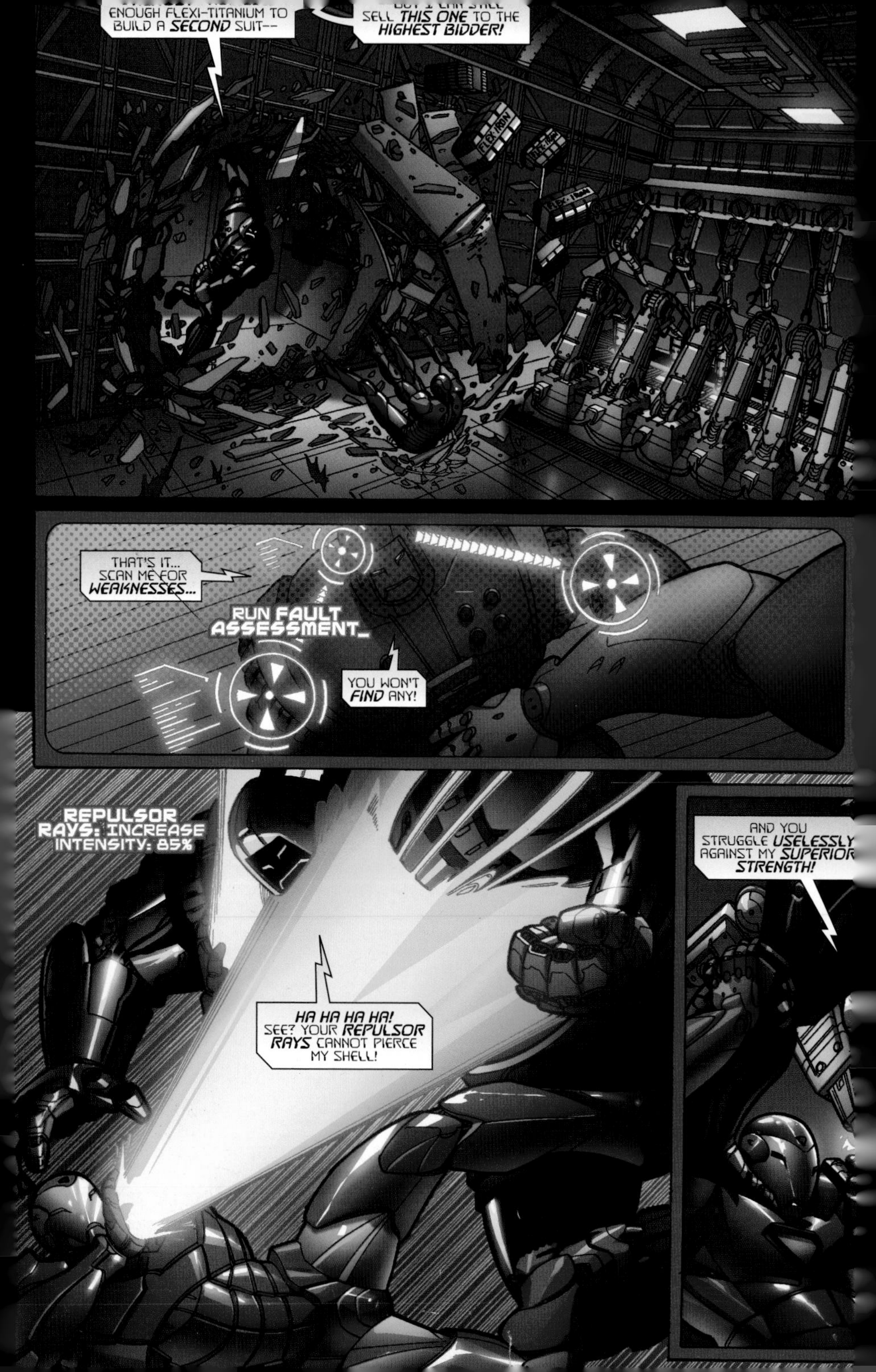
ENOUGH FLEXI-TITANIUM TO BUILD A SECOND SUIT--
SELL THIS ONE TO THE HIGHEST BIDDER!
THAT'S IT... SCAN ME FOR WEAKNESSES...
RUN FAULT ASSESSMENT_
YOU WON'T FIND ANY!
REPULSOR RAYS: INCREASE INTENSITY: 85%
HA HA HA HA! SEE? YOUR REPULSOR RAYS CANNOT PIERCE MY SHELL!
AND YOU STRUGGLE USELESSLY AGAINST MY SUPERIOR STRENGTH!

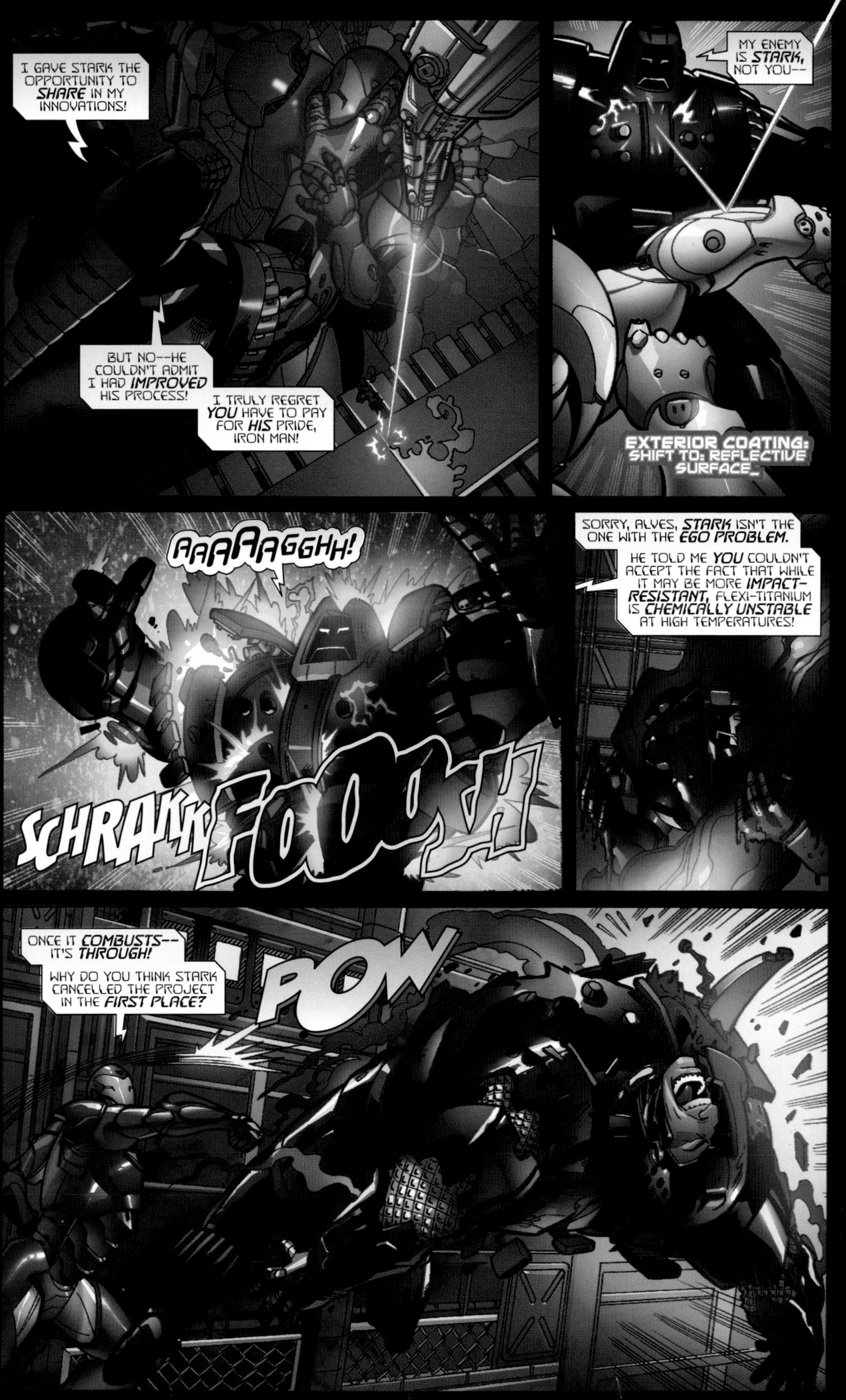

I GAVE STARK THE OPPORTUNITY TO SHARE IN MY INNOVATIONS!
BUT NO--HE COULDN'T ADMIT I HAD IMPROVED HIS PROCESS!
I TRULY REGRET YOU HAVE TO PAY FOR HIS PRIDE, IRON MAN!
MY ENEMY IS STARK, NOT YOU--
EXTERIOR COATING: SHIFT TO: REFLECTIVE SURFACE_
AAAAAGGHH!
SCHRAKK FOOM!
SORRY, ALVES, STARK ISN'T THE ONE WITH THE EGO PROBLEM.
HE TOLD ME YOU COULDN'T ACCEPT THE FACT THAT WHILE IT MAY BE MORE IMPACT-RESISTANT, FLEXI-TITANIUM IS CHEMICALLY UNSTABLE AT HIGH TEMPERATURES!
ONCE IT COMBUSTS-- IT'S THROUGH!
WHY DO YOU THINK STARK CANCELLED THE PROJECT IN THE FIRST PLACE?
POW

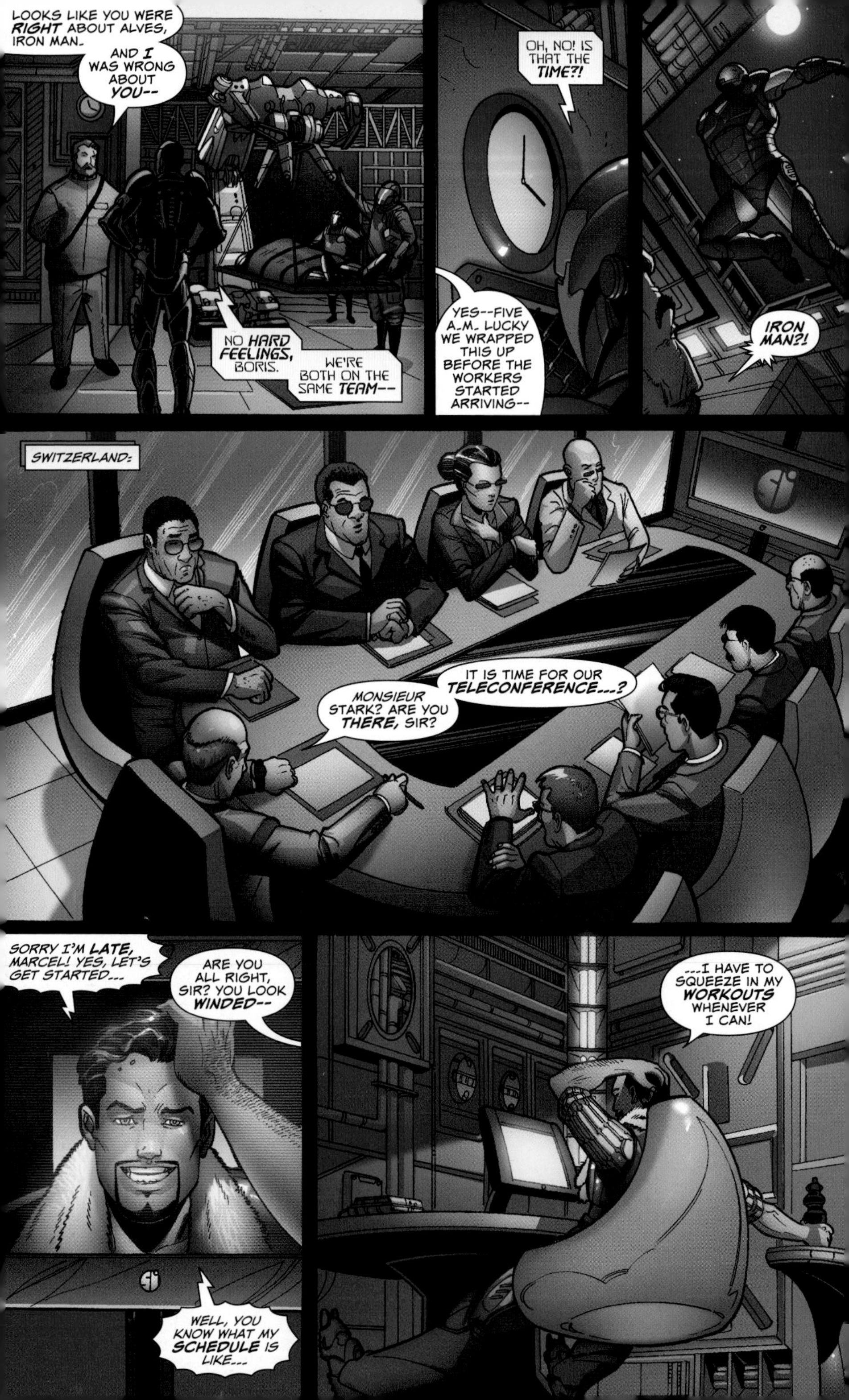
LOOKS LIKE YOU WERE RIGHT ABOUT ALVES, IRON MAN.
AND I WAS WRONG ABOUT YOU--
NO HARD FEELINGS, BORIS.
WE'RE BOTH ON THE SAME TEAM--
OH, NO! IS THAT THE TIME?!
YES--FIVE A.M. LUCKY WE WRAPPED THIS UP BEFORE THE WORKERS STARTED ARRIVING--
IRON MAN?!
SWITZERLAND:
MONSIEUR STARK? ARE YOU THERE, SIR?
IT IS TIME FOR OUR TELECONFERENCE...?
SORRY I'M LATE, MARCEL! YES, LET'S GET STARTED...
ARE YOU ALL RIGHT, SIR? YOU LOOK WINDED--
WELL, YOU KNOW WHAT MY SCHEDULE IS LIKE...
...I HAVE TO SQUEEZE IN MY WORKOUTS WHENEVER I CAN!

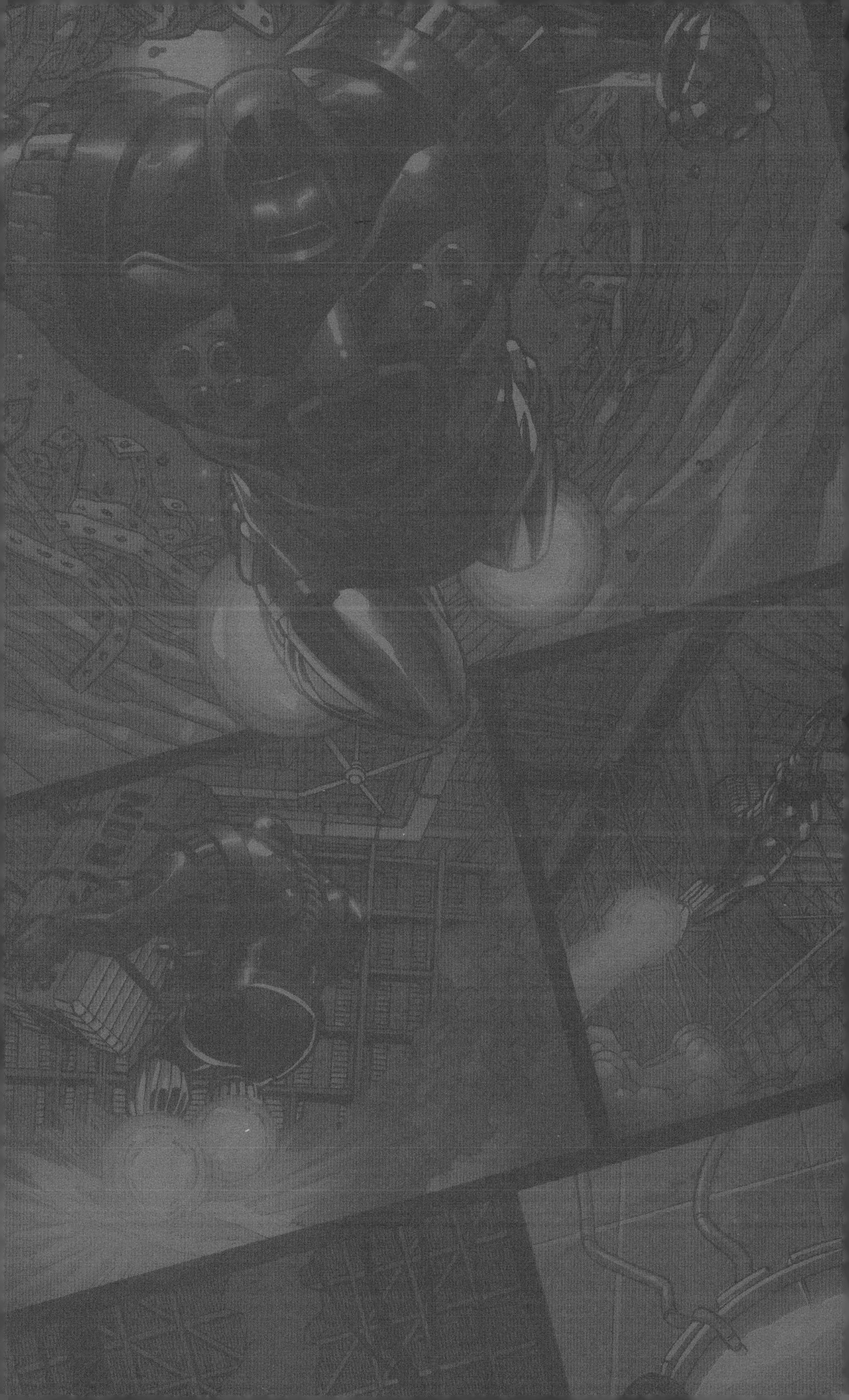

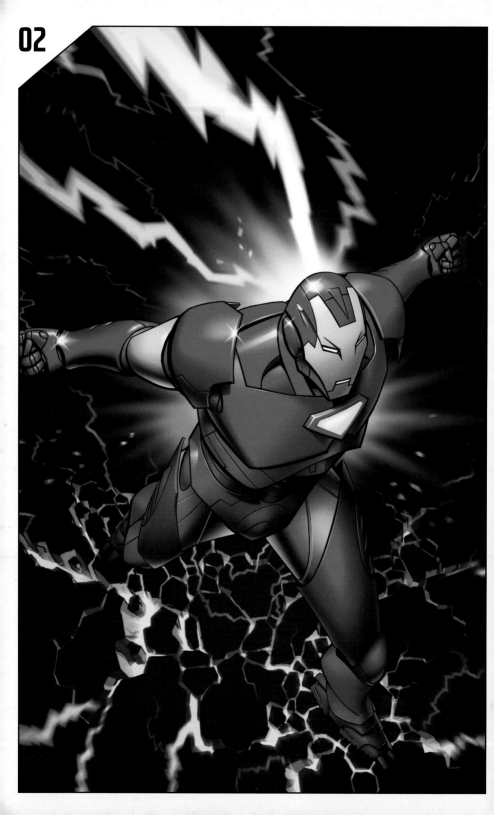

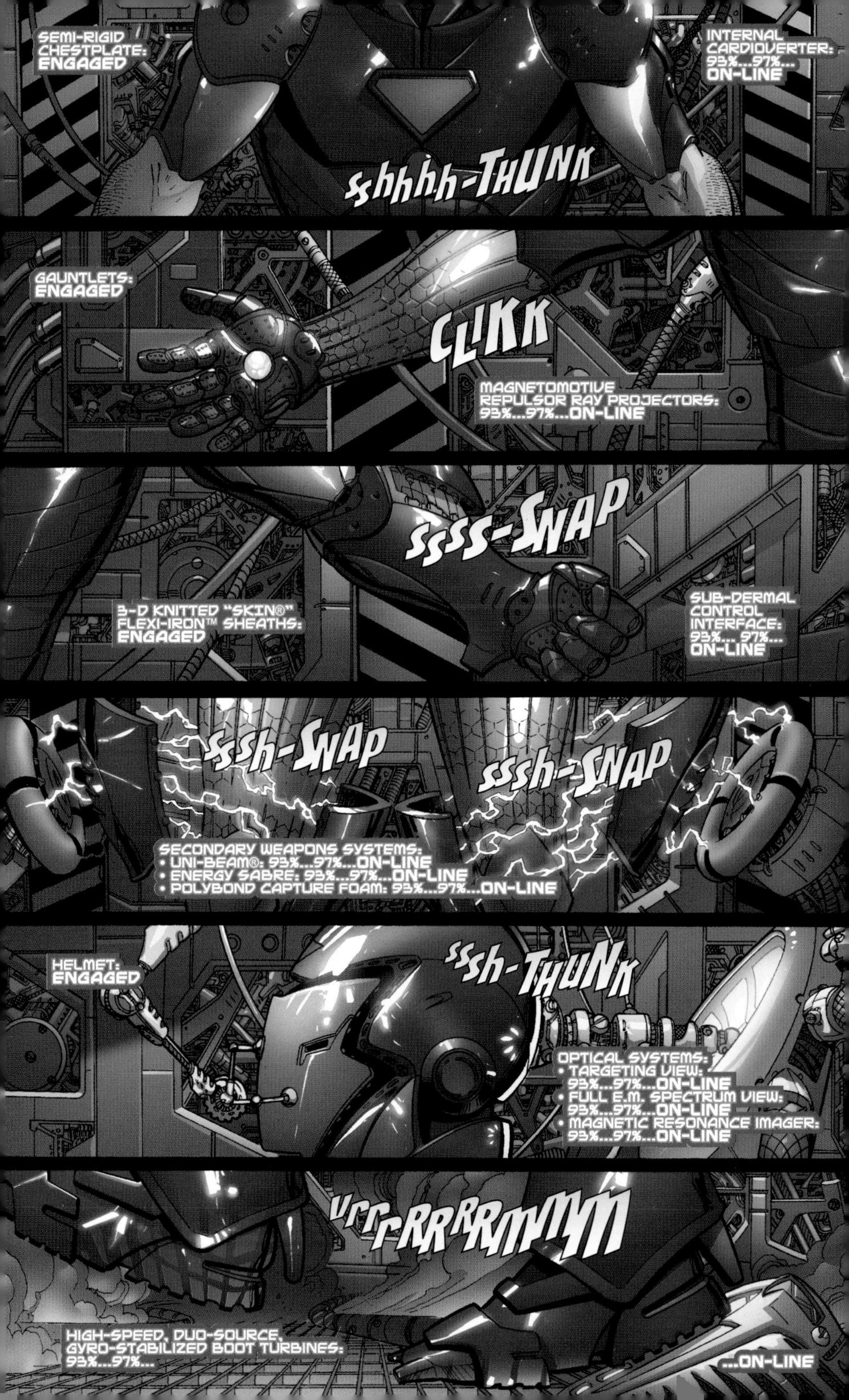
SEMI-RIGID CHESTPLATE: ENGAGED
INTERNAL CARDIOVERTER: 93%...97%... ON-LINE
SSHHHH-THUNK
GAUNTLETS: ENGAGED
CLIKK
MAGNETOMOTIVE REPULSOR RAY PROJECTORS: 93%...97%...ON-LINE
SSSS-SNAP
3-D KNITTED "SKIN®" FLEXI-IRON™ SHEATHS: ENGAGED
SUB-DERMAL CONTROL INTERFACE: 93%... 97%... ON-LINE
SSSH-SNAP
SSSH-SNAP
SECONDARY WEAPONS SYSTEMS:
• UNI-BEAM®: 93%...97%...ON-LINE
• ENERGY SABRE: 93%...97%...ON-LINE
• POLYBOND CAPTURE FOAM: 93%...97%...ON-LINE
HELMET: ENGAGED
SSSH-THUNK
OPTICAL SYSTEMS:
• TARGETING VIEW: 93%...97%...ON-LINE
• FULL E.M. SPECTRUM VIEW: 93%...97%...ON-LINE
• MAGNETIC RESONANCE IMAGER: 93%...97%...ON-LINE
VRRRRRRRMMMM
HIGH-SPEED, DUO-SOURCE, GYRO-STABILIZED BOOT TURBINES: 93%...97%...
...ON-LINE

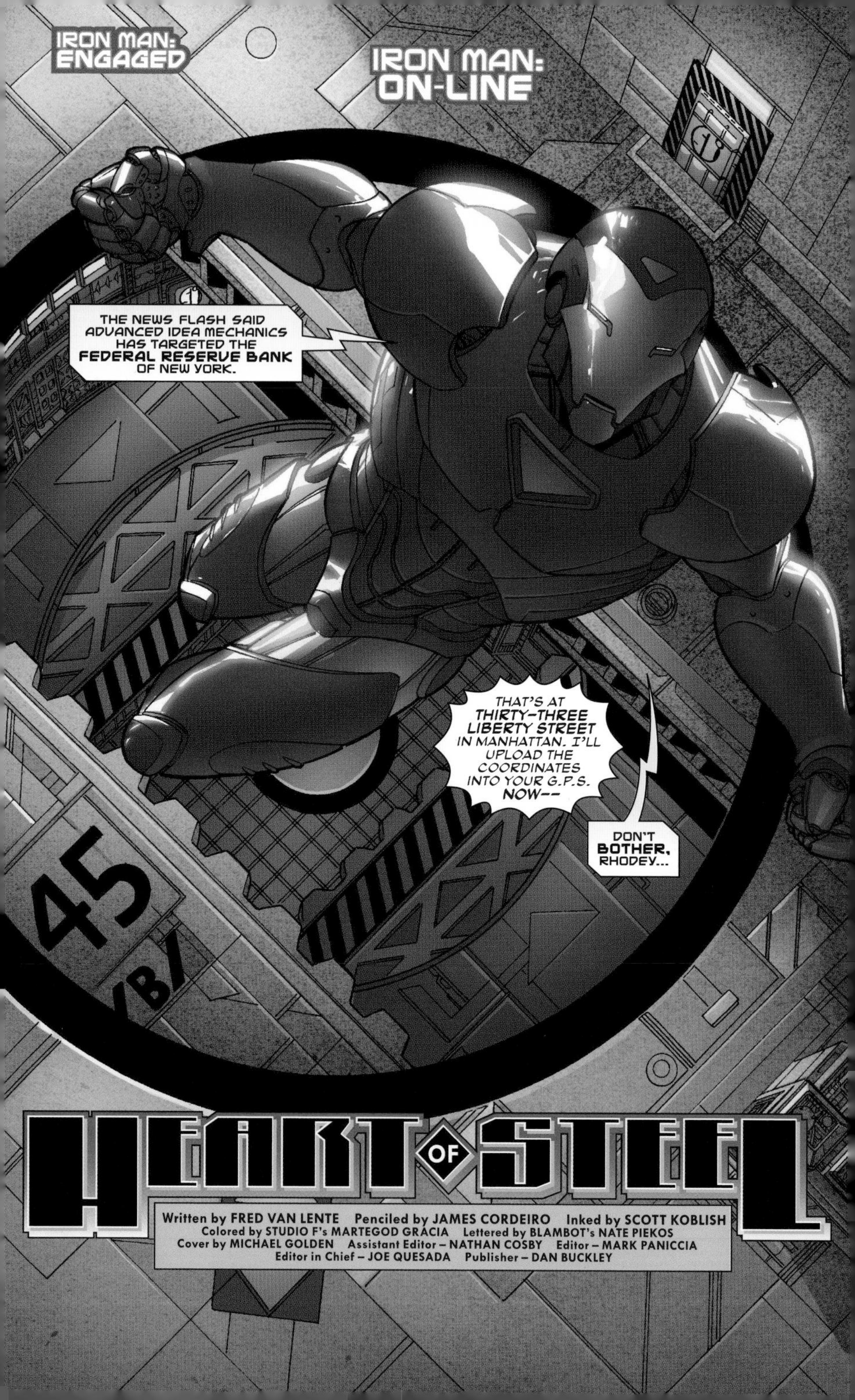
IRON MAN: ENGAGED
IRON MAN: ON-LINE
THE NEWS FLASH SAID ADVANCED IDEA MECHANICS HAS TARGETED THE FEDERAL RESERVE BANK OF NEW YORK.
THAT'S AT THIRTY-THREE LIBERTY STREET IN MANHATTAN. I'LL UPLOAD THE COORDINATES INTO YOUR G.P.S. NOW--
DON'T BOTHER, RHODEY...
45 /B/
HEART OF STEEL
Written by FRED VAN LENTE Penciled by JAMES CORDEIRO Inked by SCOTT KOBLISH
Colored by STUDIO F's MARTEGOD GRACIA Lettered by BLAMBOT's NATE PIEKOS
Cover by MICHAEL GOLDEN Assistant Editor – NATHAN COSBY Editor – MARK PANICCIA
Editor in Chief – JOE QUESADA Publisher – DAN BUCKLEY

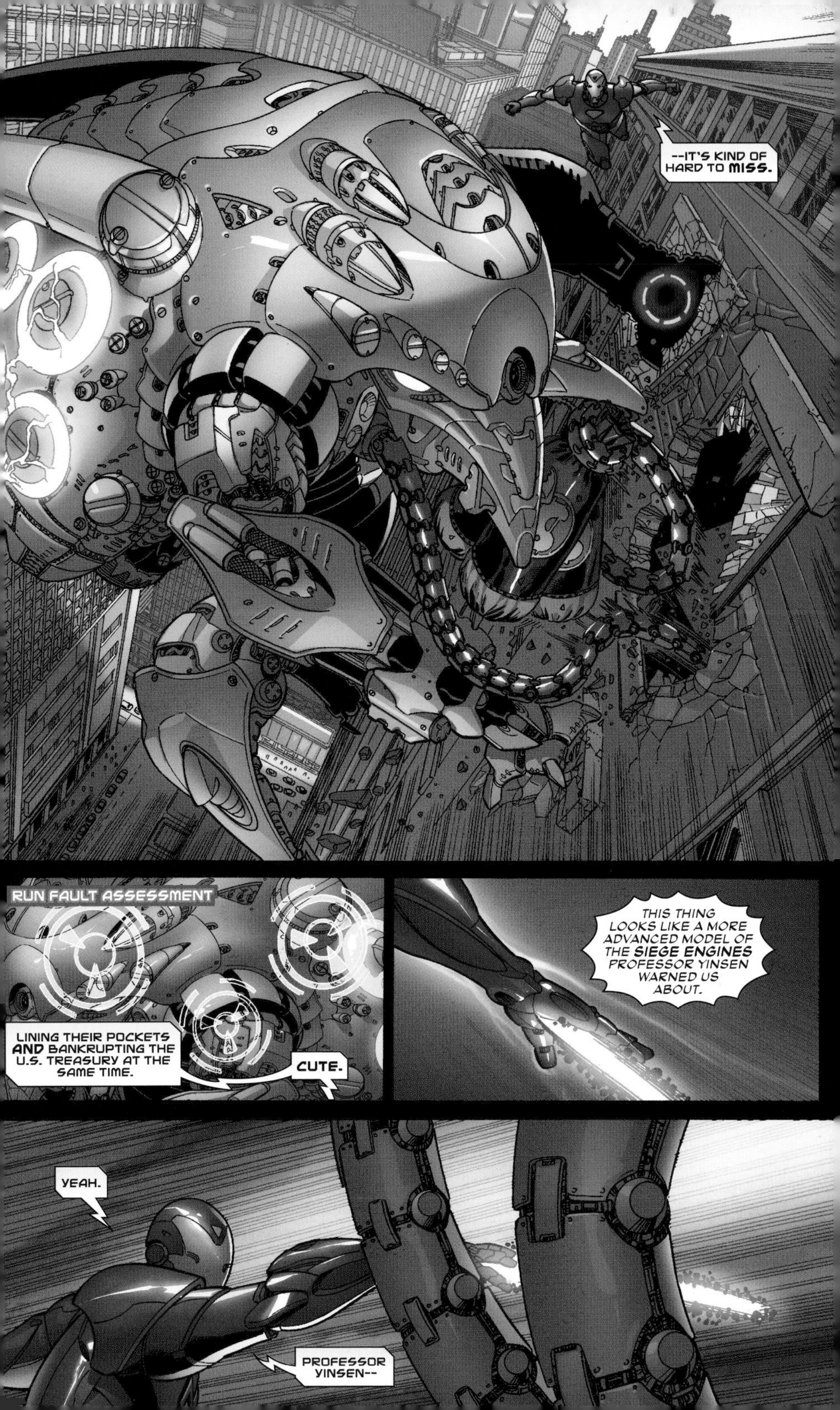
--IT'S KIND OF HARD TO MISS.
RUN FAULT ASSESSMENT
LINING THEIR POCKETS AND BANKRUPTING THE U.S. TREASURY AT THE SAME TIME.
CUTE.
THIS THING LOOKS LIKE A MORE ADVANCED MODEL OF THE SIEGE ENGINES PROFESSOR YINSEN WARNED US ABOUT.
YEAH.
PROFESSOR YINSEN--

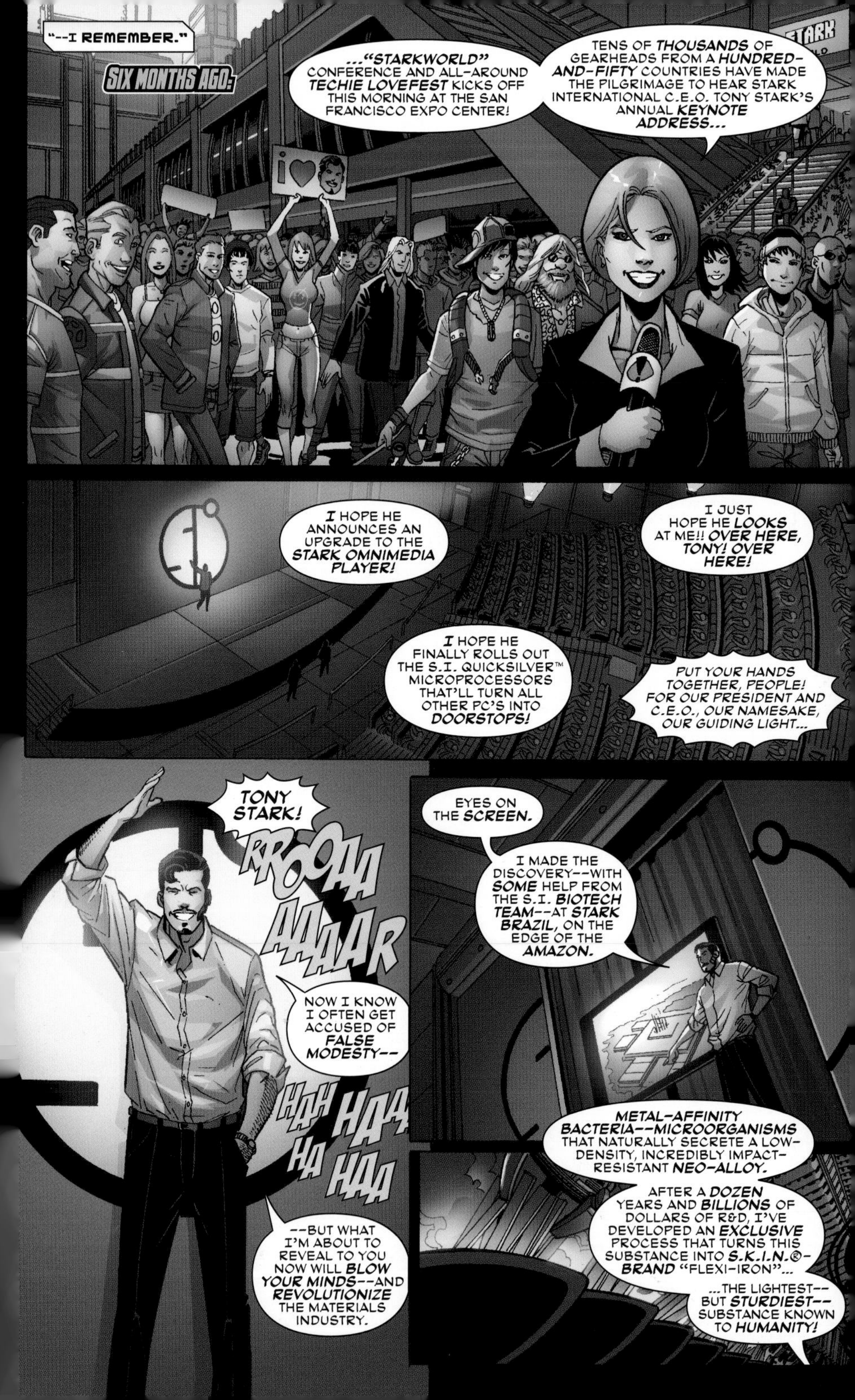
"--I REMEMBER."
SIX MONTHS AGO:
..."STARKWORLD" CONFERENCE AND ALL-AROUND TECHIE LOVEFEST KICKS OFF THIS MORNING AT THE SAN FRANCISCO EXPO CENTER!
TENS OF THOUSANDS OF GEARHEADS FROM A HUNDRED-AND-FIFTY COUNTRIES HAVE MADE THE PILGRIMAGE TO HEAR STARK INTERNATIONAL C.E.O. TONY STARK'S ANNUAL KEYNOTE ADDRESS...
I HOPE HE ANNOUNCES AN UPGRADE TO THE STARK OMNIMEDIA PLAYER!
I JUST HOPE HE LOOKS AT ME!! OVER HERE, TONY! OVER HERE!
I HOPE HE FINALLY ROLLS OUT THE S.I. QUICKSILVER™ MICROPROCESSORS THAT'LL TURN ALL OTHER PC'S INTO DOORSTOPS!
PUT YOUR HANDS TOGETHER, PEOPLE! FOR OUR PRESIDENT AND C.E.O., OUR NAMESAKE, OUR GUIDING LIGHT...
TONY STARK!
RROOAAAAAAR
NOW I KNOW I OFTEN GET ACCUSED OF FALSE MODESTY--
HAH HAA HA HAA
--BUT WHAT I'M ABOUT TO REVEAL TO YOU NOW WILL BLOW YOUR MINDS--AND REVOLUTIONIZE THE MATERIALS INDUSTRY.
EYES ON THE SCREEN.
I MADE THE DISCOVERY--WITH SOME HELP FROM THE S.I. BIOTECH TEAM--AT STARK BRAZIL, ON THE EDGE OF THE AMAZON.
METAL-AFFINITY BACTERIA--MICROORGANISMS THAT NATURALLY SECRETE A LOW-DENSITY, INCREDIBLY IMPACT-RESISTANT NEO-ALLOY.
AFTER A DOZEN YEARS AND BILLIONS OF DOLLARS OF R&D, I'VE DEVELOPED AN EXCLUSIVE PROCESS THAT TURNS THIS SUBSTANCE INTO S.K.I.N.®-BRAND "FLEXI-IRON"...
...THE LIGHTEST--BUT STURDIEST--SUBSTANCE KNOWN TO HUMANITY!

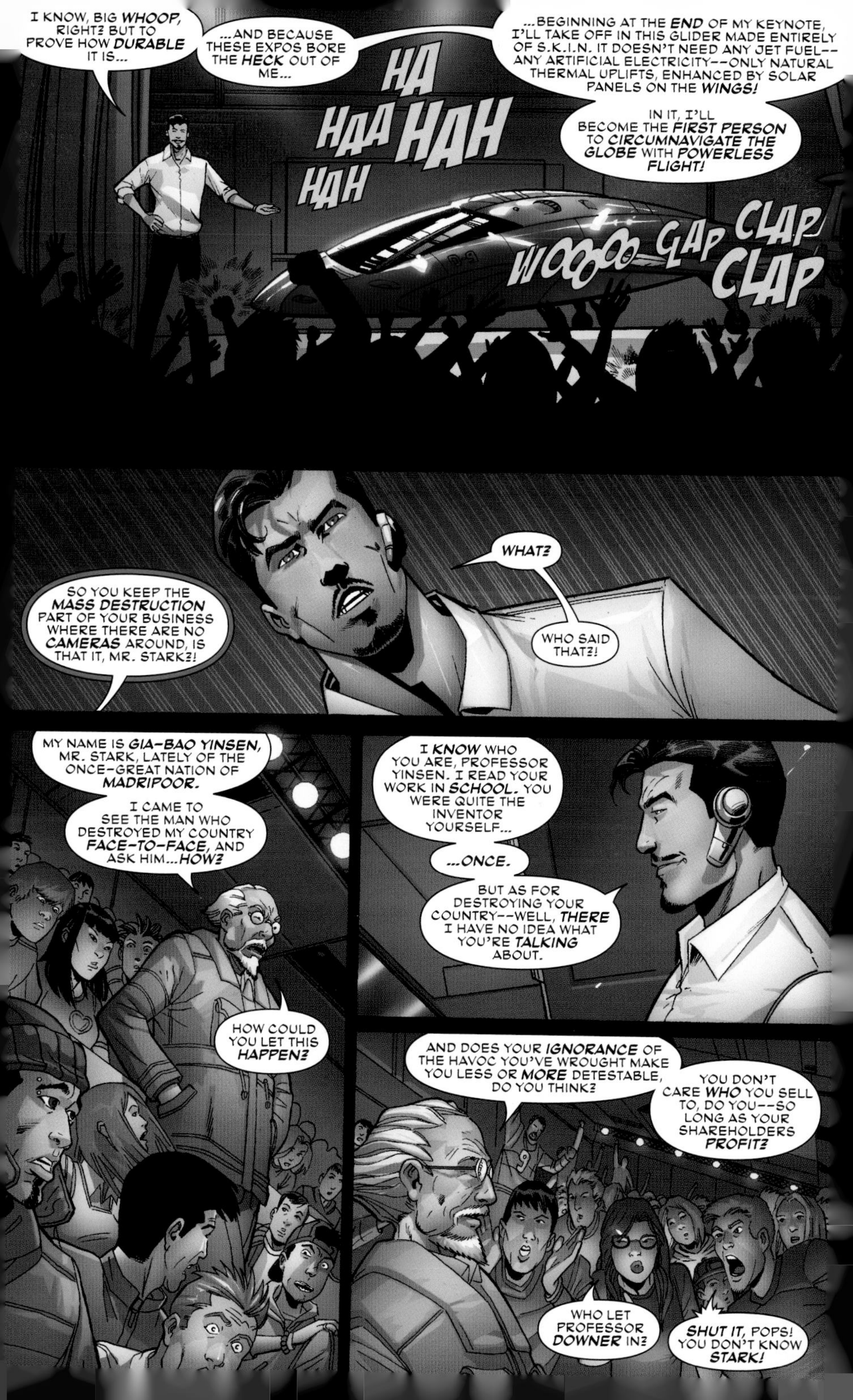
I KNOW, BIG WHOOP, RIGHT? BUT TO PROVE HOW DURABLE IT IS...
...AND BECAUSE THESE EXPOS BORE THE HECK OUT OF ME...
...BEGINNING AT THE END OF MY KEYNOTE, I'LL TAKE OFF IN THIS GLIDER MADE ENTIRELY OF S.K.I.N. IT DOESN'T NEED ANY JET FUEL-- ANY ARTIFICIAL ELECTRICITY--ONLY NATURAL THERMAL UPLIFTS, ENHANCED BY SOLAR PANELS ON THE WINGS!
IN IT, I'LL BECOME THE FIRST PERSON TO CIRCUMNAVIGATE THE GLOBE WITH POWERLESS FLIGHT!
HA HAA HAH HAH
WOOOOO CLAP CLAP CLAP
SO YOU KEEP THE MASS DESTRUCTION PART OF YOUR BUSINESS WHERE THERE ARE NO CAMERAS AROUND, IS THAT IT, MR. STARK?!
WHAT?
WHO SAID THAT?!
MY NAME IS GIA-BAO YINSEN, MR. STARK, LATELY OF THE ONCE-GREAT NATION OF MADRIPOOR.
I CAME TO SEE THE MAN WHO DESTROYED MY COUNTRY FACE-TO-FACE, AND ASK HIM...HOW?
HOW COULD YOU LET THIS HAPPEN?
I KNOW WHO YOU ARE, PROFESSOR YINSEN. I READ YOUR WORK IN SCHOOL. YOU WERE QUITE THE INVENTOR YOURSELF...
...ONCE.
BUT AS FOR DESTROYING YOUR COUNTRY--WELL, THERE I HAVE NO IDEA WHAT YOU'RE TALKING ABOUT.
AND DOES YOUR IGNORANCE OF THE HAVOC YOU'VE WROUGHT MAKE YOU LESS OR MORE DETESTABLE, DO YOU THINK?
YOU DON'T CARE WHO YOU SELL TO, DO YOU--SO LONG AS YOUR SHAREHOLDERS PROFIT?
WHO LET PROFESSOR DOWNER IN?
SHUT IT, POPS! YOU DON'T KNOW STARK!

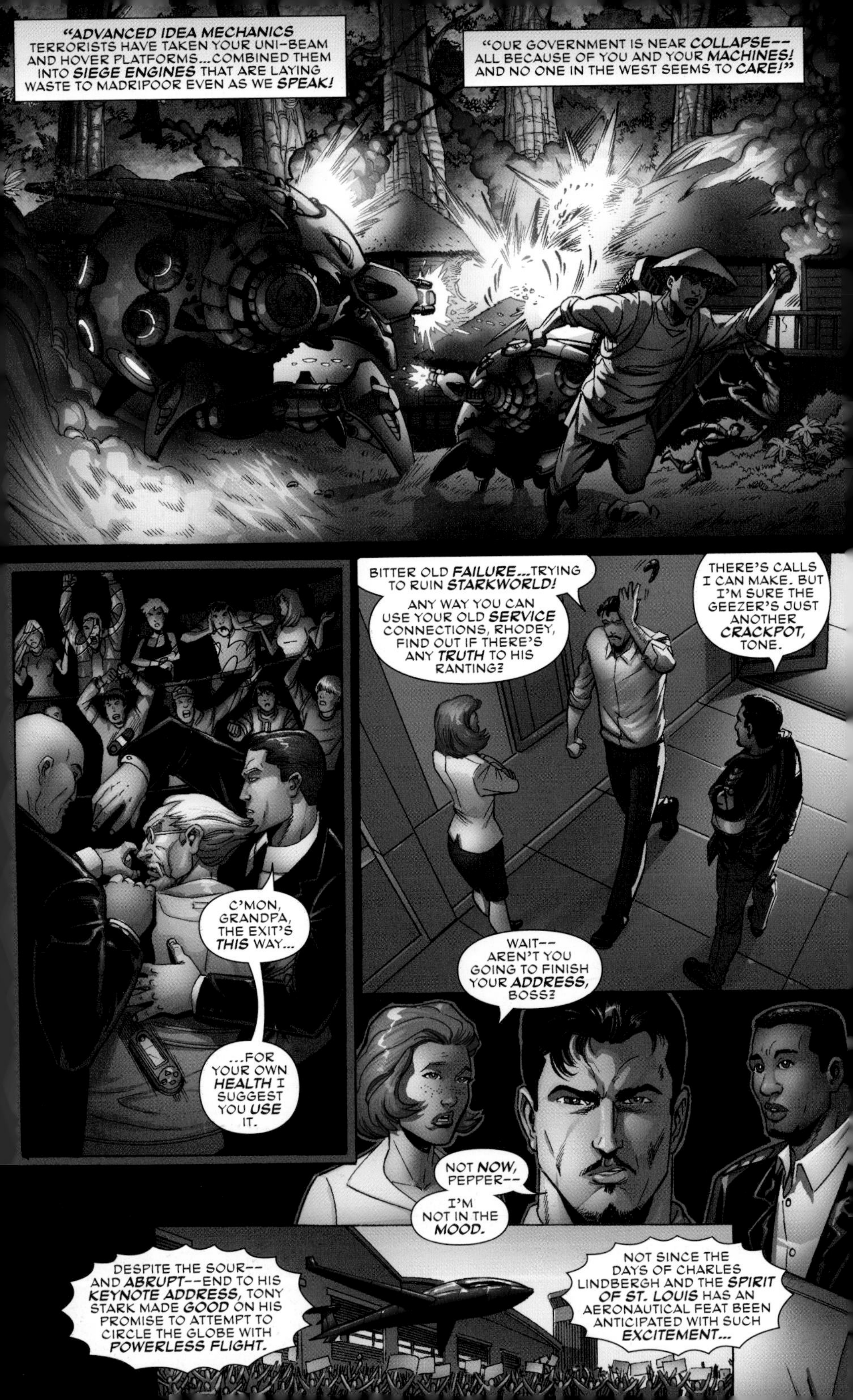
"ADVANCED IDEA MECHANICS TERRORISTS HAVE TAKEN YOUR UNI-BEAM AND HOVER PLATFORMS...COMBINED THEM INTO SIEGE ENGINES THAT ARE LAYING WASTE TO MADRIPOOR EVEN AS WE SPEAK!
"OUR GOVERNMENT IS NEAR COLLAPSE-- ALL BECAUSE OF YOU AND YOUR MACHINES! AND NO ONE IN THE WEST SEEMS TO CARE!"
C'MON, GRANDPA, THE EXIT'S THIS WAY...
...FOR YOUR OWN HEALTH I SUGGEST YOU USE IT.
BITTER OLD FAILURE...TRYING TO RUIN STARKWORLD!
ANY WAY YOU CAN USE YOUR OLD SERVICE CONNECTIONS, RHODEY, FIND OUT IF THERE'S ANY TRUTH TO HIS RANTING?
THERE'S CALLS I CAN MAKE. BUT I'M SURE THE GEEZER'S JUST ANOTHER CRACKPOT, TONE.
WAIT-- AREN'T YOU GOING TO FINISH YOUR ADDRESS, BOSS?
NOT NOW, PEPPER--
I'M NOT IN THE MOOD.
DESPITE THE SOUR-- AND ABRUPT--END TO HIS KEYNOTE ADDRESS, TONY STARK MADE GOOD ON HIS PROMISE TO ATTEMPT TO CIRCLE THE GLOBE WITH POWERLESS FLIGHT.
NOT SINCE THE DAYS OF CHARLES LINDBERGH AND THE SPIRIT OF ST. LOUIS HAS AN AERONAUTICAL FEAT BEEN ANTICIPATED WITH SUCH EXCITEMENT...

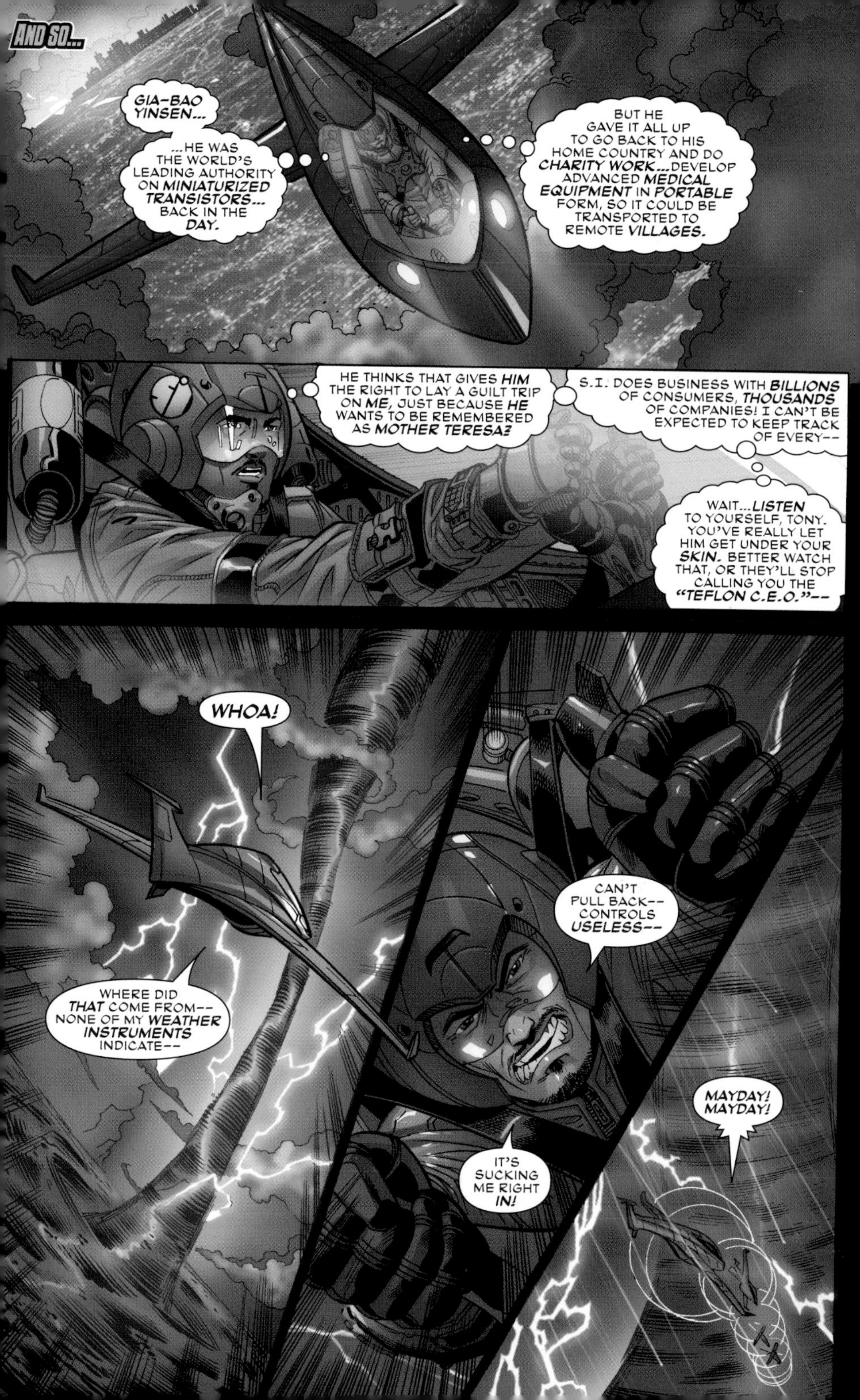
AND SO...
GIA-BAO YINSEN...
...HE WAS THE WORLD'S LEADING AUTHORITY ON MINIATURIZED TRANSISTORS... BACK IN THE DAY.
BUT HE GAVE IT ALL UP TO GO BACK TO HIS HOME COUNTRY AND DO CHARITY WORK... DEVELOP ADVANCED MEDICAL EQUIPMENT IN PORTABLE FORM, SO IT COULD BE TRANSPORTED TO REMOTE VILLAGES.
HE THINKS THAT GIVES HIM THE RIGHT TO LAY A GUILT TRIP ON ME, JUST BECAUSE HE WANTS TO BE REMEMBERED AS MOTHER TERESA?
S.I. DOES BUSINESS WITH BILLIONS OF CONSUMERS, THOUSANDS OF COMPANIES! I CAN'T BE EXPECTED TO KEEP TRACK OF EVERY--
WAIT... LISTEN TO YOURSELF, TONY. YOU'VE REALLY LET HIM GET UNDER YOUR SKIN. BETTER WATCH THAT, OR THEY'LL STOP CALLING YOU THE "TEFLON C.E.O."--
WHOA!
WHERE DID THAT COME FROM-- NONE OF MY WEATHER INSTRUMENTS INDICATE--
CAN'T PULL BACK-- CONTROLS USELESS--
IT'S SUCKING ME RIGHT IN!
MAYDAY! MAYDAY!

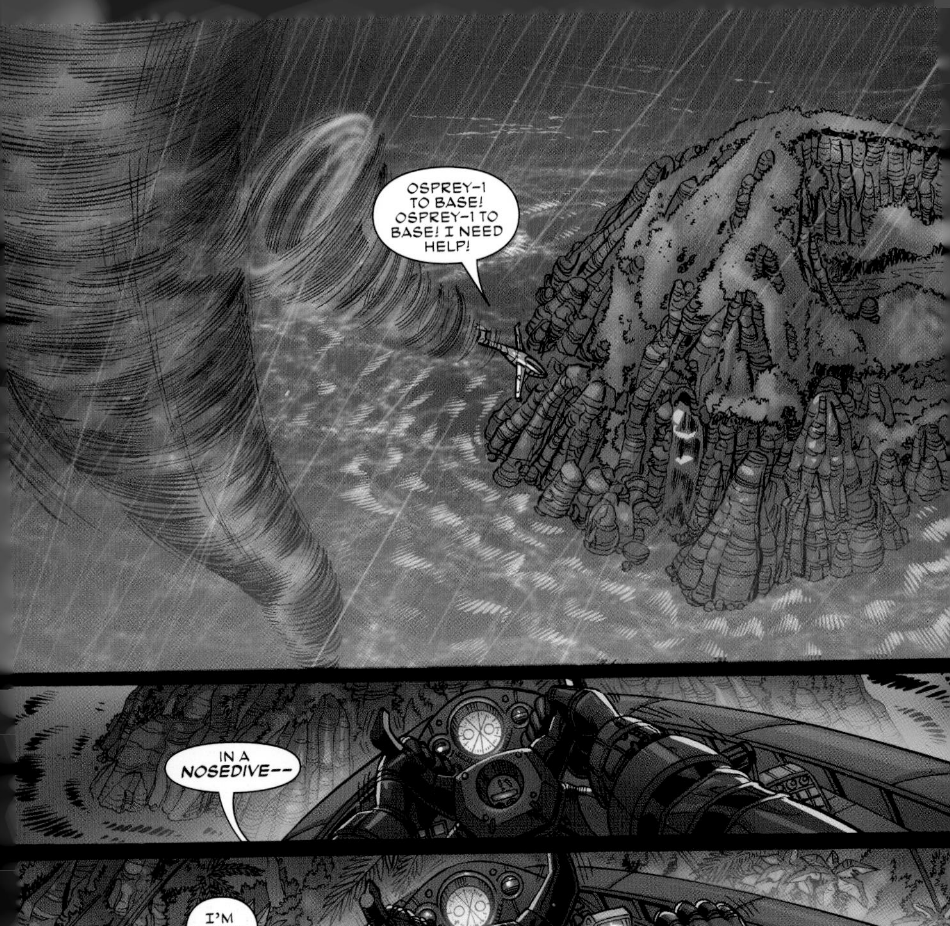
OSPREY-1 TO BASE! OSPREY-1 TO BASE! I NEED HELP!
IN A NOSEDIVE--
I'M GOING TO--
KRASHHH

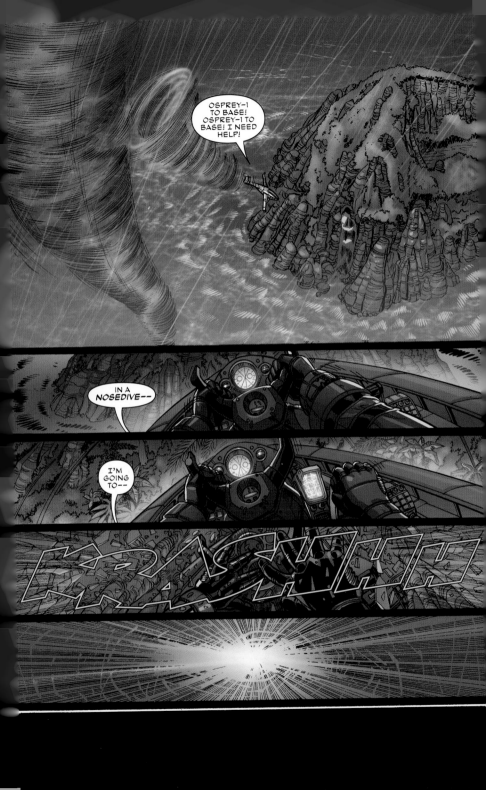

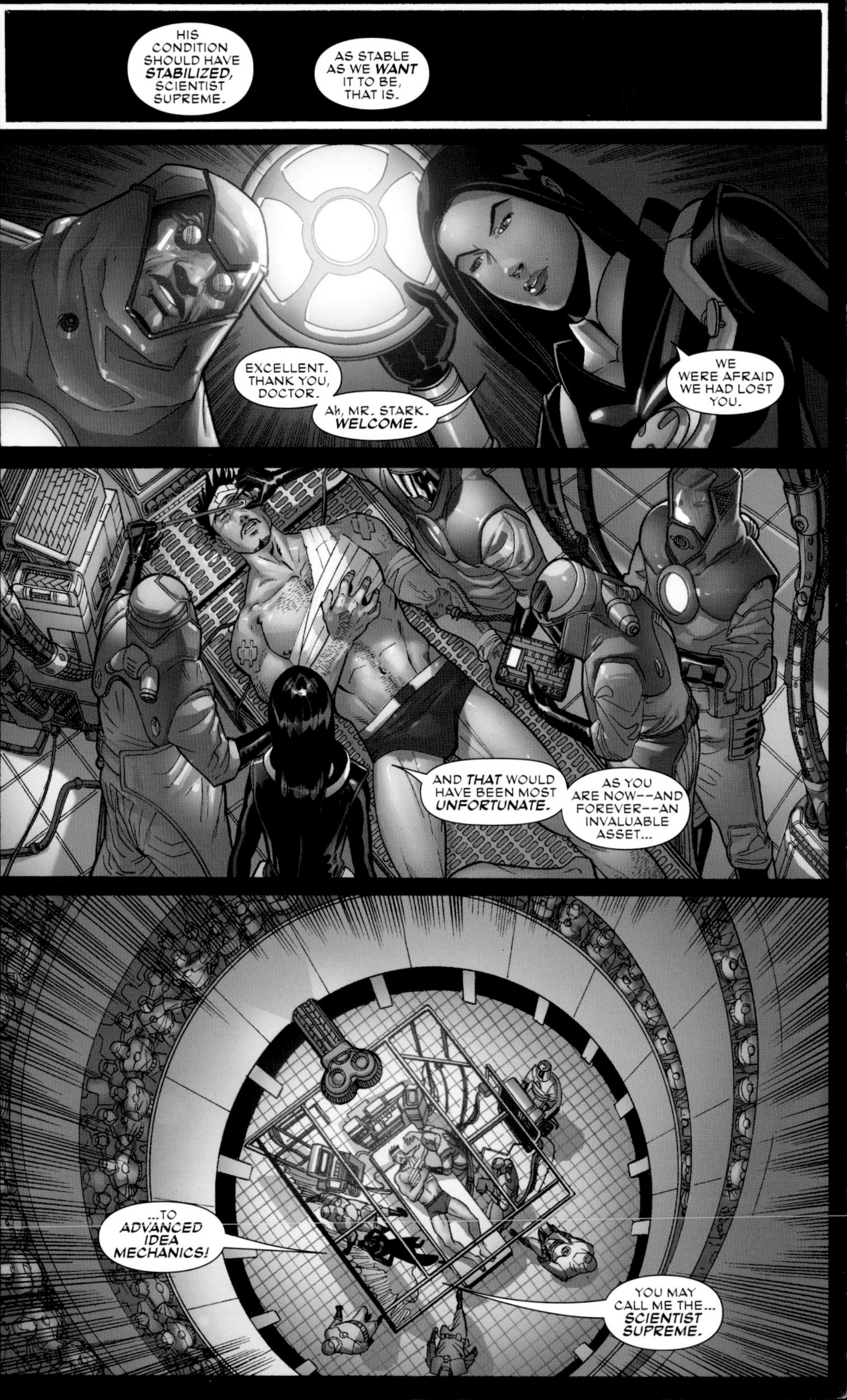
HIS CONDITION SHOULD HAVE STABILIZED, SCIENTIST SUPREME.
AS STABLE AS WE WANT IT TO BE, THAT IS.
EXCELLENT. THANK YOU, DOCTOR.
Ah, MR. STARK. WELCOME.
WE WERE AFRAID WE HAD LOST YOU.
AND THAT WOULD HAVE BEEN MOST UNFORTUNATE.
AS YOU ARE NOW--AND FOREVER--AN INVALUABLE ASSET...
...TO ADVANCED IDEA MECHANICS!
YOU MAY CALL ME THE... SCIENTIST SUPREME.

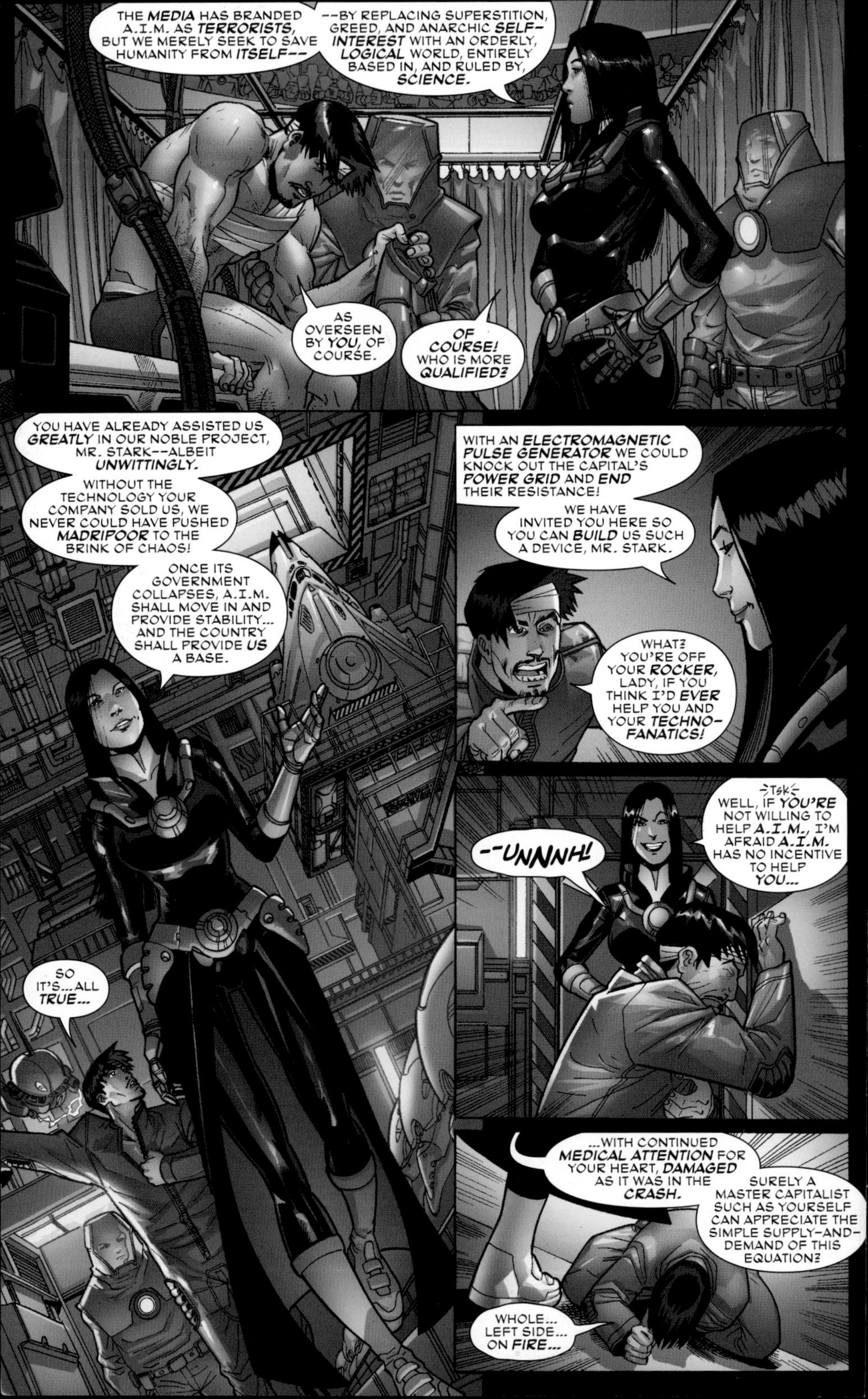
THE MEDIA HAS BRANDED A.I.M. AS TERRORISTS, BUT WE MERELY SEEK TO SAVE HUMANITY FROM ITSELF--
--BY REPLACING SUPERSTITION, GREED, AND ANARCHIC SELF-INTEREST WITH AN ORDERLY, LOGICAL WORLD, ENTIRELY BASED IN, AND RULED BY, SCIENCE.
AS OVERSEEN BY YOU, OF COURSE.
OF COURSE! WHO IS MORE QUALIFIED?
YOU HAVE ALREADY ASSISTED US GREATLY IN OUR NOBLE PROJECT, MR. STARK--ALBEIT UNWITTINGLY.
WITHOUT THE TECHNOLOGY YOUR COMPANY SOLD US, WE NEVER COULD HAVE PUSHED MADRIPOOR TO THE BRINK OF CHAOS!
ONCE ITS GOVERNMENT COLLAPSES, A.I.M. SHALL MOVE IN AND PROVIDE STABILITY... AND THE COUNTRY SHALL PROVIDE US A BASE.
SO IT'S...ALL TRUE...
WITH AN ELECTROMAGNETIC PULSE GENERATOR WE COULD KNOCK OUT THE CAPITAL'S POWER GRID AND END THEIR RESISTANCE!
WE HAVE INVITED YOU HERE SO YOU CAN BUILD US SUCH A DEVICE, MR. STARK.
WHAT? YOU'RE OFF YOUR ROCKER, LADY, IF YOU THINK I'D EVER HELP YOU AND YOUR TECHNO-FANATICS!
TSK
WELL, IF YOU'RE NOT WILLING TO HELP A.I.M., I'M AFRAID A.I.M. HAS NO INCENTIVE TO HELP YOU...
--UNNNH!
...WITH CONTINUED MEDICAL ATTENTION FOR YOUR HEART, DAMAGED AS IT WAS IN THE CRASH.
SURELY A MASTER CAPITALIST SUCH AS YOURSELF CAN APPRECIATE THE SIMPLE SUPPLY-AND-DEMAND OF THIS EQUATION?
WHOLE... LEFT SIDE... ON FIRE...

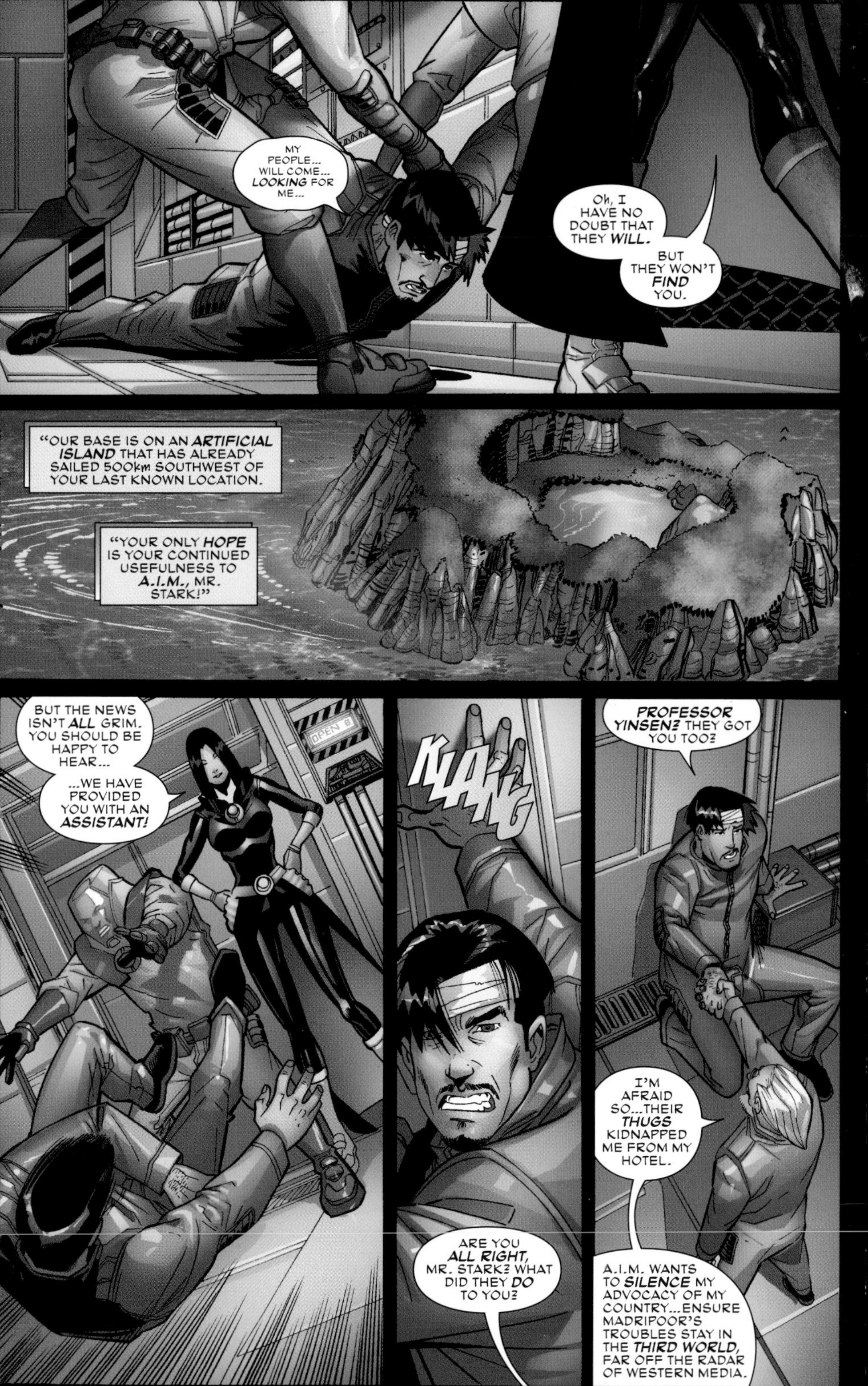
MY PEOPLE... WILL COME... LOOKING FOR ME...
Oh, I HAVE NO DOUBT THAT THEY WILL.
BUT THEY WON'T FIND YOU.
"OUR BASE IS ON AN ARTIFICIAL ISLAND THAT HAS ALREADY SAILED 500km SOUTHWEST OF YOUR LAST KNOWN LOCATION.
"YOUR ONLY HOPE IS YOUR CONTINUED USEFULNESS TO A.I.M., MR. STARK!"
BUT THE NEWS ISN'T ALL GRIM. YOU SHOULD BE HAPPY TO HEAR...
...WE HAVE PROVIDED YOU WITH AN ASSISTANT!
OPEN
KLANG
ARE YOU ALL RIGHT, MR. STARK? WHAT DID THEY DO TO YOU?
PROFESSOR YINSEN? THEY GOT YOU TOO?
I'M AFRAID SO...THEIR THUGS KIDNAPPED ME FROM MY HOTEL.
A.I.M. WANTS TO SILENCE MY ADVOCACY OF MY COUNTRY...ENSURE MADRIPOOR'S TROUBLES STAY IN THE THIRD WORLD, FAR OFF THE RADAR OF WESTERN MEDIA.

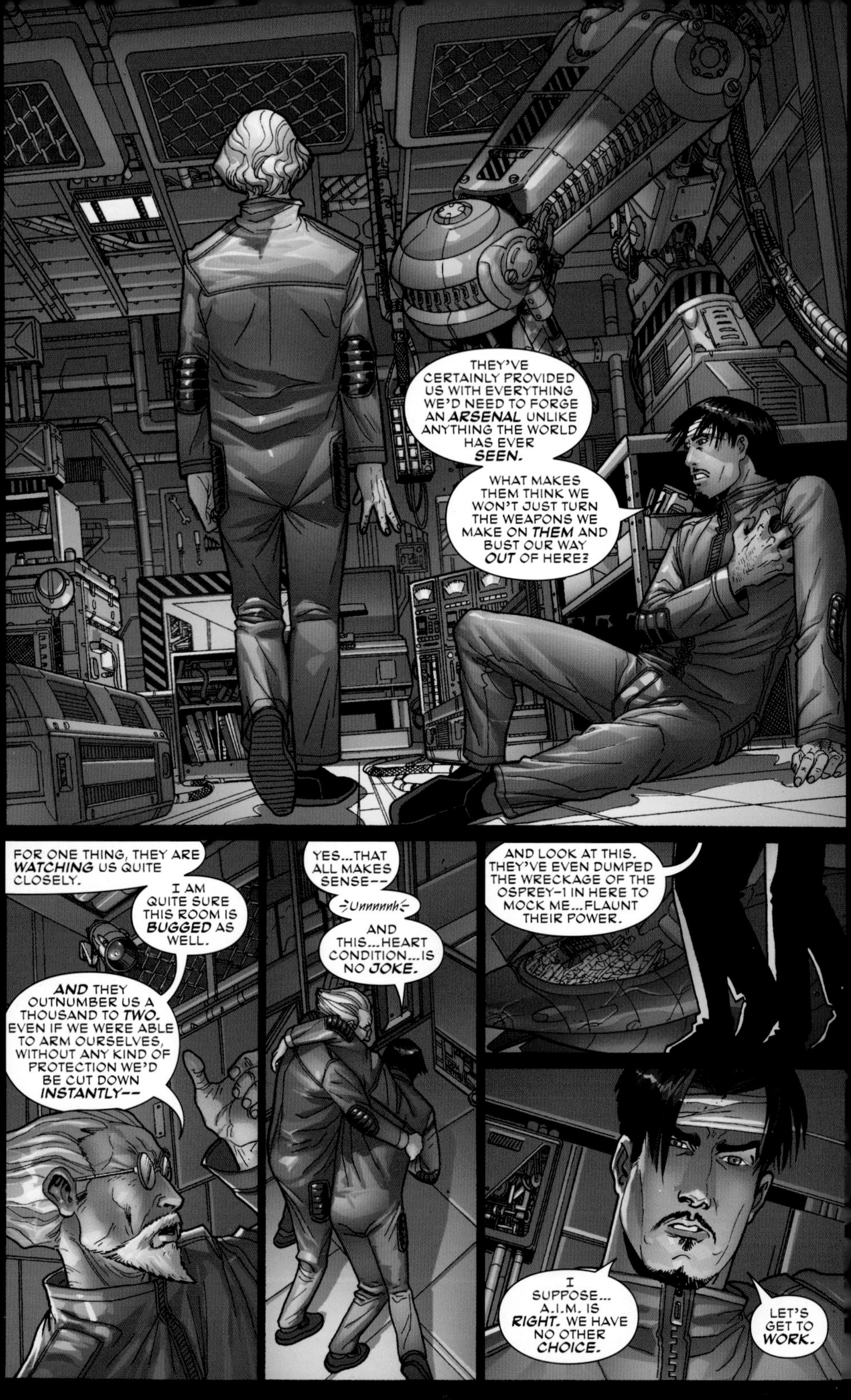
THEY'VE CERTAINLY PROVIDED US WITH EVERYTHING WE'D NEED TO FORGE AN ARSENAL UNLIKE ANYTHING THE WORLD HAS EVER SEEN.
WHAT MAKES THEM THINK WE WON'T JUST TURN THE WEAPONS WE MAKE ON THEM AND BUST OUR WAY OUT OF HERE?
FOR ONE THING, THEY ARE WATCHING US QUITE CLOSELY.
I AM QUITE SURE THIS ROOM IS BUGGED AS WELL.
AND THEY OUTNUMBER US A THOUSAND TO TWO. EVEN IF WE WERE ABLE TO ARM OURSELVES, WITHOUT ANY KIND OF PROTECTION WE'D BE CUT DOWN INSTANTLY--
YES...THAT ALL MAKES SENSE--
Unnnnnh
AND THIS...HEART CONDITION...IS NO JOKE.
AND LOOK AT THIS. THEY'VE EVEN DUMPED THE WRECKAGE OF THE OSPREY-1 IN HERE TO MOCK ME...FLAUNT THEIR POWER.
I SUPPOSE... A.I.M. IS RIGHT. WE HAVE NO OTHER CHOICE.
LET'S GET TO WORK.

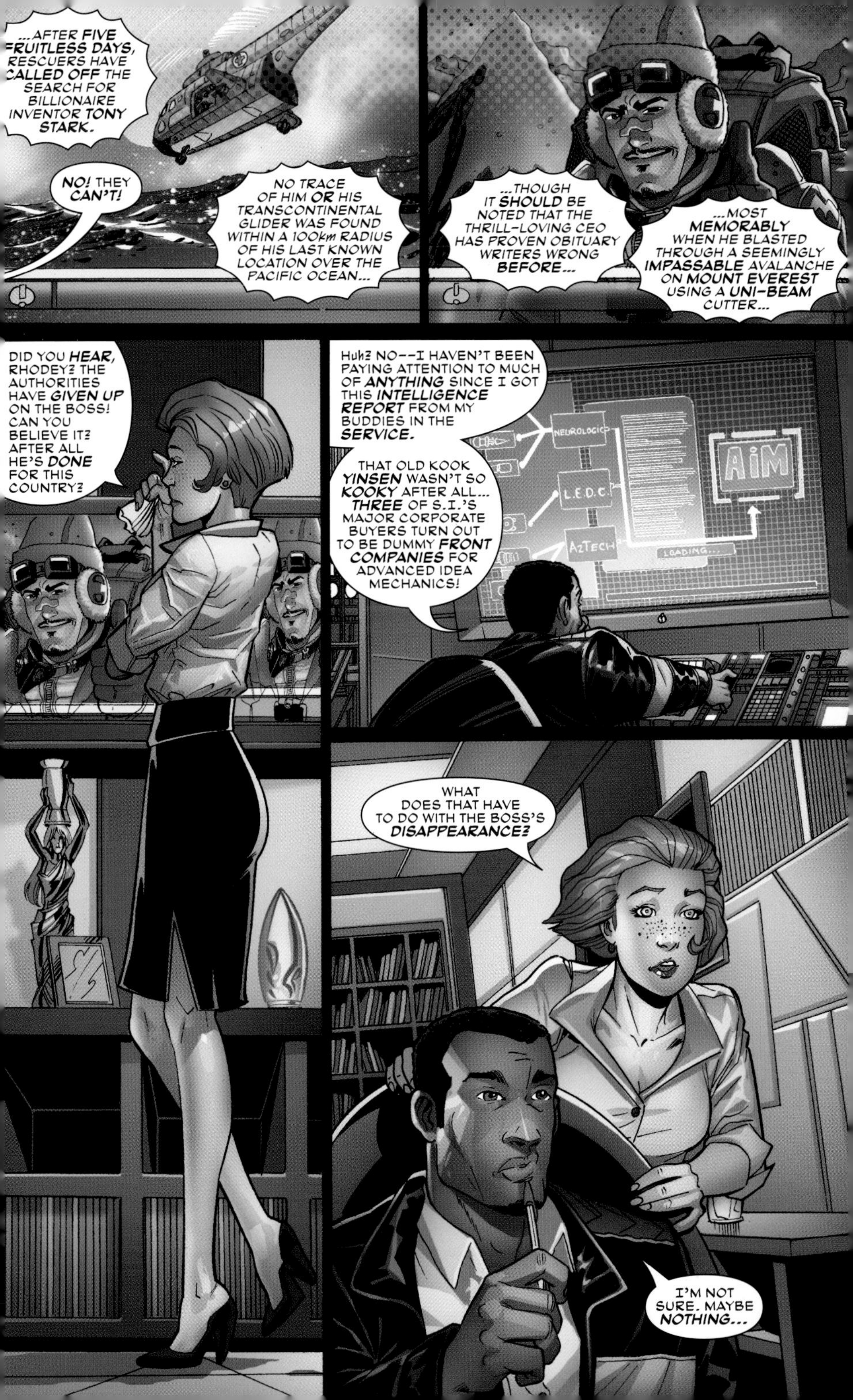
...AFTER FIVE FRUITLESS DAYS, RESCUERS HAVE CALLED OFF THE SEARCH FOR BILLIONAIRE INVENTOR TONY STARK.
NO! THEY CAN'T!
NO TRACE OF HIM OR HIS TRANSCONTINENTAL GLIDER WAS FOUND WITHIN A 100km RADIUS OF HIS LAST KNOWN LOCATION OVER THE PACIFIC OCEAN...
...THOUGH IT SHOULD BE NOTED THAT THE THRILL-LOVING CEO HAS PROVEN OBITUARY WRITERS WRONG BEFORE...
...MOST MEMORABLY WHEN HE BLASTED THROUGH A SEEMINGLY IMPASSABLE AVALANCHE ON MOUNT EVEREST USING A UNI-BEAM CUTTER...
DID YOU HEAR, RHODEY? THE AUTHORITIES HAVE GIVEN UP ON THE BOSS! CAN YOU BELIEVE IT? AFTER ALL HE'S DONE FOR THIS COUNTRY?
Huh? NO--I HAVEN'T BEEN PAYING ATTENTION TO MUCH OF ANYTHING SINCE I GOT THIS INTELLIGENCE REPORT FROM MY BUDDIES IN THE SERVICE.
THAT OLD KOOK YINSEN WASN'T SO KOOKY AFTER ALL... THREE OF S.I.'S MAJOR CORPORATE BUYERS TURN OUT TO BE DUMMY FRONT COMPANIES FOR ADVANCED IDEA MECHANICS!
NEUROLOGIC
L.E.D.C.
AzTECH
AIM
LOADING...
WHAT DOES THAT HAVE TO DO WITH THE BOSS'S DISAPPEARANCE?
I'M NOT SURE. MAYBE NOTHING...

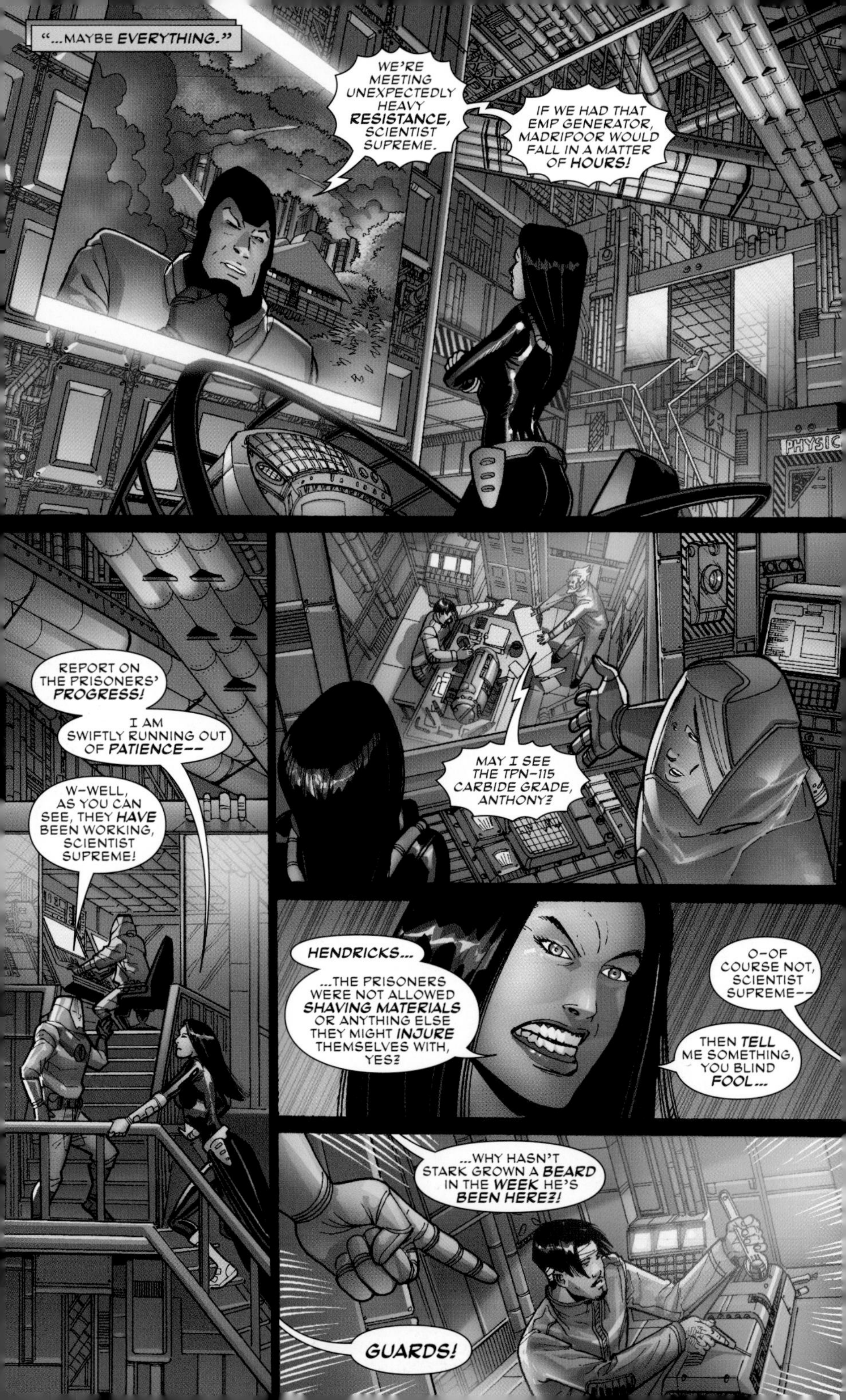
"...MAYBE EVERYTHING."
WE'RE MEETING UNEXPECTEDLY HEAVY RESISTANCE, SCIENTIST SUPREME.
IF WE HAD THAT EMP GENERATOR, MADRIPOOR WOULD FALL IN A MATTER OF HOURS!
PHYSIC
REPORT ON THE PRISONERS' PROGRESS!
I AM SWIFTLY RUNNING OUT OF PATIENCE--
W-WELL, AS YOU CAN SEE, THEY HAVE BEEN WORKING, SCIENTIST SUPREME!
MAY I SEE THE TPN-115 CARBIDE GRADE, ANTHONY?
HENDRICKS...
...THE PRISONERS WERE NOT ALLOWED SHAVING MATERIALS OR ANYTHING ELSE THEY MIGHT INJURE THEMSELVES WITH, YES?
O-OF COURSE NOT, SCIENTIST SUPREME--
THEN TELL ME SOMETHING, YOU BLIND FOOL...
...WHY HASN'T STARK GROWN A BEARD IN THE WEEK HE'S BEEN HERE?!
GUARDS!

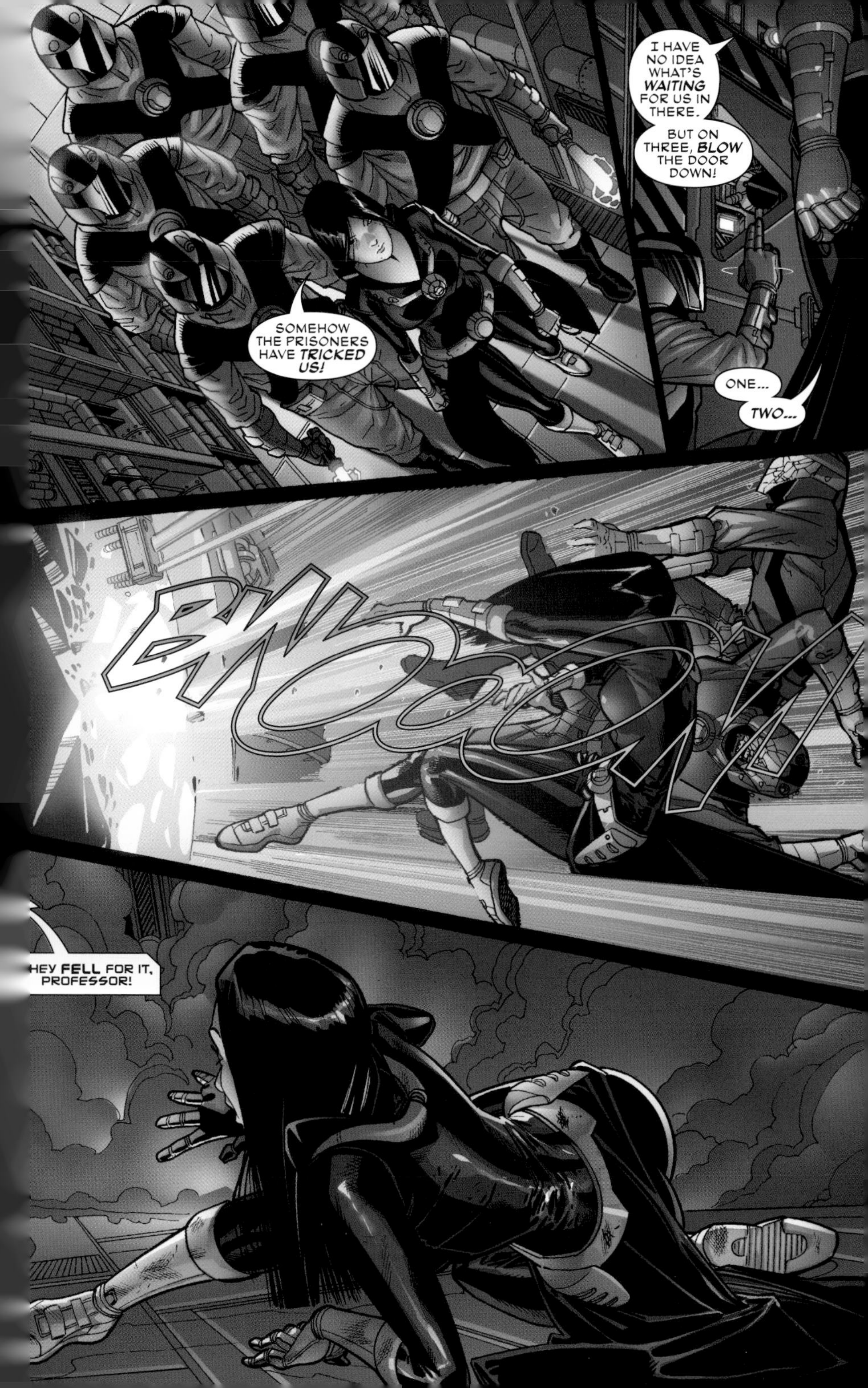

I HAVE NO IDEA WHAT'S WAITING FOR US IN THERE.
BUT ON THREE, BLOW THE DOOR DOWN!
SOMEHOW THE PRISONERS HAVE TRICKED US!
ONE...
TWO...
BWOOOM
HEY FELL FOR IT, PROFESSOR!

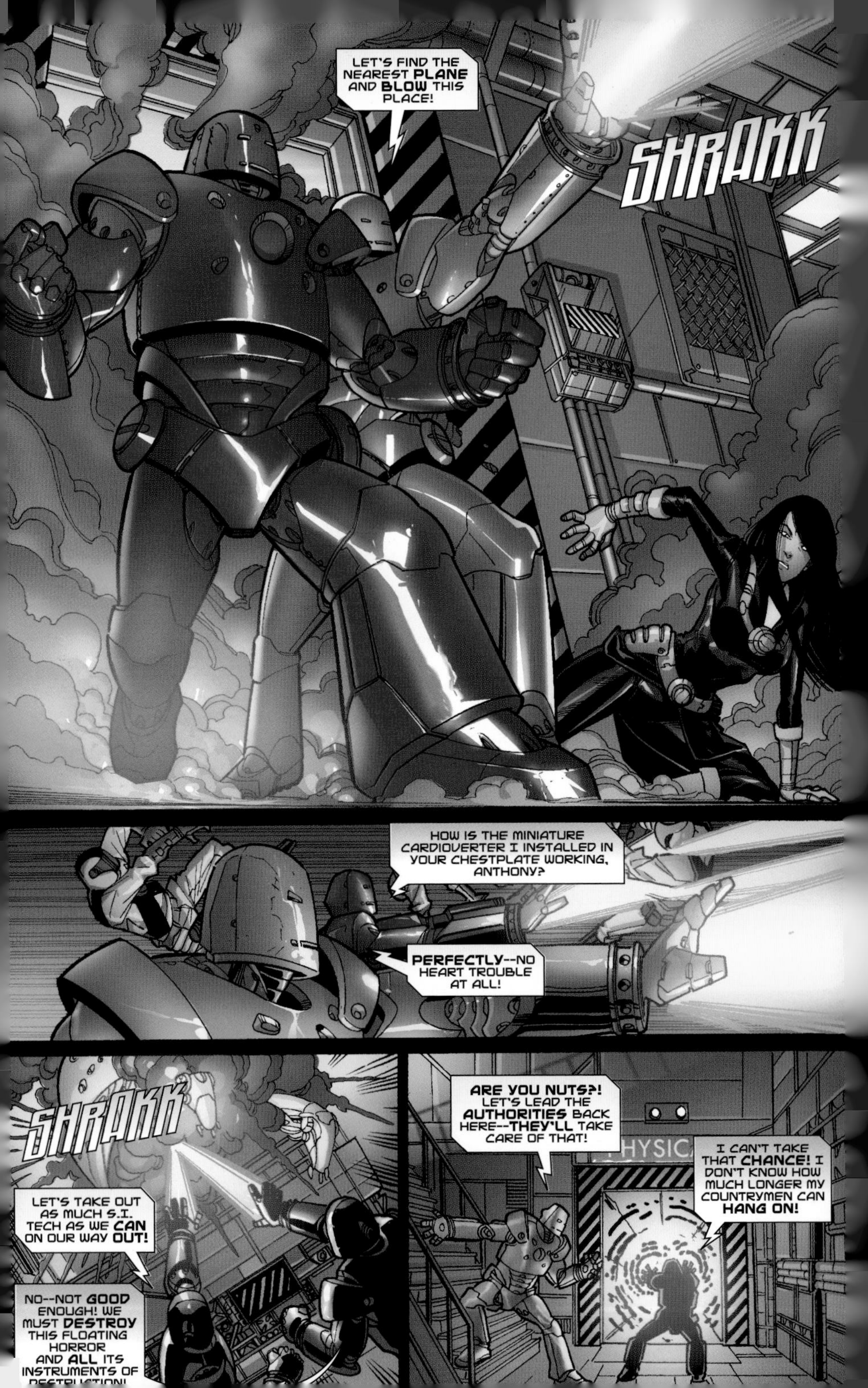
LET'S FIND THE NEAREST PLANE AND BLOW THIS PLACE!
SHRAKK
HOW IS THE MINIATURE CARDIOVERTER I INSTALLED IN YOUR CHESTPLATE WORKING, ANTHONY?
PERFECTLY--NO HEART TROUBLE AT ALL!
SHRAKK
LET'S TAKE OUT AS MUCH S.I. TECH AS WE CAN ON OUR WAY OUT!
NO--NOT GOOD ENOUGH! WE MUST DESTROY THIS FLOATING HORROR AND ALL ITS INSTRUMENTS OF
ARE YOU NUTS?! LET'S LEAD THE AUTHORITIES BACK HERE--THEY'LL TAKE CARE OF THAT!
I CAN'T TAKE THAT CHANCE! I DON'T KNOW HOW MUCH LONGER MY COUNTRYMEN CAN HANG ON!

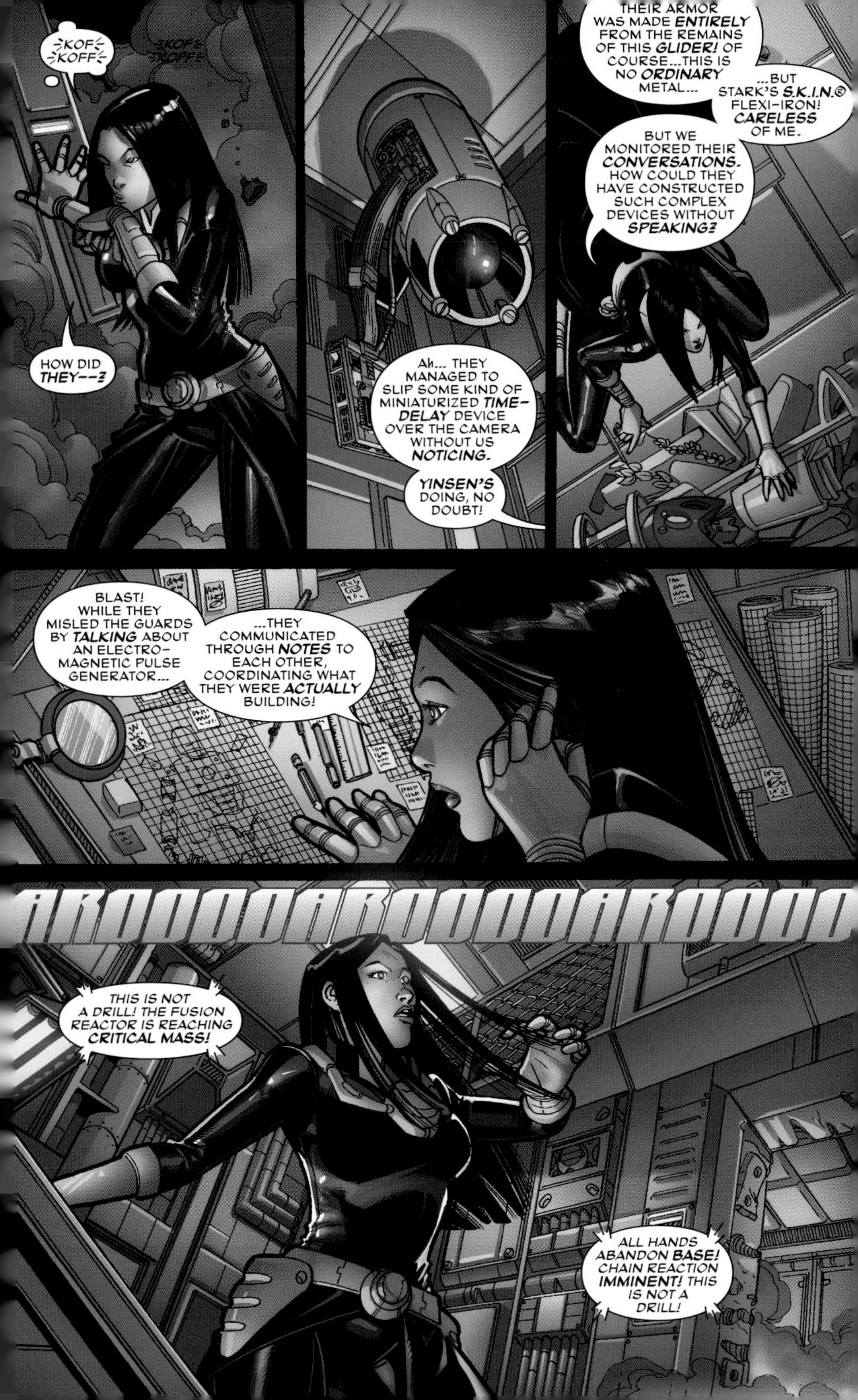

KOF KOFF
KOF KOFF
HOW DID THEY--?
Ah... THEY MANAGED TO SLIP SOME KIND OF MINIATURIZED TIME-DELAY DEVICE OVER THE CAMERA WITHOUT US NOTICING.
YINSEN'S DOING, NO DOUBT!
THEIR ARMOR WAS MADE ENTIRELY FROM THE REMAINS OF THIS GLIDER! OF COURSE... THIS IS NO ORDINARY METAL...
...BUT STARK'S S.K.I.N.® FLEXI-IRON! CARELESS OF ME.
BUT WE MONITORED THEIR CONVERSATIONS. HOW COULD THEY HAVE CONSTRUCTED SUCH COMPLEX DEVICES WITHOUT SPEAKING?
BLAST! WHILE THEY MISLED THE GUARDS BY TALKING ABOUT AN ELECTRO-MAGNETIC PULSE GENERATOR...
...THEY COMMUNICATED THROUGH NOTES TO EACH OTHER, COORDINATING WHAT THEY WERE ACTUALLY BUILDING!
AROOOOAROOOOOAROOOO
THIS IS NOT A DRILL! THE FUSION REACTOR IS REACHING CRITICAL MASS!
ALL HANDS ABANDON BASE! CHAIN REACTION IMMINENT! THIS IS NOT A DRILL!

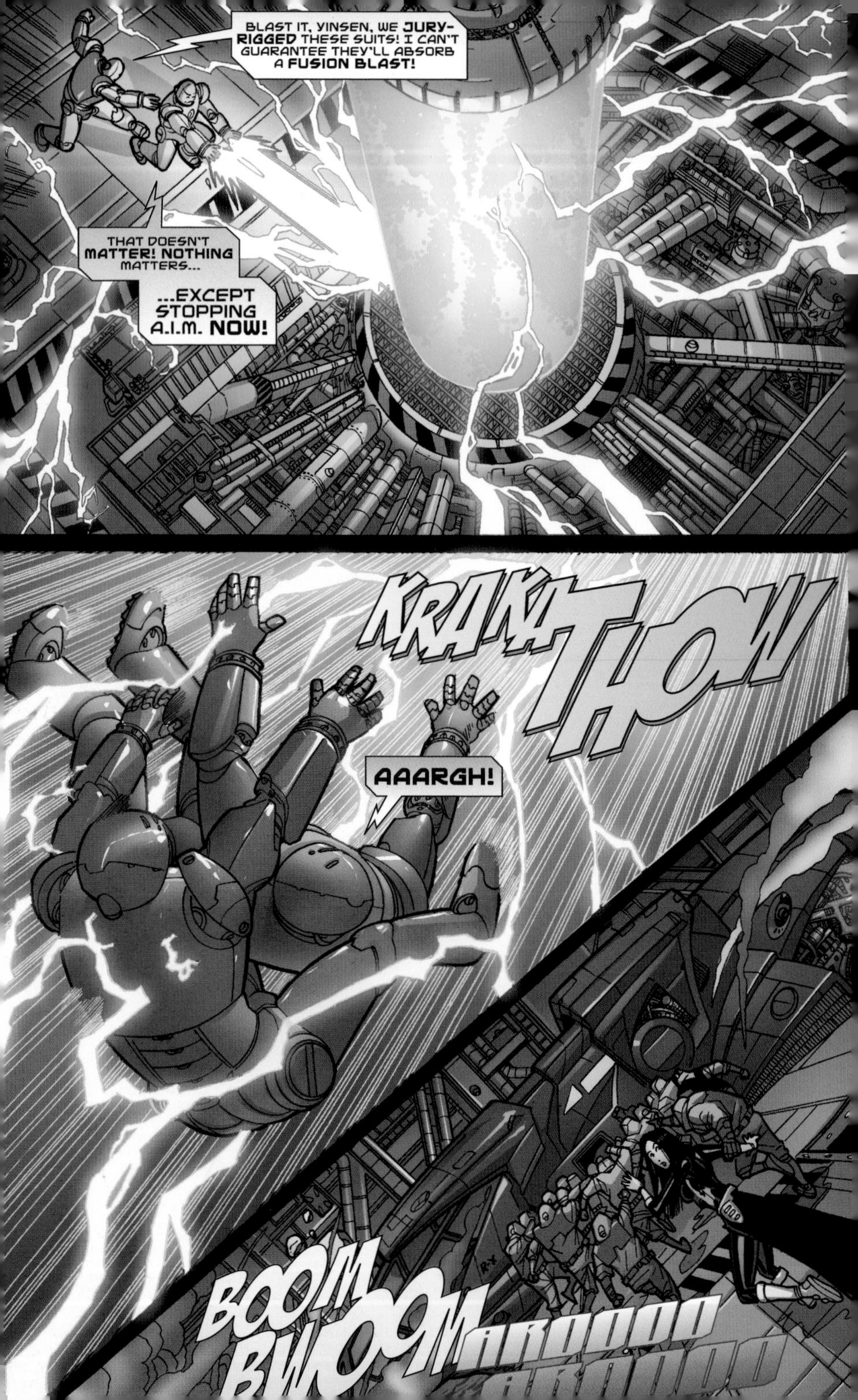
BLAST IT, YINSEN, WE JURY-RIGGED THESE SUITS! I CAN'T GUARANTEE THEY'LL ABSORB A FUSION BLAST!
THAT DOESN'T MATTER! NOTHING MATTERS...
...EXCEPT STOPPING A.I.M. NOW!
KRAKA THOOW
AAARGH!
BOOM
BWOOM
ARRRRRR

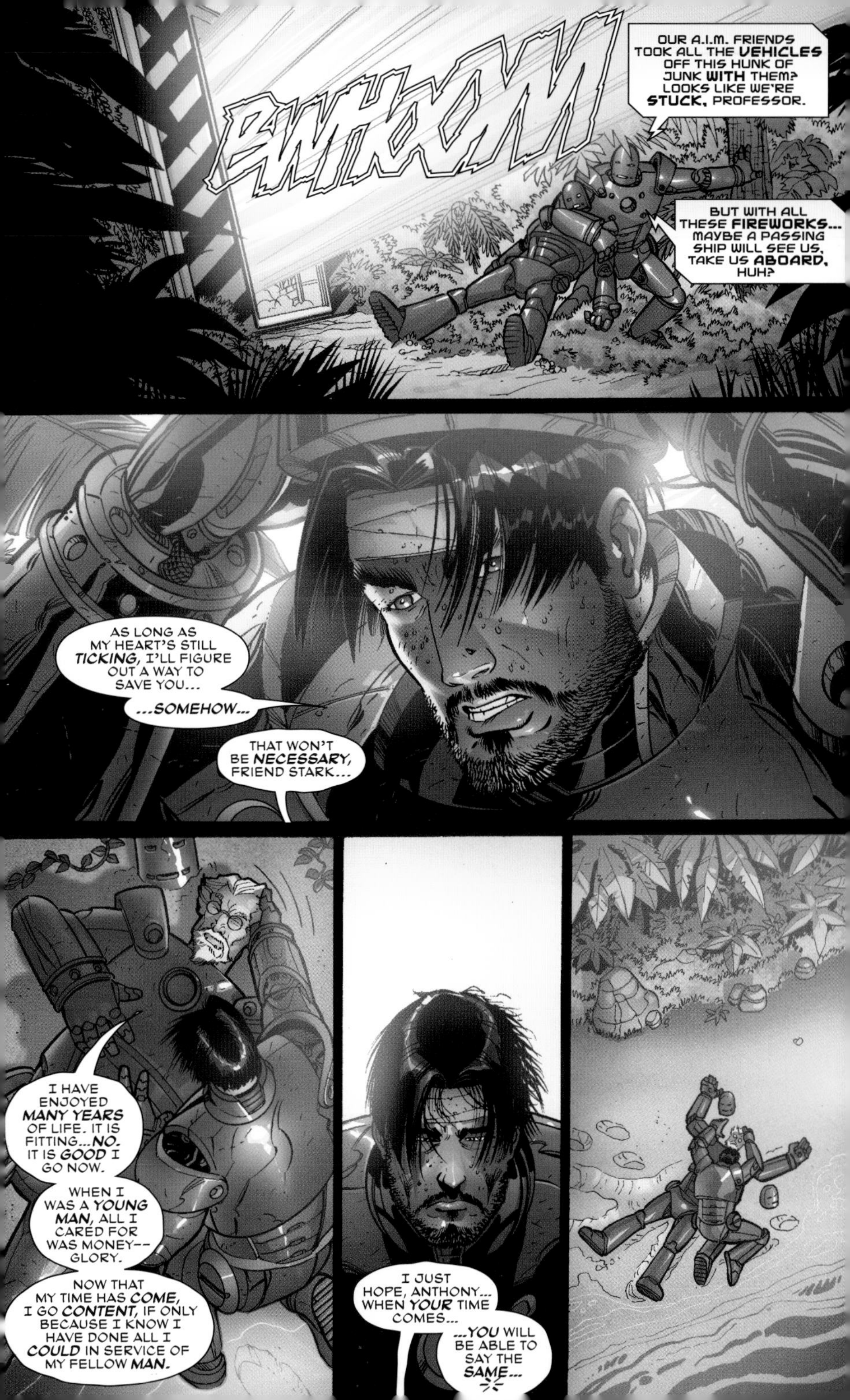
BWHOOM
OUR A.I.M. FRIENDS TOOK ALL THE VEHICLES OFF THIS HUNK OF JUNK WITH THEM? LOOKS LIKE WE'RE STUCK, PROFESSOR.
BUT WITH ALL THESE FIREWORKS... MAYBE A PASSING SHIP WILL SEE US, TAKE US ABOARD, HUH?
AS LONG AS MY HEART'S STILL TICKING, I'LL FIGURE OUT A WAY TO SAVE YOU...
...SOMEHOW...
THAT WON'T BE NECESSARY, FRIEND STARK...
I HAVE ENJOYED MANY YEARS OF LIFE. IT IS FITTING...NO. IT IS GOOD I GO NOW.
WHEN I WAS A YOUNG MAN, ALL I CARED FOR WAS MONEY-- GLORY.
NOW THAT MY TIME HAS COME, I GO CONTENT, IF ONLY BECAUSE I KNOW I HAVE DONE ALL I COULD IN SERVICE OF MY FELLOW MAN.
I JUST HOPE, ANTHONY... WHEN YOUR TIME COMES...
...YOU WILL BE ABLE TO SAY THE SAME...

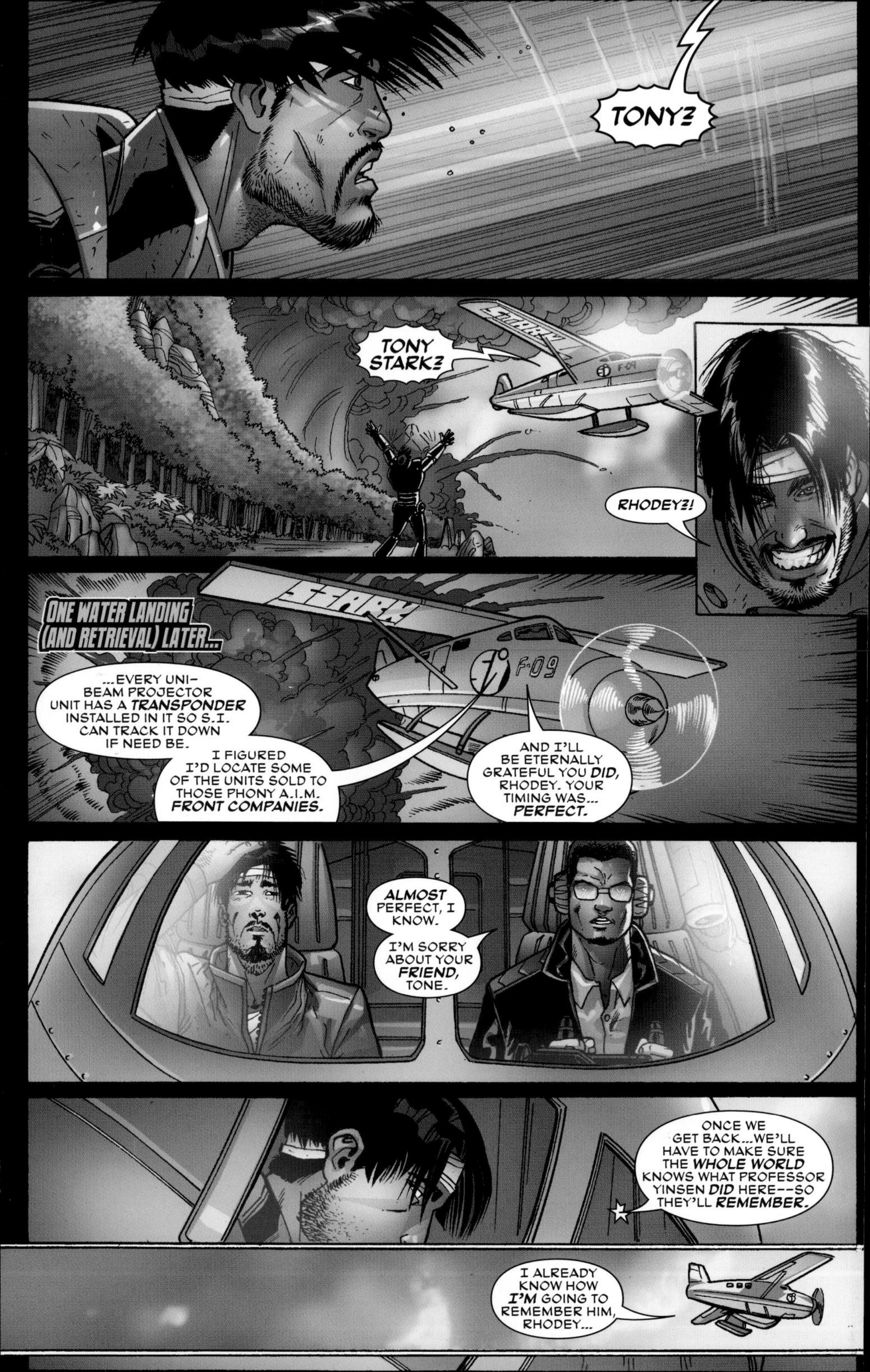
TONY?
TONY STARK?
RHODEY?!
ONE WATER LANDING (AND RETRIEVAL) LATER...
...EVERY UNI-BEAM PROJECTOR UNIT HAS A TRANSPONDER INSTALLED IN IT SO S.I. CAN TRACK IT DOWN IF NEED BE.
I FIGURED I'D LOCATE SOME OF THE UNITS SOLD TO THOSE PHONY A.I.M. FRONT COMPANIES.
AND I'LL BE ETERNALLY GRATEFUL YOU DID, RHODEY. YOUR TIMING WAS... PERFECT.
ALMOST PERFECT, I KNOW.
I'M SORRY ABOUT YOUR FRIEND, TONE.
ONCE WE GET BACK...WE'LL HAVE TO MAKE SURE THE WHOLE WORLD KNOWS WHAT PROFESSOR YINSEN DID HERE--SO THEY'LL REMEMBER.
I ALREADY KNOW HOW I'M GOING TO REMEMBER HIM, RHODEY...

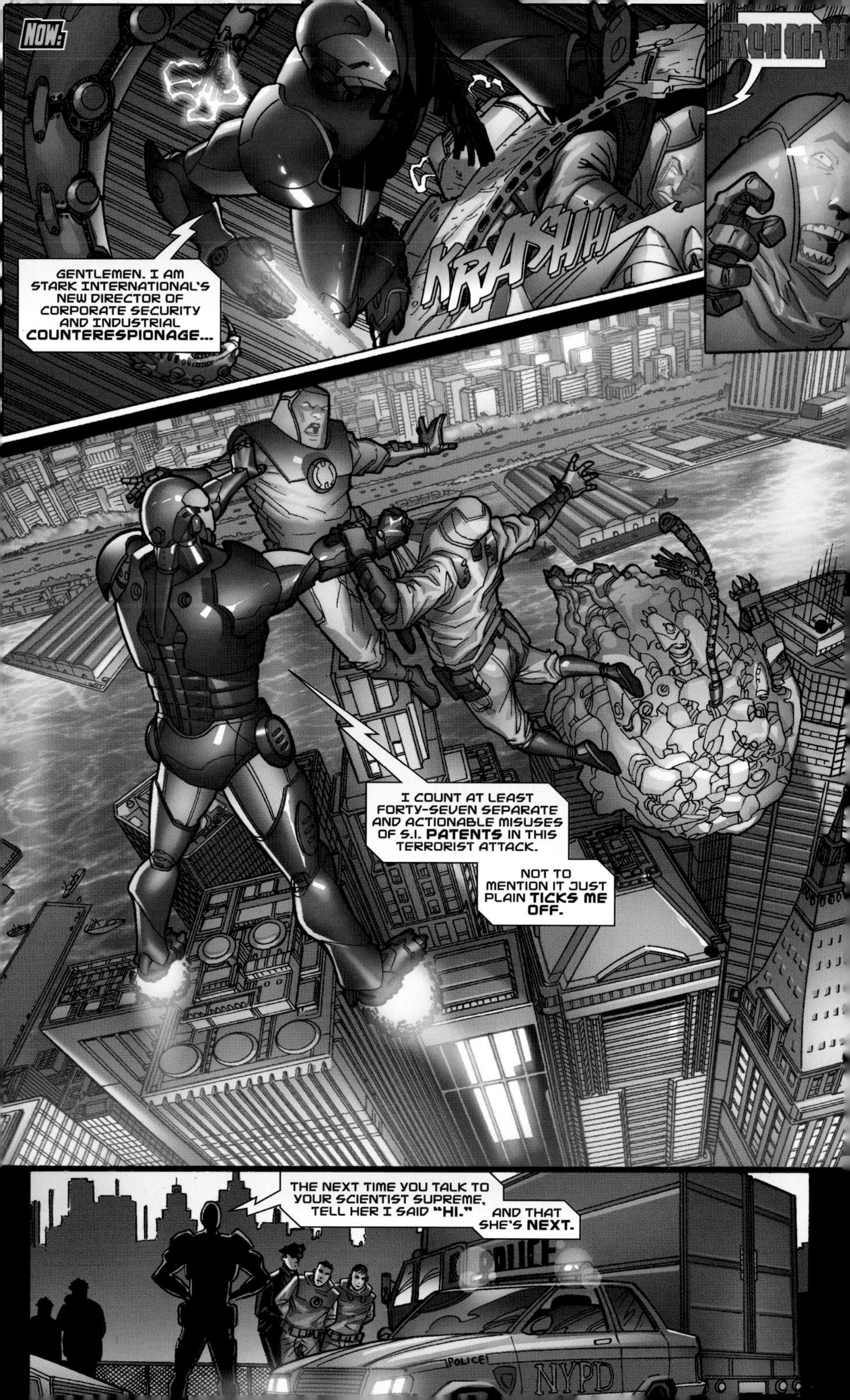
NOW:
IRON MAN
GENTLEMEN. I AM STARK INTERNATIONAL'S NEW DIRECTOR OF CORPORATE SECURITY AND INDUSTRIAL COUNTERESPIONAGE...
KRASHH
I COUNT AT LEAST FORTY-SEVEN SEPARATE AND ACTIONABLE MISUSES OF S.I. PATENTS IN THIS TERRORIST ATTACK.
NOT TO MENTION IT JUST PLAIN TICKS ME OFF.
THE NEXT TIME YOU TALK TO YOUR SCIENTIST SUPREME, TELL HER I SAID "HI."
AND THAT SHE'S NEXT.
POLICE
NYPD

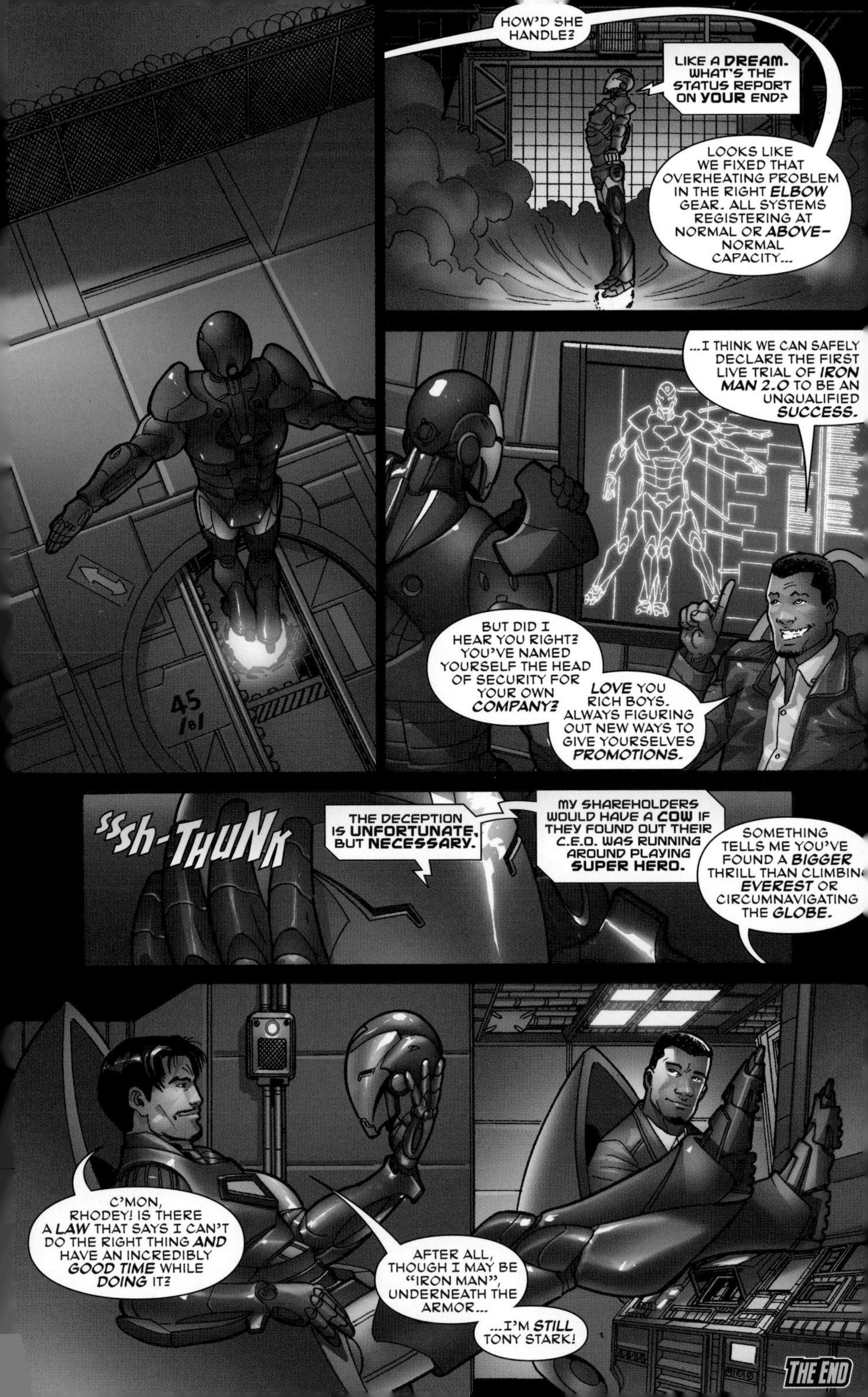
HOW'D SHE HANDLE?
LIKE A DREAM. WHAT'S THE STATUS REPORT ON YOUR END?
LOOKS LIKE WE FIXED THAT OVERHEATING PROBLEM IN THE RIGHT ELBOW GEAR. ALL SYSTEMS REGISTERING AT NORMAL OR ABOVE-NORMAL CAPACITY...
...I THINK WE CAN SAFELY DECLARE THE FIRST LIVE TRIAL OF IRON MAN 2.0 TO BE AN UNQUALIFIED SUCCESS.
BUT DID I HEAR YOU RIGHT? YOU'VE NAMED YOURSELF THE HEAD OF SECURITY FOR YOUR OWN COMPANY?
LOVE YOU RICH BOYS. ALWAYS FIGURING OUT NEW WAYS TO GIVE YOURSELVES PROMOTIONS.
45
/8/
SSSH-THUNK
THE DECEPTION IS UNFORTUNATE, BUT NECESSARY.
MY SHAREHOLDERS WOULD HAVE A COW IF THEY FOUND OUT THEIR C.E.O. WAS RUNNING AROUND PLAYING SUPER HERO.
SOMETHING TELLS ME YOU'VE FOUND A BIGGER THRILL THAN CLIMBIN EVEREST OR CIRCUMNAVIGATING THE GLOBE.
C'MON, RHODEY! IS THERE A LAW THAT SAYS I CAN'T DO THE RIGHT THING AND HAVE AN INCREDIBLY GOOD TIME WHILE DOING IT?
AFTER ALL, THOUGH I MAY BE "IRON MAN", UNDERNEATH THE ARMOR...
...I'M STILL TONY STARK!
THE END

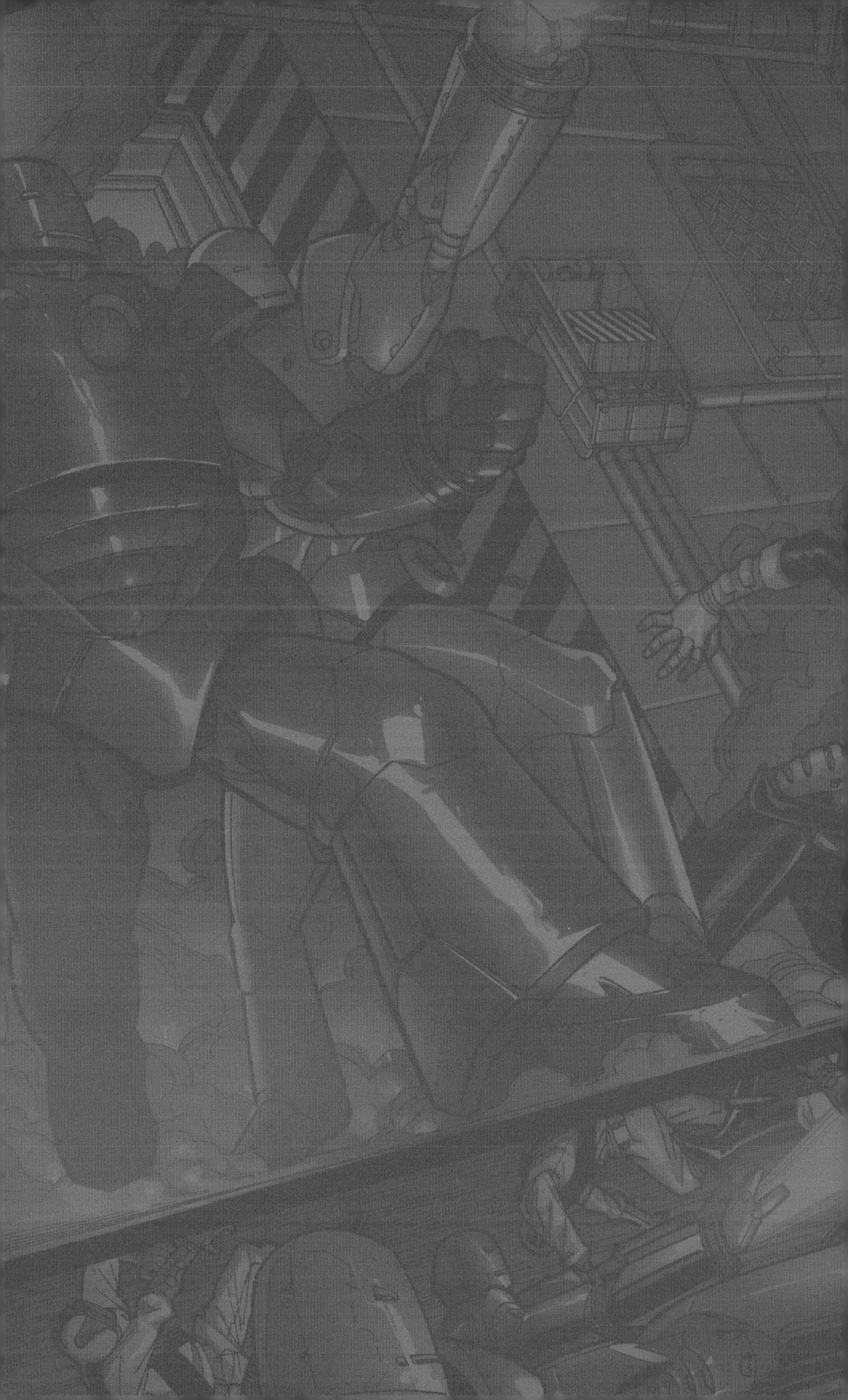

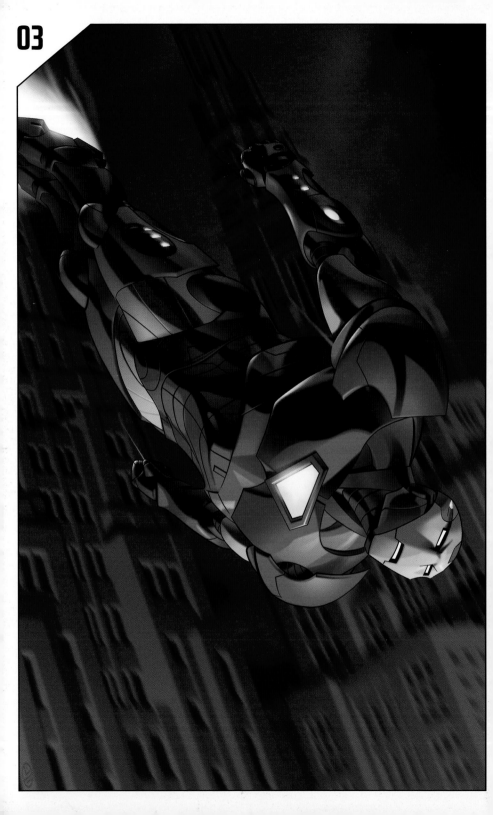

03

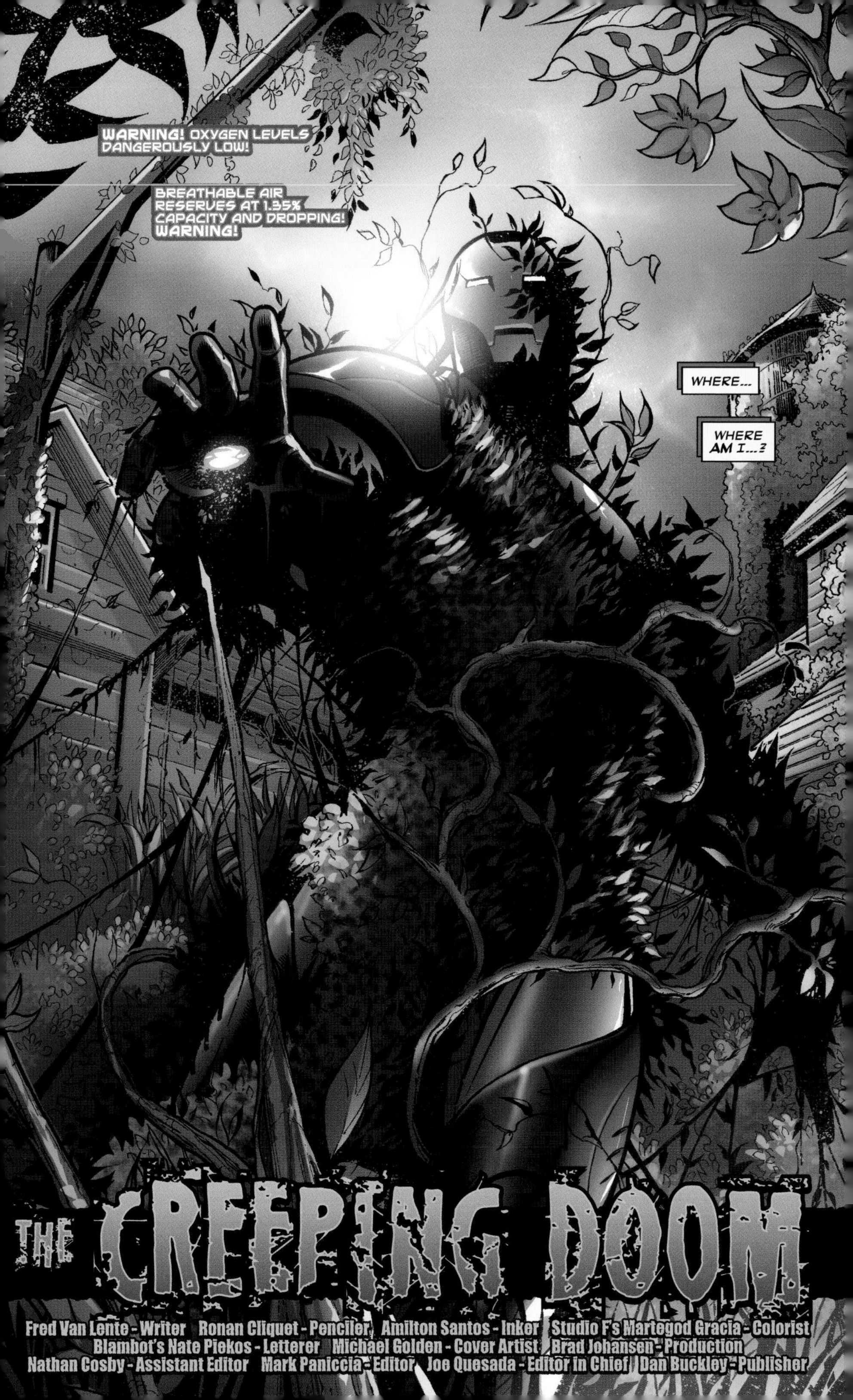
WARNING! OXYGEN LEVELS DANGEROUSLY LOW!
BREATHABLE AIR RESERVES AT 1.35% CAPACITY AND DROPPING! WARNING!
WHERE...
WHERE AM I...?
THE CREEPING DOOM
Fred Van Lente - Writer Ronan Cliquet - Penciler Amilton Santos - Inker Studio F's Martegod Gracia - Colorist
Blambot's Nate Piekos - Letterer Michael Golden - Cover Artist Brad Johansen - Production
Nathan Cosby - Assistant Editor Mark Paniccia - Editor Joe Quesada - Editor in Chief Dan Buckley - Publisher

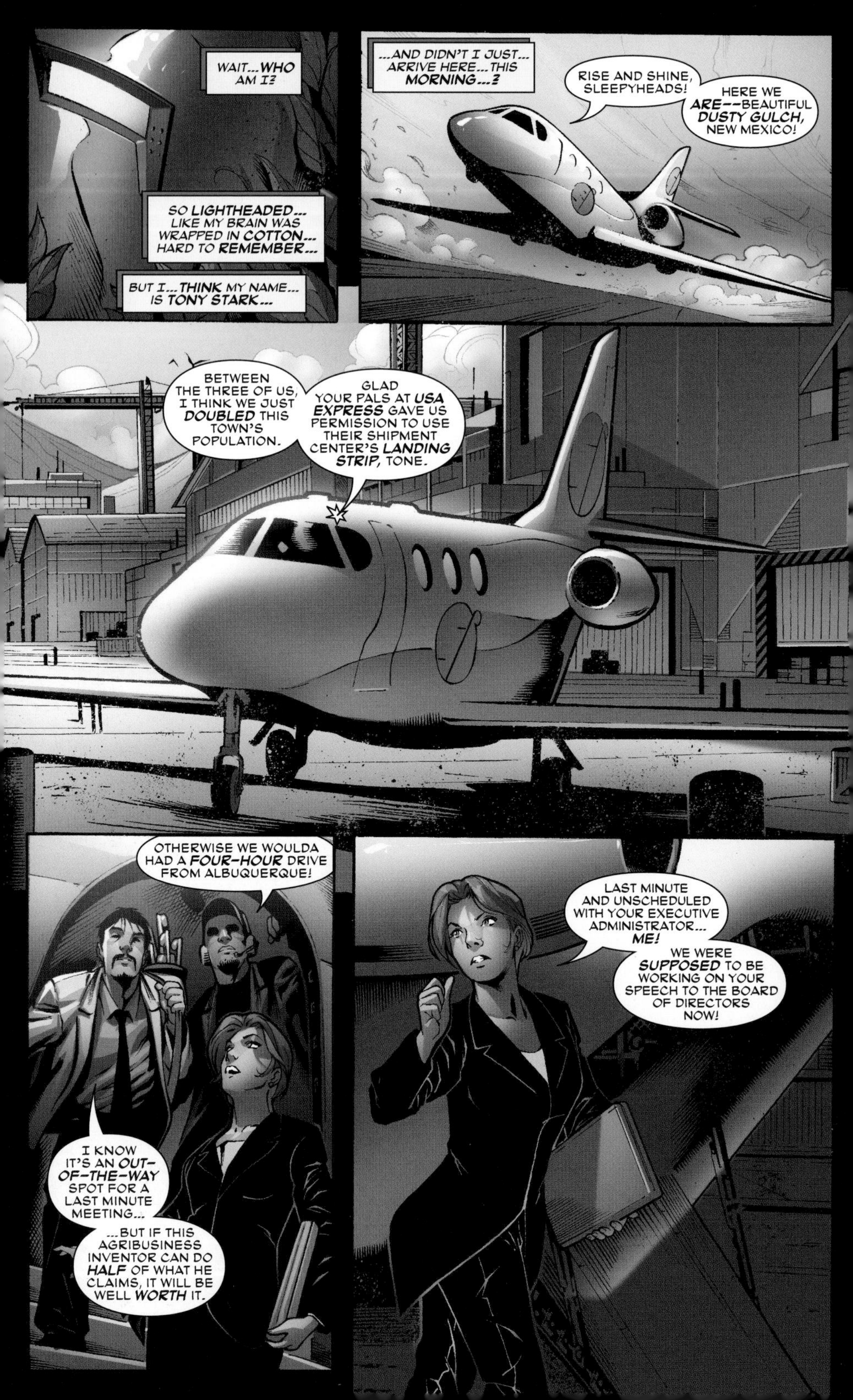

WAIT...WHO AM I?
SO LIGHTHEADED... LIKE MY BRAIN WAS WRAPPED IN COTTON... HARD TO REMEMBER...
BUT I...THINK MY NAME... IS TONY STARK...
...AND DIDN'T I JUST... ARRIVE HERE...THIS MORNING...?
RISE AND SHINE, SLEEPYHEADS!
HERE WE ARE--BEAUTIFUL DUSTY GULCH, NEW MEXICO!
BETWEEN THE THREE OF US, I THINK WE JUST DOUBLED THIS TOWN'S POPULATION.
GLAD YOUR PALS AT USA EXPRESS GAVE US PERMISSION TO USE THEIR SHIPMENT CENTER'S LANDING STRIP, TONE.
OTHERWISE WE WOULDA HAD A FOUR-HOUR DRIVE FROM ALBUQUERQUE!
I KNOW IT'S AN OUT-OF-THE-WAY SPOT FOR A LAST MINUTE MEETING...
...BUT IF THIS AGRIBUSINESS INVENTOR CAN DO HALF OF WHAT HE CLAIMS, IT WILL BE WELL WORTH IT.
LAST MINUTE AND UNSCHEDULED WITH YOUR EXECUTIVE ADMINISTRATOR... ME!
WE WERE SUPPOSED TO BE WORKING ON YOUR SPEECH TO THE BOARD OF DIRECTORS NOW!

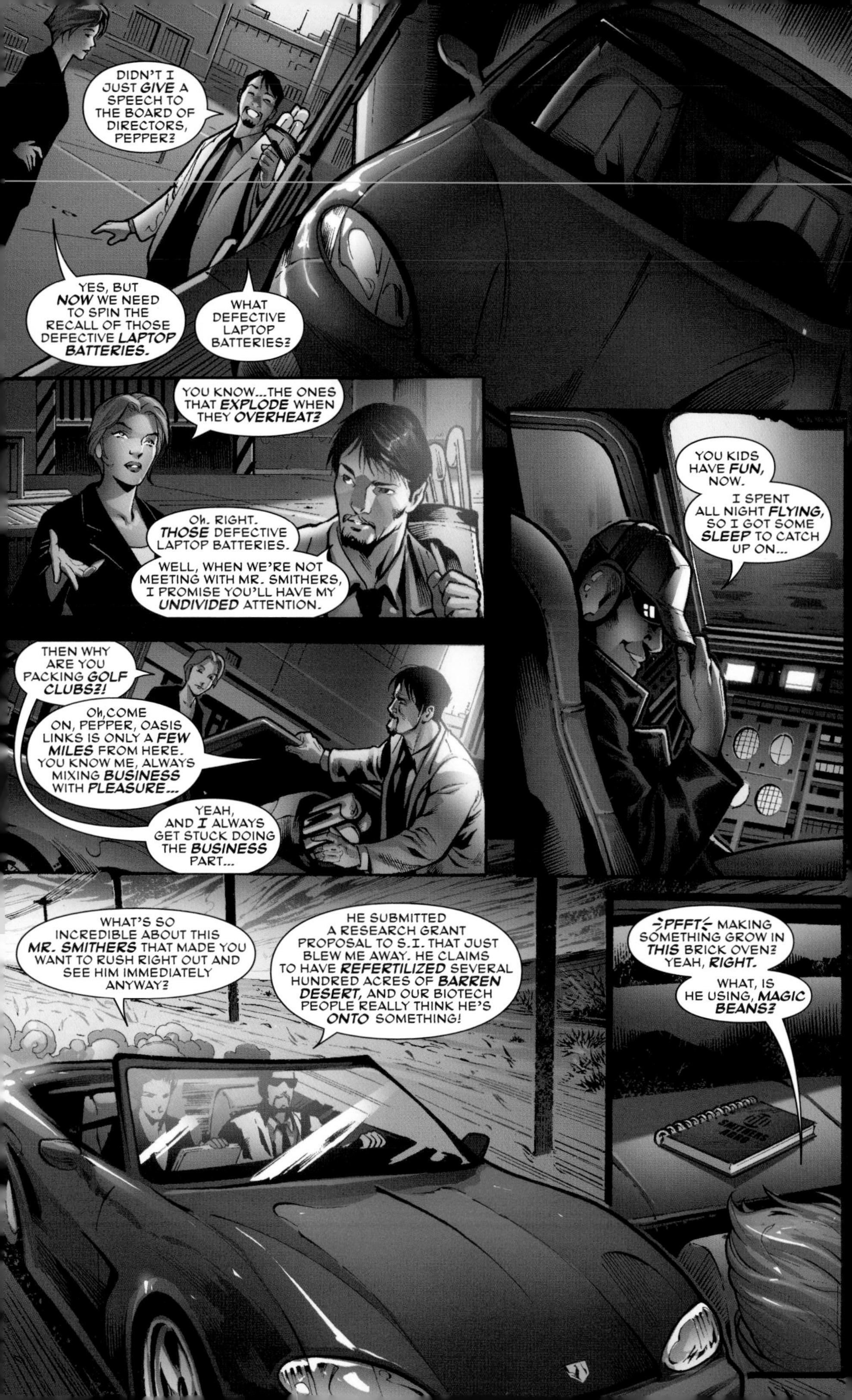
DIDN'T I JUST GIVE A SPEECH TO THE BOARD OF DIRECTORS, PEPPER?
YES, BUT NOW WE NEED TO SPIN THE RECALL OF THOSE DEFECTIVE LAPTOP BATTERIES.
WHAT DEFECTIVE LAPTOP BATTERIES?
YOU KNOW...THE ONES THAT EXPLODE WHEN THEY OVERHEAT?
OH. RIGHT. THOSE DEFECTIVE LAPTOP BATTERIES.
WELL, WHEN WE'RE NOT MEETING WITH MR. SMITHERS, I PROMISE YOU'LL HAVE MY UNDIVIDED ATTENTION.
YOU KIDS HAVE FUN, NOW.
I SPENT ALL NIGHT FLYING, SO I GOT SOME SLEEP TO CATCH UP ON...
THEN WHY ARE YOU PACKING GOLF CLUBS?!
OH, COME ON, PEPPER, OASIS LINKS IS ONLY A FEW MILES FROM HERE. YOU KNOW ME, ALWAYS MIXING BUSINESS WITH PLEASURE...
YEAH, AND I ALWAYS GET STUCK DOING THE BUSINESS PART...
WHAT'S SO INCREDIBLE ABOUT THIS MR. SMITHERS THAT MADE YOU WANT TO RUSH RIGHT OUT AND SEE HIM IMMEDIATELY ANYWAY?
HE SUBMITTED A RESEARCH GRANT PROPOSAL TO S.I. THAT JUST BLEW ME AWAY. HE CLAIMS TO HAVE REFERTILIZED SEVERAL HUNDRED ACRES OF BARREN DESERT, AND OUR BIOTECH PEOPLE REALLY THINK HE'S ONTO SOMETHING!
PFFT MAKING SOMETHING GROW IN THIS BRICK OVEN? YEAH, RIGHT.
WHAT, IS HE USING, MAGIC BEANS?

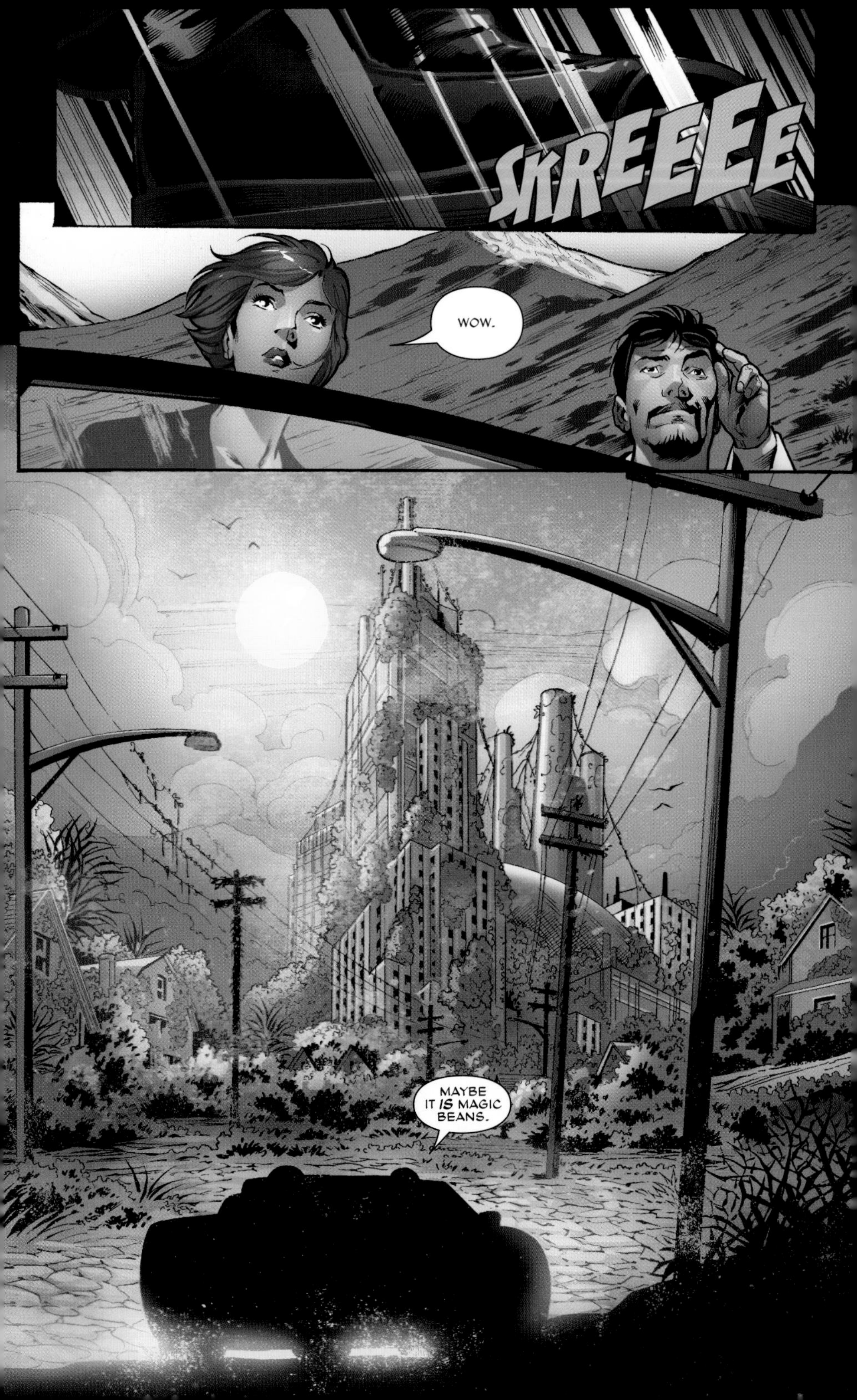
SKREEEE
WOW.
MAYBE IT IS MAGIC BEANS.

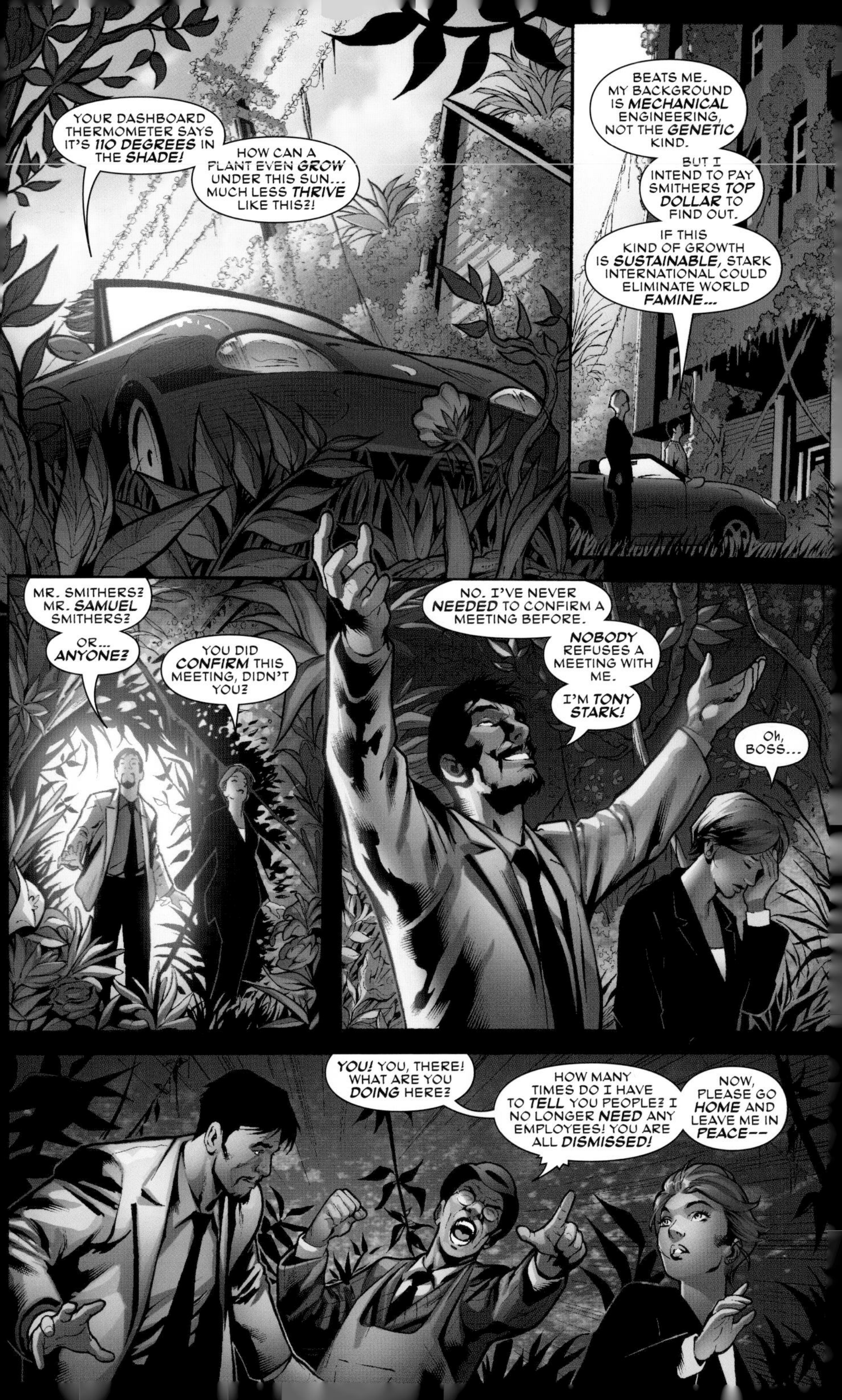

YOUR DASHBOARD THERMOMETER SAYS IT'S 110 DEGREES IN THE SHADE!
HOW CAN A PLANT EVEN GROW UNDER THIS SUN... MUCH LESS THRIVE LIKE THIS?!
BEATS ME. MY BACKGROUND IS MECHANICAL ENGINEERING, NOT THE GENETIC KIND.
BUT I INTEND TO PAY SMITHERS TOP DOLLAR TO FIND OUT.
IF THIS KIND OF GROWTH IS SUSTAINABLE, STARK INTERNATIONAL COULD ELIMINATE WORLD FAMINE...
MR. SMITHERS? MR. SAMUEL SMITHERS?
OR... ANYONE?
YOU DID CONFIRM THIS MEETING, DIDN'T YOU?
NO. I'VE NEVER NEEDED TO CONFIRM A MEETING BEFORE.
NOBODY REFUSES A MEETING WITH ME.
I'M TONY STARK!
Oh, BOSS...
YOU! YOU, THERE! WHAT ARE YOU DOING HERE?
HOW MANY TIMES DO I HAVE TO TELL YOU PEOPLE? I NO LONGER NEED ANY EMPLOYEES! YOU ARE ALL DISMISSED!
NOW, PLEASE GO HOME AND LEAVE ME IN PEACE--

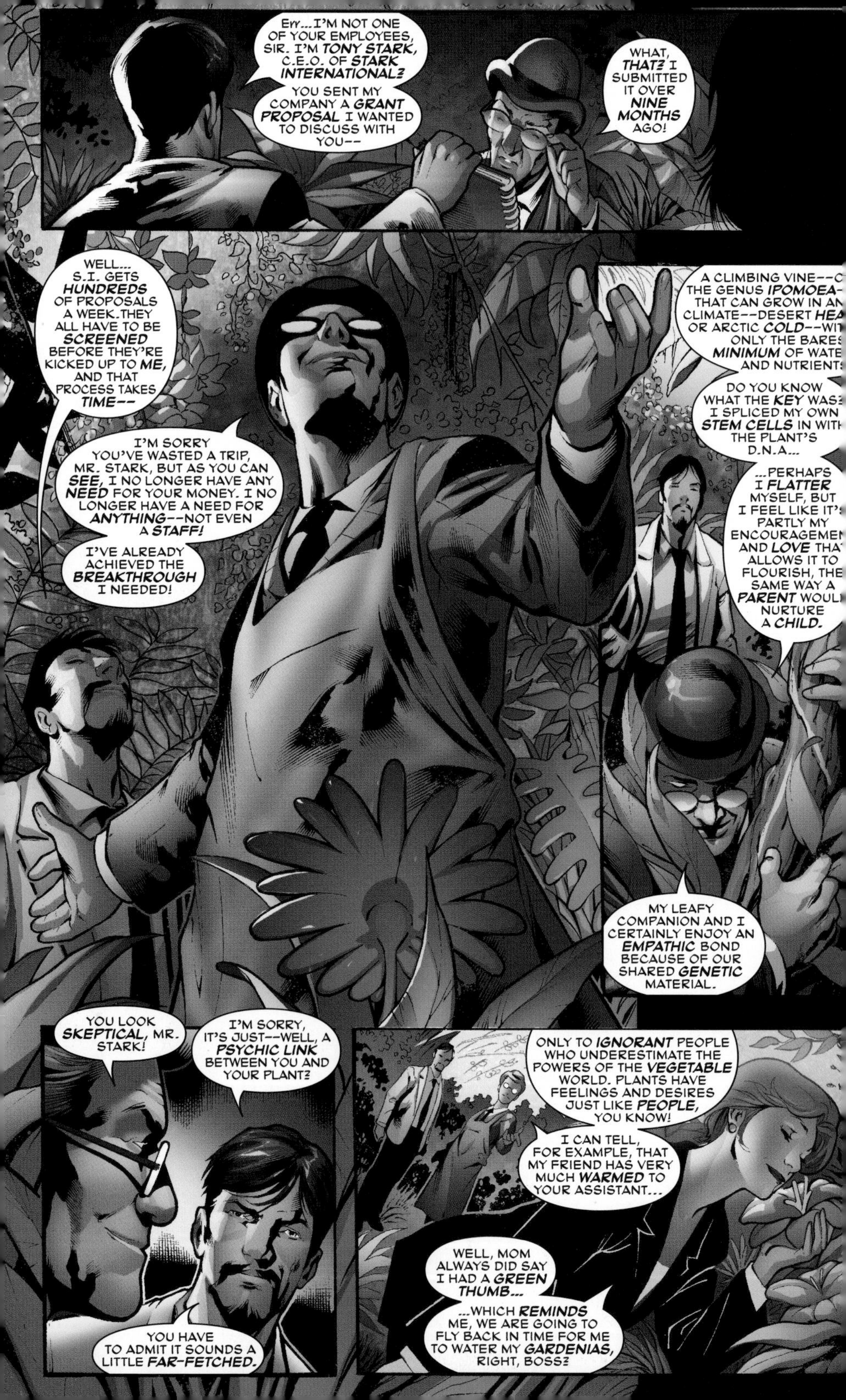
Err... I'M NOT ONE OF YOUR EMPLOYEES, SIR. I'M TONY STARK, C.E.O. OF STARK INTERNATIONAL?
YOU SENT MY COMPANY A GRANT PROPOSAL I WANTED TO DISCUSS WITH YOU--
WHAT, THAT? I SUBMITTED IT OVER NINE MONTHS AGO!
WELL... S.I. GETS HUNDREDS OF PROPOSALS A WEEK. THEY ALL HAVE TO BE SCREENED BEFORE THEY'RE KICKED UP TO ME, AND THAT PROCESS TAKES TIME--
I'M SORRY YOU'VE WASTED A TRIP, MR. STARK, BUT AS YOU CAN SEE, I NO LONGER HAVE ANY NEED FOR YOUR MONEY. I NO LONGER HAVE A NEED FOR ANYTHING--NOT EVEN A STAFF!
I'VE ALREADY ACHIEVED THE BREAKTHROUGH I NEEDED!
A CLIMBING VINE--C THE GENUS IPOMOEA- THAT CAN GROW IN AN CLIMATE--DESERT HEA OR ARCTIC COLD--WIT ONLY THE BARES MINIMUM OF WATE AND NUTRIENTS
DO YOU KNOW WHAT THE KEY WAS? I SPLICED MY OWN STEM CELLS IN WITH THE PLANT'S D.N.A...
...PERHAPS I FLATTER MYSELF, BUT I FEEL LIKE IT'S PARTLY MY ENCOURAGEMEN AND LOVE THAT ALLOWS IT TO FLOURISH, THE SAME WAY A PARENT WOUL NURTURE A CHILD.
MY LEAFY COMPANION AND I CERTAINLY ENJOY AN EMPATHIC BOND BECAUSE OF OUR SHARED GENETIC MATERIAL.
YOU LOOK SKEPTICAL, MR. STARK!
I'M SORRY, IT'S JUST--WELL, A PSYCHIC LINK BETWEEN YOU AND YOUR PLANT?
YOU HAVE TO ADMIT IT SOUNDS A LITTLE FAR-FETCHED.
ONLY TO IGNORANT PEOPLE WHO UNDERESTIMATE THE POWERS OF THE VEGETABLE WORLD. PLANTS HAVE FEELINGS AND DESIRES JUST LIKE PEOPLE, YOU KNOW!
I CAN TELL, FOR EXAMPLE, THAT MY FRIEND HAS VERY MUCH WARMED TO YOUR ASSISTANT...
WELL, MOM ALWAYS DID SAY I HAD A GREEN THUMB...
...WHICH REMINDS ME, WE ARE GOING TO FLY BACK IN TIME FOR ME TO WATER MY GARDENIAS, RIGHT, BOSS?

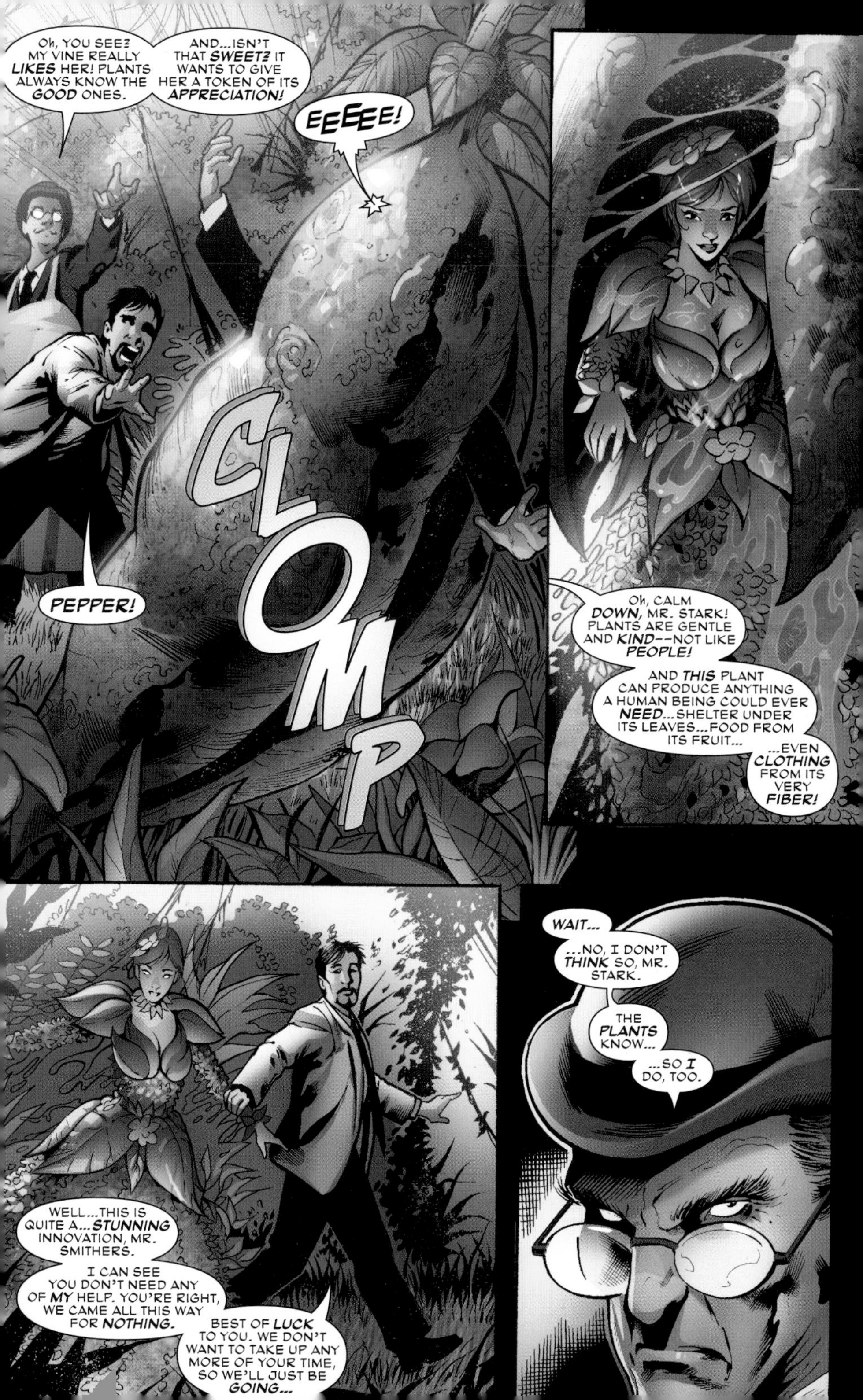
Oh, YOU SEE? MY VINE REALLY LIKES HER! PLANTS ALWAYS KNOW THE GOOD ONES.
AND...ISN'T THAT SWEET? IT WANTS TO GIVE HER A TOKEN OF ITS APPRECIATION!
EEEEE!
CLOMP
PEPPER!
Oh, CALM DOWN, MR. STARK! PLANTS ARE GENTLE AND KIND--NOT LIKE PEOPLE!
AND THIS PLANT CAN PRODUCE ANYTHING A HUMAN BEING COULD EVER NEED...SHELTER UNDER ITS LEAVES...FOOD FROM ITS FRUIT...
...EVEN CLOTHING FROM ITS VERY FIBER!
WELL...THIS IS QUITE A...STUNNING INNOVATION, MR. SMITHERS.
I CAN SEE YOU DON'T NEED ANY OF MY HELP. YOU'RE RIGHT, WE CAME ALL THIS WAY FOR NOTHING.
BEST OF LUCK TO YOU. WE DON'T WANT TO TAKE UP ANY MORE OF YOUR TIME, SO WE'LL JUST BE GOING...
WAIT...
...NO, I DON'T THINK SO, MR. STARK.
THE PLANTS KNOW...
...SO I DO, TOO.

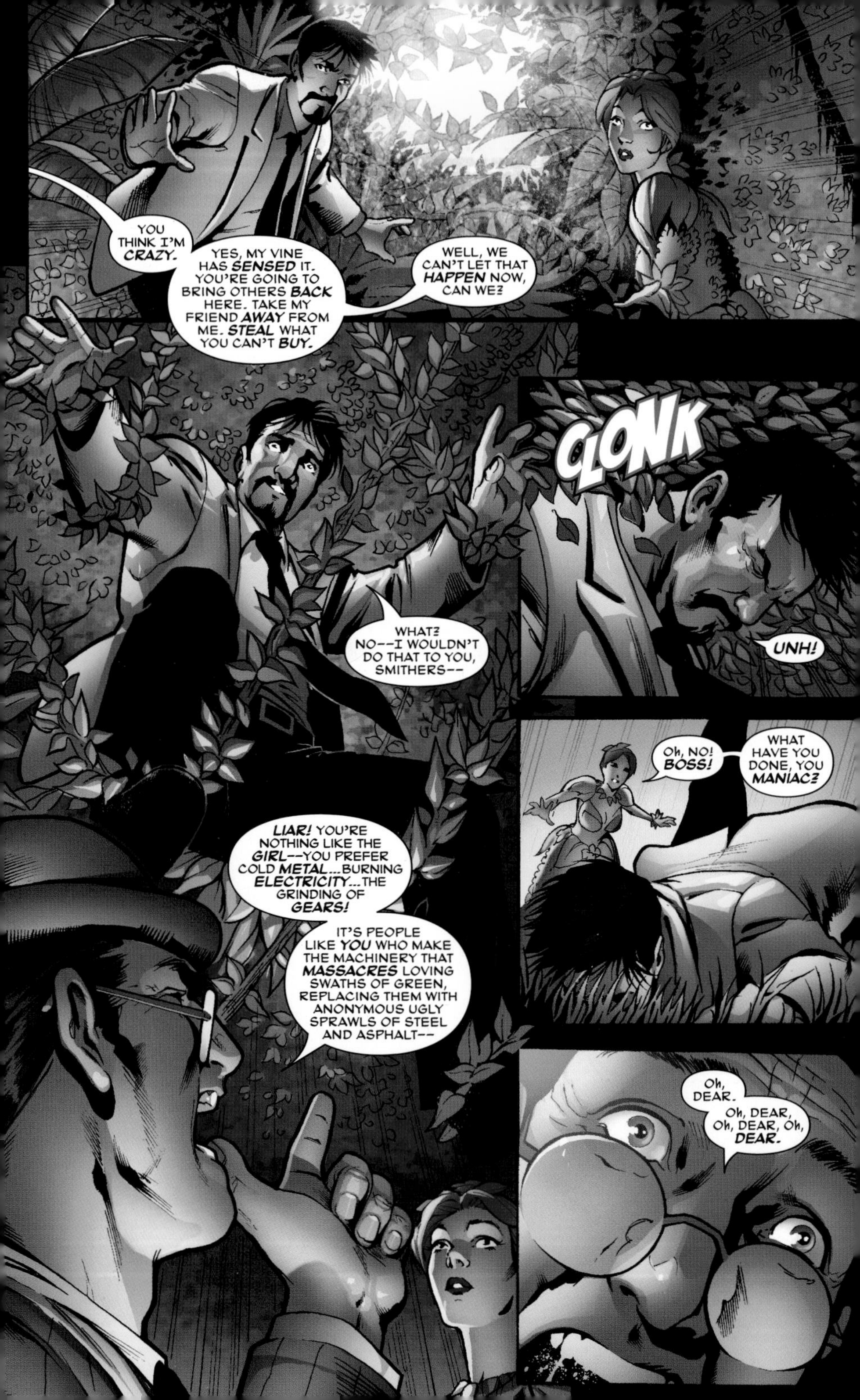
YOU THINK I'M CRAZY.
YES, MY VINE HAS SENSED IT. YOU'RE GOING TO BRING OTHERS BACK HERE. TAKE MY FRIEND AWAY FROM ME. STEAL WHAT YOU CAN'T BUY.
WELL, WE CAN'T LET THAT HAPPEN NOW, CAN WE?
WHAT? NO--I WOULDN'T DO THAT TO YOU, SMITHERS--
LIAR! YOU'RE NOTHING LIKE THE GIRL--YOU PREFER COLD METAL...BURNING ELECTRICITY...THE GRINDING OF GEARS!
IT'S PEOPLE LIKE YOU WHO MAKE THE MACHINERY THAT MASSACRES LOVING SWATHS OF GREEN, REPLACING THEM WITH ANONYMOUS UGLY SPRAWLS OF STEEL AND ASPHALT--
CLONK
UNH!
Oh, NO! BOSS!
WHAT HAVE YOU DONE, YOU MANIAC?
Oh, DEAR.
Oh, DEAR, Oh, DEAR, Oh, DEAR.

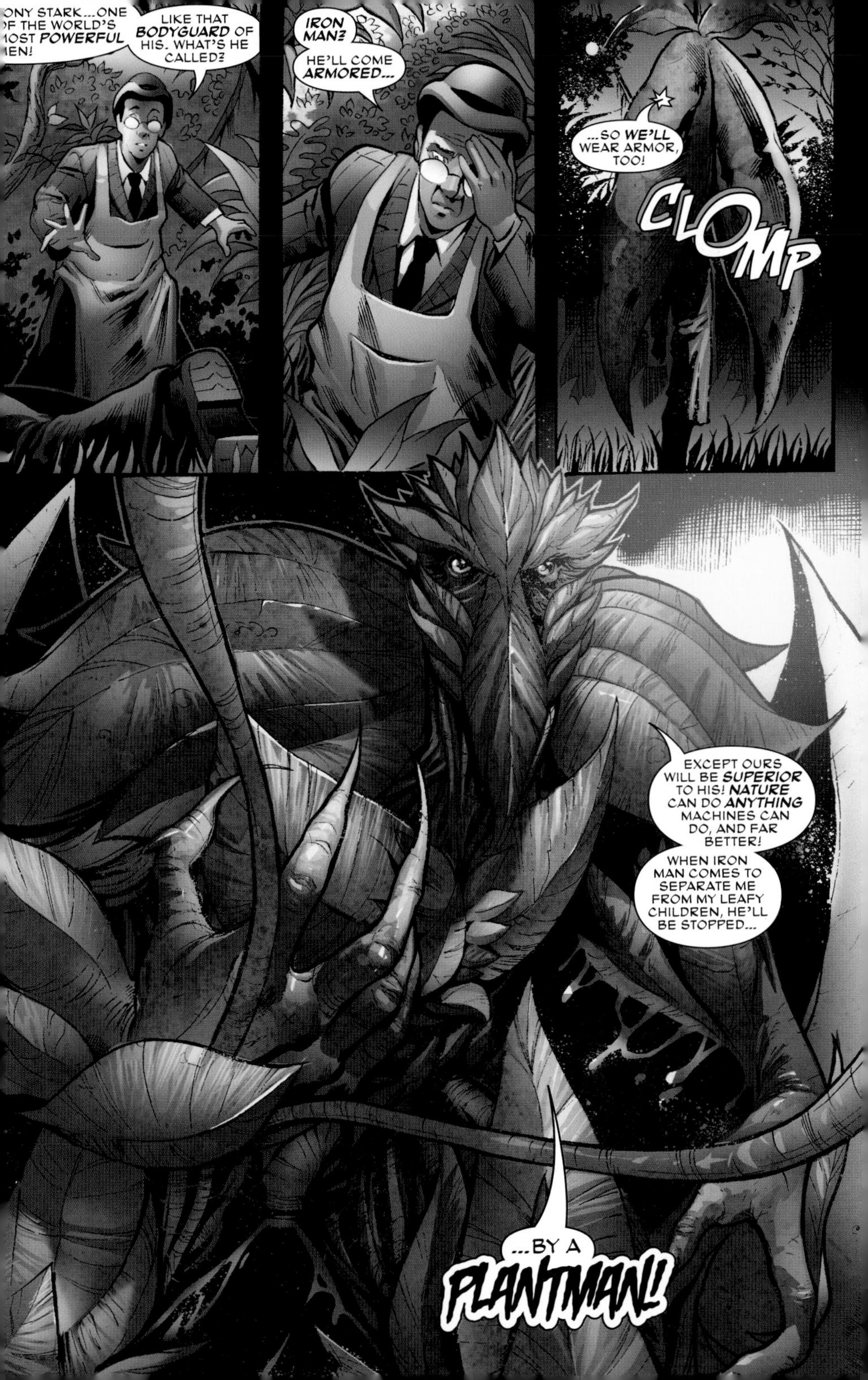

ONY STARK...ONE
OF THE WORLD'S
MOST POWERFUL
MEN!
LIKE THAT BODYGUARD OF HIS. WHAT'S HE CALLED?
IRON MAN?
HE'LL COME ARMORED...
...SO WE'LL WEAR ARMOR, TOO!
CLOMP
EXCEPT OURS WILL BE SUPERIOR TO HIS! NATURE CAN DO ANYTHING MACHINES CAN DO, AND FAR BETTER!
WHEN IRON MAN COMES TO SEPARATE ME FROM MY LEAFY CHILDREN, HE'LL BE STOPPED...
...BY A
PLANTMAN!

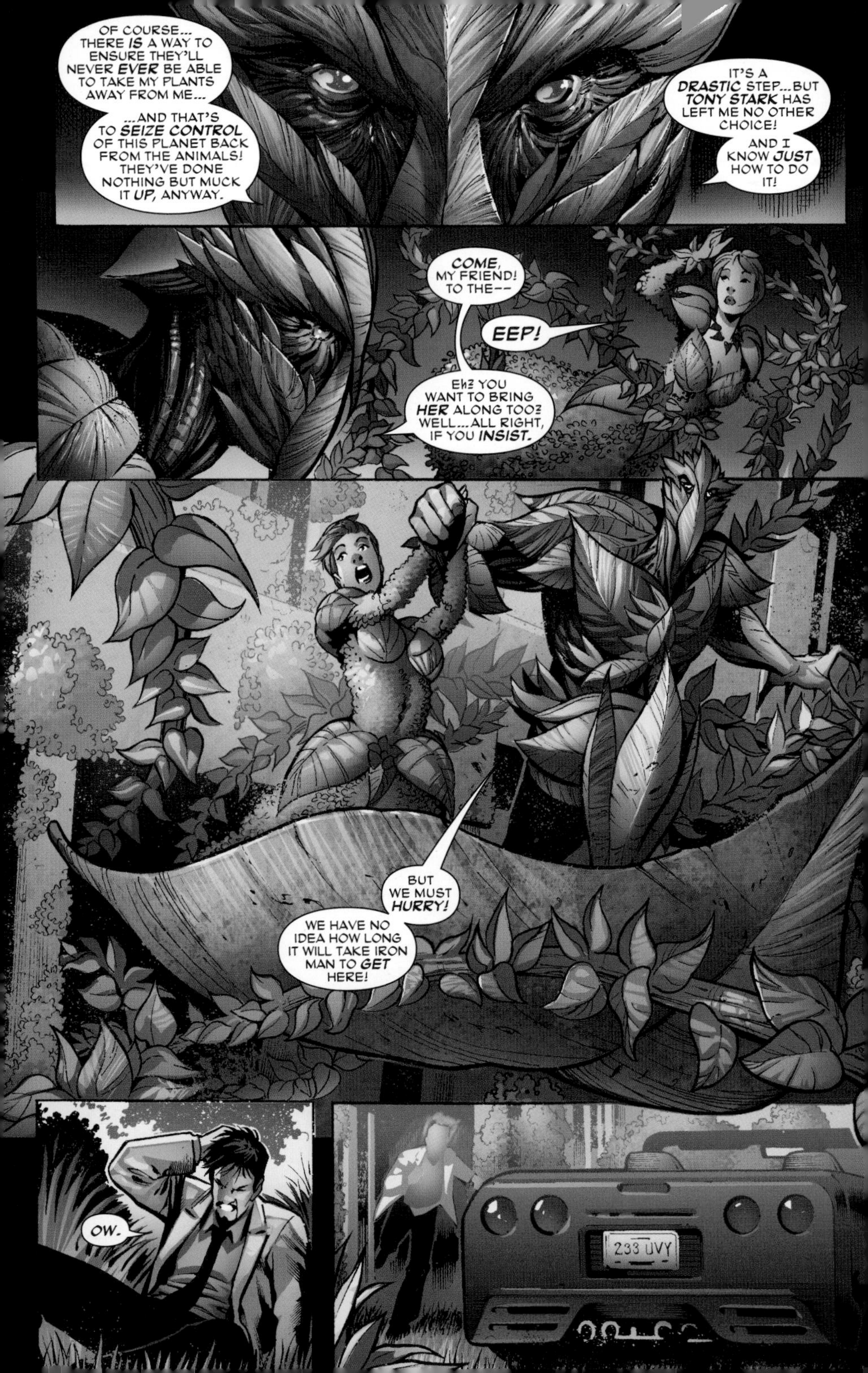
OF COURSE... THERE IS A WAY TO ENSURE THEY'LL NEVER EVER BE ABLE TO TAKE MY PLANTS AWAY FROM ME...
...AND THAT'S TO SEIZE CONTROL OF THIS PLANET BACK FROM THE ANIMALS! THEY'VE DONE NOTHING BUT MUCK IT UP, ANYWAY.
IT'S A DRASTIC STEP...BUT TONY STARK HAS LEFT ME NO OTHER CHOICE!
AND I KNOW JUST HOW TO DO IT!
COME, MY FRIEND! TO THE--
EEP!
EH? YOU WANT TO BRING HER ALONG TOO? WELL...ALL RIGHT, IF YOU INSIST.
BUT WE MUST HURRY!
WE HAVE NO IDEA HOW LONG IT WILL TAKE IRON MAN TO GET HERE!
OW.
233 UVY

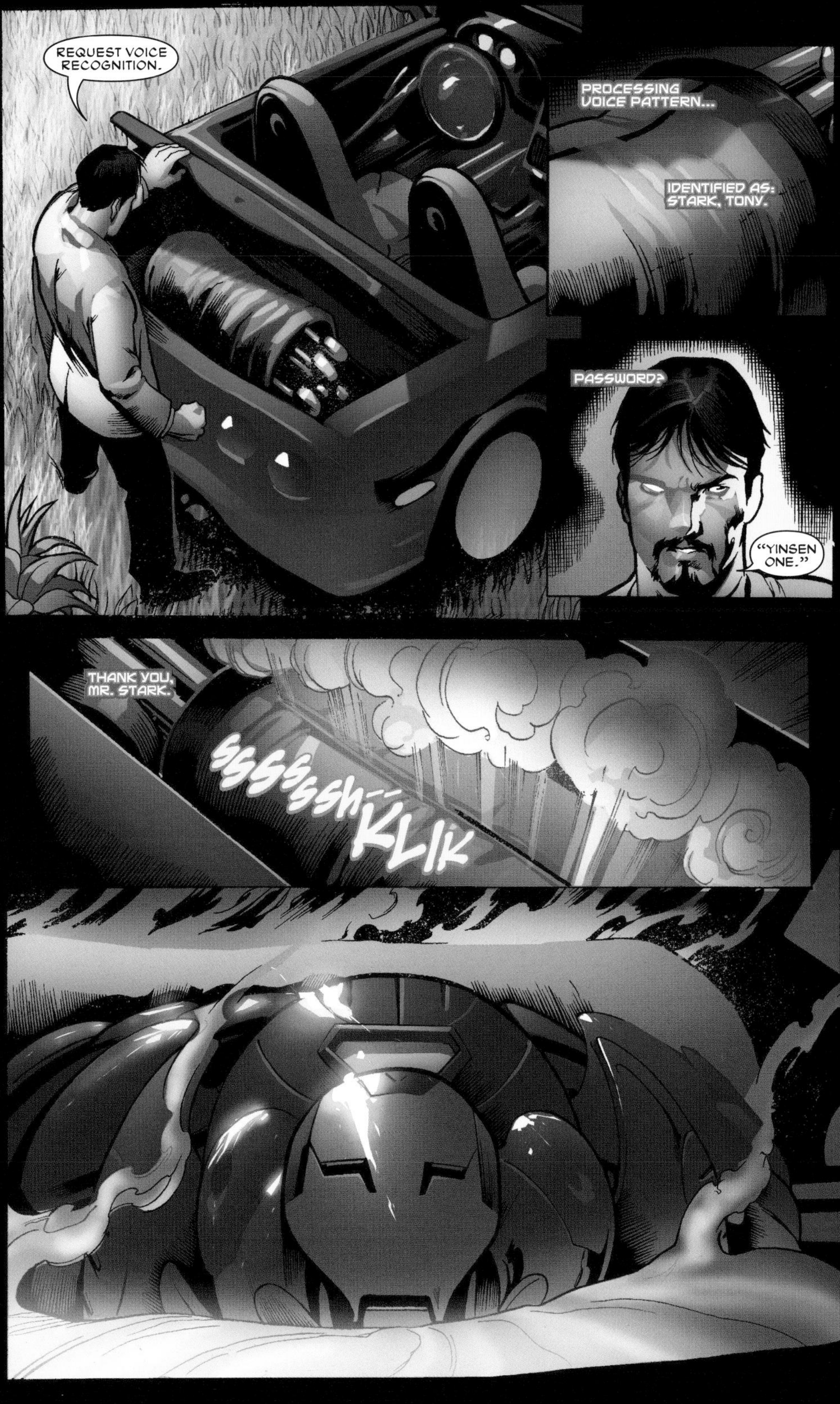
REQUEST VOICE RECOGNITION.
PROCESSING VOICE PATTERN...
IDENTIFIED AS: STARK, TONY.
PASSWORD?
"YINSEN ONE."
THANK YOU, MR. STARK.
SSSSSSH--KLIK

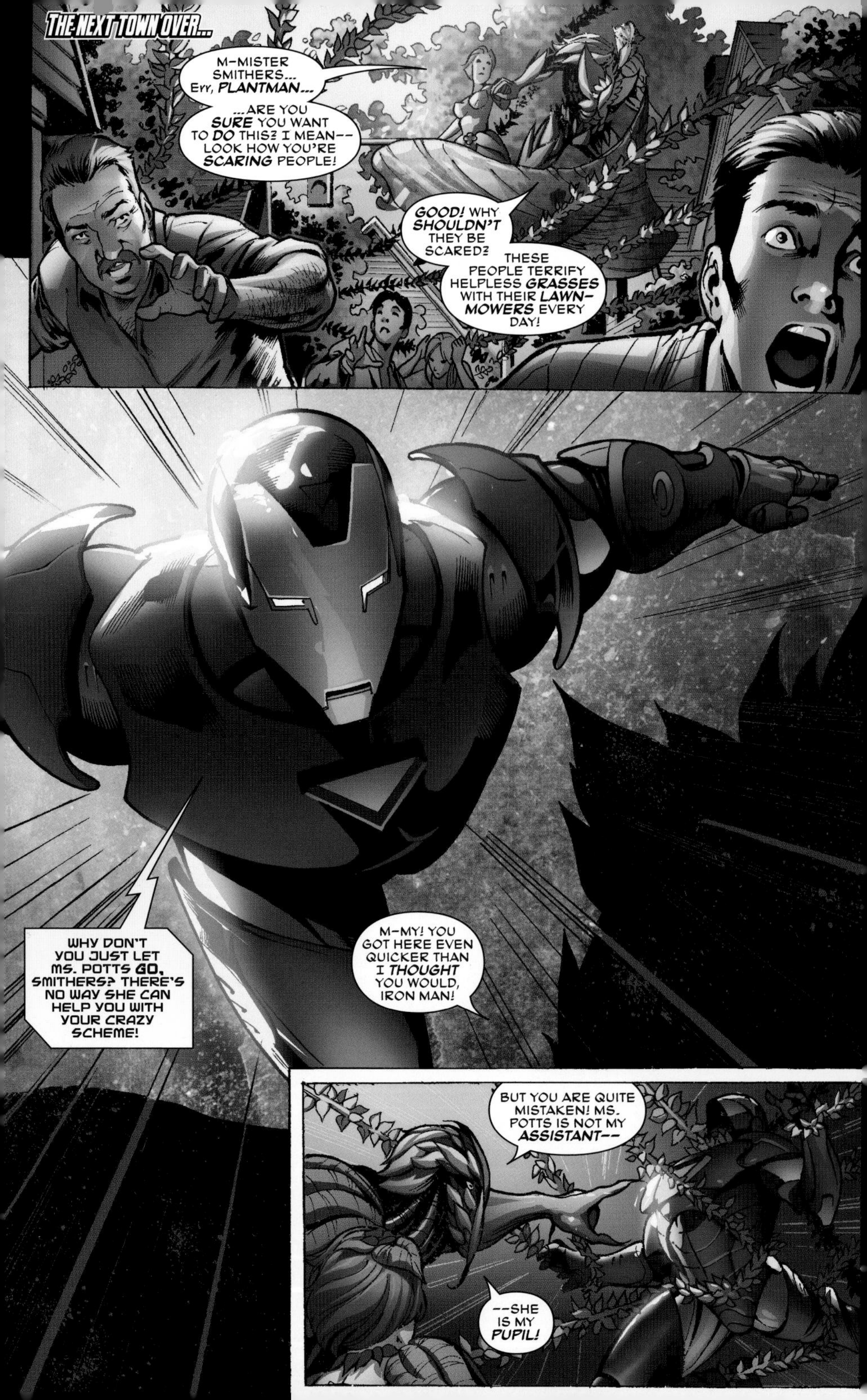
THE NEXT TOWN OVER...
M-MISTER SMITHERS... Err, PLANTMAN...
...ARE YOU SURE YOU WANT TO DO THIS? I MEAN-- LOOK HOW YOU'RE SCARING PEOPLE!
GOOD! WHY SHOULDN'T THEY BE SCARED?
THESE PEOPLE TERRIFY HELPLESS GRASSES WITH THEIR LAWN-MOWERS EVERY DAY!
WHY DON'T YOU JUST LET MS. POTTS GO, SMITHERS? THERE'S NO WAY SHE CAN HELP YOU WITH YOUR CRAZY SCHEME!
M-MY! YOU GOT HERE EVEN QUICKER THAN I THOUGHT YOU WOULD, IRON MAN!
BUT YOU ARE QUITE MISTAKEN! MS. POTTS IS NOT MY ASSISTANT--
--SHE IS MY PUPIL!

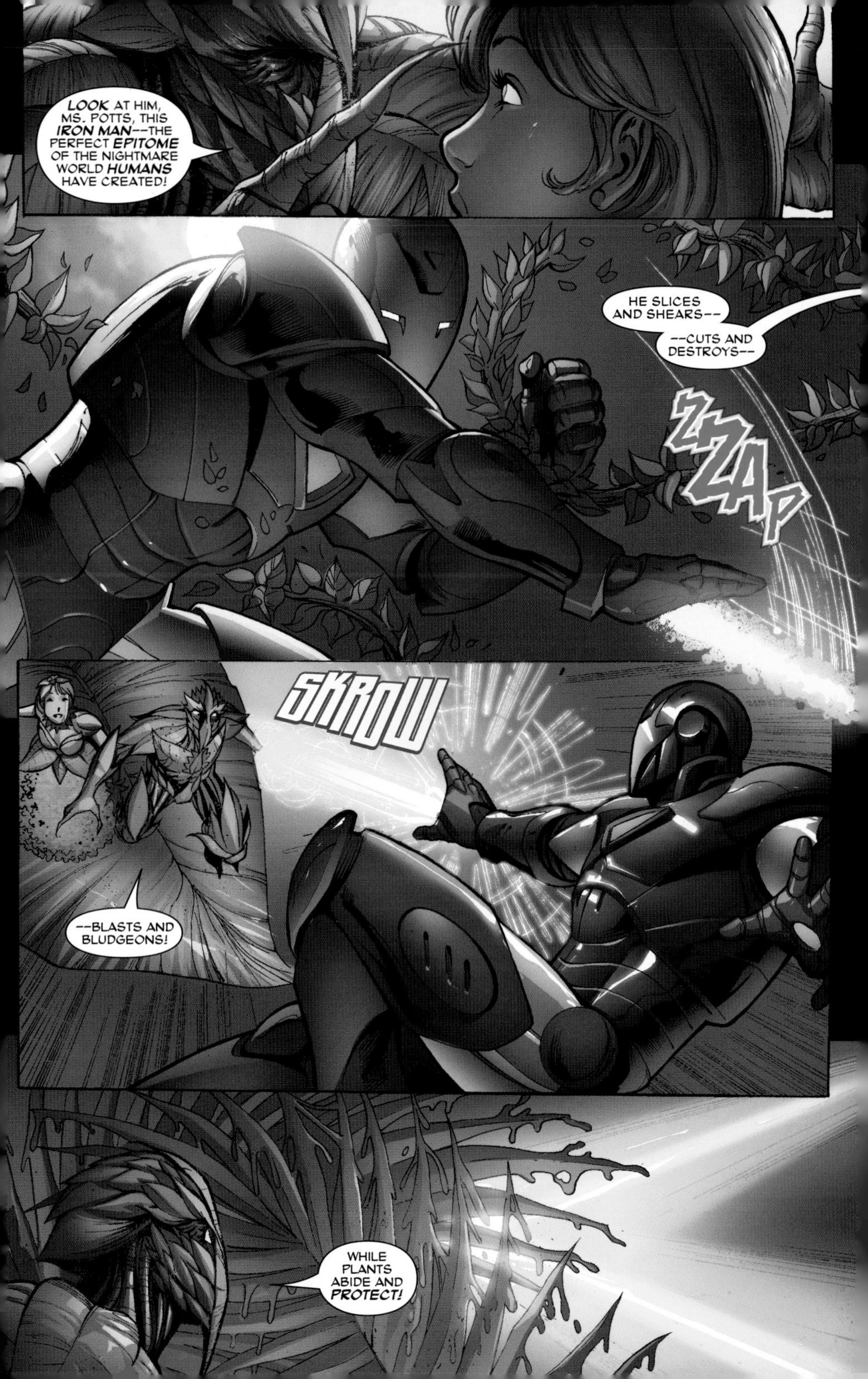
LOOK AT HIM, MS. POTTS, THIS IRON MAN--THE PERFECT EPITOME OF THE NIGHTMARE WORLD HUMANS HAVE CREATED!
HE SLICES AND SHEARS--
--CUTS AND DESTROYS--
ZZZAP
SKROW
--BLASTS AND BLUDGEONS!
WHILE PLANTS ABIDE AND PROTECT!

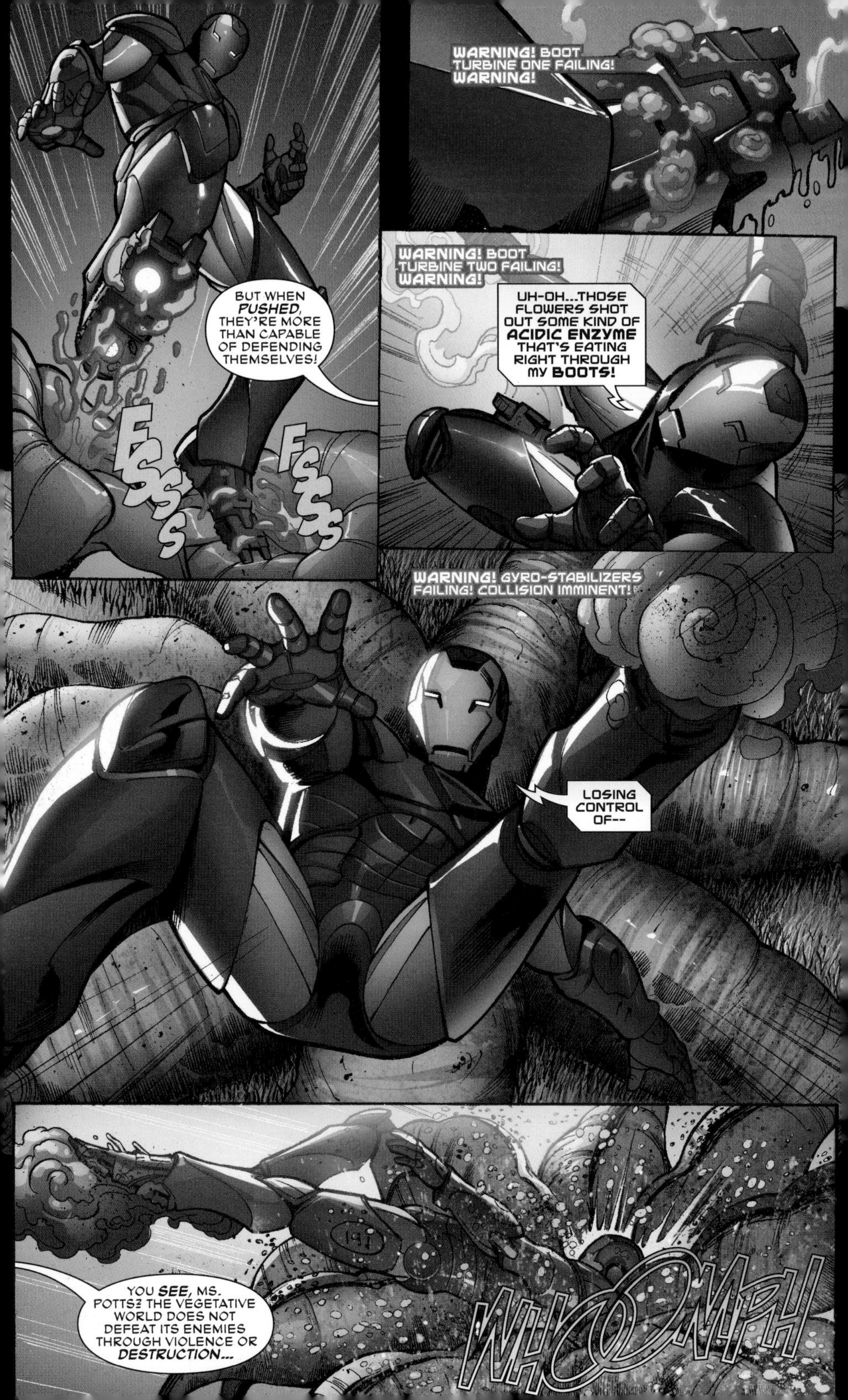
BUT WHEN PUSHED, THEY'RE MORE THAN CAPABLE OF DEFENDING THEMSELVES!
FSSSS
FSSSS
WARNING! BOOT TURBINE ONE FAILING! WARNING!
WARNING! BOOT TURBINE TWO FAILING! WARNING!
UH-OH...THOSE FLOWERS SHOT OUT SOME KIND OF ACIDIC ENZYME THAT'S EATING RIGHT THROUGH MY BOOTS!
WARNING! GYRO-STABILIZERS FAILING! COLLISION IMMINENT!
LOSING CONTROL OF--
YOU SEE, MS. POTTS? THE VEGETATIVE WORLD DOES NOT DEFEAT ITS ENEMIES THROUGH VIOLENCE OR DESTRUCTION...
WHOOMPH

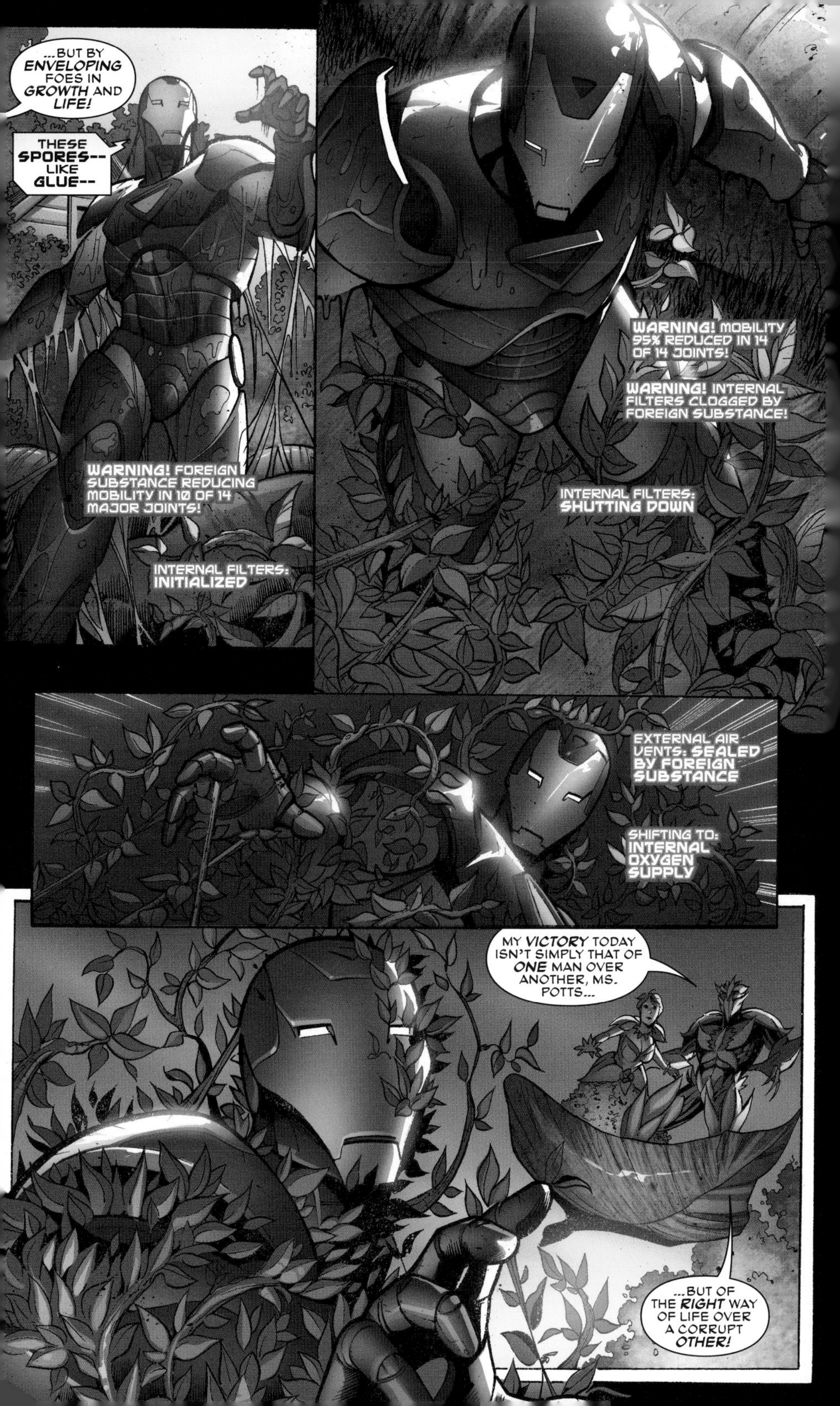

...BUT BY ENVELOPING FOES IN GROWTH AND LIFE!
THESE SPORES-- LIKE GLUE--
WARNING! FOREIGN SUBSTANCE REDUCING MOBILITY IN 10 OF 14 MAJOR JOINTS!
INTERNAL FILTERS: INITIALIZED
WARNING! MOBILITY 95% REDUCED IN 14 OF 14 JOINTS!
WARNING! INTERNAL FILTERS CLOGGED BY FOREIGN SUBSTANCE!
INTERNAL FILTERS: SHUTTING DOWN
EXTERNAL AIR VENTS: SEALED BY FOREIGN SUBSTANCE
SHIFTING TO: INTERNAL OXYGEN SUPPLY
MY VICTORY TODAY ISN'T SIMPLY THAT OF ONE MAN OVER ANOTHER, MS. POTTS...
...BUT OF THE RIGHT WAY OF LIFE OVER A CORRUPT OTHER!

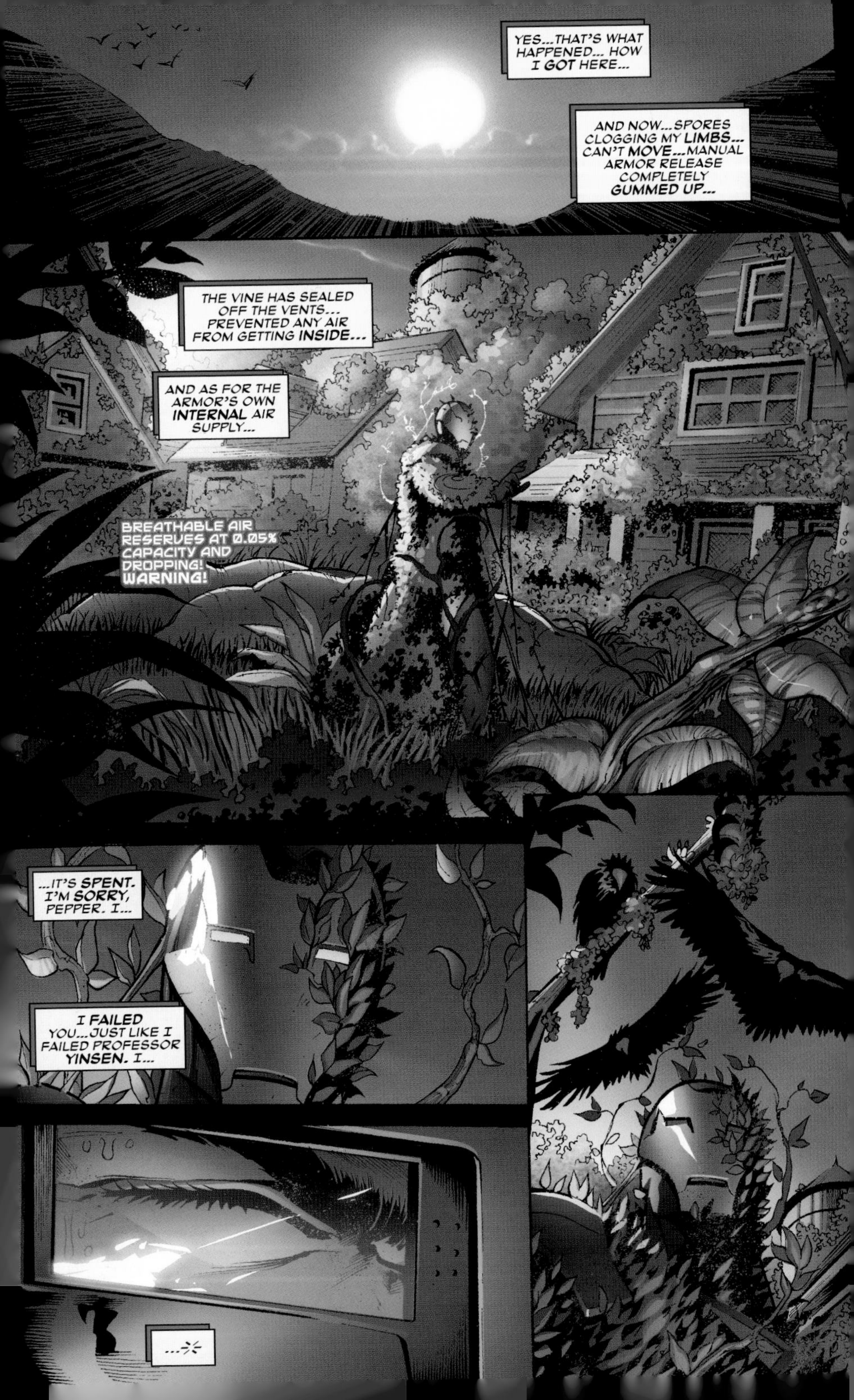
YES...THAT'S WHAT HAPPENED... HOW I GOT HERE...
AND NOW...SPORES CLOGGING MY LIMBS... CAN'T MOVE...MANUAL ARMOR RELEASE COMPLETELY GUMMED UP...
THE VINE HAS SEALED OFF THE VENTS... PREVENTED ANY AIR FROM GETTING INSIDE...
AND AS FOR THE ARMOR'S OWN INTERNAL AIR SUPPLY...
BREATHABLE AIR RESERVES AT 0.05% CAPACITY AND DROPPING! WARNING!
...IT'S SPENT. I'M SORRY, PEPPER. I...
I FAILED YOU...JUST LIKE I FAILED PROFESSOR YINSEN. I...
...*

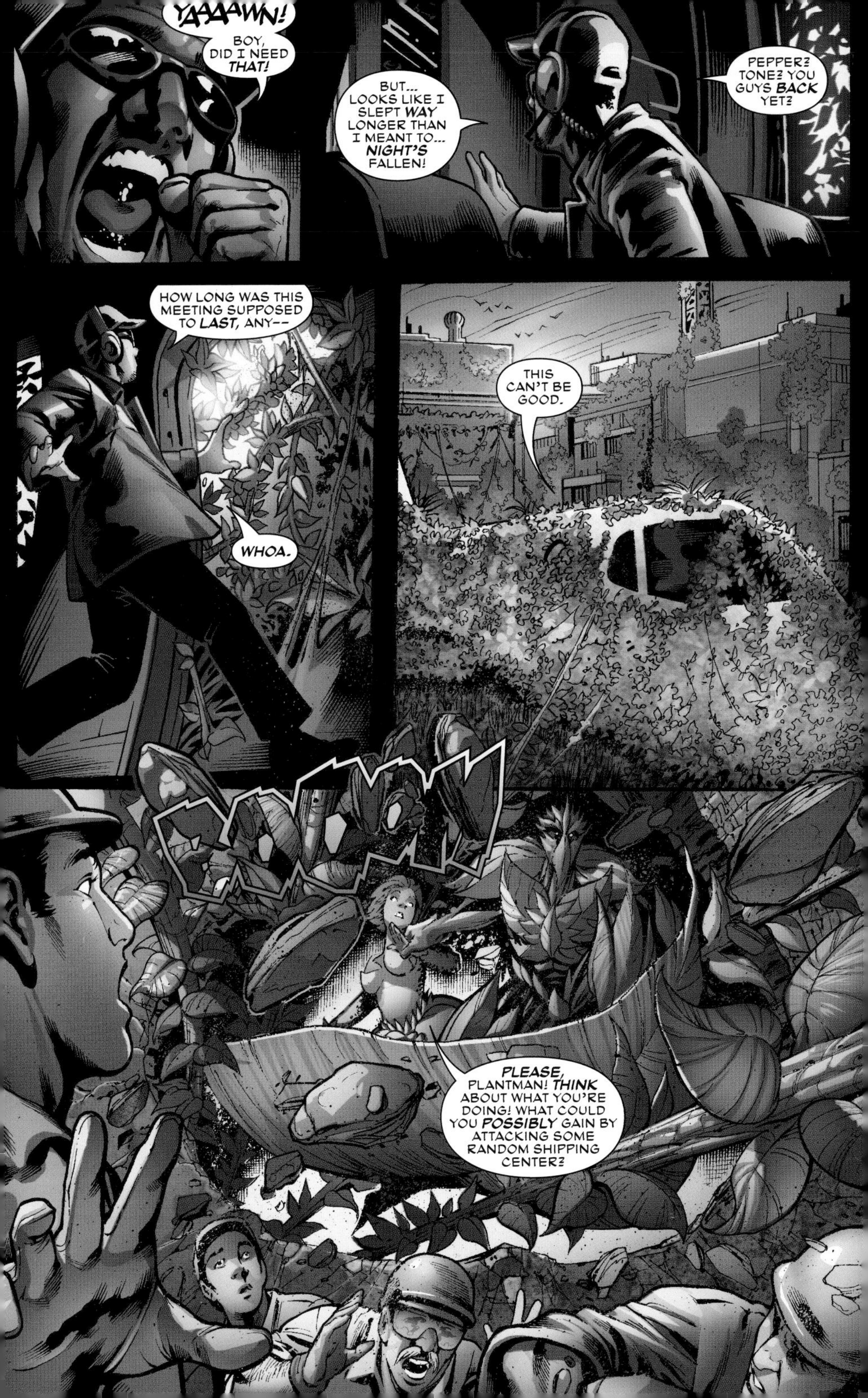
YAAAAWN!
BOY, DID I NEED THAT!
BUT... LOOKS LIKE I SLEPT WAY LONGER THAN I MEANT TO... NIGHT'S FALLEN!
PEPPER? TONE? YOU GUYS BACK YET?
HOW LONG WAS THIS MEETING SUPPOSED TO LAST, ANY--
WHOA.
THIS CAN'T BE GOOD.
PLEASE, PLANTMAN! THINK ABOUT WHAT YOU'RE DOING! WHAT COULD YOU POSSIBLY GAIN BY ATTACKING SOME RANDOM SHIPPING CENTER?

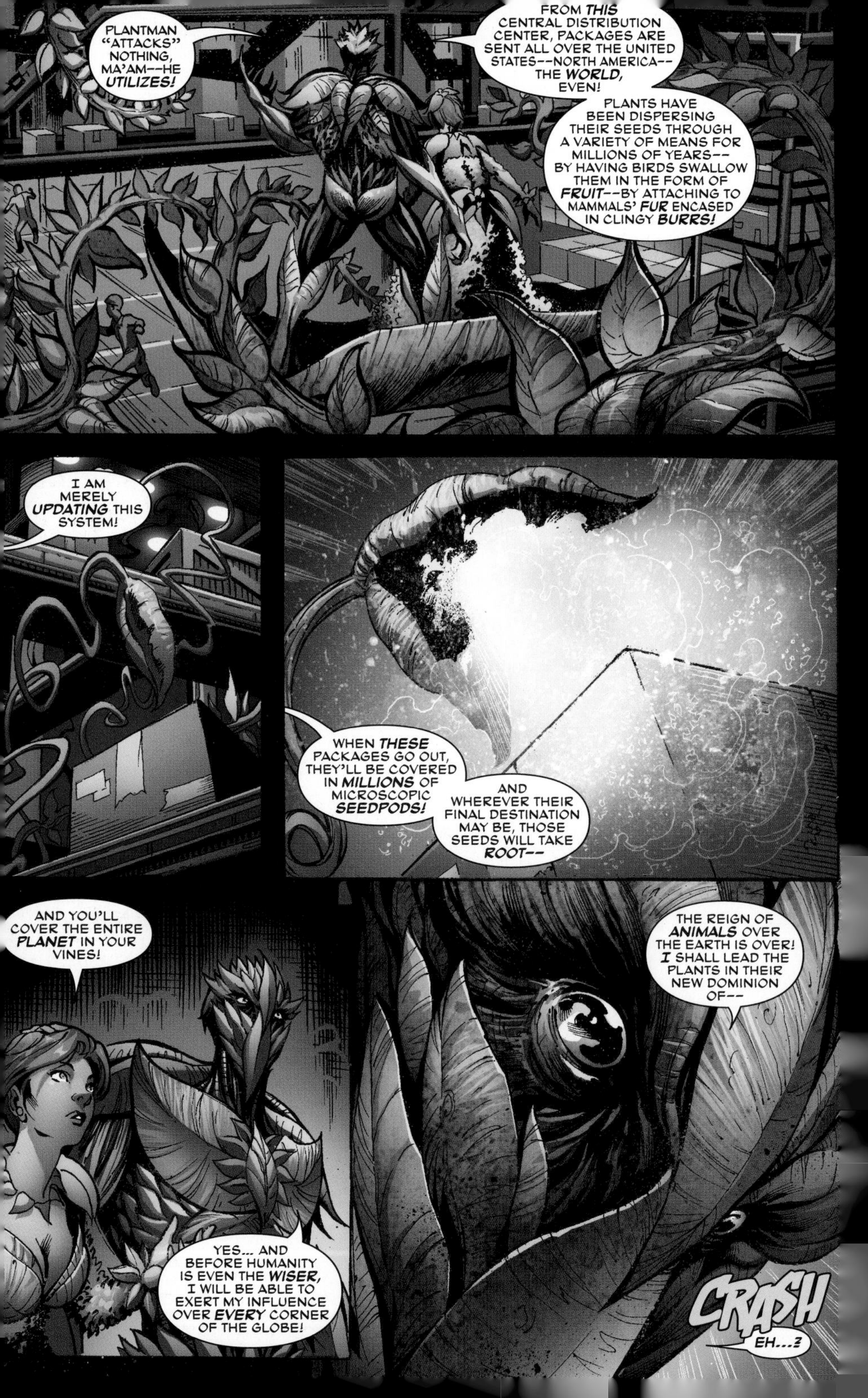
PLANTMAN "ATTACKS" NOTHING, MA'AM--HE UTILIZES!
FROM THIS CENTRAL DISTRIBUTION CENTER, PACKAGES ARE SENT ALL OVER THE UNITED STATES--NORTH AMERICA--THE WORLD, EVEN!
PLANTS HAVE BEEN DISPERSING THEIR SEEDS THROUGH A VARIETY OF MEANS FOR MILLIONS OF YEARS--BY HAVING BIRDS SWALLOW THEM IN THE FORM OF FRUIT--BY ATTACHING TO MAMMALS' FUR ENCASED IN CLINGY BURRS!
I AM MERELY UPDATING THIS SYSTEM!
WHEN THESE PACKAGES GO OUT, THEY'LL BE COVERED IN MILLIONS OF MICROSCOPIC SEEDPODS!
AND WHEREVER THEIR FINAL DESTINATION MAY BE, THOSE SEEDS WILL TAKE ROOT--
AND YOU'LL COVER THE ENTIRE PLANET IN YOUR VINES!
YES... AND BEFORE HUMANITY IS EVEN THE WISER, I WILL BE ABLE TO EXERT MY INFLUENCE OVER EVERY CORNER OF THE GLOBE!
THE REIGN OF ANIMALS OVER THE EARTH IS OVER! I SHALL LEAD THE PLANTS IN THEIR NEW DOMINION OF--
CRASH
EH...?

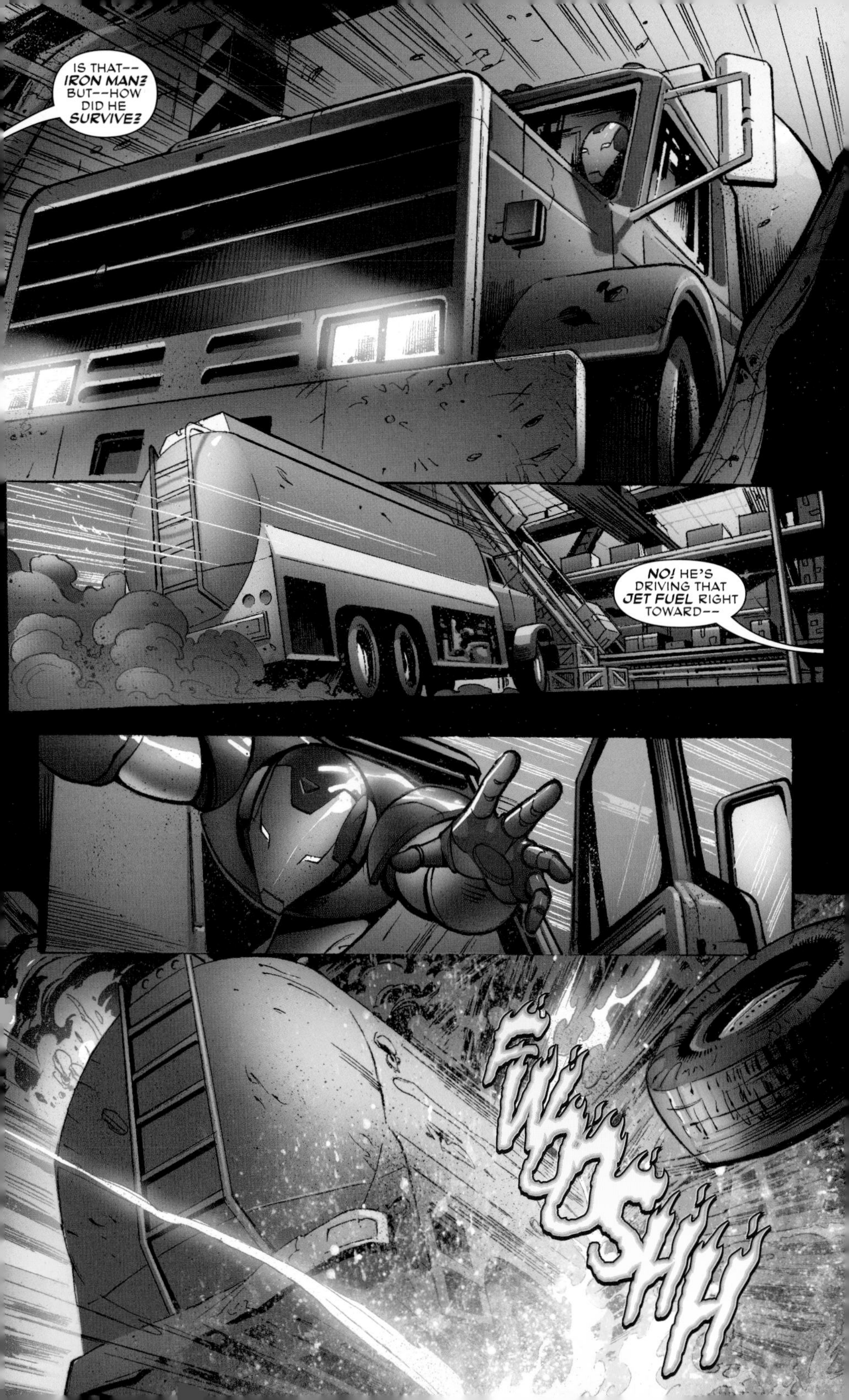
IS THAT-- IRON MAN? BUT--HOW DID HE SURVIVE?
NO! HE'S DRIVING THAT JET FUEL RIGHT TOWARD--
FWOOSHH

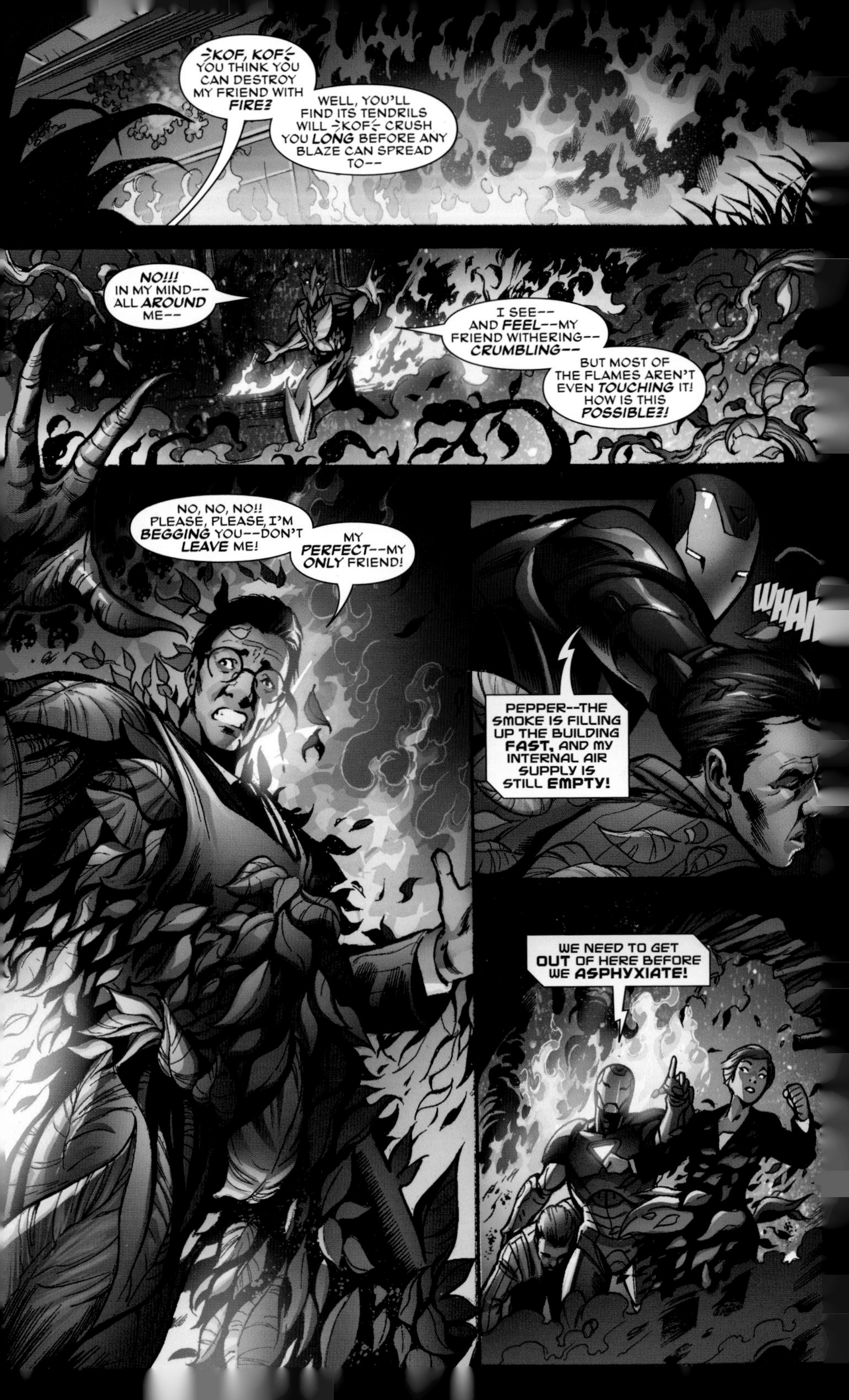

⊰KOF, KOF⊱ YOU THINK YOU CAN DESTROY MY FRIEND WITH FIRE?
WELL, YOU'LL FIND ITS TENDRILS WILL ⊰KOF⊱ CRUSH YOU LONG BEFORE ANY BLAZE CAN SPREAD TO--
NO!!! IN MY MIND-- ALL AROUND ME--
I SEE-- AND FEEL--MY FRIEND WITHERING-- CRUMBLING--
BUT MOST OF THE FLAMES AREN'T EVEN TOUCHING IT! HOW IS THIS POSSIBLE?!
NO, NO, NO!! PLEASE, PLEASE, I'M BEGGING YOU--DON'T LEAVE ME!
MY PERFECT--MY ONLY FRIEND!
WHAM
PEPPER--THE SMOKE IS FILLING UP THE BUILDING FAST, AND MY INTERNAL AIR SUPPLY IS STILL EMPTY!
WE NEED TO GET OUT OF HERE BEFORE WE ASPHYXIATE!

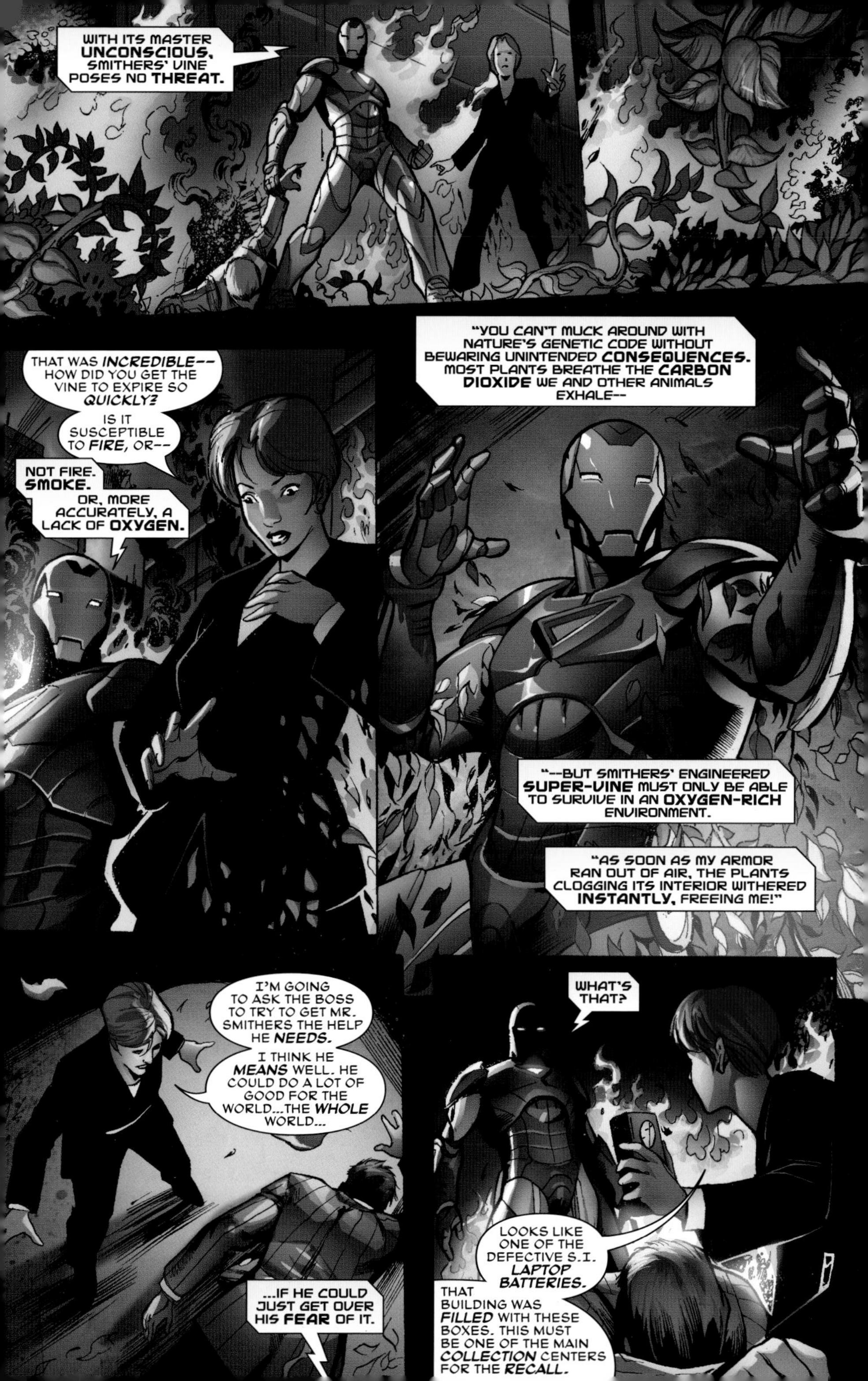
WITH ITS MASTER UNCONSCIOUS, SMITHERS' VINE POSES NO THREAT.
THAT WAS INCREDIBLE-- HOW DID YOU GET THE VINE TO EXPIRE SO QUICKLY?
IS IT SUSCEPTIBLE TO FIRE, OR--
NOT FIRE. SMOKE.
OR, MORE ACCURATELY, A LACK OF OXYGEN.
"YOU CAN'T MUCK AROUND WITH NATURE'S GENETIC CODE WITHOUT BEWARING UNINTENDED CONSEQUENCES. MOST PLANTS BREATHE THE CARBON DIOXIDE WE AND OTHER ANIMALS EXHALE--
"--BUT SMITHERS' ENGINEERED SUPER-VINE MUST ONLY BE ABLE TO SURVIVE IN AN OXYGEN-RICH ENVIRONMENT.
"AS SOON AS MY ARMOR RAN OUT OF AIR, THE PLANTS CLOGGING ITS INTERIOR WITHERED INSTANTLY, FREEING ME!"
I'M GOING TO ASK THE BOSS TO TRY TO GET MR. SMITHERS THE HELP HE NEEDS.
I THINK HE MEANS WELL. HE COULD DO A LOT OF GOOD FOR THE WORLD...THE WHOLE WORLD...
...IF HE COULD JUST GET OVER HIS FEAR OF IT.
WHAT'S THAT?
LOOKS LIKE ONE OF THE DEFECTIVE S.I. LAPTOP BATTERIES.
THAT BUILDING WAS FILLED WITH THESE BOXES. THIS MUST BE ONE OF THE MAIN COLLECTION CENTERS FOR THE RECALL.

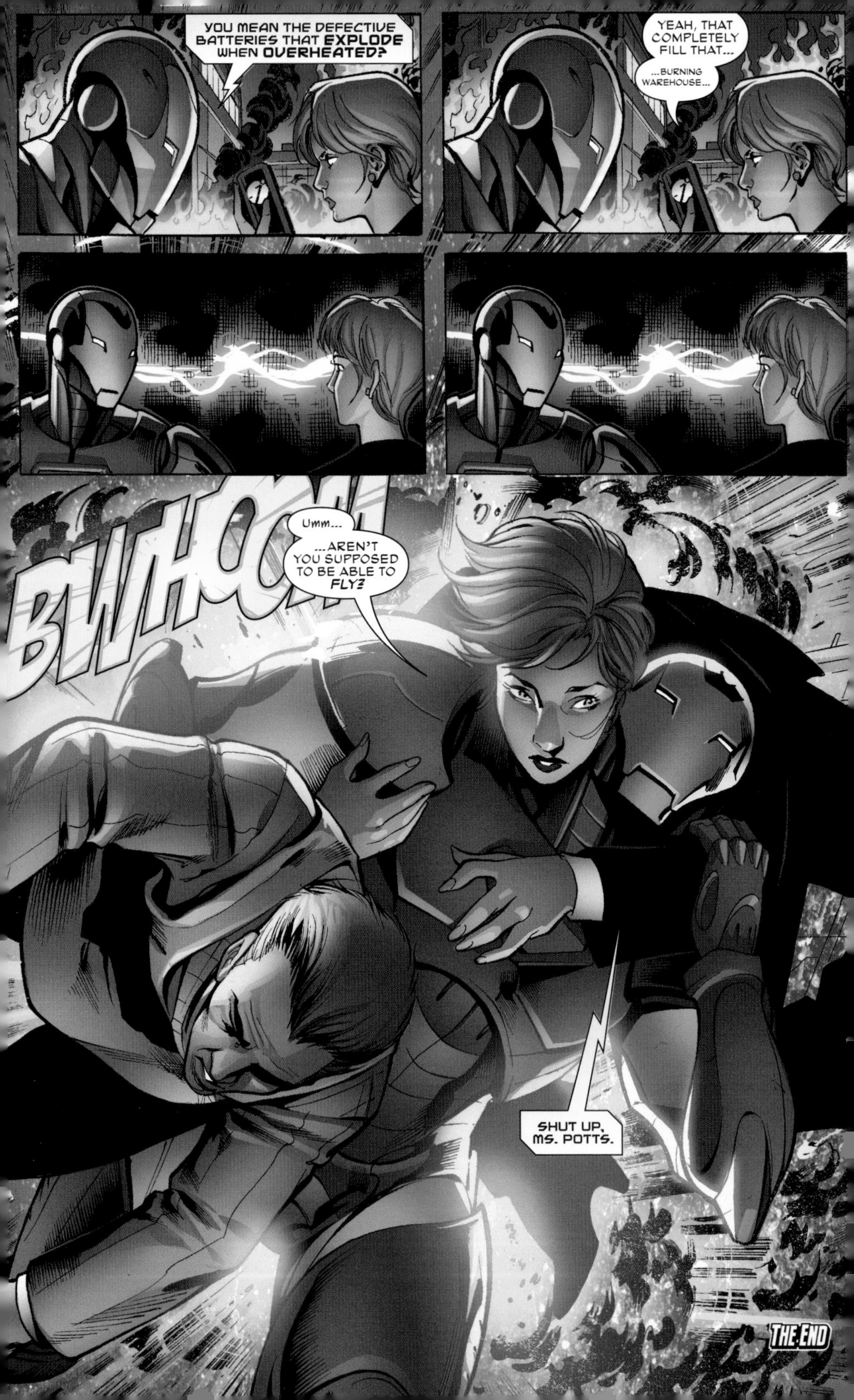
YOU MEAN THE DEFECTIVE BATTERIES THAT EXPLODE WHEN OVERHEATED?
YEAH, THAT COMPLETELY FILL THAT...
...BURNING WAREHOUSE...
BWHOOM
Umm...
...AREN'T YOU SUPPOSED TO BE ABLE TO FLY?
SHUT UP, MS. POTTS.
THE END

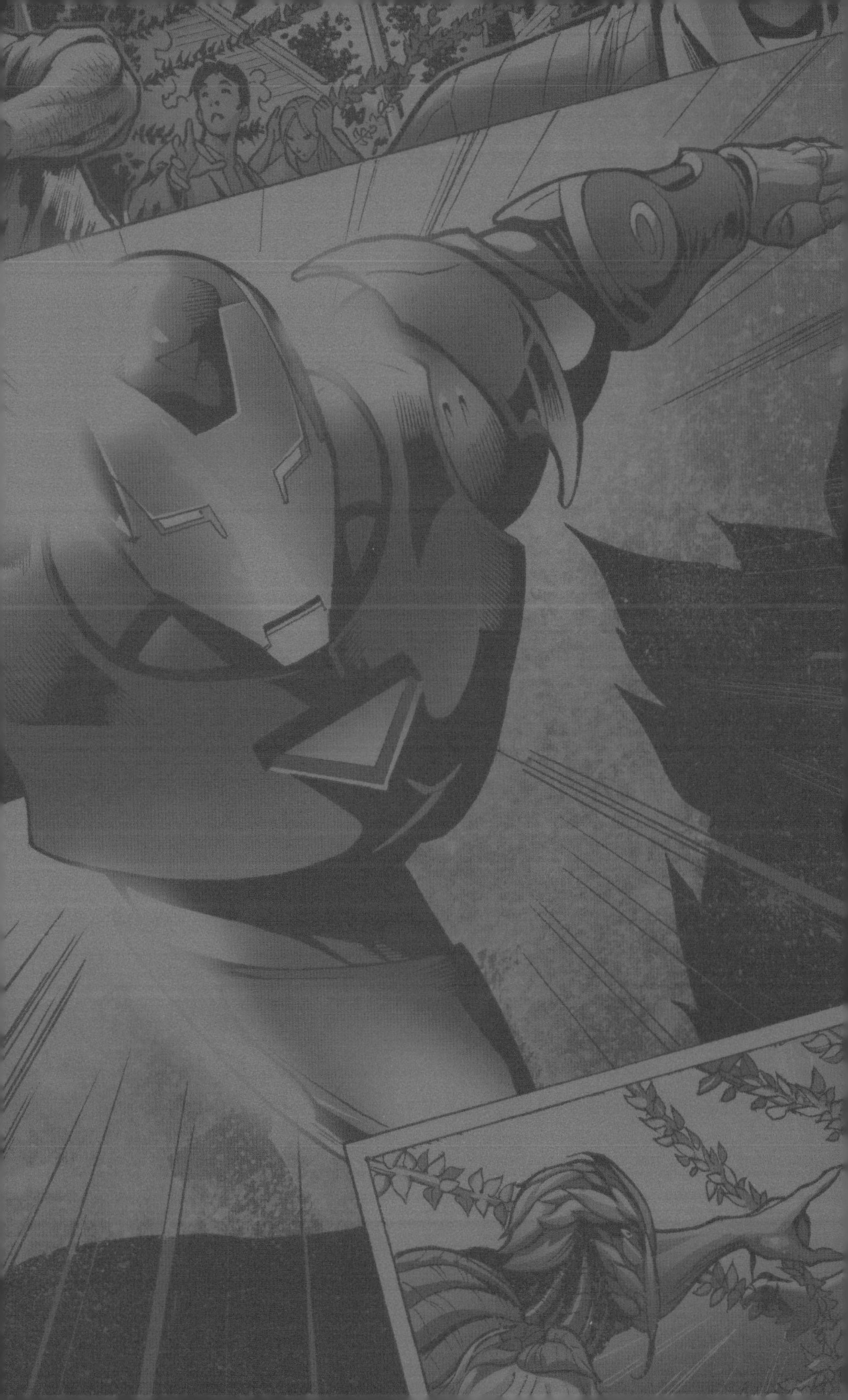

04

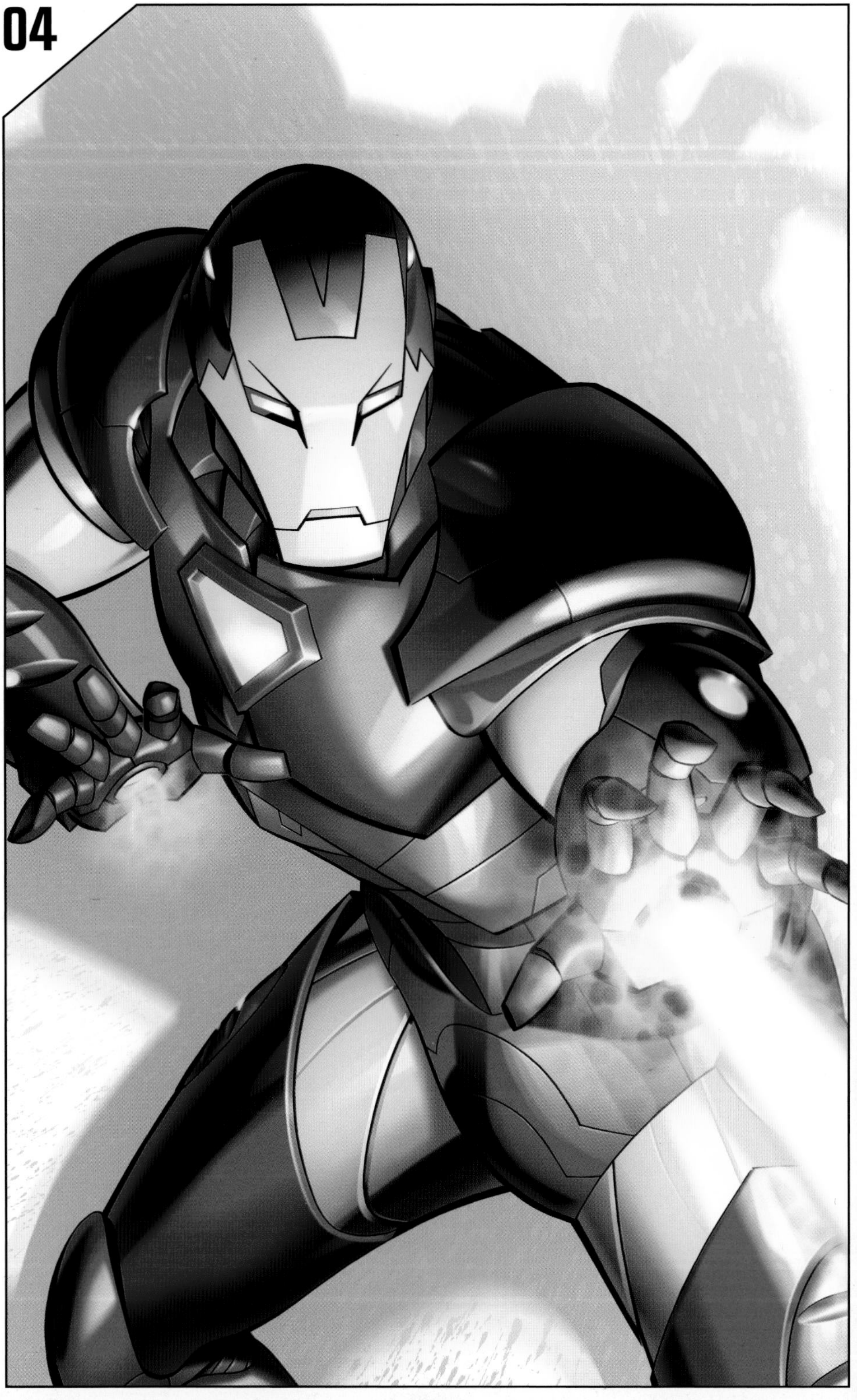

STARK INTERNATIONAL CORPORATE HEADQUARTERS, NEW YORK CITY, SUB-BASEMENT FOUR:

HOSTILE TAKEOVER

Writer: Fred Van Lente   **Penciler:** James Cordeiro   **Inker:** Gary Erskine
Colorist: Martegod Gracia   **Letterer:** Blambot's Nate Piekos   **Cover:** Michael Golden   **Production:** Rich Ginter
Assistant Editor: Nathan Cosby   **Editor:** Mark Paniccia   **Editor in Chief:** Joe Quesada   **Publisher:** Dan Buckley

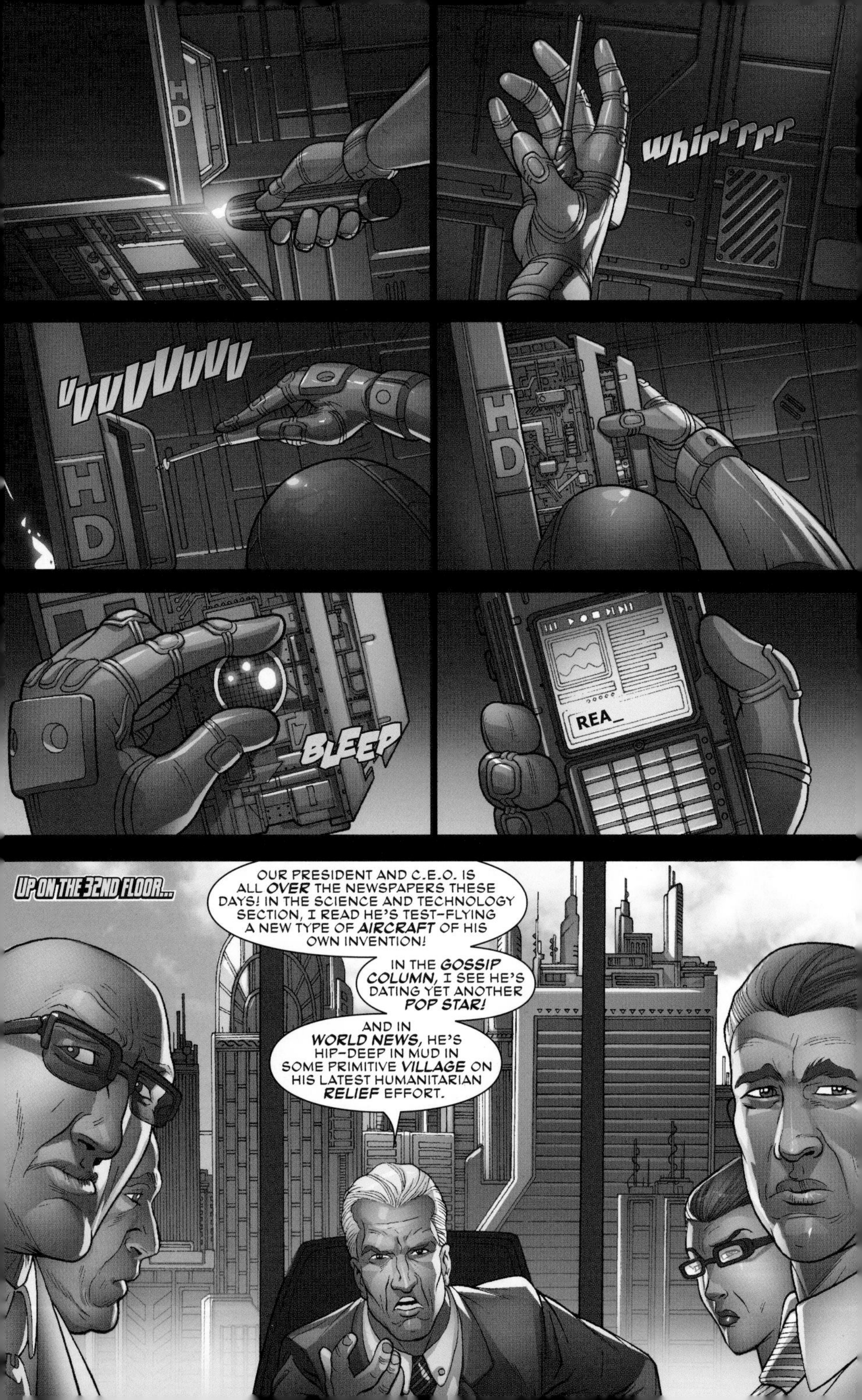
whirrrrr
vvvVVvvvv
HD
BLEEP
REA_
UP ON THE 32ND FLOOR...
OUR PRESIDENT AND C.E.O. IS ALL OVER THE NEWSPAPERS THESE DAYS! IN THE SCIENCE AND TECHNOLOGY SECTION, I READ HE'S TEST-FLYING A NEW TYPE OF AIRCRAFT OF HIS OWN INVENTION!
IN THE GOSSIP COLUMN, I SEE HE'S DATING YET ANOTHER POP STAR!
AND IN WORLD NEWS, HE'S HIP-DEEP IN MUD IN SOME PRIMITIVE VILLAGE ON HIS LATEST HUMANITARIAN RELIEF EFFORT.

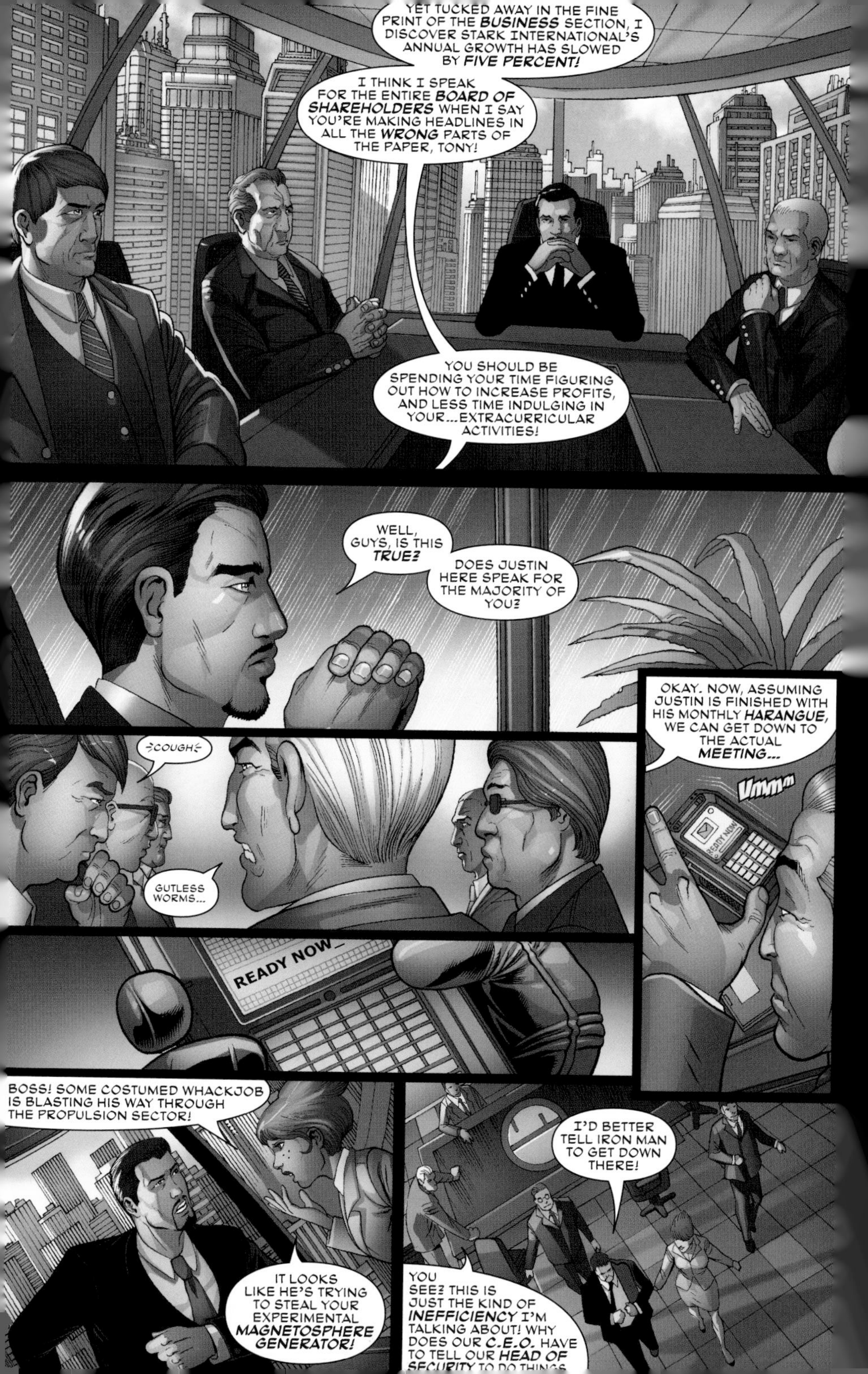
YET TUCKED AWAY IN THE FINE PRINT OF THE BUSINESS SECTION, I DISCOVER STARK INTERNATIONAL'S ANNUAL GROWTH HAS SLOWED BY FIVE PERCENT!
I THINK I SPEAK FOR THE ENTIRE BOARD OF SHAREHOLDERS WHEN I SAY YOU'RE MAKING HEADLINES IN ALL THE WRONG PARTS OF THE PAPER, TONY!
YOU SHOULD BE SPENDING YOUR TIME FIGURING OUT HOW TO INCREASE PROFITS, AND LESS TIME INDULGING IN YOUR...EXTRACURRICULAR ACTIVITIES!
WELL, GUYS, IS THIS TRUE?
DOES JUSTIN HERE SPEAK FOR THE MAJORITY OF YOU?
COUGH
GUTLESS WORMS...
OKAY. NOW, ASSUMING JUSTIN IS FINISHED WITH HIS MONTHLY HARANGUE, WE CAN GET DOWN TO THE ACTUAL MEETING...
Vmmm
READY NOW
READY NOW_
BOSS! SOME COSTUMED WHACKJOB IS BLASTING HIS WAY THROUGH THE PROPULSION SECTOR!
IT LOOKS LIKE HE'S TRYING TO STEAL YOUR EXPERIMENTAL MAGNETOSPHERE GENERATOR!
I'D BETTER TELL IRON MAN TO GET DOWN THERE!
YOU SEE? THIS IS JUST THE KIND OF INEFFICIENCY I'M TALKING ABOUT! WHY DOES OUR C.E.O. HAVE TO TELL OUR HEAD OF SECURITY TO DO THINGS

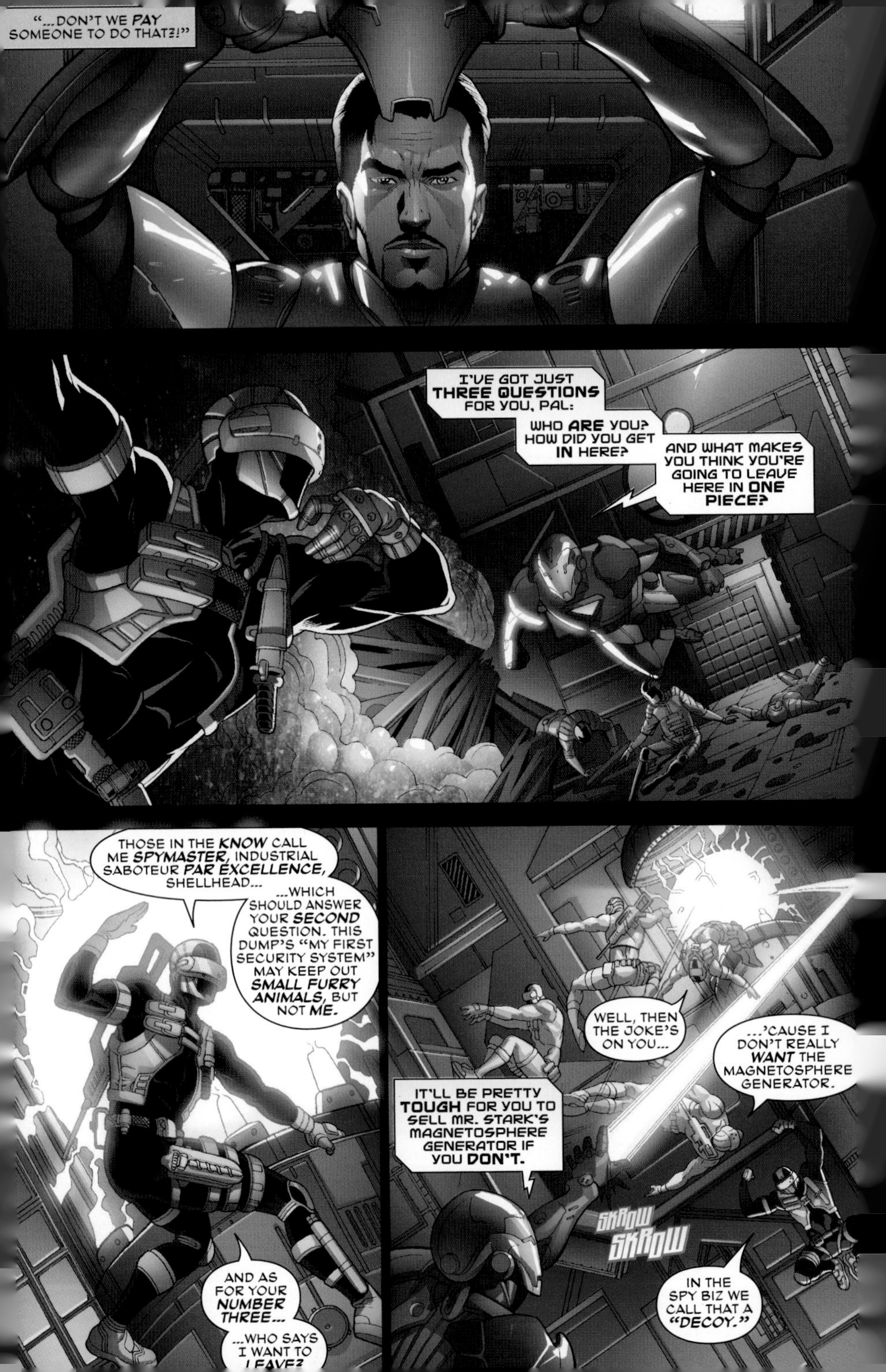
"...DON'T WE PAY SOMEONE TO DO THAT?!"
I'VE GOT JUST THREE QUESTIONS FOR YOU, PAL:
WHO ARE YOU? HOW DID YOU GET IN HERE?
AND WHAT MAKES YOU THINK YOU'RE GOING TO LEAVE HERE IN ONE PIECE?
THOSE IN THE KNOW CALL ME SPYMASTER, INDUSTRIAL SABOTEUR PAR EXCELLENCE, SHELLHEAD...
...WHICH SHOULD ANSWER YOUR SECOND QUESTION. THIS DUMP'S "MY FIRST SECURITY SYSTEM" MAY KEEP OUT SMALL FURRY ANIMALS, BUT NOT ME.
AND AS FOR YOUR NUMBER THREE...
...WHO SAYS I WANT TO LEAVE?
IT'LL BE PRETTY TOUGH FOR YOU TO SELL MR. STARK'S MAGNETOSPHERE GENERATOR IF YOU DON'T.
WELL, THEN THE JOKE'S ON YOU...
...'CAUSE I DON'T REALLY WANT THE MAGNETOSPHERE GENERATOR.
SKROW
SKROW
IN THE SPY BIZ WE CALL THAT A "DECOY."

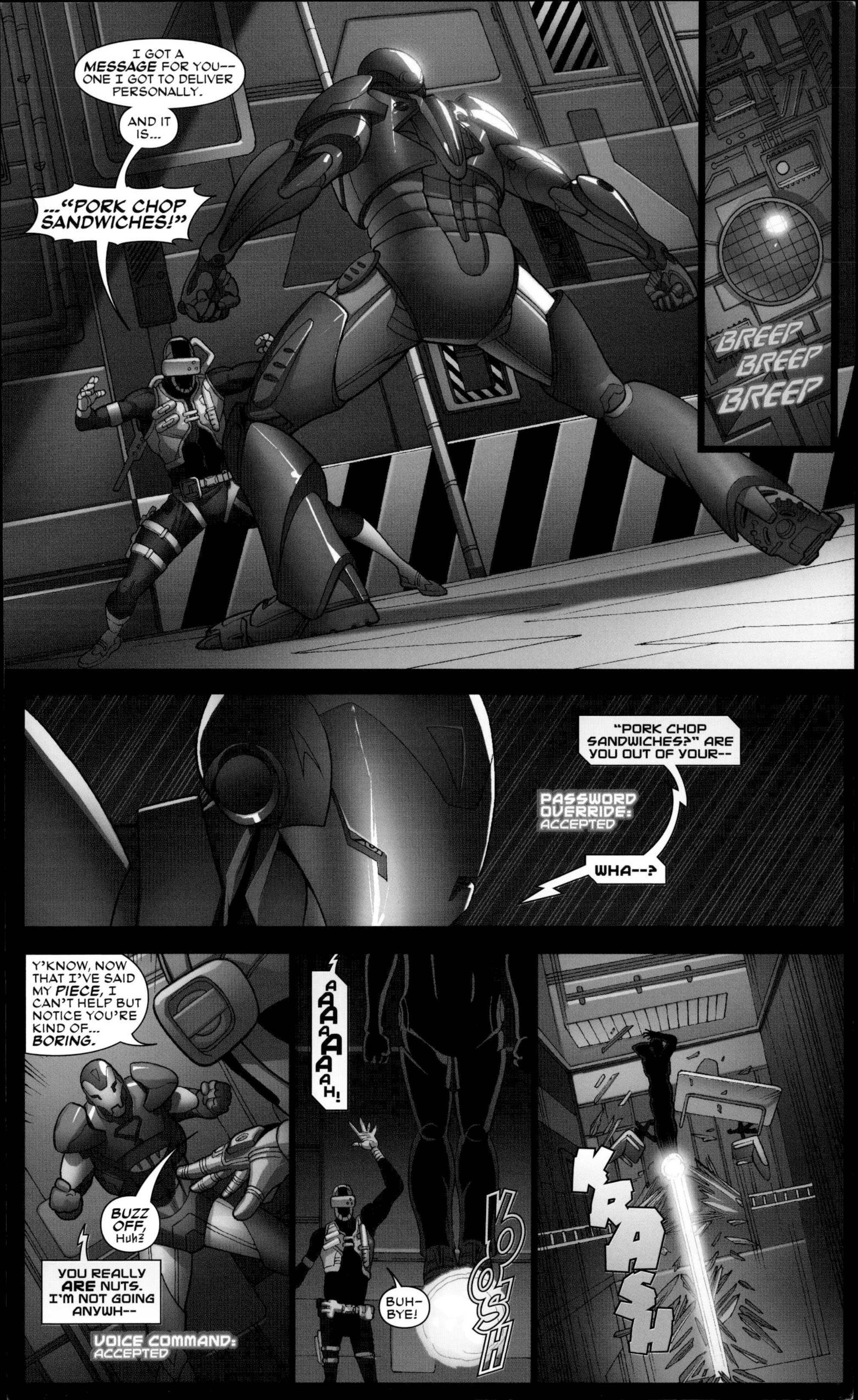
I GOT A MESSAGE FOR YOU-- ONE I GOT TO DELIVER PERSONALLY.
AND IT IS...
..."PORK CHOP SANDWICHES!"
BREEP BREEP BREEP
"PORK CHOP SANDWICHES?" ARE YOU OUT OF YOUR--
PASSWORD OVERRIDE: ACCEPTED
WHA--?
Y'KNOW, NOW THAT I'VE SAID MY PIECE, I CAN'T HELP BUT NOTICE YOU'RE KIND OF... BORING.
BUZZ OFF, HUH?
YOU REALLY ARE NUTS. I'M NOT GOING ANYWH--
VOICE COMMAND: ACCEPTED
AAAAAAAAH!
BUH-BYE!
VOOSH
KRASH

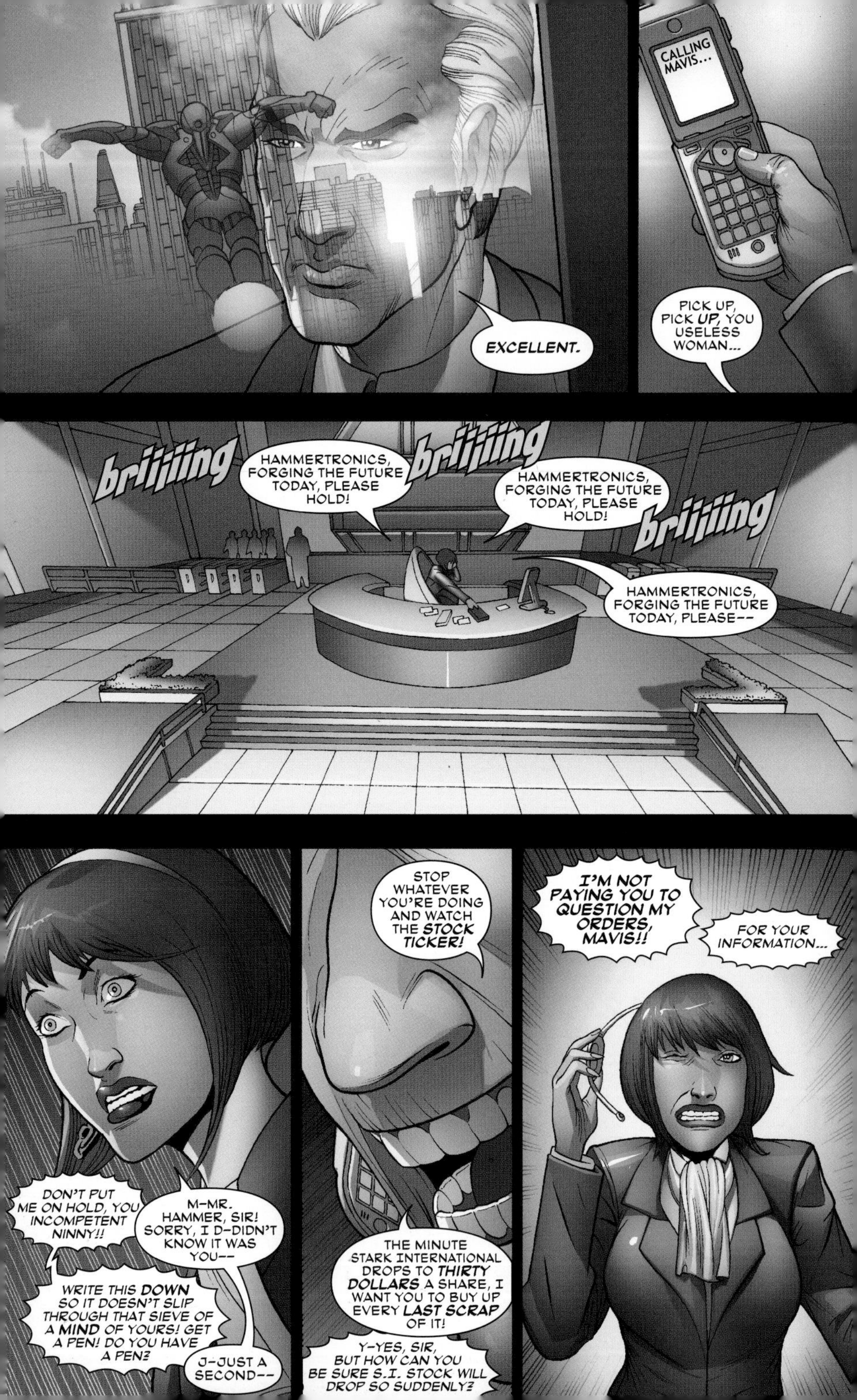

EXCELLENT.
CALLING MAVIS...
PICK UP, PICK UP, YOU USELESS WOMAN...
briiiiing
HAMMERTRONICS, FORGING THE FUTURE TODAY, PLEASE HOLD!
briiiiing
HAMMERTRONICS, FORGING THE FUTURE TODAY, PLEASE HOLD!
briiiiing
HAMMERTRONICS, FORGING THE FUTURE TODAY, PLEASE--
DON'T PUT ME ON HOLD, YOU INCOMPETENT NINNY!!
M-MR. HAMMER, SIR! SORRY, I D-DIDN'T KNOW IT WAS YOU--
WRITE THIS DOWN SO IT DOESN'T SLIP THROUGH THAT SIEVE OF A MIND OF YOURS! GET A PEN! DO YOU HAVE A PEN?
J-JUST A SECOND--
STOP WHATEVER YOU'RE DOING AND WATCH THE STOCK TICKER!
THE MINUTE STARK INTERNATIONAL DROPS TO THIRTY DOLLARS A SHARE, I WANT YOU TO BUY UP EVERY LAST SCRAP OF IT!
Y-YES, SIR, BUT HOW CAN YOU BE SURE S.I. STOCK WILL DROP SO SUDDENLY?
I'M NOT PAYING YOU TO QUESTION MY ORDERS, MAVIS!!
FOR YOUR INFORMATION...

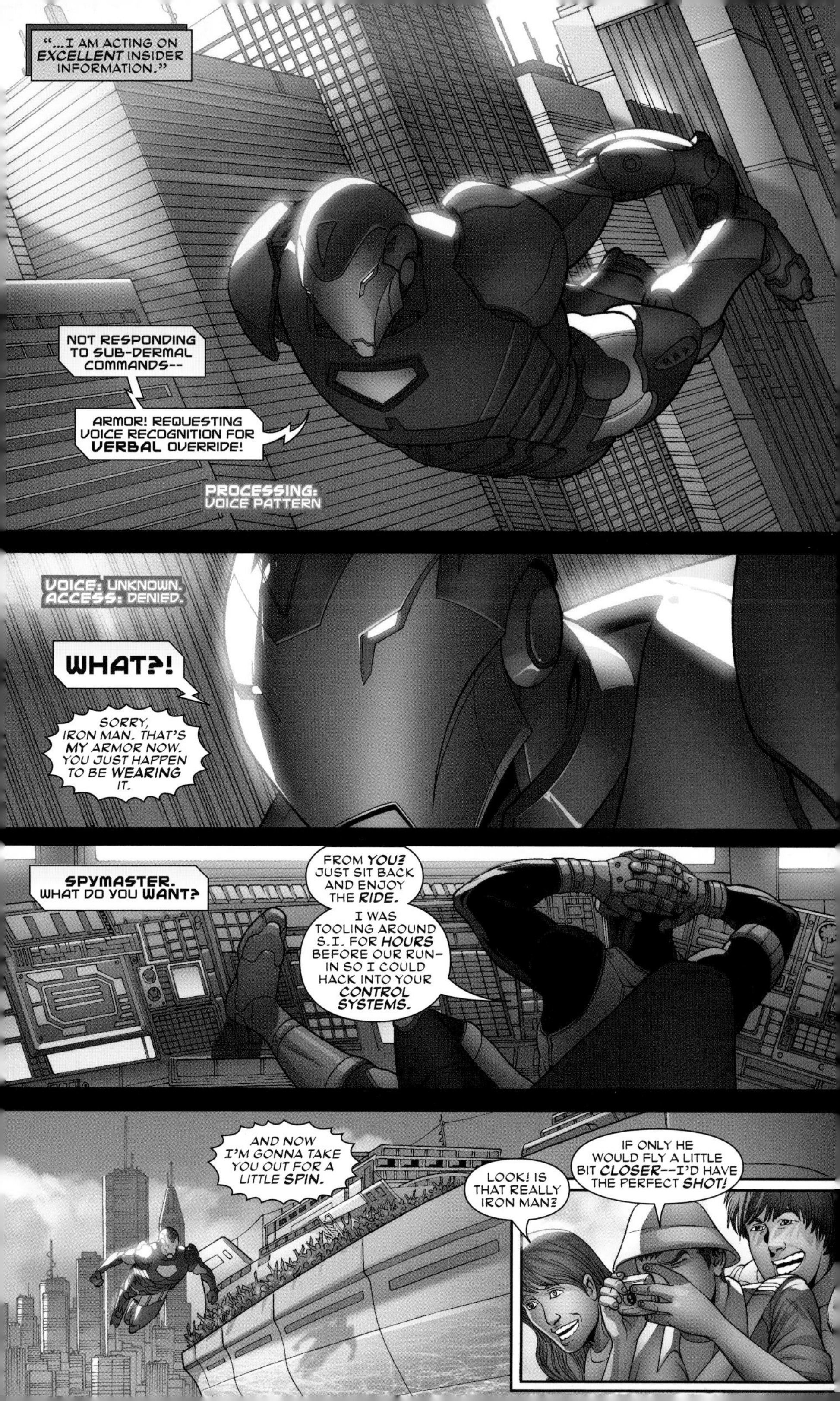

"...I AM ACTING ON EXCELLENT INSIDER INFORMATION."
NOT RESPONDING TO SUB-DERMAL COMMANDS--
ARMOR! REQUESTING VOICE RECOGNITION FOR VERBAL OVERRIDE!
PROCESSING: VOICE PATTERN
VOICE: UNKNOWN. ACCESS: DENIED.
WHAT?!
SORRY, IRON MAN. THAT'S MY ARMOR NOW. YOU JUST HAPPEN TO BE WEARING IT.
SPYMASTER. WHAT DO YOU WANT?
FROM YOU? JUST SIT BACK AND ENJOY THE RIDE.
I WAS TOOLING AROUND S.I. FOR HOURS BEFORE OUR RUN-IN SO I COULD HACK INTO YOUR CONTROL SYSTEMS.
AND NOW I'M GONNA TAKE YOU OUT FOR A LITTLE SPIN.
LOOK! IS THAT REALLY IRON MAN?
IF ONLY HE WOULD FLY A LITTLE BIT CLOSER--I'D HAVE THE PERFECT SHOT!

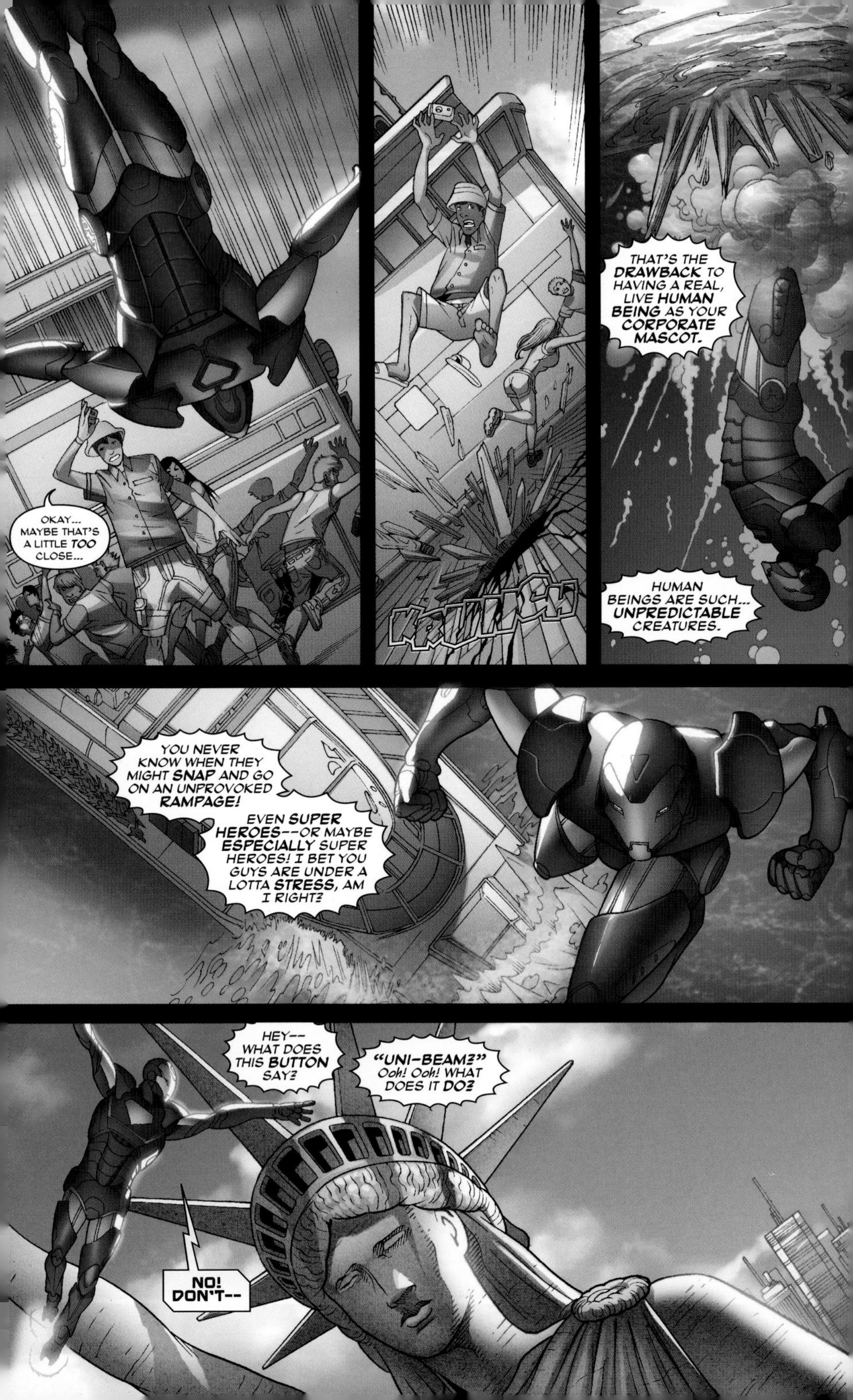
OKAY... MAYBE THAT'S A LITTLE TOO CLOSE...
THAT'S THE DRAWBACK TO HAVING A REAL, LIVE HUMAN BEING AS YOUR CORPORATE MASCOT.
HUMAN BEINGS ARE SUCH... UNPREDICTABLE CREATURES.
YOU NEVER KNOW WHEN THEY MIGHT SNAP AND GO ON AN UNPROVOKED RAMPAGE!
EVEN SUPER HEROES--OR MAYBE ESPECIALLY SUPER HEROES! I BET YOU GUYS ARE UNDER A LOTTA STRESS, AM I RIGHT?
HEY-- WHAT DOES THIS BUTTON SAY?
"UNI-BEAM?" Ooh! Ooh! WHAT DOES IT DO?
NO! DON'T--

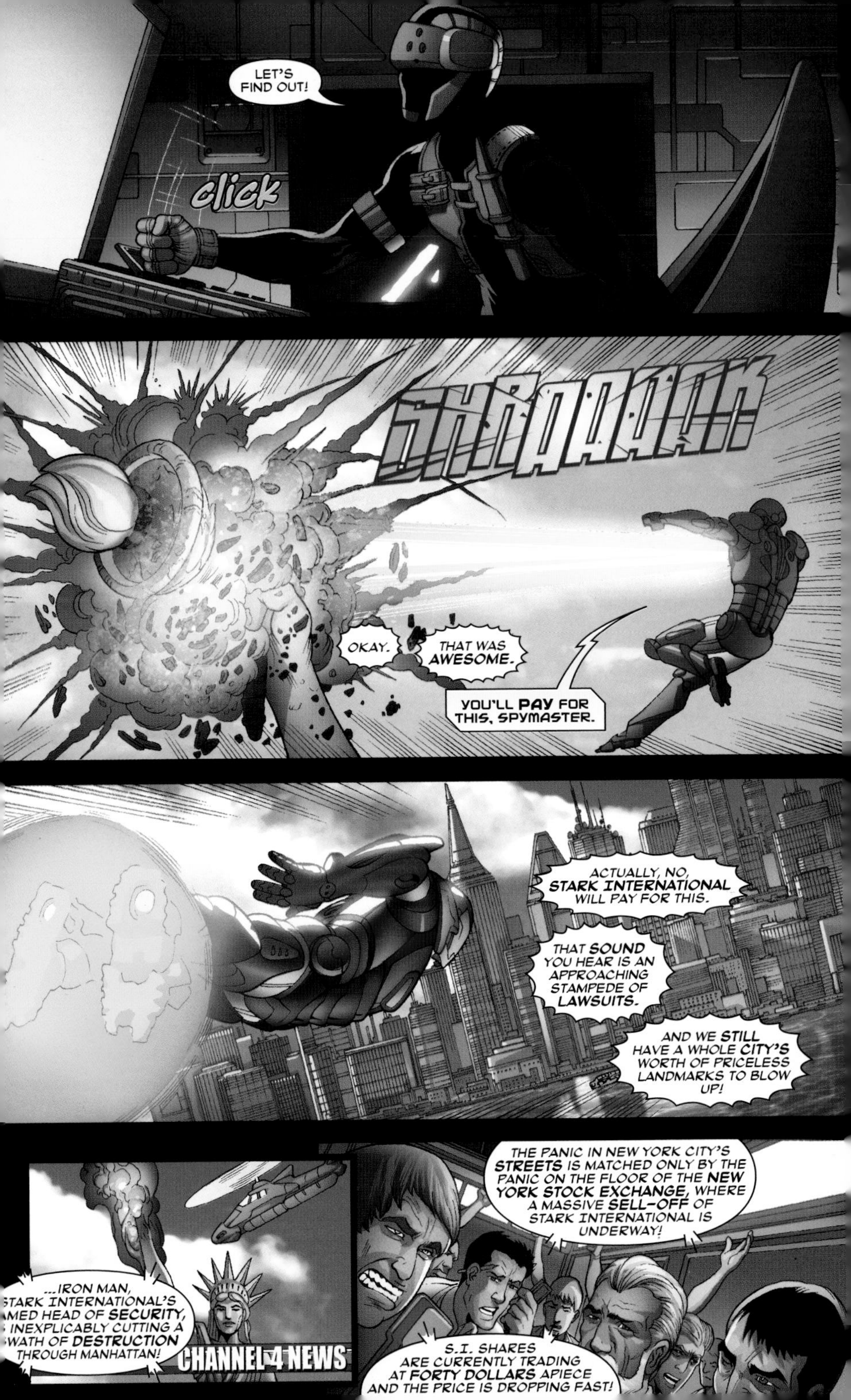
LET'S FIND OUT!
click
OKAY.
THAT WAS AWESOME.
YOU'LL PAY FOR THIS, SPYMASTER.
ACTUALLY, NO, STARK INTERNATIONAL WILL PAY FOR THIS.
THAT SOUND YOU HEAR IS AN APPROACHING STAMPEDE OF LAWSUITS.
AND WE STILL HAVE A WHOLE CITY'S WORTH OF PRICELESS LANDMARKS TO BLOW UP!
...IRON MAN, STARK INTERNATIONAL'S AMED HEAD OF SECURITY, INEXPLICABLY CUTTING A WATH OF DESTRUCTION THROUGH MANHATTAN!
CHANNEL 4 NEWS
THE PANIC IN NEW YORK CITY'S STREETS IS MATCHED ONLY BY THE PANIC ON THE FLOOR OF THE NEW YORK STOCK EXCHANGE, WHERE A MASSIVE SELL-OFF OF STARK INTERNATIONAL IS UNDERWAY!
S.I. SHARES ARE CURRENTLY TRADING AT FORTY DOLLARS APIECE AND THE PRICE IS DROPPING FAST!

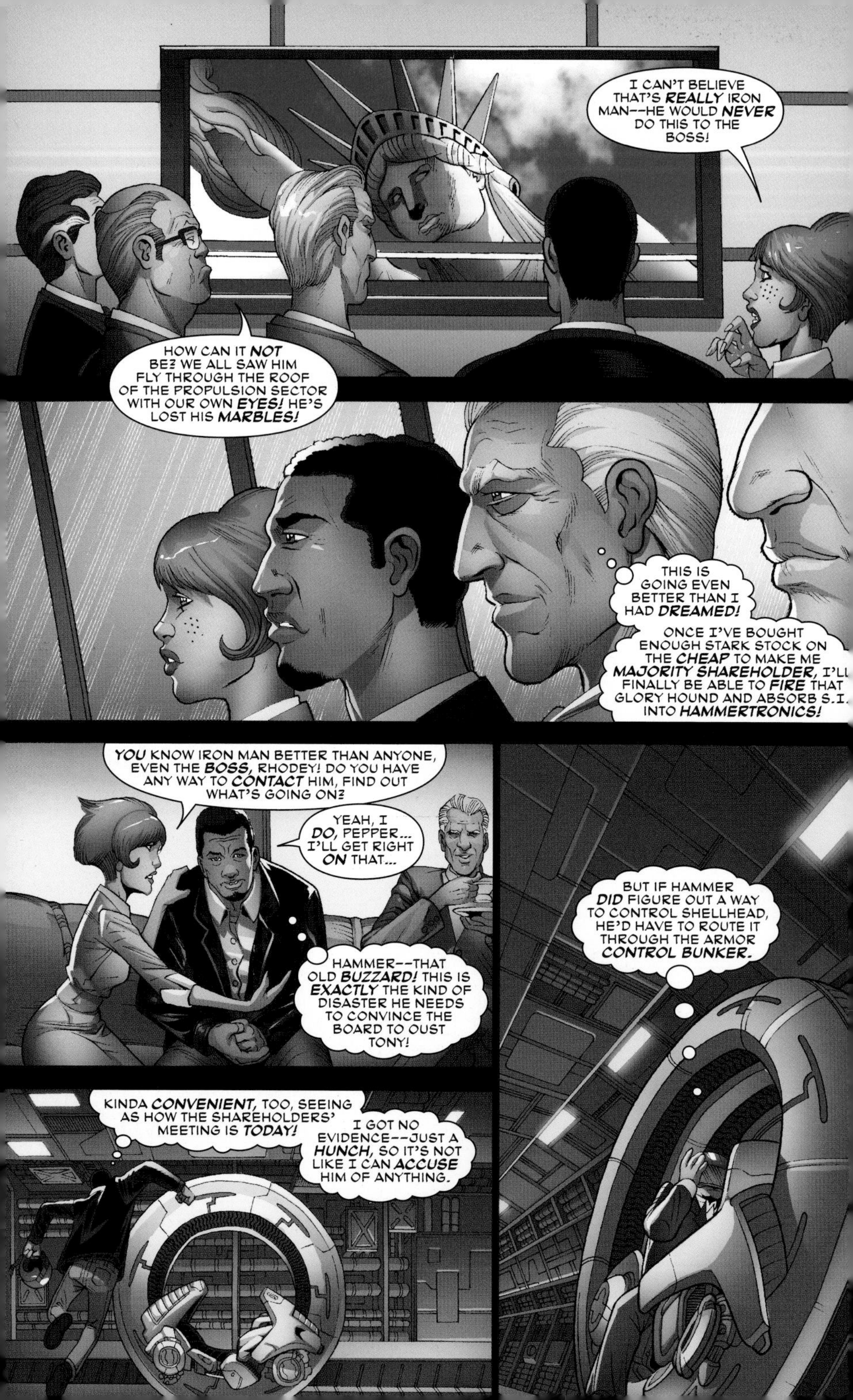
I CAN'T BELIEVE THAT'S REALLY IRON MAN--HE WOULD NEVER DO THIS TO THE BOSS!
HOW CAN IT NOT BE? WE ALL SAW HIM FLY THROUGH THE ROOF OF THE PROPULSION SECTOR WITH OUR OWN EYES! HE'S LOST HIS MARBLES!
THIS IS GOING EVEN BETTER THAN I HAD DREAMED!
ONCE I'VE BOUGHT ENOUGH STARK STOCK ON THE CHEAP TO MAKE ME MAJORITY SHAREHOLDER, I'LL FINALLY BE ABLE TO FIRE THAT GLORY HOUND AND ABSORB S.I. INTO HAMMERTRONICS!
YOU KNOW IRON MAN BETTER THAN ANYONE, EVEN THE BOSS, RHODEY! DO YOU HAVE ANY WAY TO CONTACT HIM, FIND OUT WHAT'S GOING ON?
YEAH, I DO, PEPPER... I'LL GET RIGHT ON THAT...
HAMMER--THAT OLD BUZZARD! THIS IS EXACTLY THE KIND OF DISASTER HE NEEDS TO CONVINCE THE BOARD TO OUST TONY!
KINDA CONVENIENT, TOO, SEEING AS HOW THE SHAREHOLDERS' MEETING IS TODAY!
I GOT NO EVIDENCE--JUST A HUNCH, SO IT'S NOT LIKE I CAN ACCUSE HIM OF ANYTHING.
BUT IF HAMMER DID FIGURE OUT A WAY TO CONTROL SHELLHEAD, HE'D HAVE TO ROUTE IT THROUGH THE ARMOR CONTROL BUNKER.

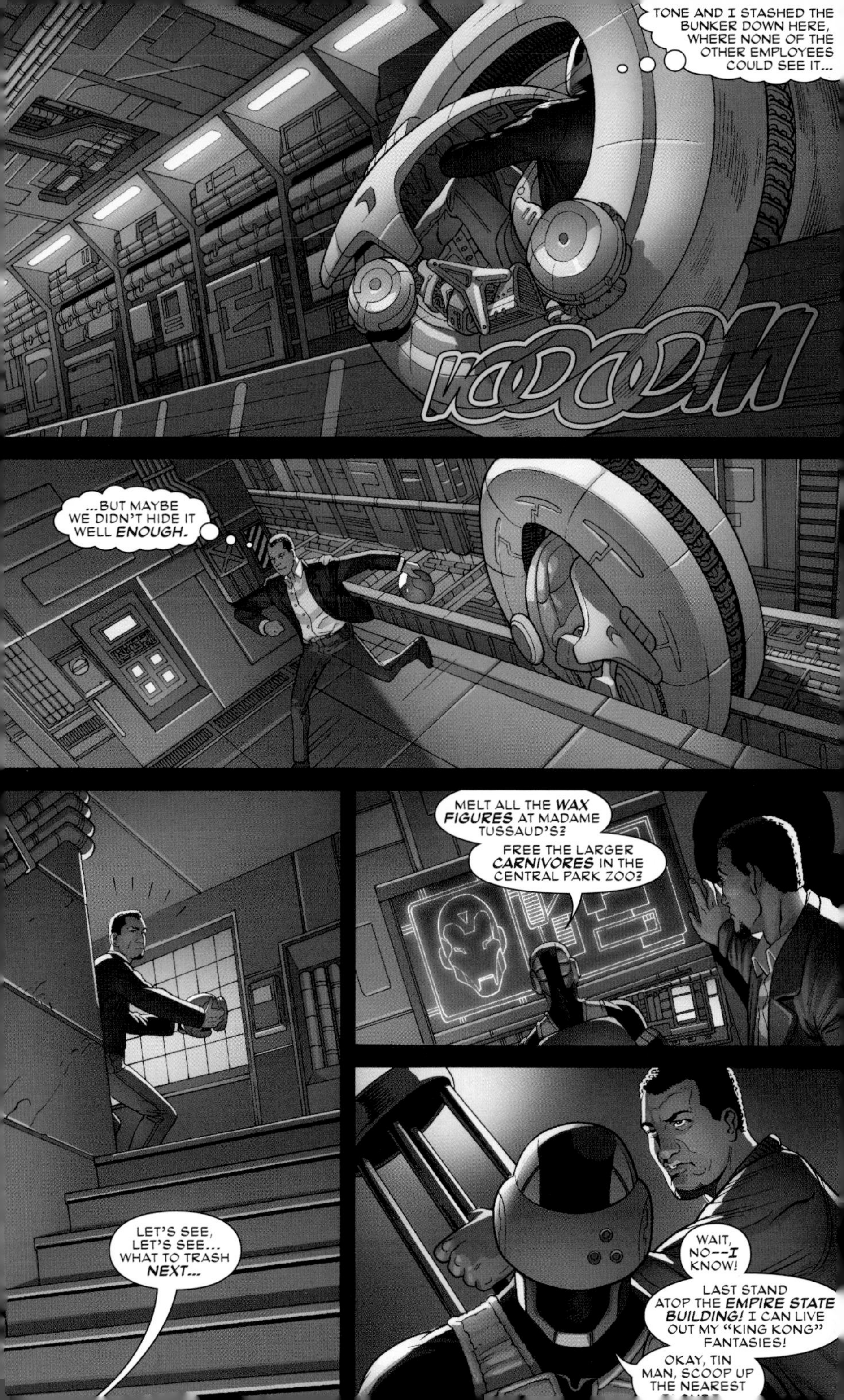
TONE AND I STASHED THE BUNKER DOWN HERE, WHERE NONE OF THE OTHER EMPLOYEES COULD SEE IT...
VROOOM
...BUT MAYBE WE DIDN'T HIDE IT WELL ENOUGH.
LET'S SEE, LET'S SEE... WHAT TO TRASH NEXT...
MELT ALL THE WAX FIGURES AT MADAME TUSSAUD'S?
FREE THE LARGER CARNIVORES IN THE CENTRAL PARK ZOO?
WAIT, NO--I KNOW!
LAST STAND ATOP THE EMPIRE STATE BUILDING! I CAN LIVE OUT MY "KING KONG" FANTASIES!
OKAY, TIN MAN, SCOOP UP THE NEAREST

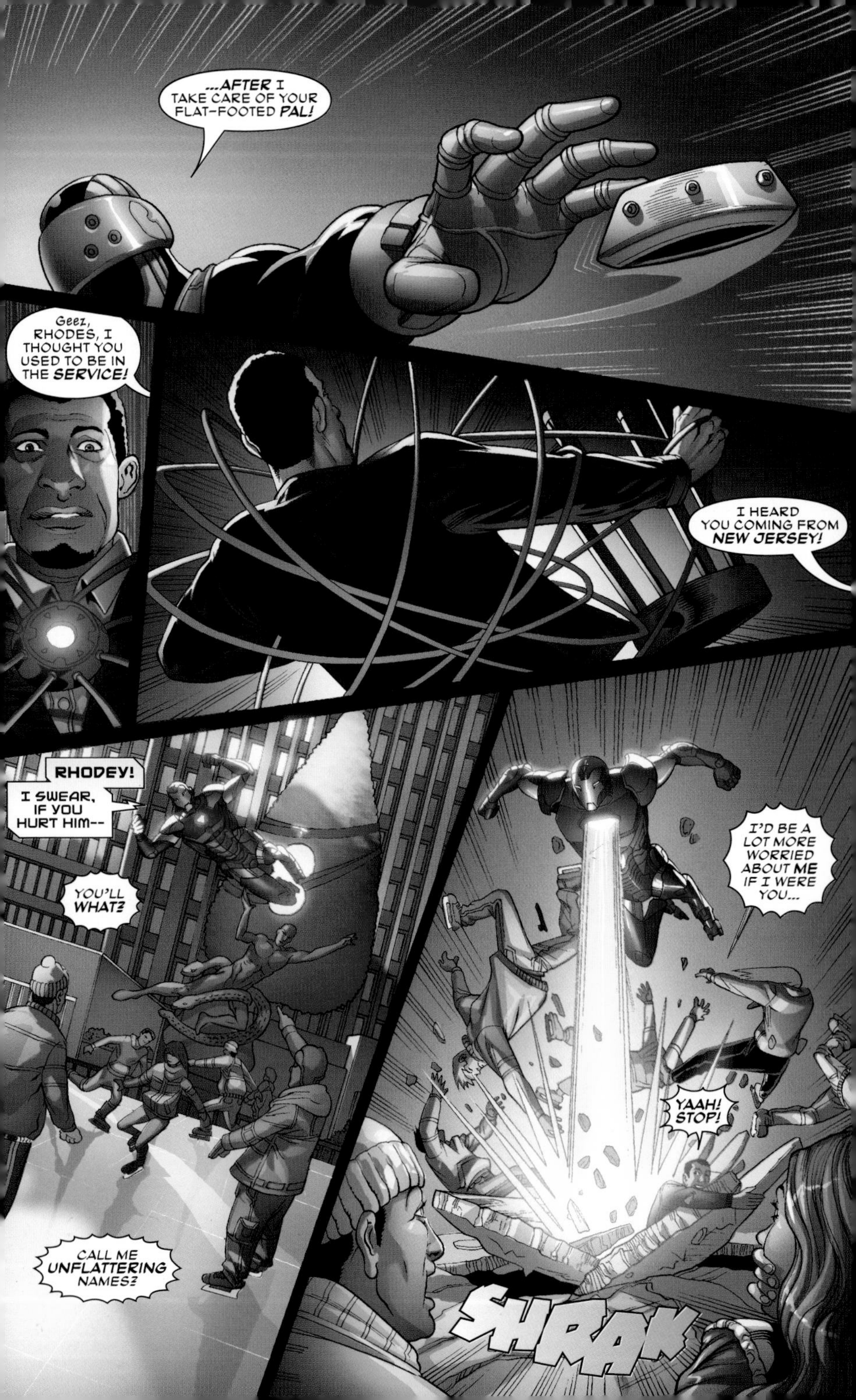
...AFTER I TAKE CARE OF YOUR FLAT-FOOTED PAL!
Geez, RHODES, I THOUGHT YOU USED TO BE IN THE SERVICE!
I HEARD YOU COMING FROM NEW JERSEY!
RHODEY!
I SWEAR, IF YOU HURT HIM--
YOU'LL WHAT?
CALL ME UNFLATTERING NAMES?
I'D BE A LOT MORE WORRIED ABOUT ME IF I WERE YOU...
YAAH! STOP!
SHRAK

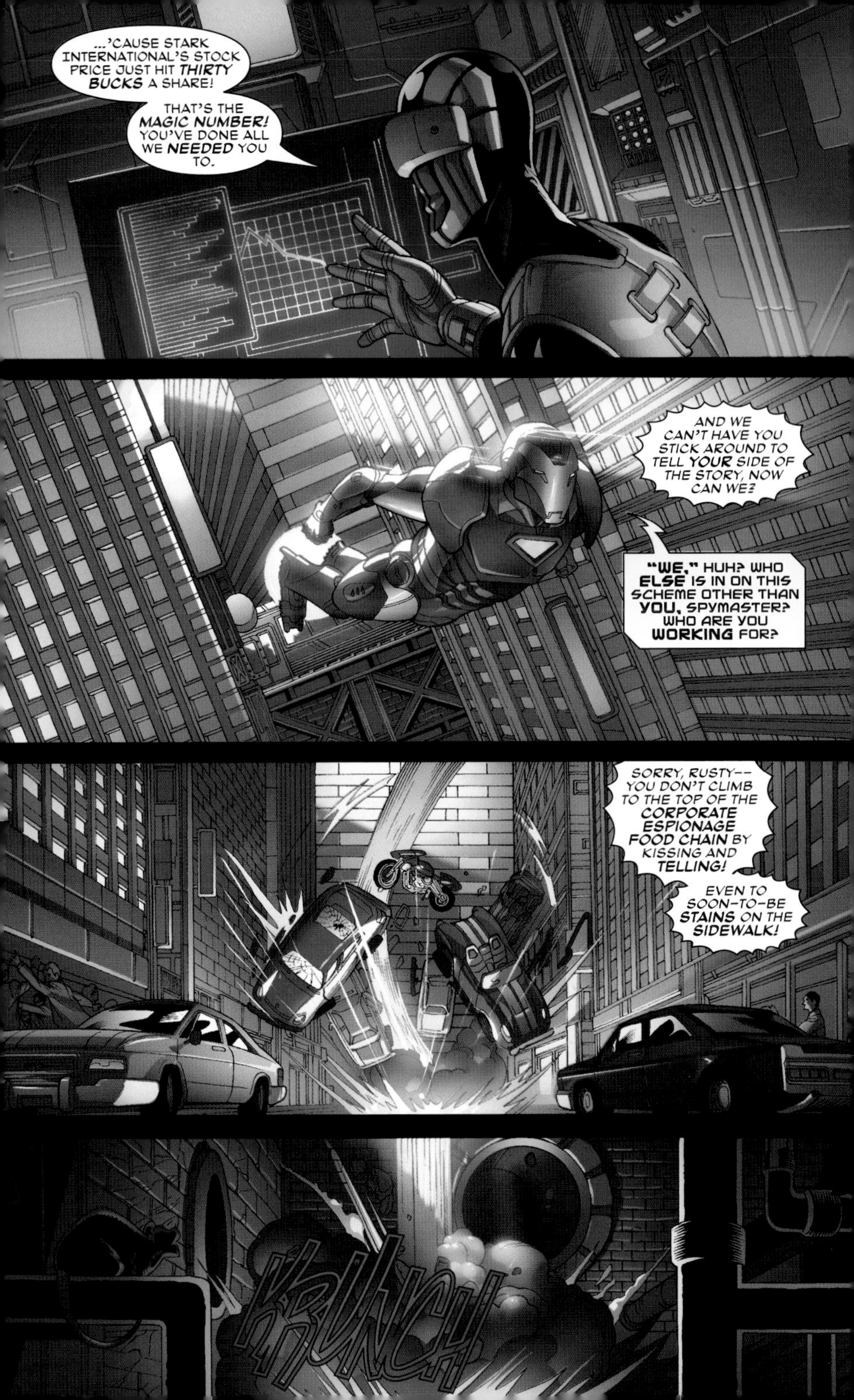
...'CAUSE STARK INTERNATIONAL'S STOCK PRICE JUST HIT THIRTY BUCKS A SHARE!
THAT'S THE MAGIC NUMBER! YOU'VE DONE ALL WE NEEDED YOU TO.
AND WE CAN'T HAVE YOU STICK AROUND TO TELL YOUR SIDE OF THE STORY, NOW CAN WE?
"WE," HUH? WHO ELSE IS IN ON THIS SCHEME OTHER THAN YOU, SPYMASTER? WHO ARE YOU WORKING FOR?
SORRY, RUSTY-- YOU DON'T CLIMB TO THE TOP OF THE CORPORATE ESPIONAGE FOOD CHAIN BY KISSING AND TELLING!
EVEN TO SOON-TO-BE STAINS ON THE SIDEWALK!
KRUNCH

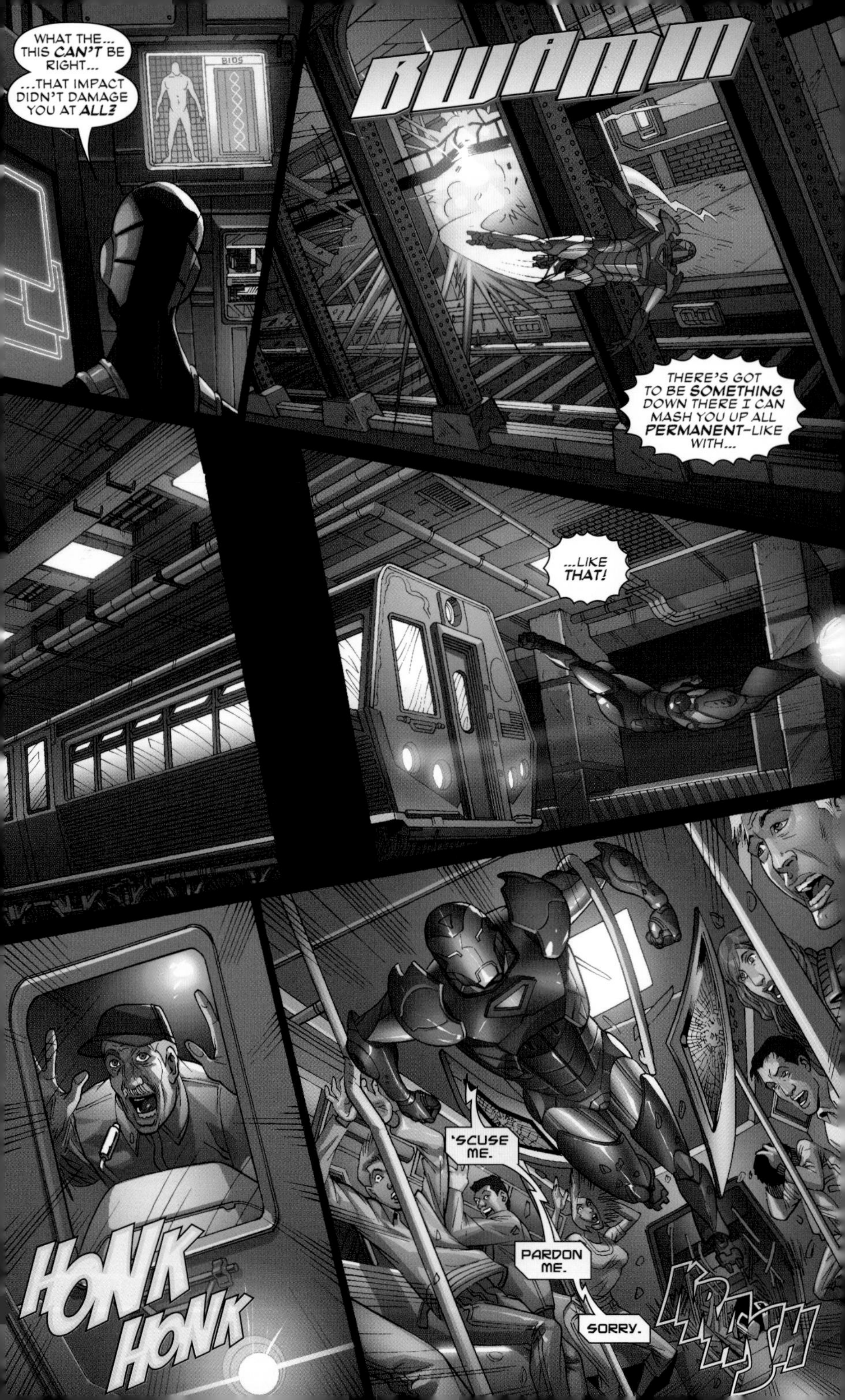
WHAT THE... THIS CAN'T BE RIGHT... ...THAT IMPACT DIDN'T DAMAGE YOU AT ALL?
BIOS
BWAMM
THERE'S GOT TO BE SOMETHING DOWN THERE I CAN MASH YOU UP ALL PERMANENT-LIKE WITH...
...LIKE THAT!
HONK HONK
'SCUSE ME.
PARDON ME.
SORRY.

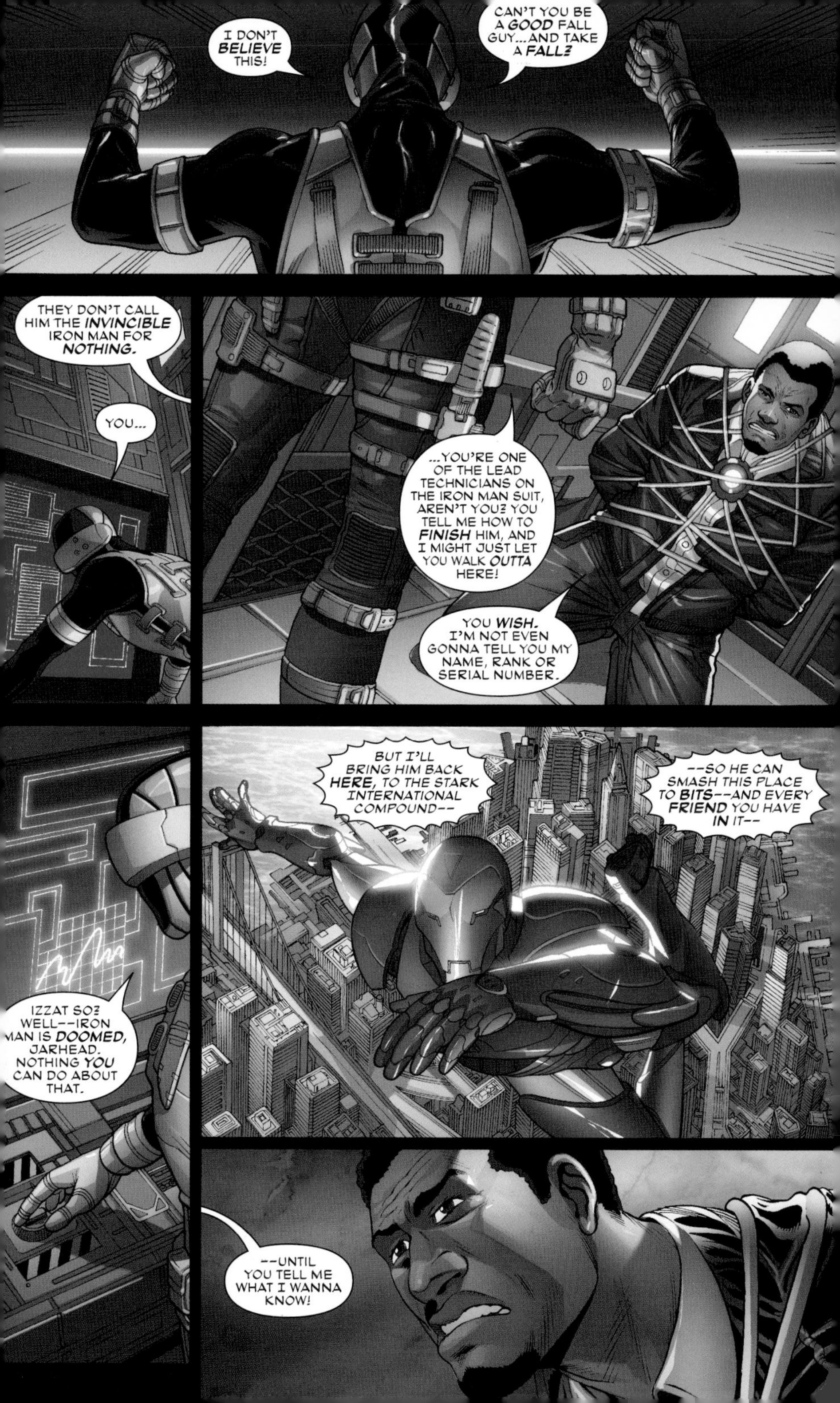
I DON'T BELIEVE THIS!
CAN'T YOU BE A GOOD FALL GUY...AND TAKE A FALL?
THEY DON'T CALL HIM THE INVINCIBLE IRON MAN FOR NOTHING.
YOU...
...YOU'RE ONE OF THE LEAD TECHNICIANS ON THE IRON MAN SUIT, AREN'T YOU? YOU TELL ME HOW TO FINISH HIM, AND I MIGHT JUST LET YOU WALK OUTTA HERE!
YOU WISH. I'M NOT EVEN GONNA TELL YOU MY NAME, RANK OR SERIAL NUMBER.
IZZAT SO? WELL--IRON MAN IS DOOMED, JARHEAD. NOTHING YOU CAN DO ABOUT THAT.
BUT I'LL BRING HIM BACK HERE, TO THE STARK INTERNATIONAL COMPOUND--
--SO HE CAN SMASH THIS PLACE TO BITS--AND EVERY FRIEND YOU HAVE IN IT--
--UNTIL YOU TELL ME WHAT I WANNA KNOW!

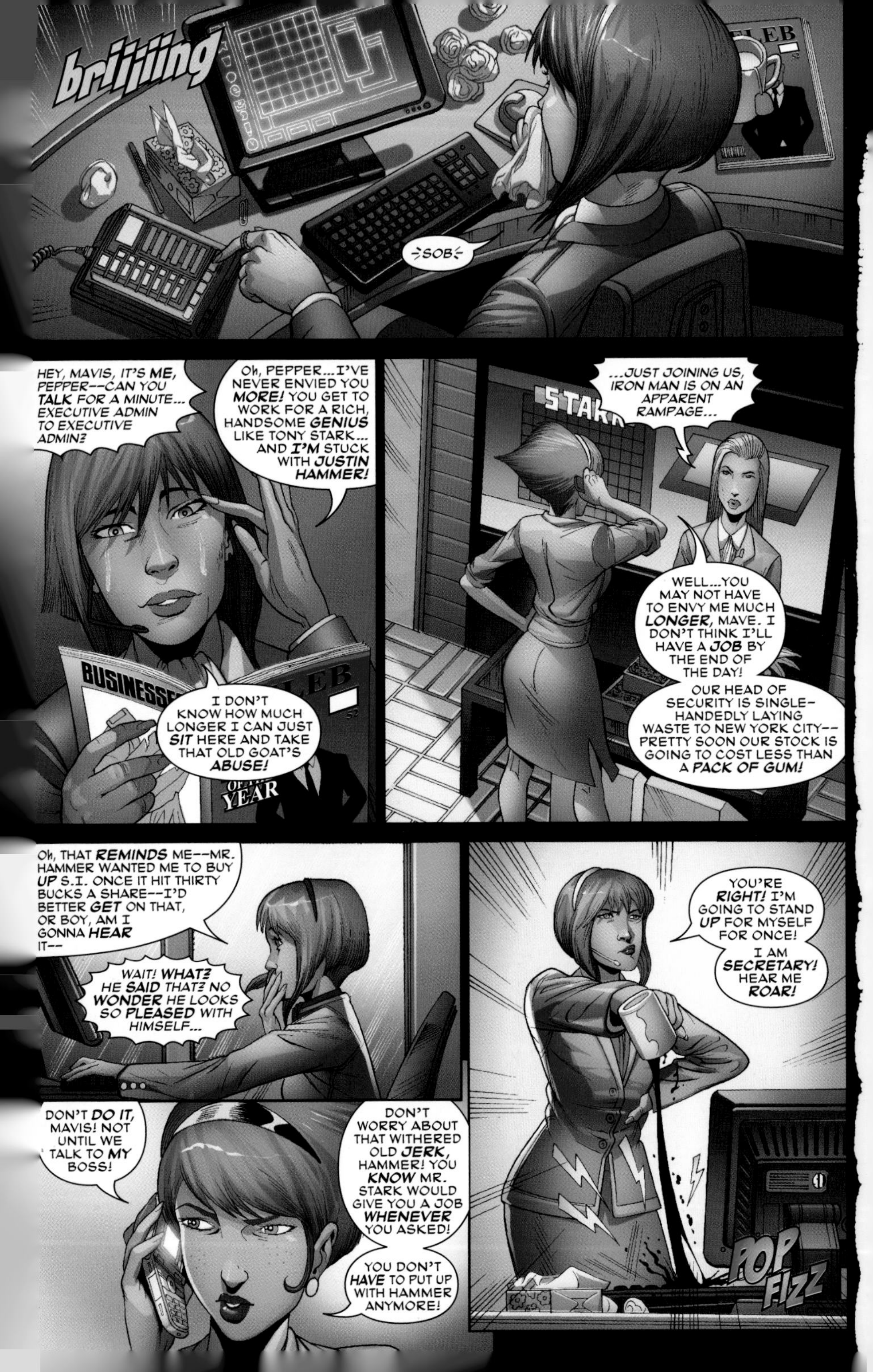
brijiiing
SOB
HEY, MAVIS, IT'S ME, PEPPER--CAN YOU TALK FOR A MINUTE... EXECUTIVE ADMIN TO EXECUTIVE ADMIN?
Oh, PEPPER...I'VE NEVER ENVIED YOU MORE! YOU GET TO WORK FOR A RICH, HANDSOME GENIUS LIKE TONY STARK... AND I'M STUCK WITH JUSTIN HAMMER!
BUSINESS
CELEB
OF THE YEAR
I DON'T KNOW HOW MUCH LONGER I CAN JUST SIT HERE AND TAKE THAT OLD GOAT'S ABUSE!
...JUST JOINING US, IRON MAN IS ON AN APPARENT RAMPAGE...
STARK
WELL...YOU MAY NOT HAVE TO ENVY ME MUCH LONGER, MAVE. I DON'T THINK I'LL HAVE A JOB BY THE END OF THE DAY!
OUR HEAD OF SECURITY IS SINGLE-HANDEDLY LAYING WASTE TO NEW YORK CITY--PRETTY SOON OUR STOCK IS GOING TO COST LESS THAN A PACK OF GUM!
Oh, THAT REMINDS ME--MR. HAMMER WANTED ME TO BUY UP S.I. ONCE IT HIT THIRTY BUCKS A SHARE--I'D BETTER GET ON THAT, OR BOY, AM I GONNA HEAR IT--
WAIT! WHAT? HE SAID THAT? NO WONDER HE LOOKS SO PLEASED WITH HIMSELF...
DON'T DO IT, MAVIS! NOT UNTIL WE TALK TO MY BOSS!
DON'T WORRY ABOUT THAT WITHERED OLD JERK, HAMMER! YOU KNOW MR. STARK WOULD GIVE YOU A JOB WHENEVER YOU ASKED!
YOU DON'T HAVE TO PUT UP WITH HAMMER ANYMORE!
YOU'RE RIGHT! I'M GOING TO STAND UP FOR MYSELF FOR ONCE!
I AM SECRETARY! HEAR ME ROAR!
POP
FIZZ

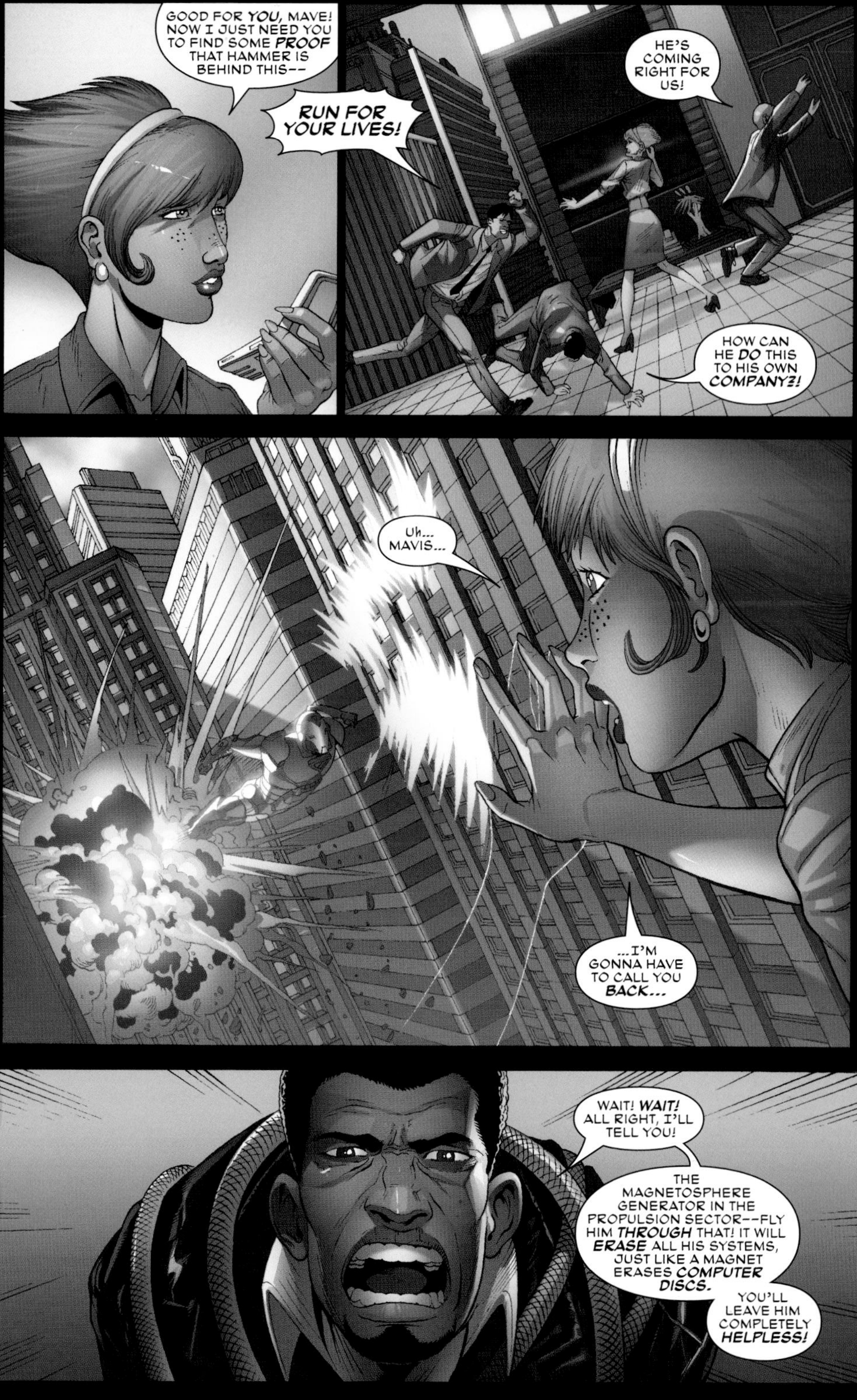
GOOD FOR YOU, MAVE! NOW I JUST NEED YOU TO FIND SOME PROOF THAT HAMMER IS BEHIND THIS--
RUN FOR YOUR LIVES!
HE'S COMING RIGHT FOR US!
HOW CAN HE DO THIS TO HIS OWN COMPANY?!
Uh... MAVIS...
...I'M GONNA HAVE TO CALL YOU BACK...
WAIT! WAIT! ALL RIGHT, I'LL TELL YOU!
THE MAGNETOSPHERE GENERATOR IN THE PROPULSION SECTOR--FLY HIM THROUGH THAT! IT WILL ERASE ALL HIS SYSTEMS, JUST LIKE A MAGNET ERASES COMPUTER DISCS.
YOU'LL LEAVE HIM COMPLETELY HELPLESS!

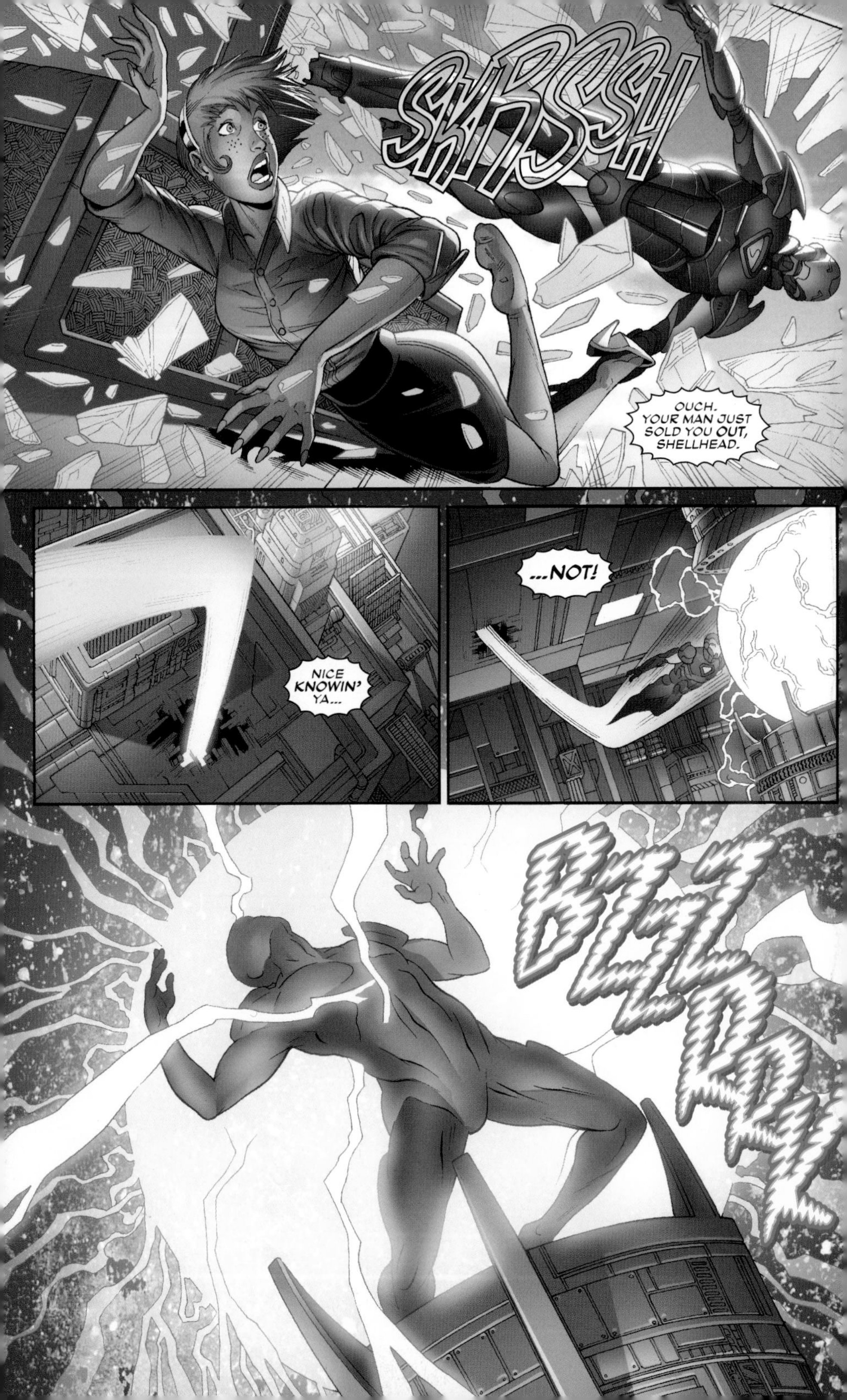
SKRSSH
OUCH. YOUR MAN JUST SOLD YOU OUT, SHELLHEAD.
NICE KNOWIN' YA...
...NOT!

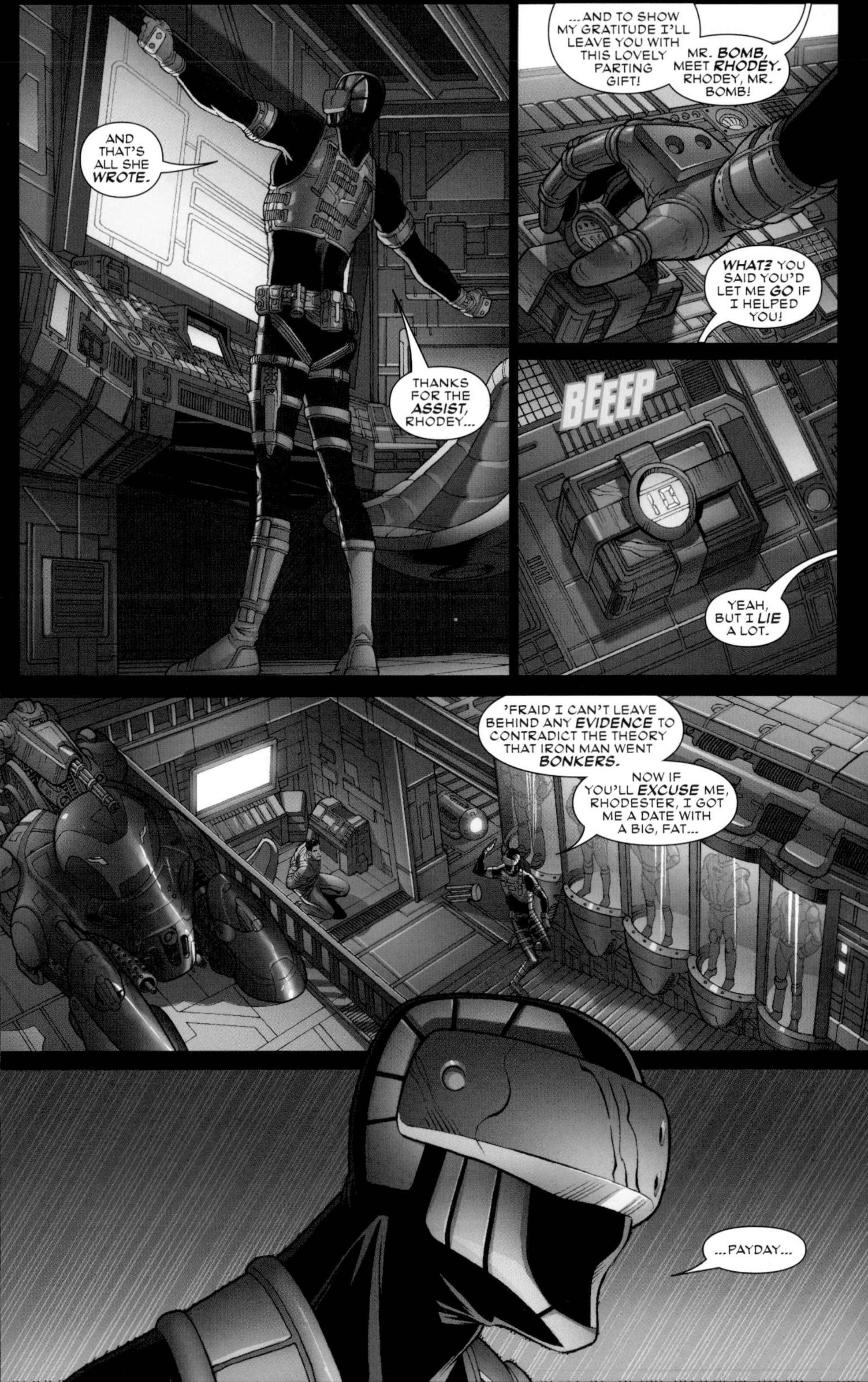
AND THAT'S ALL SHE WROTE.
THANKS FOR THE ASSIST, RHODEY...
...AND TO SHOW MY GRATITUDE I'LL LEAVE YOU WITH THIS LOVELY PARTING GIFT!
MR. BOMB, MEET RHODEY. RHODEY, MR. BOMB!
WHAT? YOU SAID YOU'D LET ME GO IF I HELPED YOU!
BEEEP
YEAH, BUT I LIE A LOT.
'FRAID I CAN'T LEAVE BEHIND ANY EVIDENCE TO CONTRADICT THE THEORY THAT IRON MAN WENT BONKERS.
NOW IF YOU'LL EXCUSE ME, RHODESTER, I GOT ME A DATE WITH A BIG, FAT...
...PAYDAY...

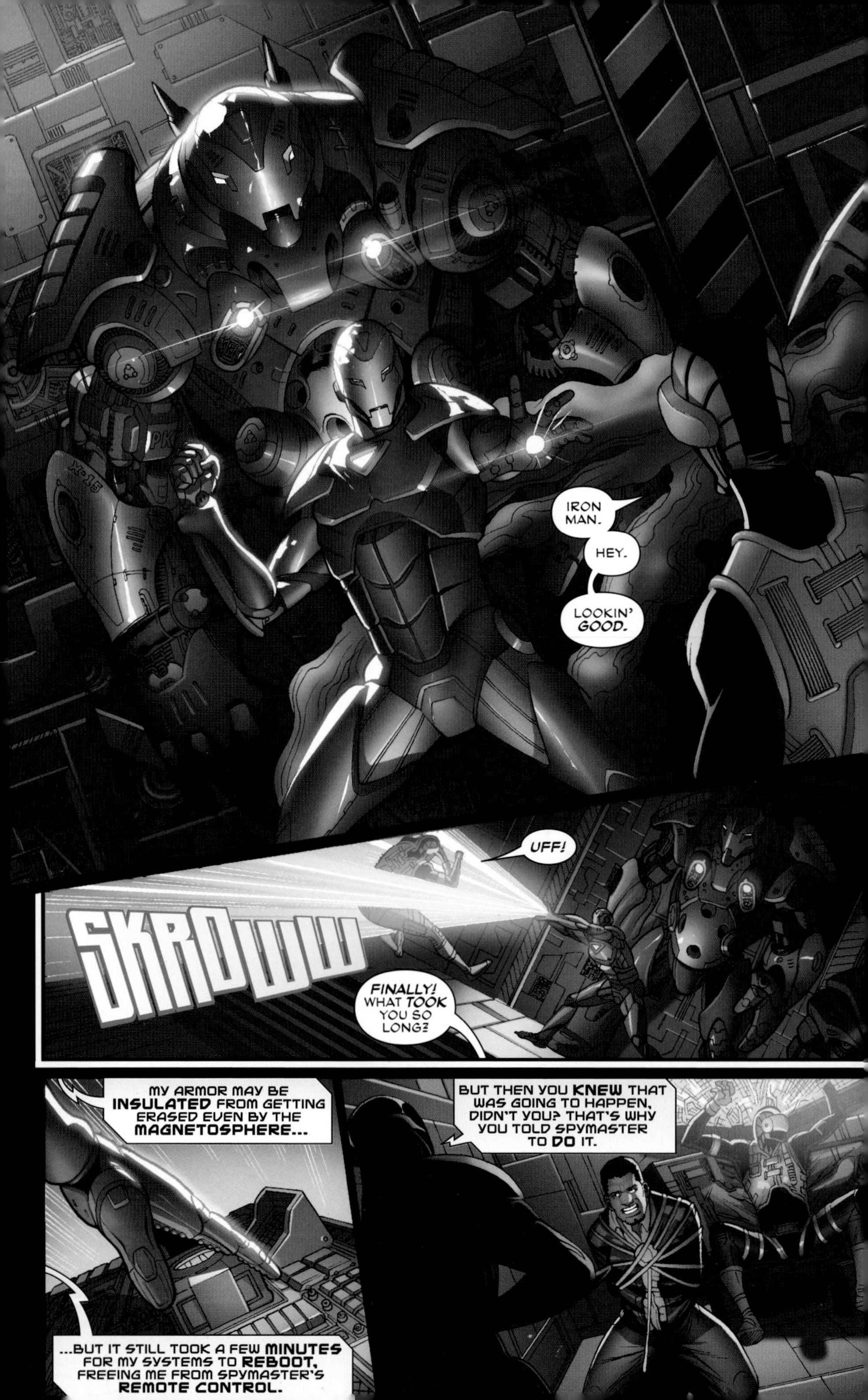
IRON MAN.
HEY.
LOOKIN' GOOD.
UFF!
SKROWW
FINALLY! WHAT TOOK YOU SO LONG?
MY ARMOR MAY BE INSULATED FROM GETTING ERASED EVEN BY THE MAGNETOSPHERE...
...BUT IT STILL TOOK A FEW MINUTES FOR MY SYSTEMS TO REBOOT, FREEING ME FROM SPYMASTER'S REMOTE CONTROL.
BUT THEN YOU KNEW THAT WAS GOING TO HAPPEN, DIDN'T YOU? THAT'S WHY YOU TOLD SPYMASTER TO DO IT.

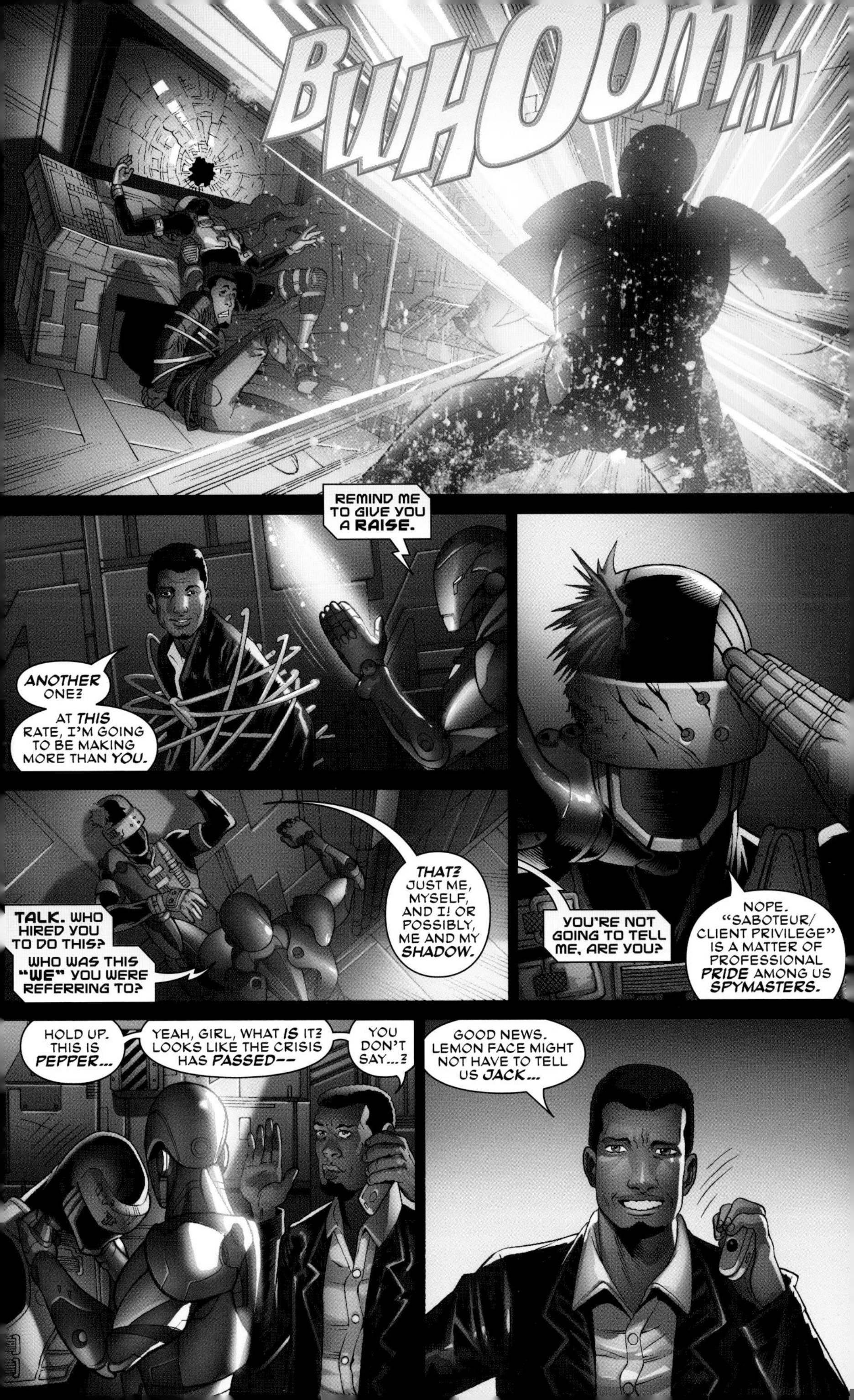
BWHOOMM
REMIND ME TO GIVE YOU A RAISE.
ANOTHER ONE?
AT THIS RATE, I'M GOING TO BE MAKING MORE THAN YOU.
TALK. WHO HIRED YOU TO DO THIS?
WHO WAS THIS "WE" YOU WERE REFERRING TO?
THAT? JUST ME, MYSELF, AND I! OR POSSIBLY, ME AND MY SHADOW.
YOU'RE NOT GOING TO TELL ME, ARE YOU?
NOPE. "SABOTEUR/ CLIENT PRIVILEGE" IS A MATTER OF PROFESSIONAL PRIDE AMONG US SPYMASTERS.
HOLD UP. THIS IS PEPPER...
YEAH, GIRL, WHAT IS IT? LOOKS LIKE THE CRISIS HAS PASSED--
YOU DON'T SAY...?
GOOD NEWS. LEMON FACE MIGHT NOT HAVE TO TELL US JACK...

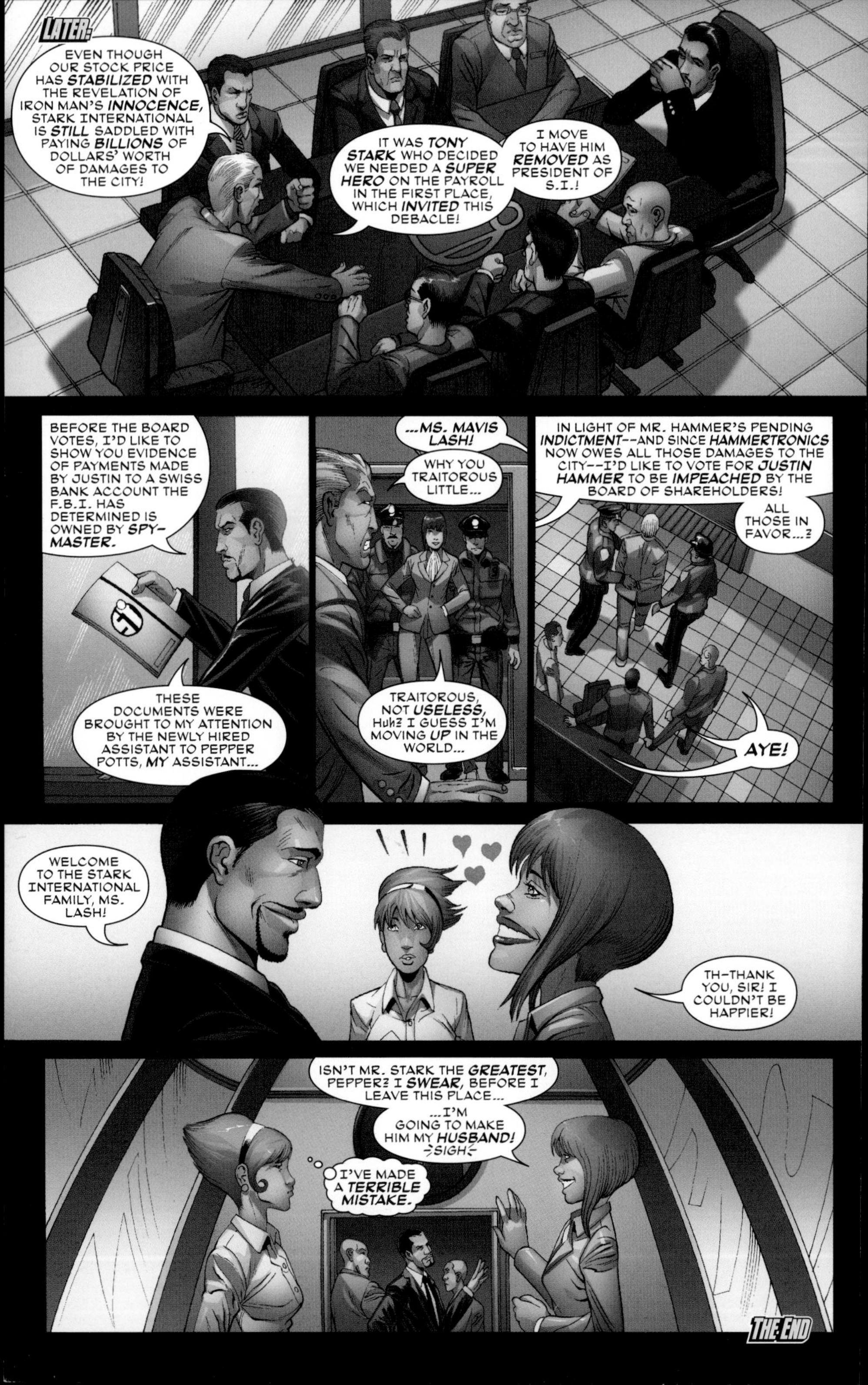
LATER:
EVEN THOUGH OUR STOCK PRICE HAS STABILIZED WITH THE REVELATION OF IRON MAN'S INNOCENCE, STARK INTERNATIONAL IS STILL SADDLED WITH PAYING BILLIONS OF DOLLARS' WORTH OF DAMAGES TO THE CITY!
IT WAS TONY STARK WHO DECIDED WE NEEDED A SUPER HERO ON THE PAYROLL IN THE FIRST PLACE, WHICH INVITED THIS DEBACLE!
I MOVE TO HAVE HIM REMOVED AS PRESIDENT OF S.I.!
BEFORE THE BOARD VOTES, I'D LIKE TO SHOW YOU EVIDENCE OF PAYMENTS MADE BY JUSTIN TO A SWISS BANK ACCOUNT THE F.B.I. HAS DETERMINED IS OWNED BY SPY-MASTER.
THESE DOCUMENTS WERE BROUGHT TO MY ATTENTION BY THE NEWLY HIRED ASSISTANT TO PEPPER POTTS, MY ASSISTANT...
...MS. MAVIS LASH!
WHY YOU TRAITOROUS LITTLE...
TRAITOROUS, NOT USELESS, Huh? I GUESS I'M MOVING UP IN THE WORLD...
IN LIGHT OF MR. HAMMER'S PENDING INDICTMENT--AND SINCE HAMMERTRONICS NOW OWES ALL THOSE DAMAGES TO THE CITY--I'D LIKE TO VOTE FOR JUSTIN HAMMER TO BE IMPEACHED BY THE BOARD OF SHAREHOLDERS!
ALL THOSE IN FAVOR...?
AYE!
WELCOME TO THE STARK INTERNATIONAL FAMILY, MS. LASH!
TH-THANK YOU, SIR! I COULDN'T BE HAPPIER!
ISN'T MR. STARK THE GREATEST, PEPPER? I SWEAR, BEFORE I LEAVE THIS PLACE...
...I'M GOING TO MAKE HIM MY HUSBAND! *SIGH*
I'VE MADE A TERRIBLE MISTAKE.
THE END

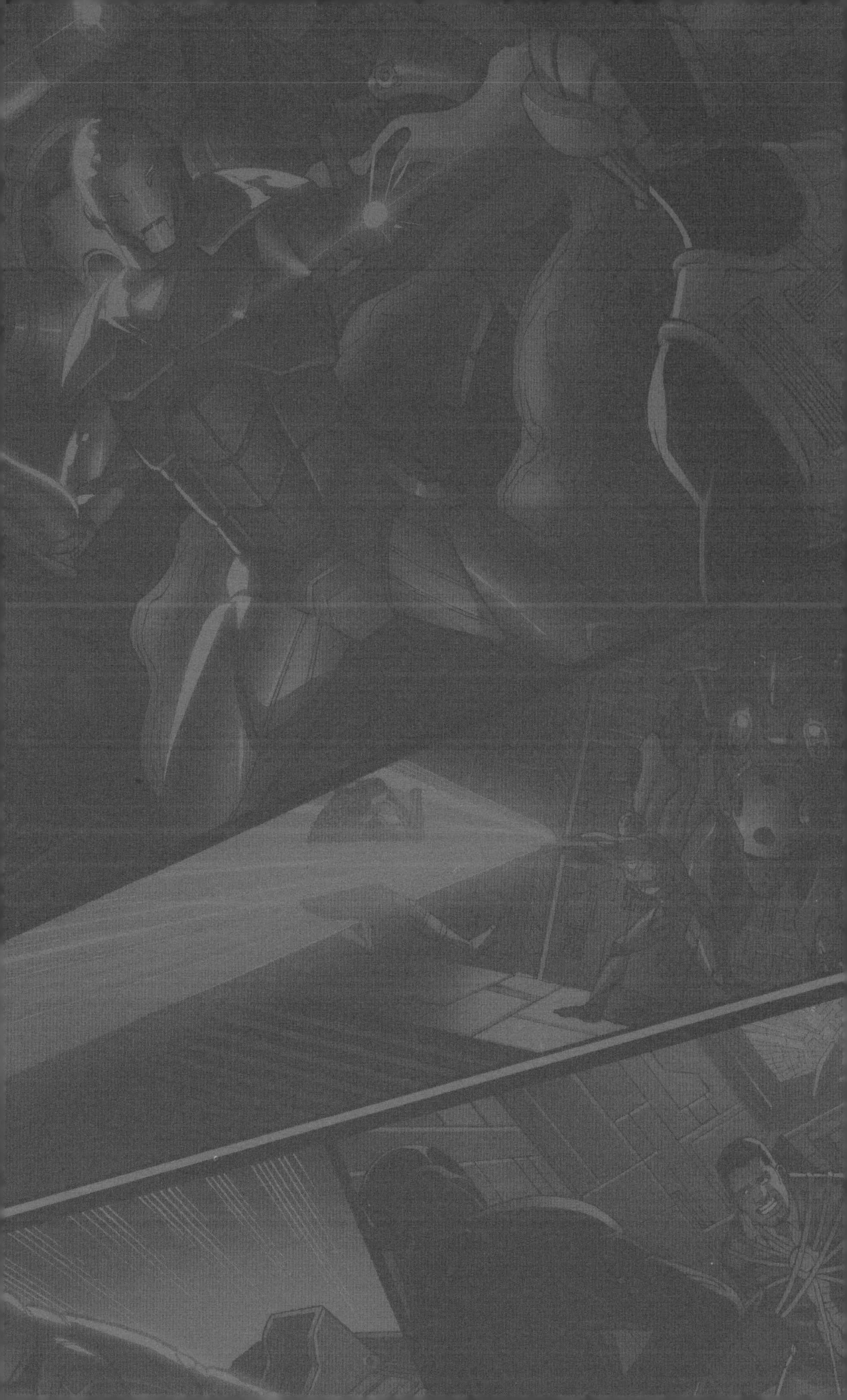

05

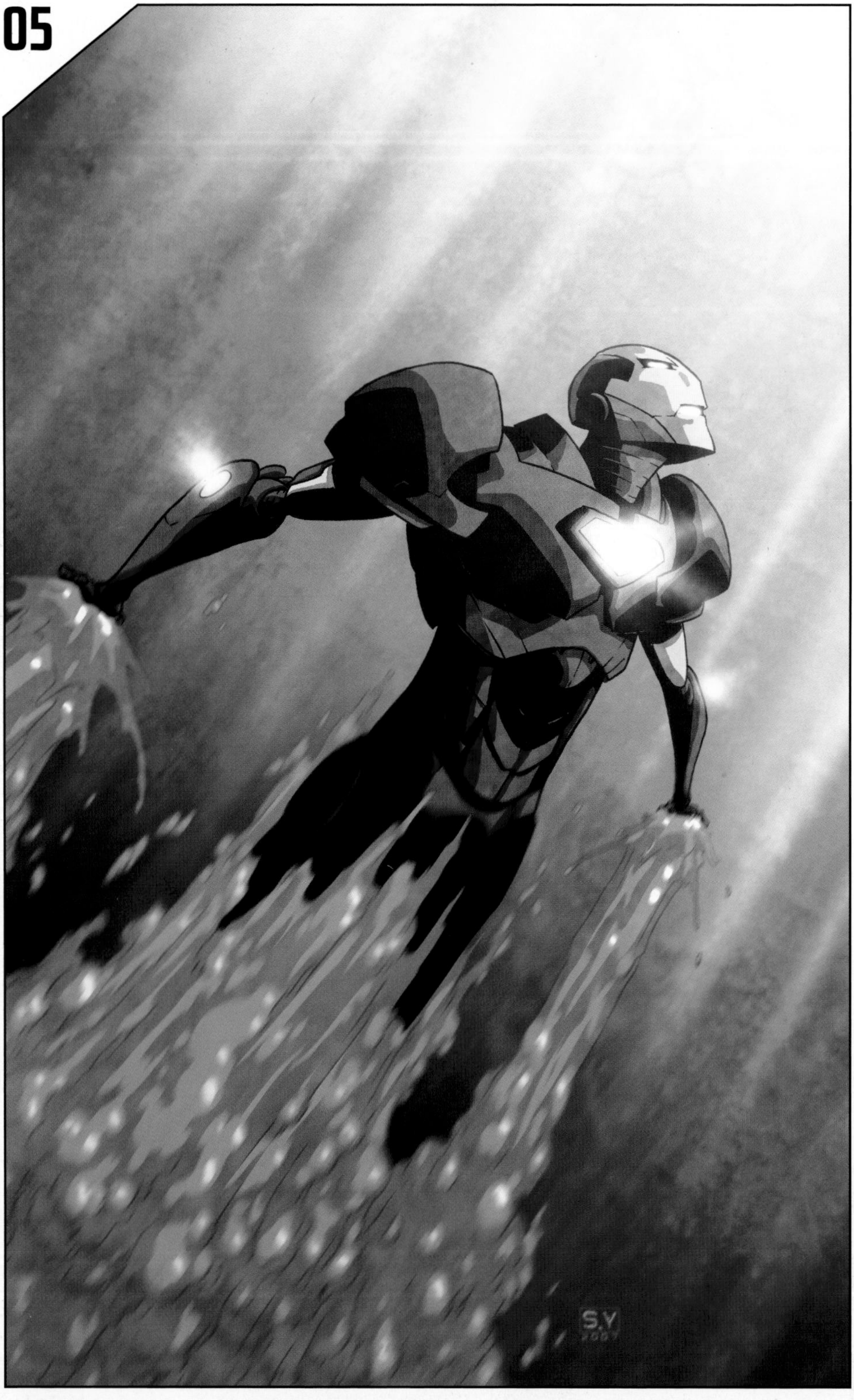

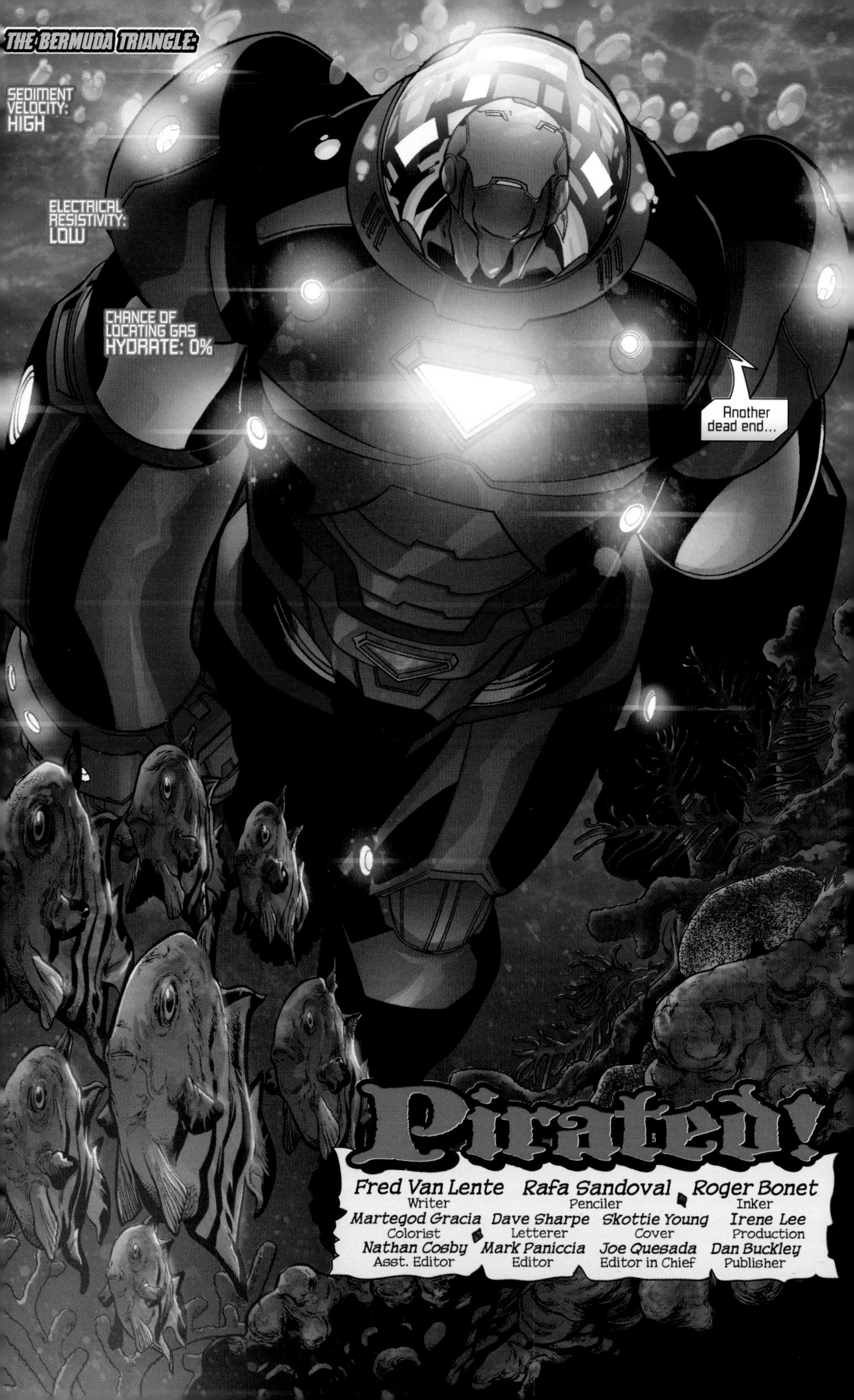

THE BERMUDA TRIANGLE:
SEDIMENT VELOCITY: HIGH
ELECTRICAL RESISTIVITY: LOW
CHANCE OF LOCATING GAS HYDRATE: 0%
Another dead end...
Pirated!
Fred Van Lente Writer
Rafa Sandoval Penciler
Roger Bonet Inker
Martegod Gracia Colorist
Dave Sharpe Letterer
Skottie Young Cover
Irene Lee Production
Nathan Cosby Asst. Editor
Mark Paniccia Editor
Joe Quesada Editor in Chief
Dan Buckley Publisher

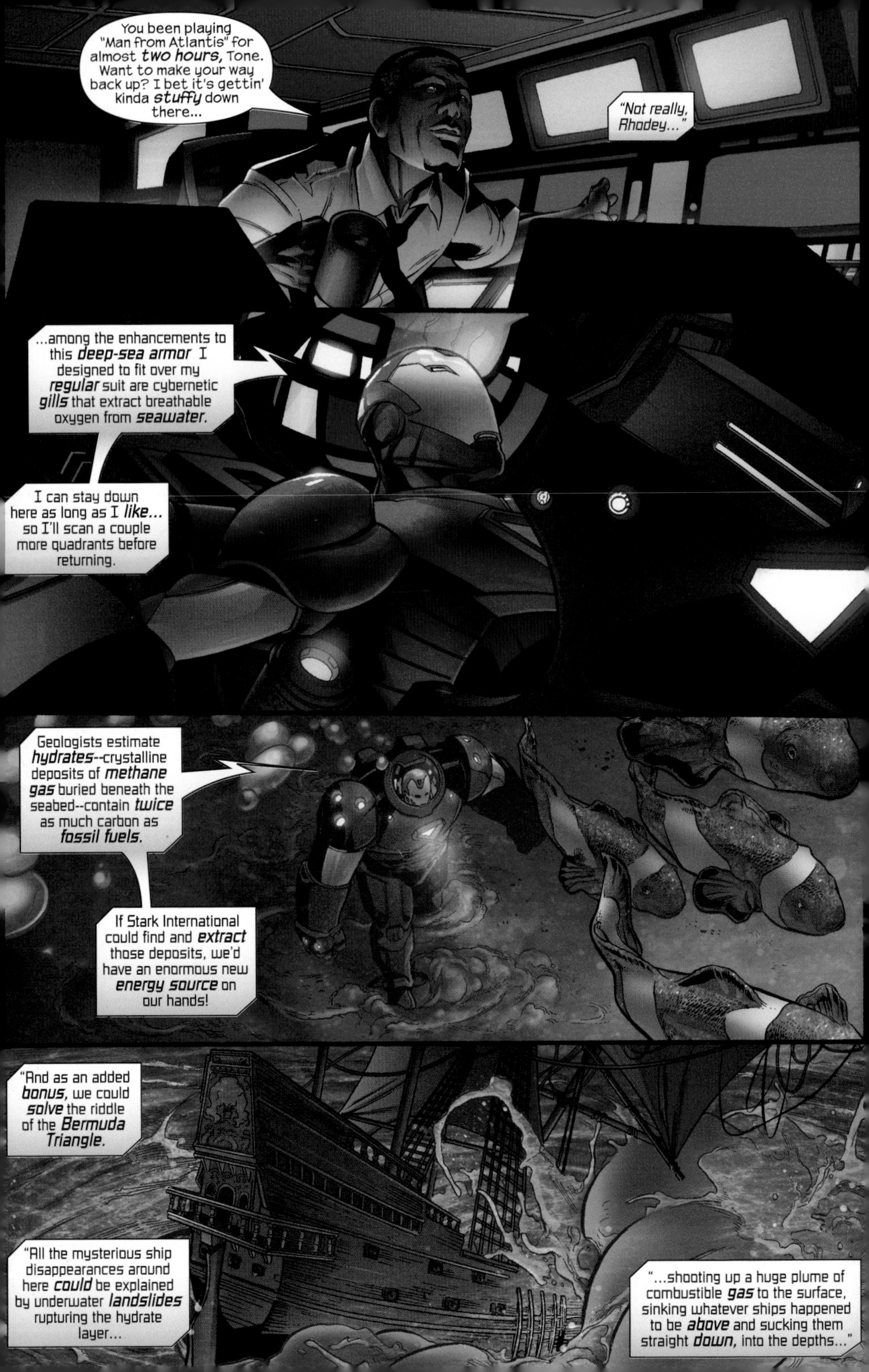

You been playing "Man from Atlantis" for almost two hours, Tone. Want to make your way back up? I bet it's gettin' kinda stuffy down there...
"Not really, Rhodey..."
...among the enhancements to this deep-sea armor I designed to fit over my regular suit are cybernetic gills that extract breathable oxygen from seawater.
I can stay down here as long as I like... so I'll scan a couple more quadrants before returning.
Geologists estimate hydrates--crystalline deposits of methane gas buried beneath the seabed--contain twice as much carbon as fossil fuels.
If Stark International could find and extract those deposits, we'd have an enormous new energy source on our hands!
"And as an added bonus, we could solve the riddle of the Bermuda Triangle.
"All the mysterious ship disappearances around here could be explained by underwater landslides rupturing the hydrate layer...
"...shooting up a huge plume of combustible gas to the surface, sinking whatever ships happened to be above and sucking them straight down, into the depths..."

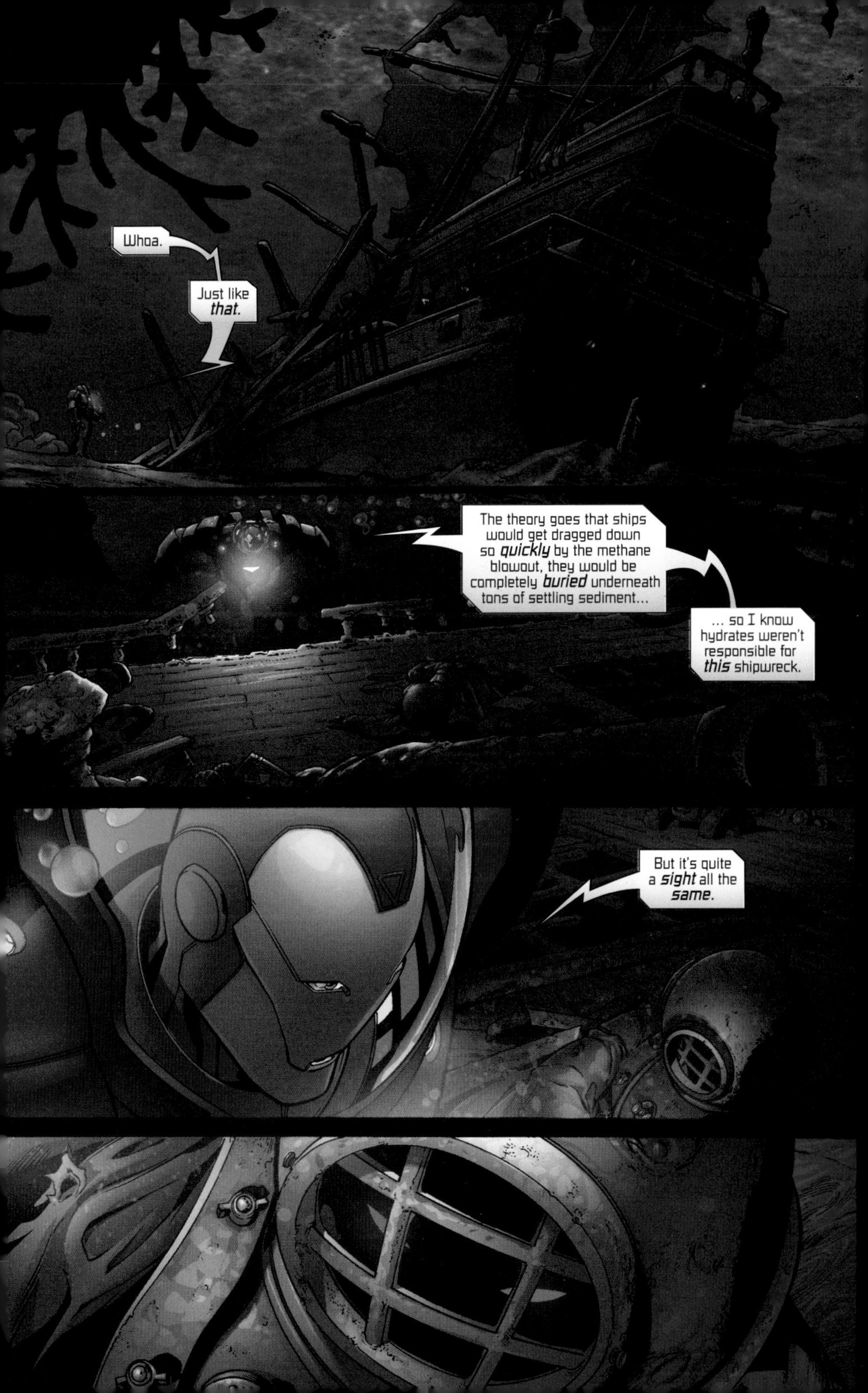

Whoa.
Just like *that*.
The theory goes that ships would get dragged down so *quickly* by the methane blowout, they would be completely *buried* underneath tons of settling sediment...
... so I know hydrates weren't responsible for *this* shipwreck.
But it's quite a *sight* all the *same*.

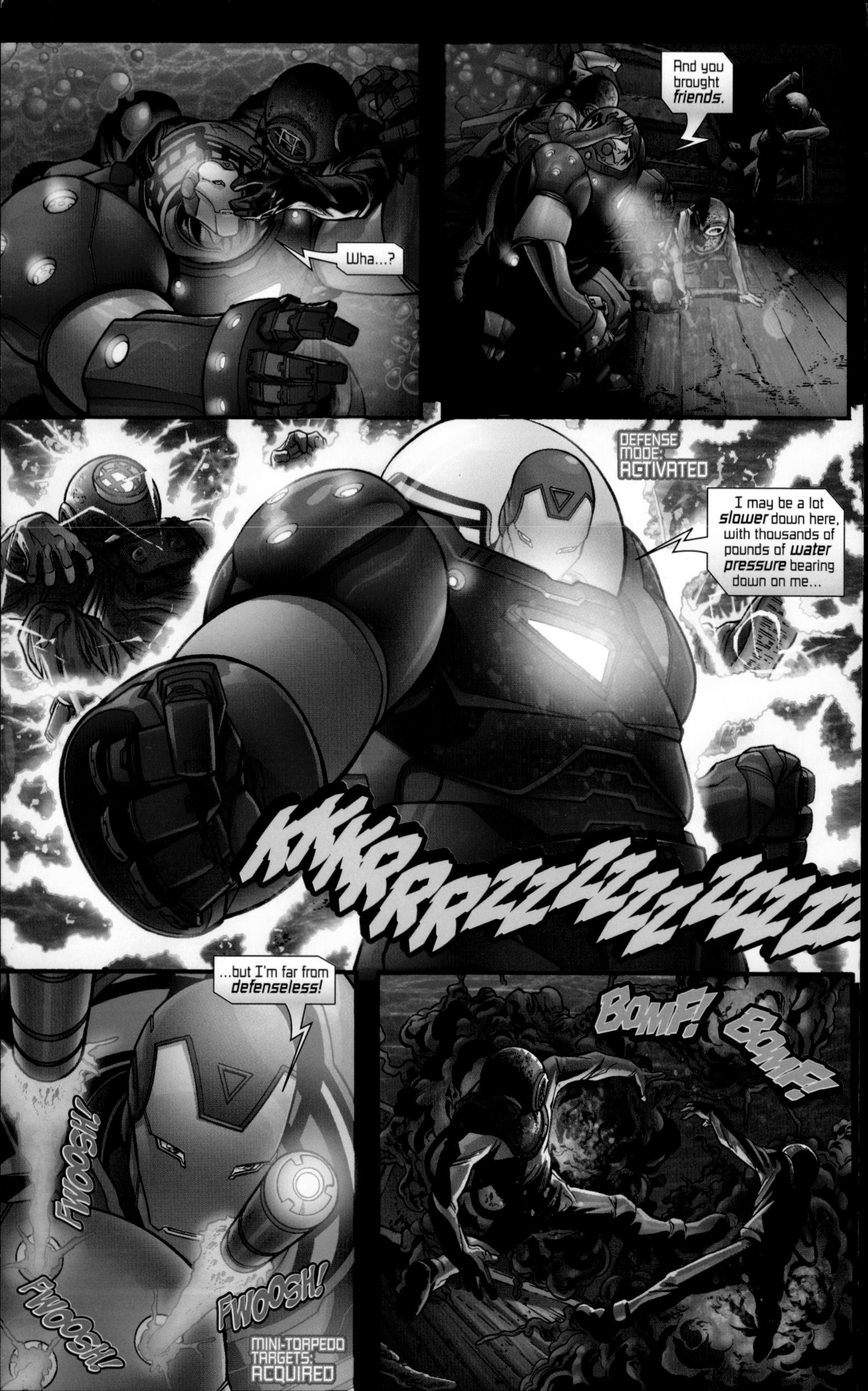
Wha...?
And you brought friends.
DEFENSE MODE: ACTIVATED
I may be a lot slower down here, with thousands of pounds of water pressure bearing down on me...
KKKRRRZZZZZZZZZZZ
...but I'm far from defenseless!
FWOOSH!
FWOOSH!
FWOOSH!
FWOOSH!
MINI-TORPEDO TARGETS: ACQUIRED
BOMF! BOMF!

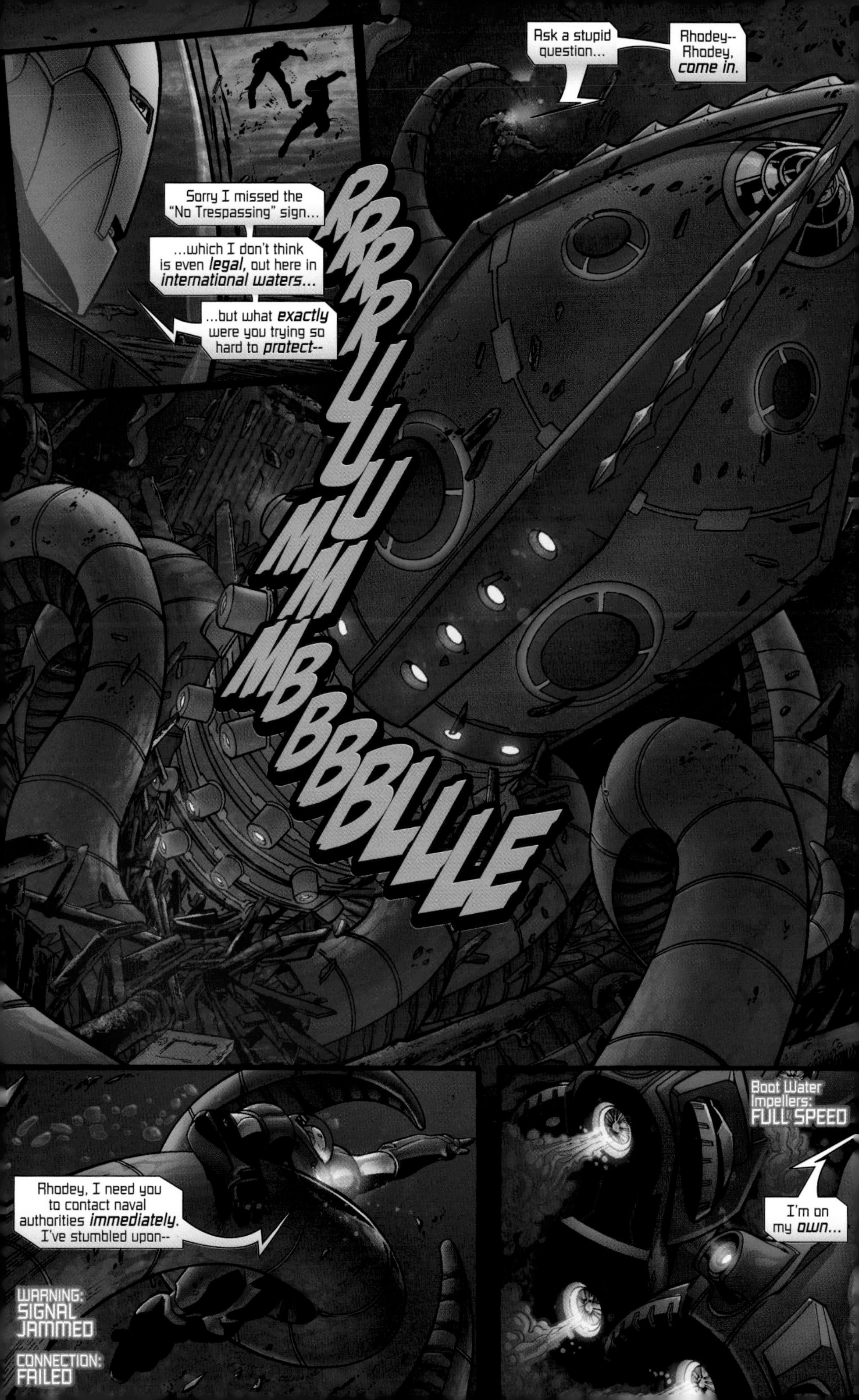
Sorry I missed the "No Trespassing" sign...
...which I don't think is even *legal*, out here in *international waters*...
...but what *exactly* were you trying so hard to *protect*--
RRRRUUUMMMBBBLLE
Ask a stupid question...
Rhodey-- Rhodey, *come in*.
Rhodey, I need you to contact naval authorities *immediately*. I've stumbled upon--
WARNING: SIGNAL JAMMED
CONNECTION: FAILED
Boot Water Impellers: FULL SPEED
I'm on my *own*...

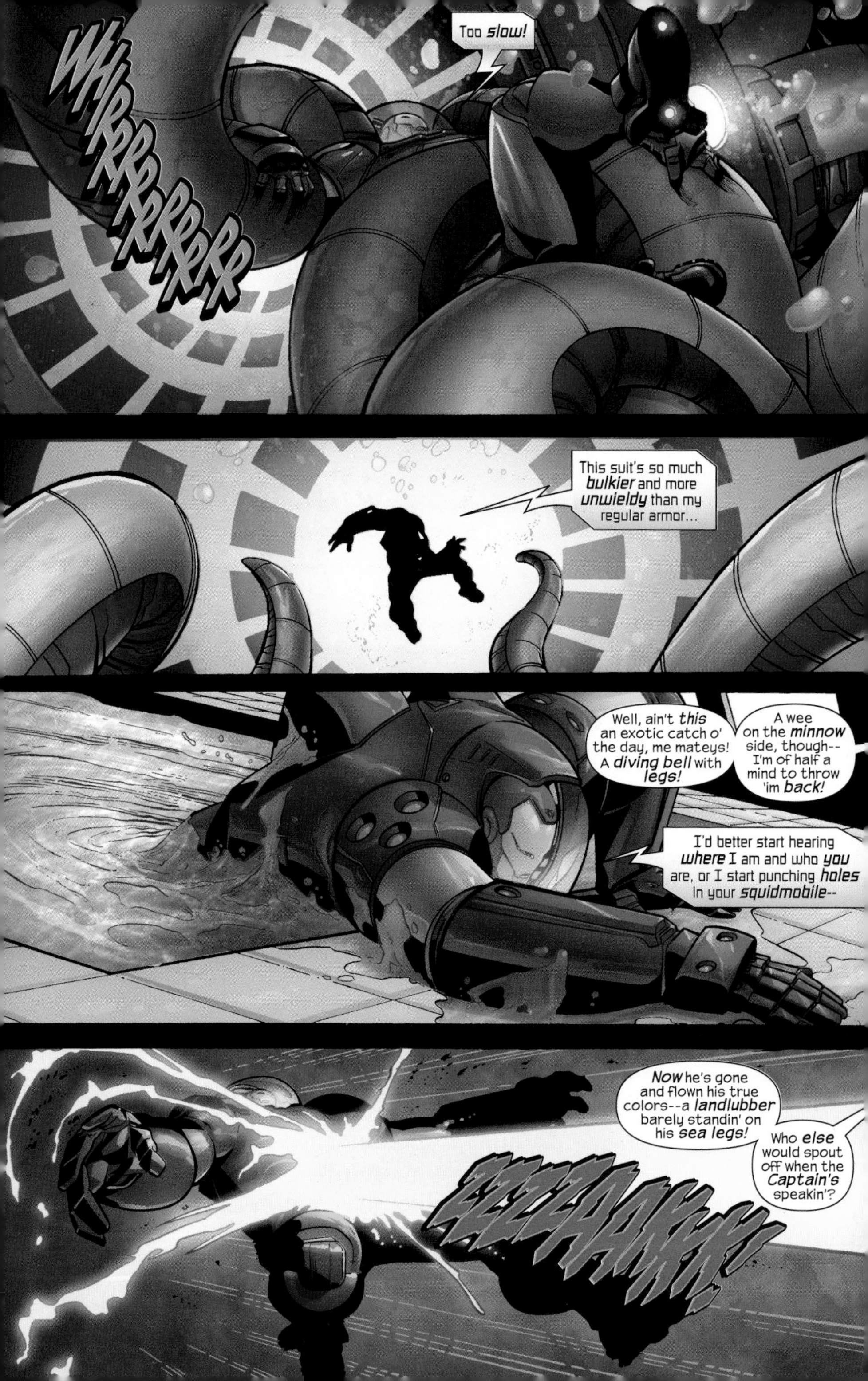
WHIRRRRRRRRRRR
Too slow!
This suit's so much bulkier and more unwieldy than my regular armor...
Well, ain't this an exotic catch o' the day, me mateys! A diving bell with legs!
A wee on the minnow side, though--I'm of half a mind to throw 'im back!
I'd better start hearing where I am and who you are, or I start punching holes in your squidmobile--
Now he's gone and flown his true colors--a landlubber barely standin' on his sea legs!
Who else would spout off when the Captain's speakin'?
ZZZZAAKKK!

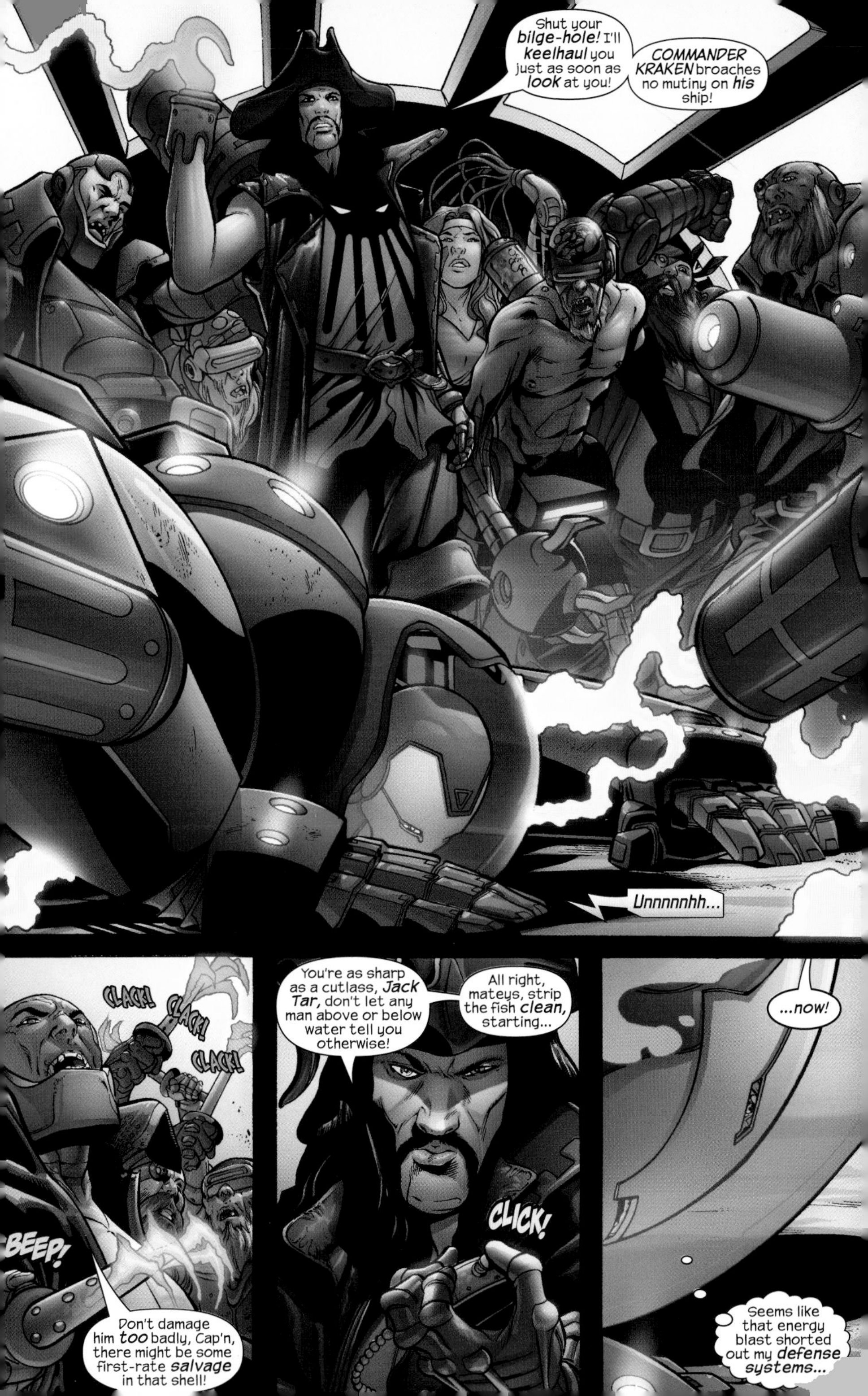
Shut your bilge-hole! I'll keelhaul you just as soon as look at you!
COMMANDER KRAKEN broaches no mutiny on his ship!
Unnnnnhh...
CLACK! CLACK! CLACK!
BEEP!
Don't damage him too badly, Cap'n, there might be some first-rate salvage in that shell!
You're as sharp as a cutlass, Jack Tar, don't let any man above or below water tell you otherwise!
All right, mateys, strip the fish clean, starting...
CLICK!
...now!
Seems like that energy blast shorted out my defense systems...

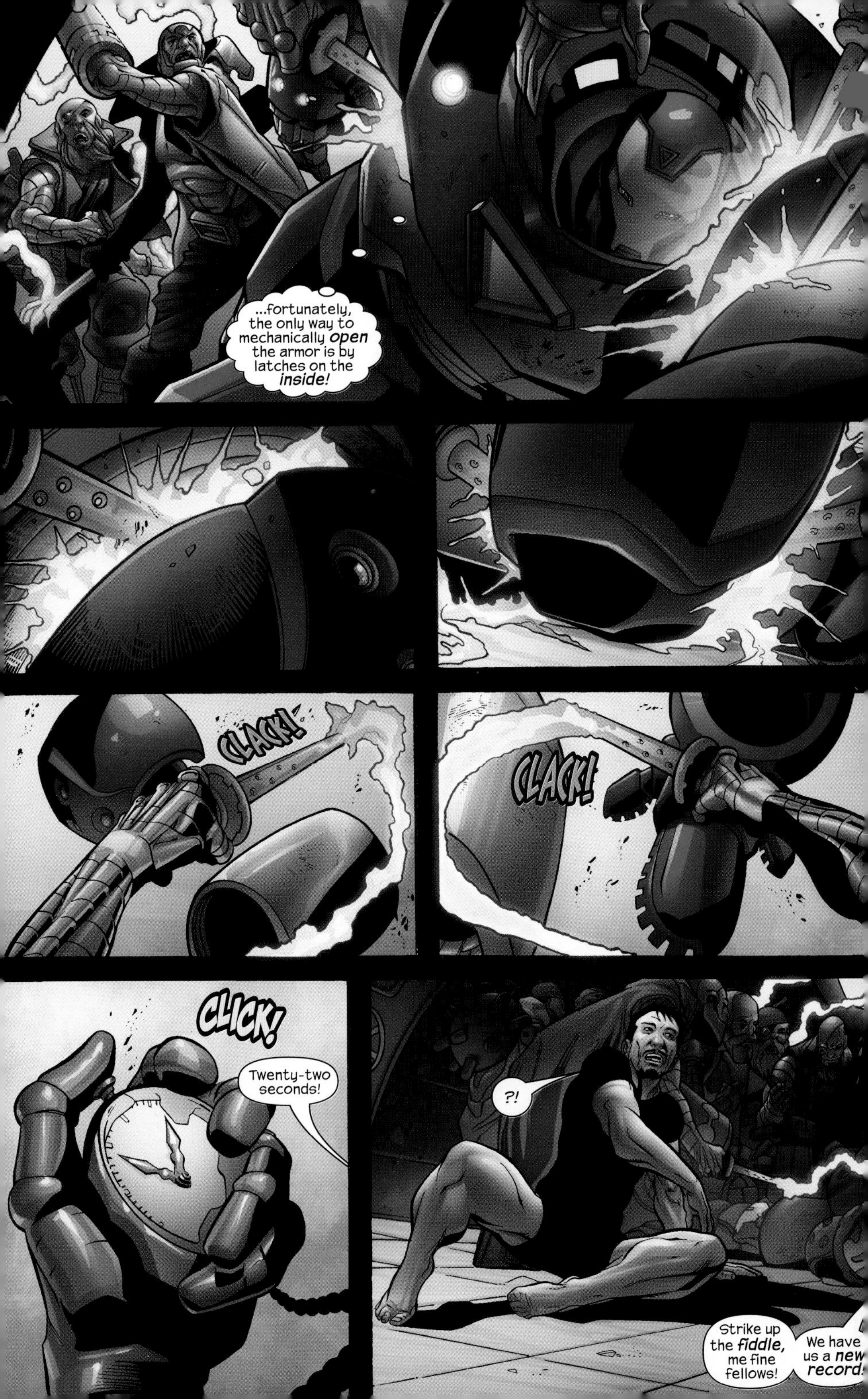
...fortunately, the only way to mechanically open the armor is by latches on the inside!
CLACK!
CLACK!
CLICK!
Twenty-two seconds!
?!
Strike up the fiddle, me fine fellows!
We have us a new record!

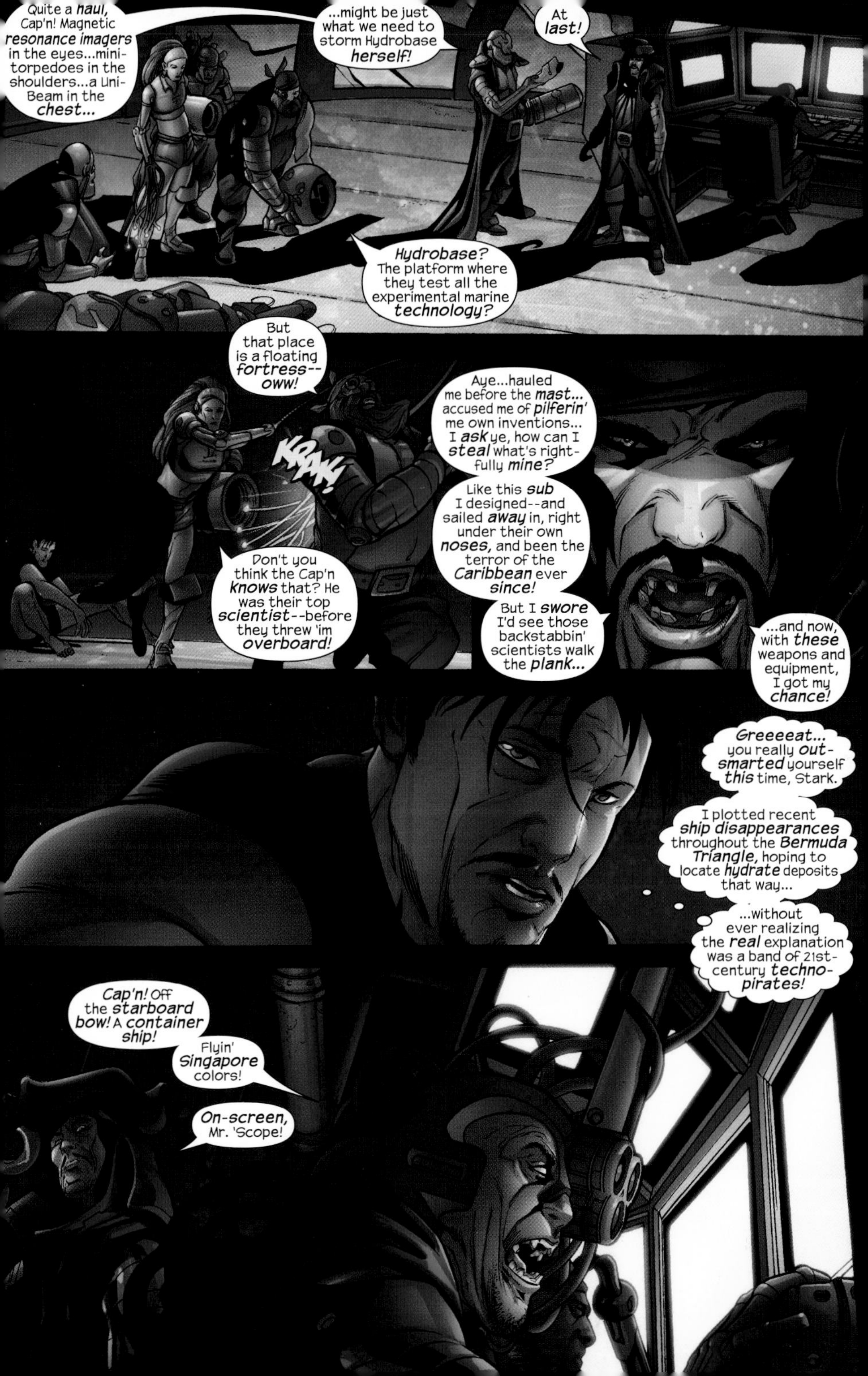
Quite a *haul*, Cap'n! Magnetic *resonance imagers* in the eyes...mini-torpedoes in the shoulders...a Uni-Beam in the *chest...*
...might be just what we need to storm Hydrobase *herself!*
At *last!*
Hydrobase? The platform where they test all the experimental marine *technology?*
But that place is a floating *fortress-- oww!*
KRAK!
Don't you think the Cap'n *knows* that? He was their top *scientist*--before they threw 'im *overboard!*
Aye...hauled me before the *mast...* accused me of *pilferin'* me own inventions... I *ask* ye, how can I *steal* what's rightfully *mine?*
Like this *sub* I designed--and sailed *away* in, right under their own *noses,* and been the terror of the *Caribbean* ever *since!*
But I *swore* I'd see those backstabbin' scientists walk the *plank...*
...and now, with *these* weapons and equipment, I got my *chance!*
Greeeeat... you really *out-smarted* yourself *this* time, Stark.
I plotted recent *ship disappearances* throughout the *Bermuda Triangle,* hoping to locate *hydrate* deposits that way...
...without ever realizing the *real* explanation was a band of 21st-century *techno-pirates!*
Cap'n! Off the *starboard bow!* A *container ship!*
Flyin' *Singapore* colors!
On-screen, Mr. 'Scope!

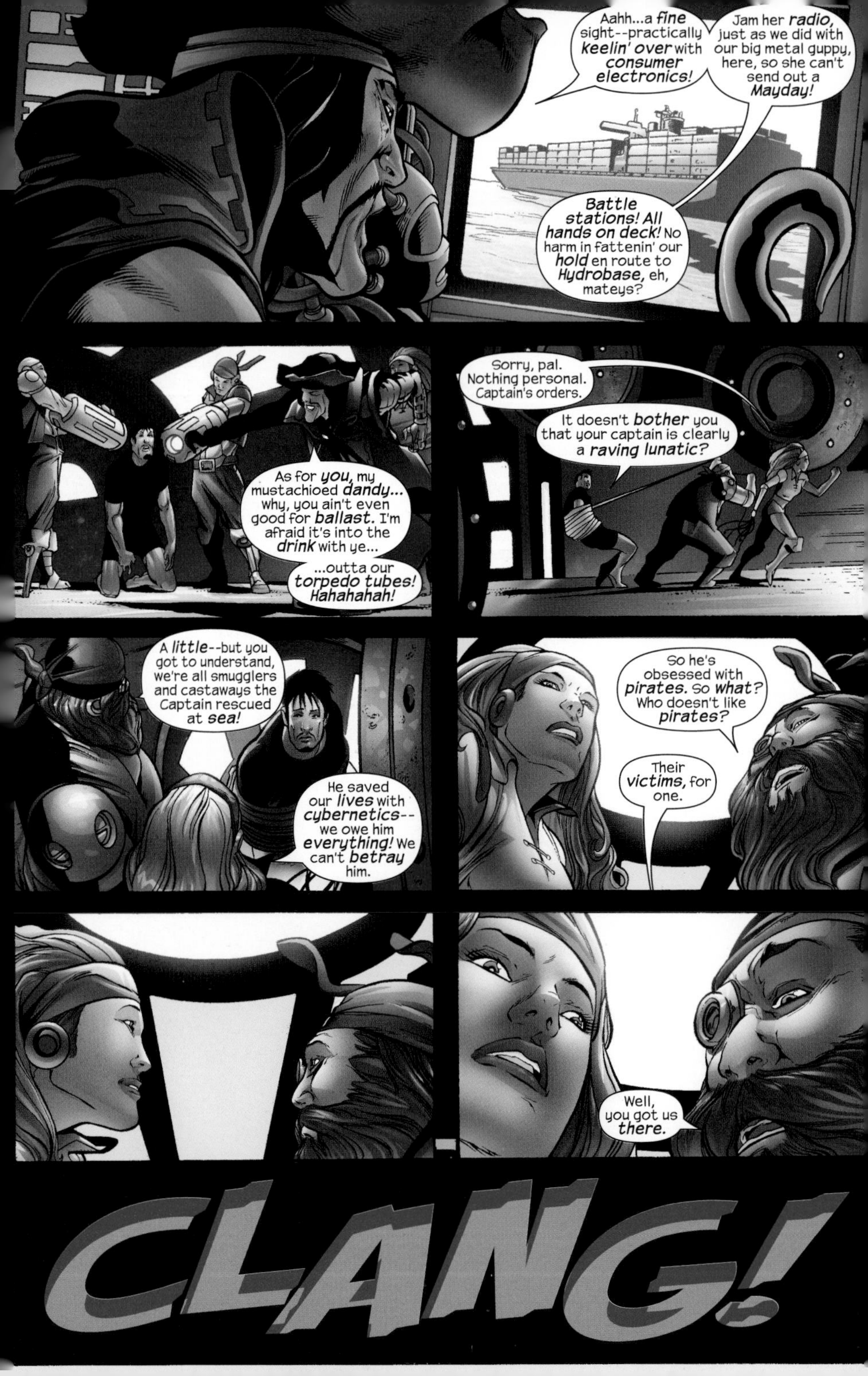
Aahh...a fine sight--practically keelin' over with consumer electronics!
Jam her radio, just as we did with our big metal guppy, here, so she can't send out a Mayday!
Battle stations! All hands on deck! No harm in fattenin' our hold en route to Hydrobase, eh, mateys?
As for you, my mustachioed dandy... why, you ain't even good for ballast. I'm afraid it's into the drink with ye...
...outta our torpedo tubes! Hahahahah!
Sorry, pal. Nothing personal. Captain's orders.
It doesn't bother you that your captain is clearly a raving lunatic?
A little--but you got to understand, we're all smugglers and castaways the Captain rescued at sea!
He saved our lives with cybernetics--we owe him everything! We can't betray him.
So he's obsessed with pirates. So what? Who doesn't like pirates?
Their victims, for one.
Well, you got us there.
CLANG!

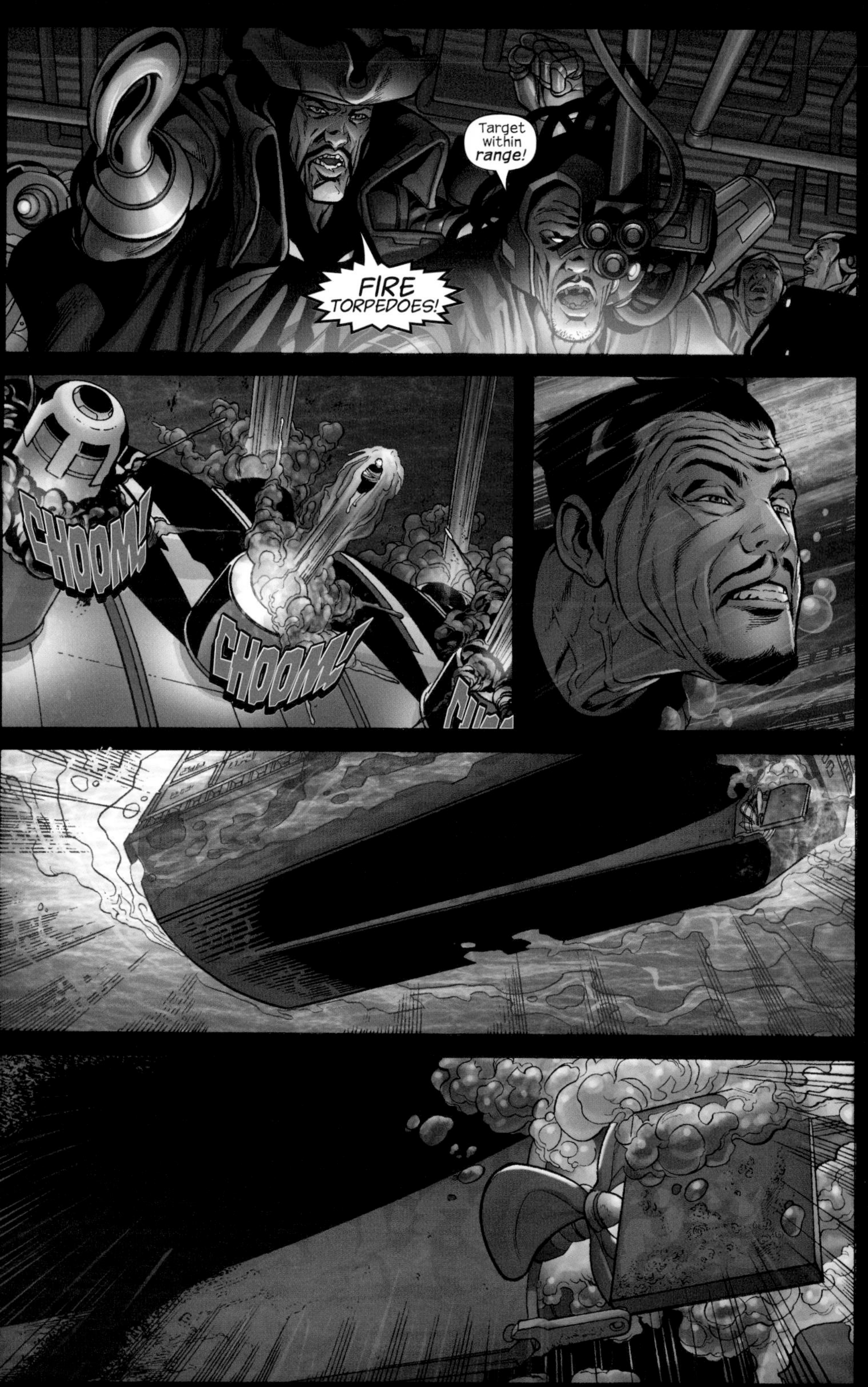
Target within range!
FIRE TORPEDOES!
CHOOM!
CHOOM!

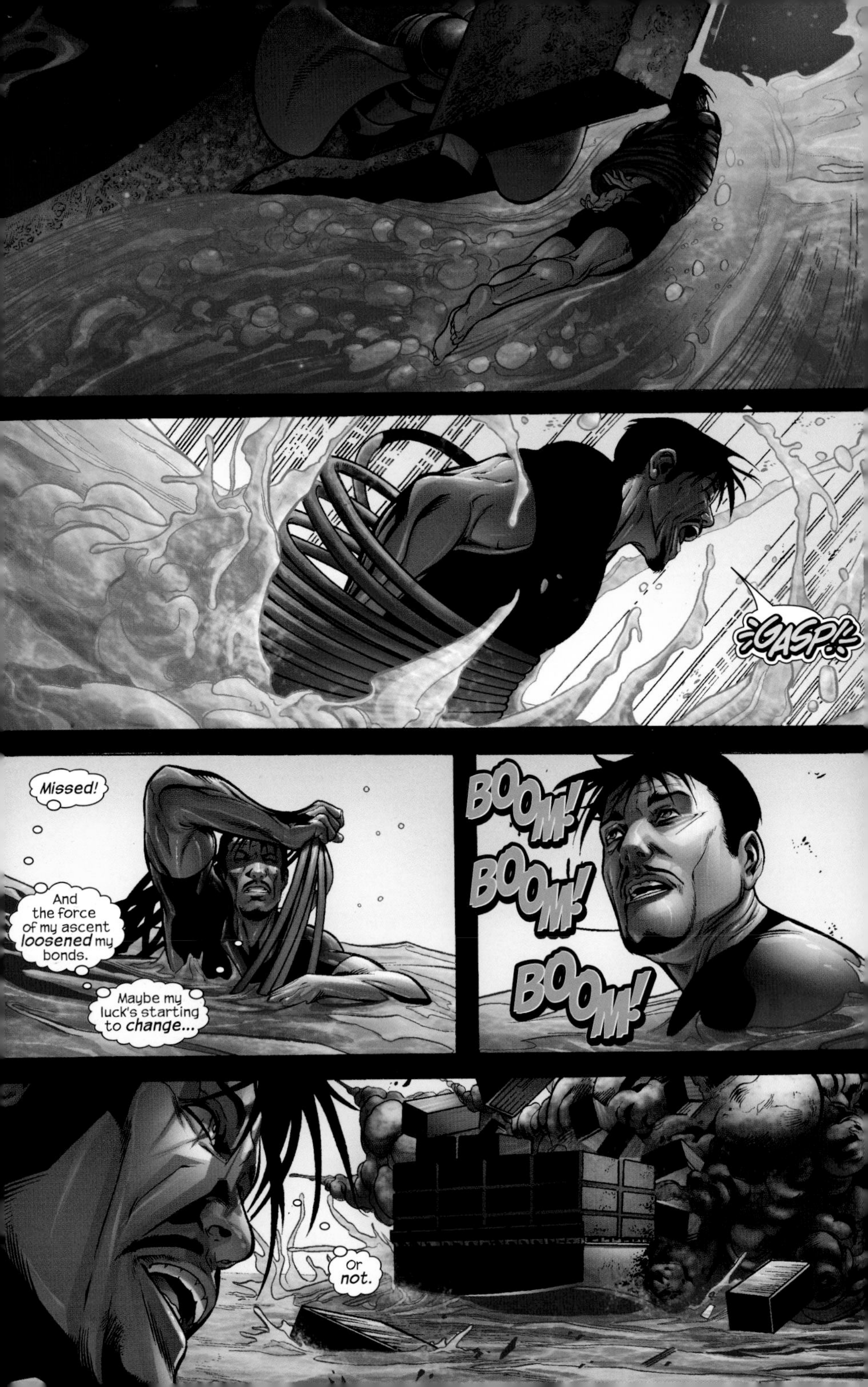
GASP!
Missed!
And the force of my ascent loosened my bonds.
Maybe my luck's starting to change...
BOOM!
BOOM!
BOOM!
Or not.

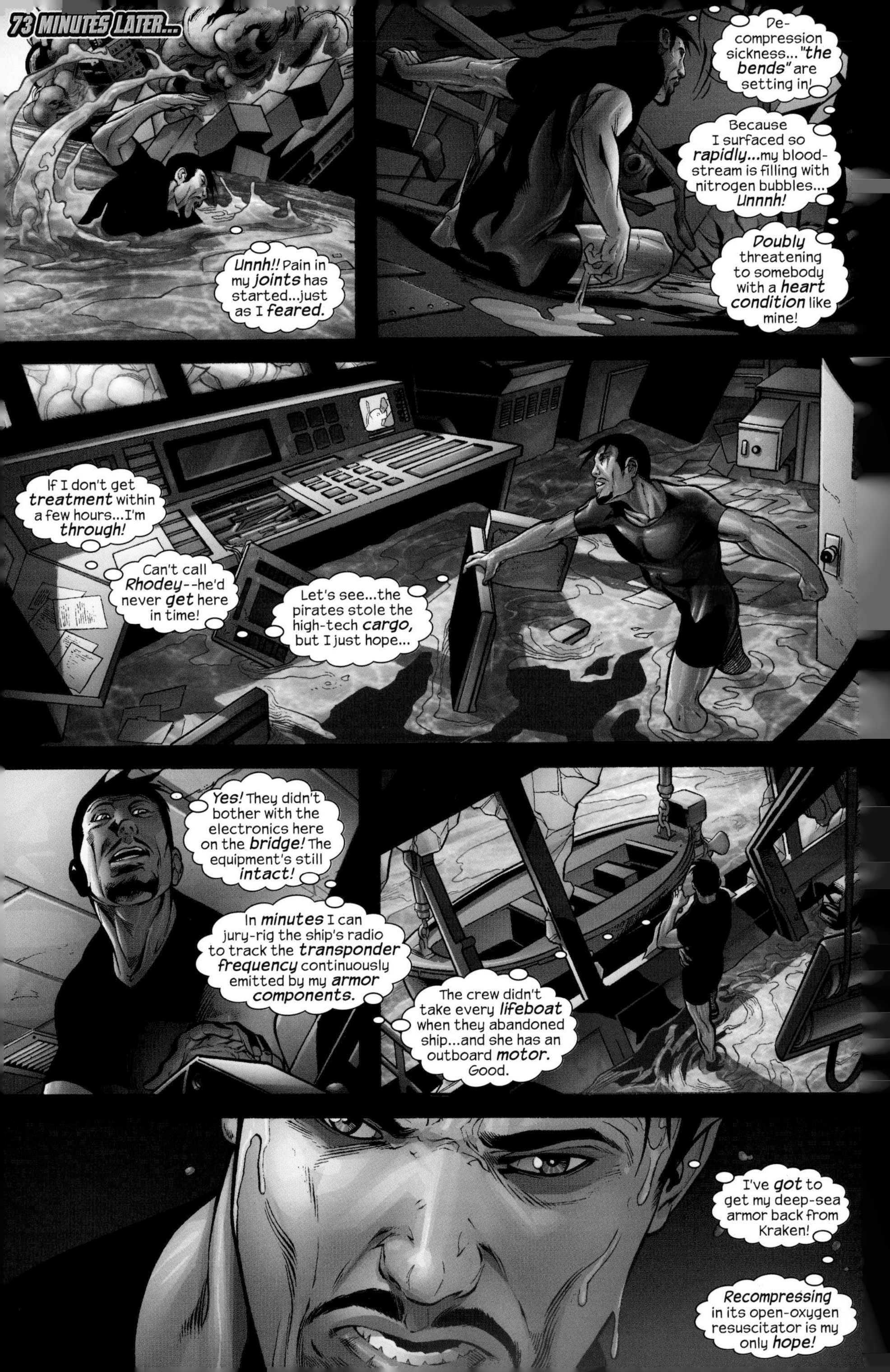
73 MINUTES LATER...
Unnh!! Pain in my joints has started...just as I feared.
De-compression sickness... "the bends" are setting in!
Because I surfaced so rapidly...my blood-stream is filling with nitrogen bubbles... Unnnh!
Doubly threatening to somebody with a heart condition like mine!
If I don't get treatment within a few hours...I'm through!
Can't call Rhodey--he'd never get here in time!
Let's see...the pirates stole the high-tech cargo, but I just hope...
Yes! They didn't bother with the electronics here on the bridge! The equipment's still intact!
In minutes I can jury-rig the ship's radio to track the transponder frequency continuously emitted by my armor components.
The crew didn't take every lifeboat when they abandoned ship...and she has an outboard motor. Good.
I've got to get my deep-sea armor back from Kraken!
Recompressing in its open-oxygen resuscitator is my only hope!

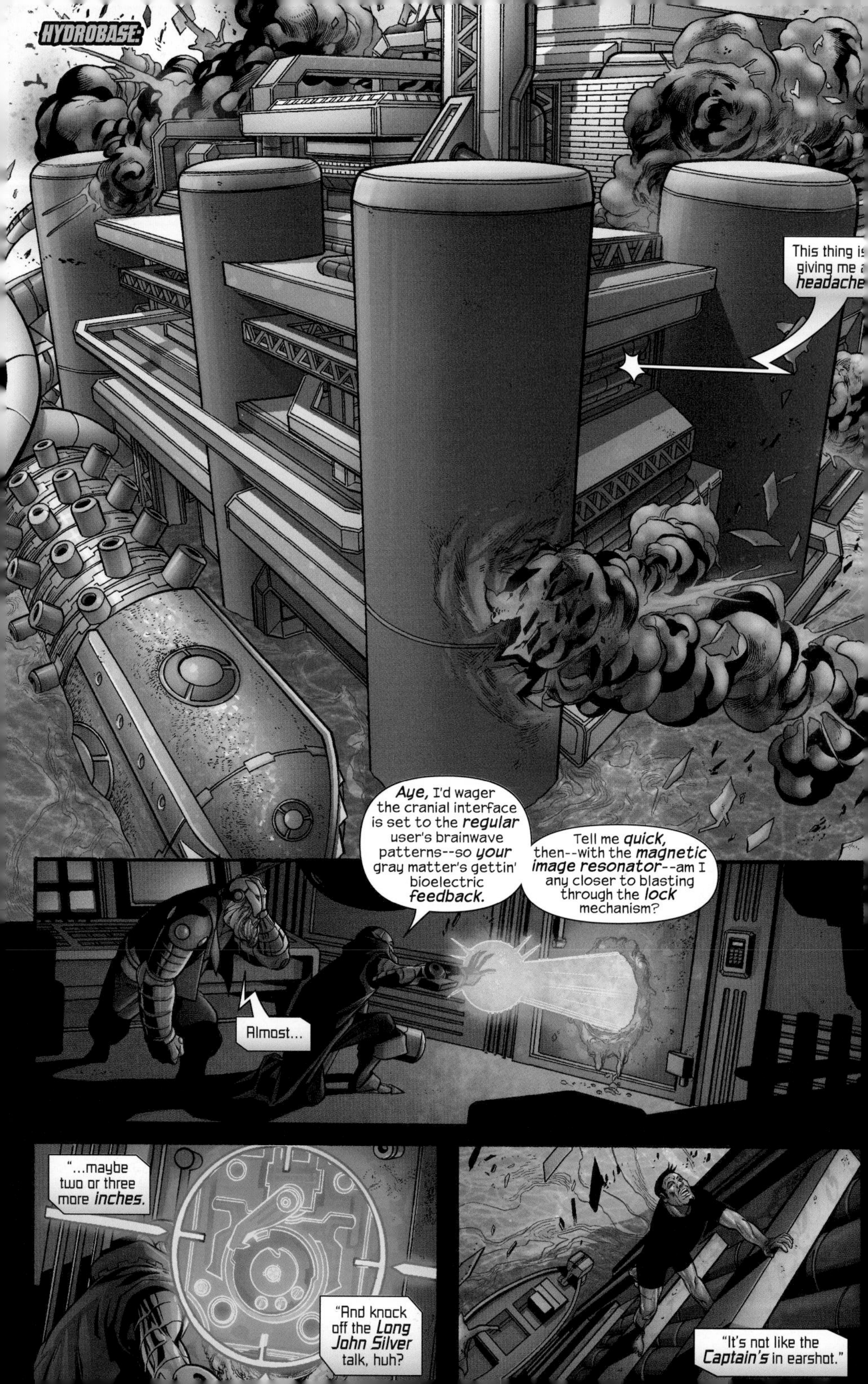
HYDROBASE:
This thing is giving me a headache
Aye, I'd wager the cranial interface is set to the regular user's brainwave patterns--so your gray matter's gettin' bioelectric feedback.
Tell me quick, then--with the magnetic image resonator--am I any closer to blasting through the lock mechanism?
Almost...
"...maybe two or three more inches.
"And knock off the Long John Silver talk, huh?
"It's not like the Captain's in earshot."

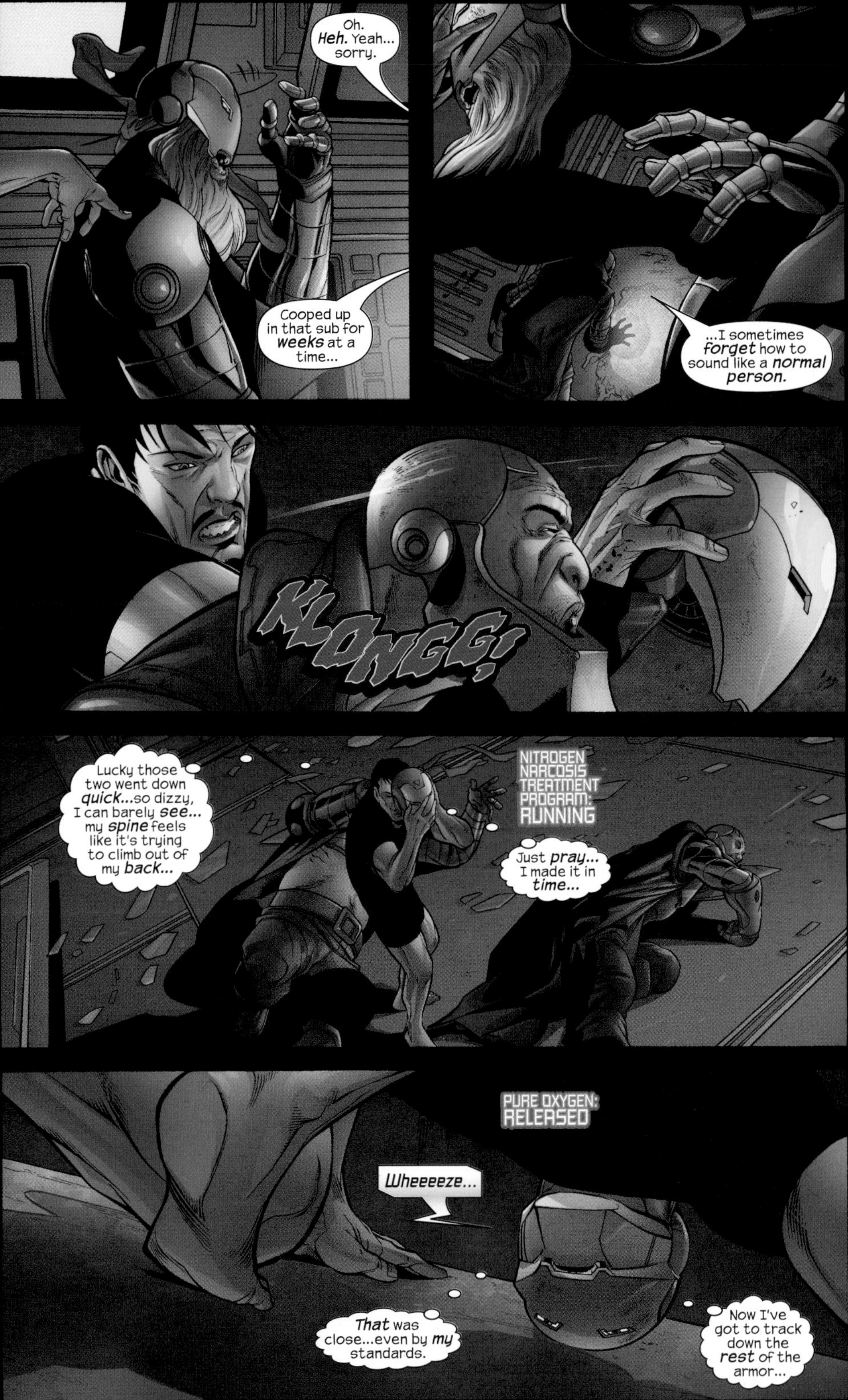
Oh. Heh. Yeah... sorry.
Cooped up in that sub for weeks at a time...
...I sometimes forget how to sound like a normal person.
KLONGG!
Lucky those two went down quick...so dizzy, I can barely see... my spine feels like it's trying to climb out of my back...
NITROGEN NARCOSIS TREATMENT PROGRAM: RUNNING
Just pray... I made it in time...
PURE OXYGEN: RELEASED
Wheeeeze...
That was close...even by my standards.
Now I've got to track down the rest of the armor...

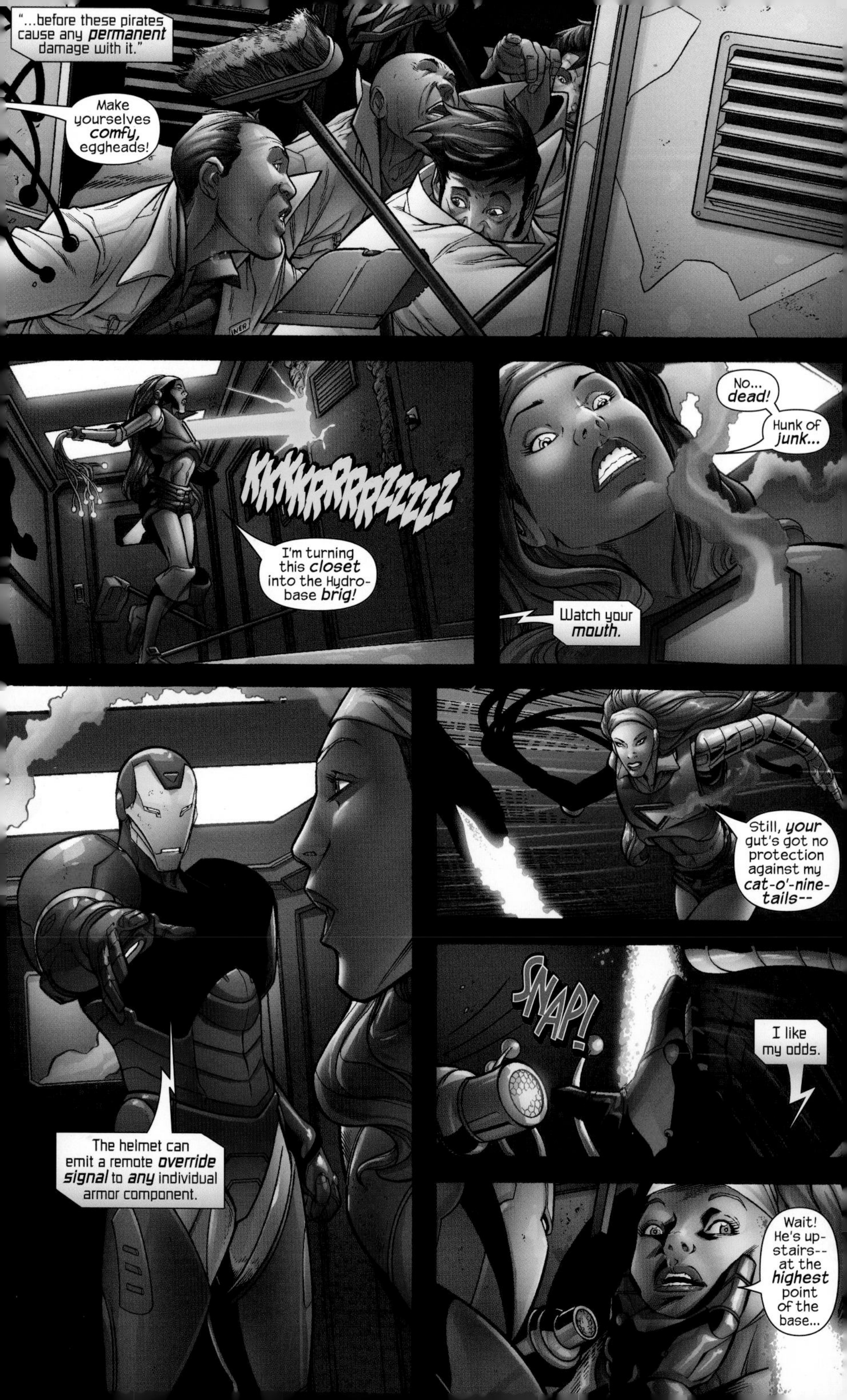
"...before these pirates cause any *permanent* damage with it."
Make yourselves *comfy*, eggheads!
KKKKRRRRRZZZZZ
I'm turning this *closet* into the Hydro-base *brig!*
No... *dead!*
Hunk of *junk...*
Watch your *mouth*.
The helmet can emit a remote *override signal* to *any* individual armor component.
Still, *your* gut's got no protection against my *cat-o'-nine-tails--*
SNAP!
I like my odds.
Wait! He's up-stairs-- at the *highest* point of the base...

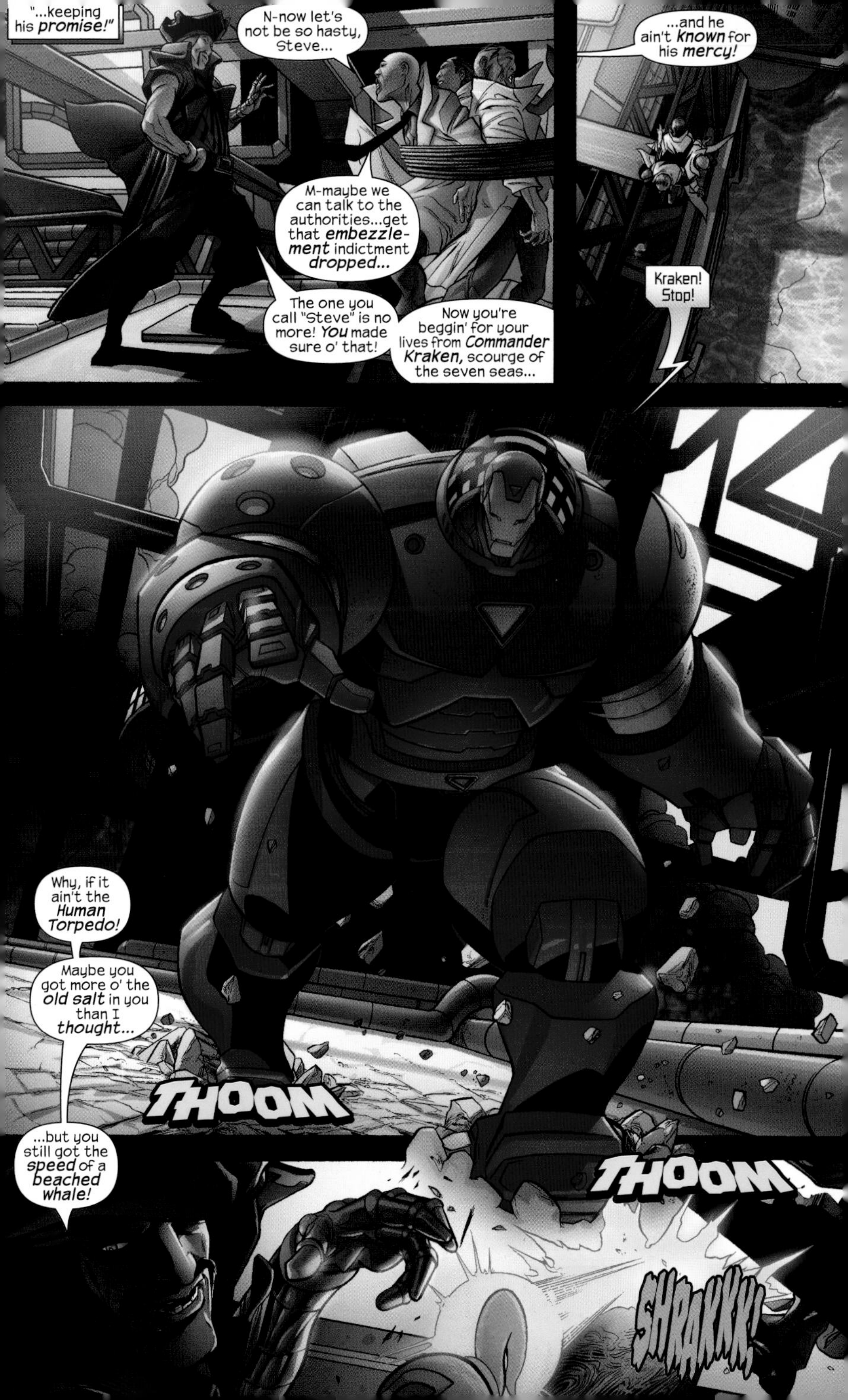
"...keeping his promise!"
N-now let's not be so hasty, Steve...
M-maybe we can talk to the authorities...get that embezzlement indictment dropped...
The one you call "Steve" is no more! You made sure o' that!
Now you're beggin' for your lives from Commander Kraken, scourge of the seven seas...
...and he ain't known for his mercy!
Kraken! Stop!
Why, if it ain't the Human Torpedo!
Maybe you got more o' the old salt in you than I thought...
THOOM
...but you still got the speed of a beached whale!
THOOM!
SHRAKKK!

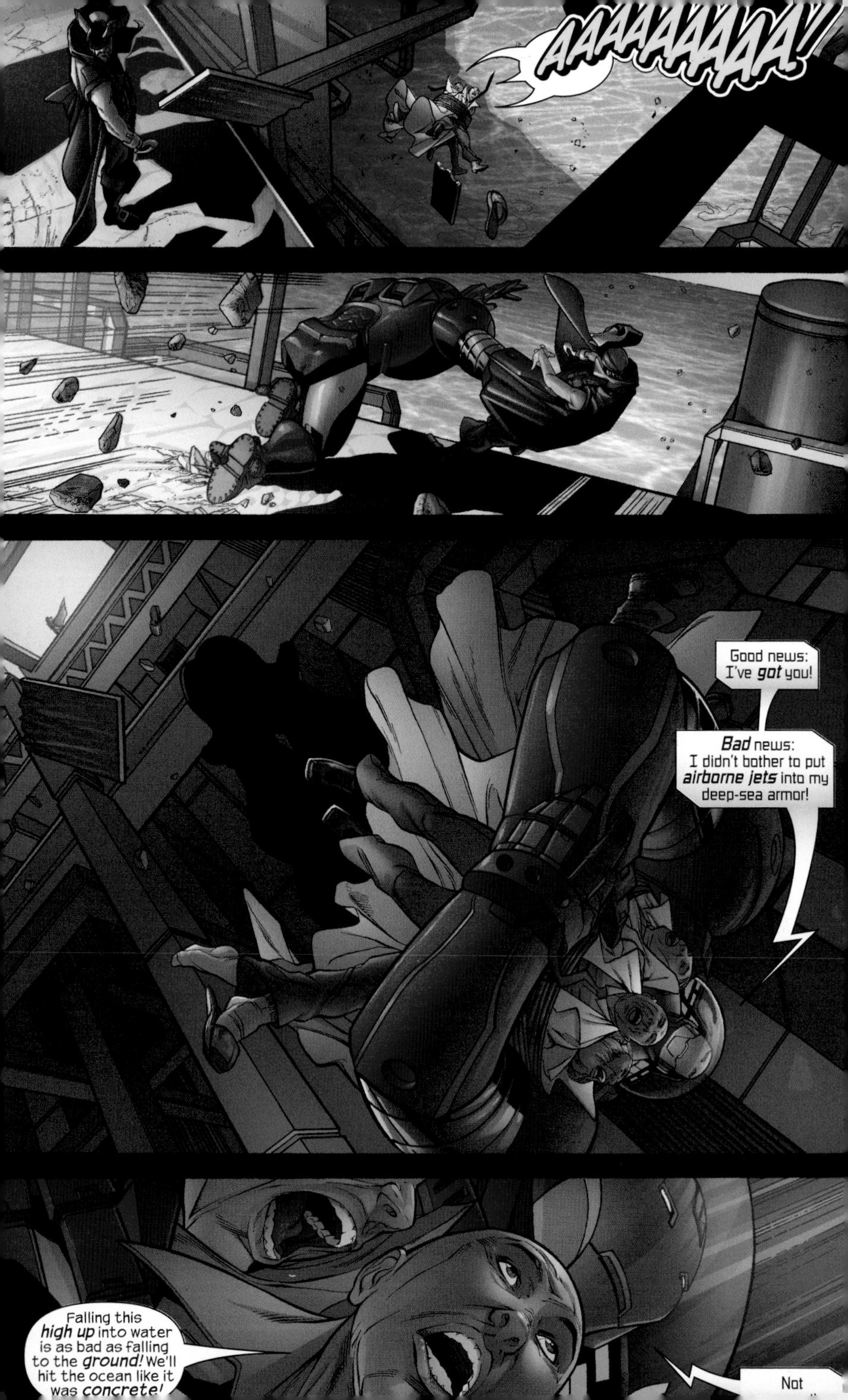
AAAAAAAAAA!
Good news: I've *got* you!
Bad news: I didn't bother to put *airborne jets* into my deep-sea armor!
Falling this *high up* into water is as bad as falling to the *ground!* We'll hit the ocean like it was *concrete!*
Not

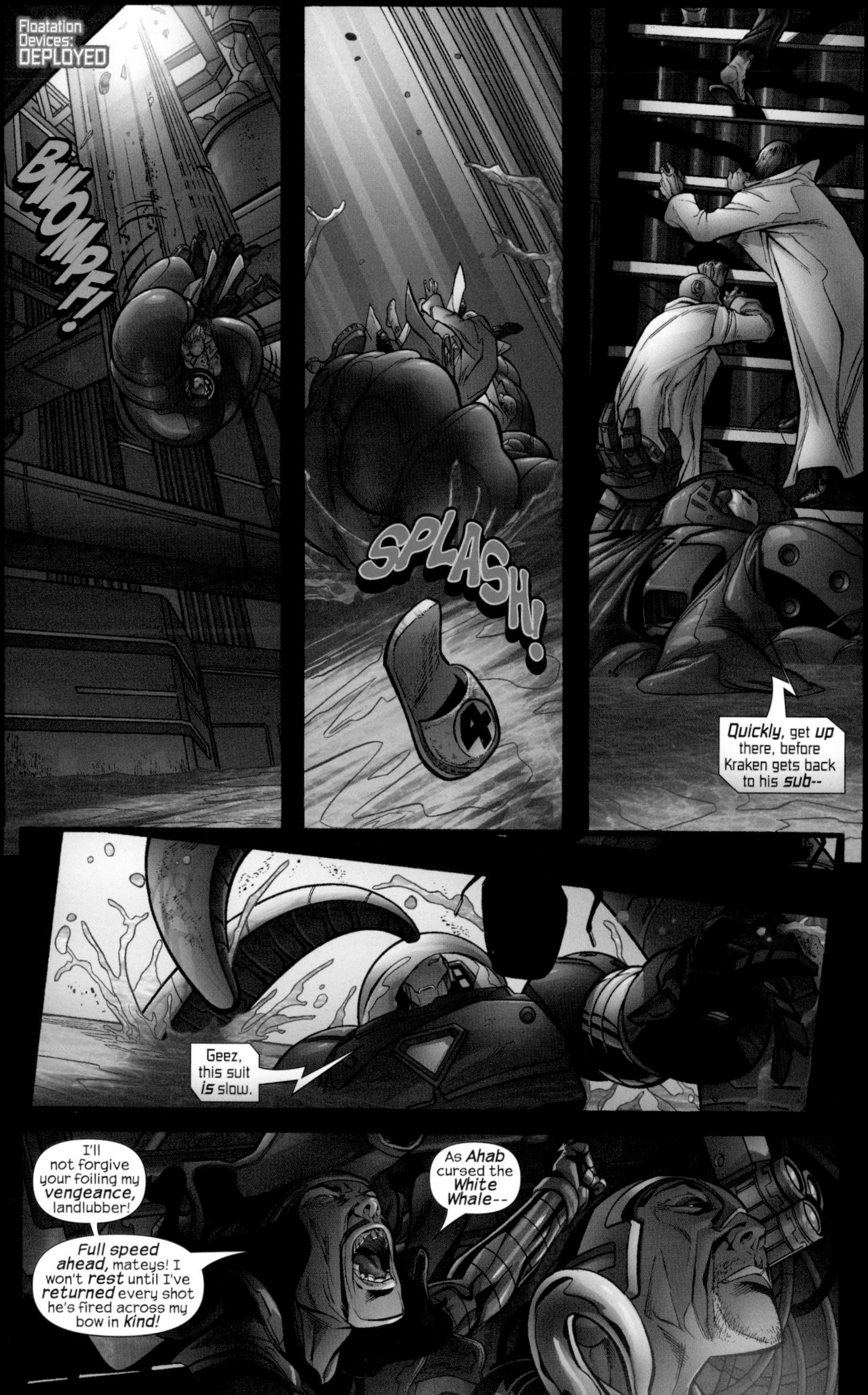
Floatation Devices: DEPLOYED
BWOMPF!
SPLASH!
Quickly, get up there, before Kraken gets back to his sub--
Geez, this suit is slow.
I'll not forgive your foiling my vengeance, landlubber!
Full speed ahead, mateys! I won't rest until I've returned every shot he's fired across my bow in kind!
As Ahab cursed the White Whale--

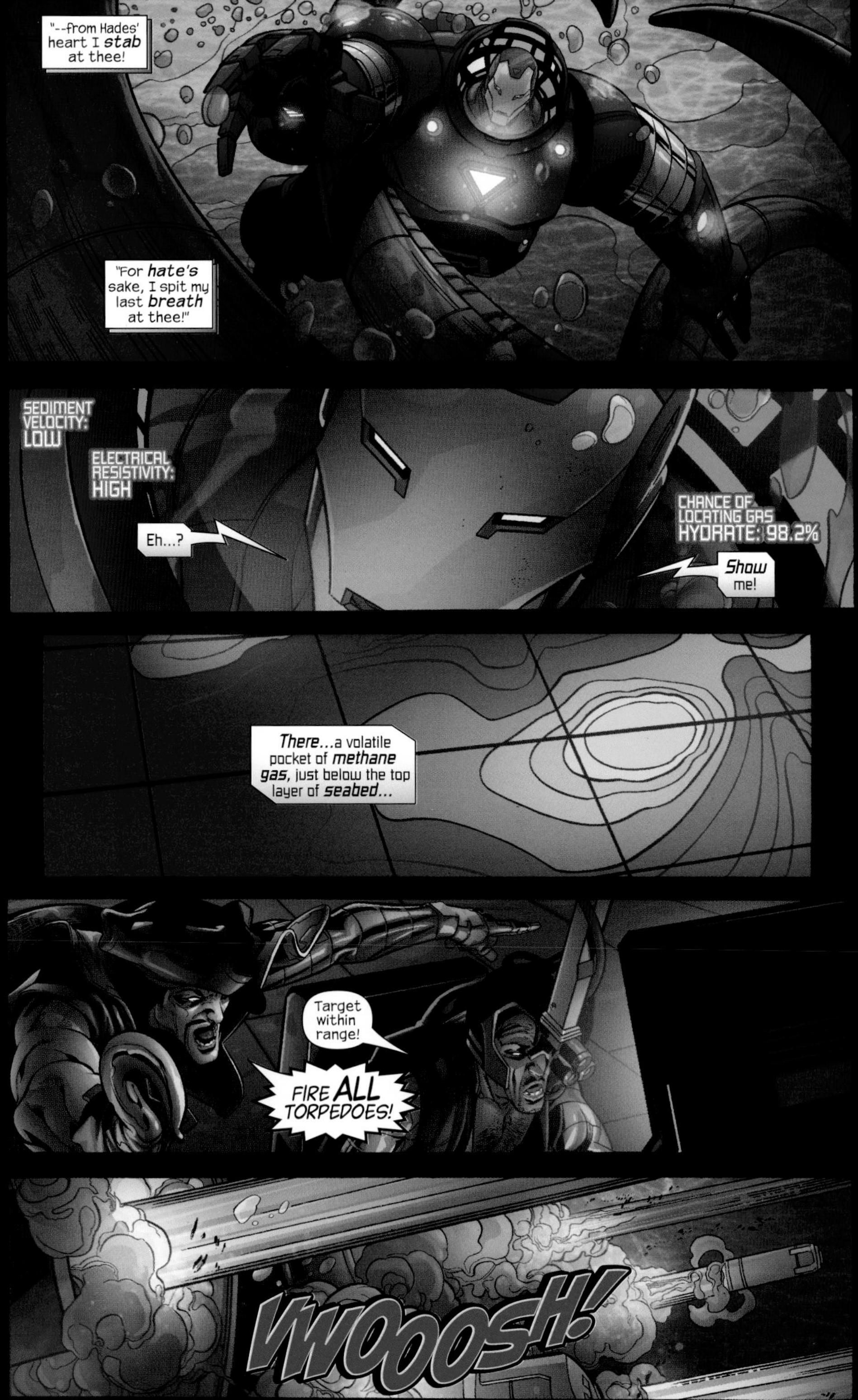
"--from Hades' heart I *stab* at thee!
"For *hate's* sake, I spit my last *breath* at thee!"
SEDIMENT VELOCITY: LOW
ELECTRICAL RESISTIVITY: HIGH
Eh...?
CHANCE OF LOCATING GAS HYDRATE: 98.2%
Show me!
There...a volatile pocket of *methane gas*, just below the top layer of *seabed*...
Target within range!
FIRE ALL TORPEDOES!
VWOOOSH!

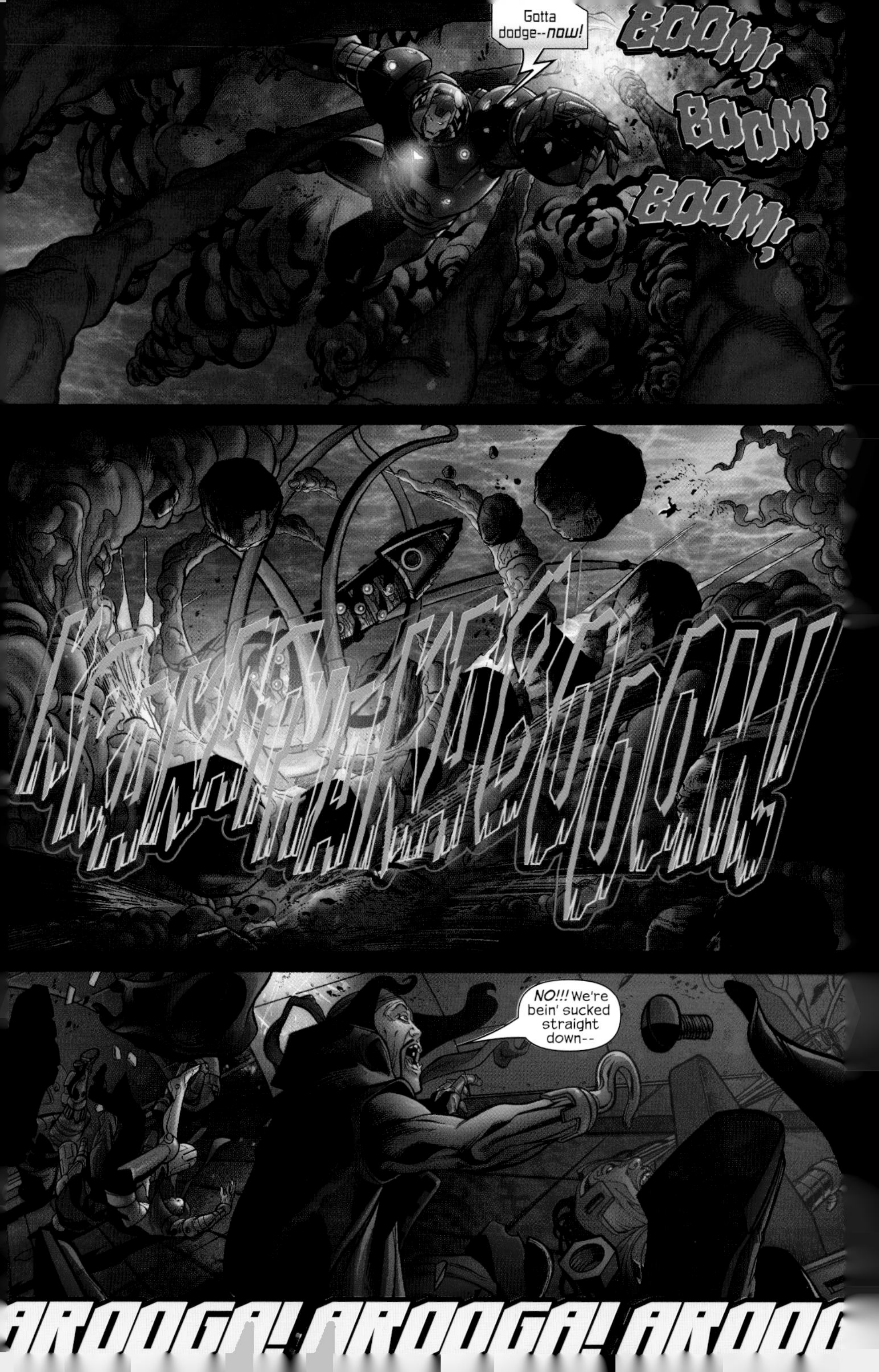
Gotta dodge--*now!*
BOOM!
BOOM!
BOOM!
NO!!! We're bein' sucked straight down--
AROOGA! AROOGA!

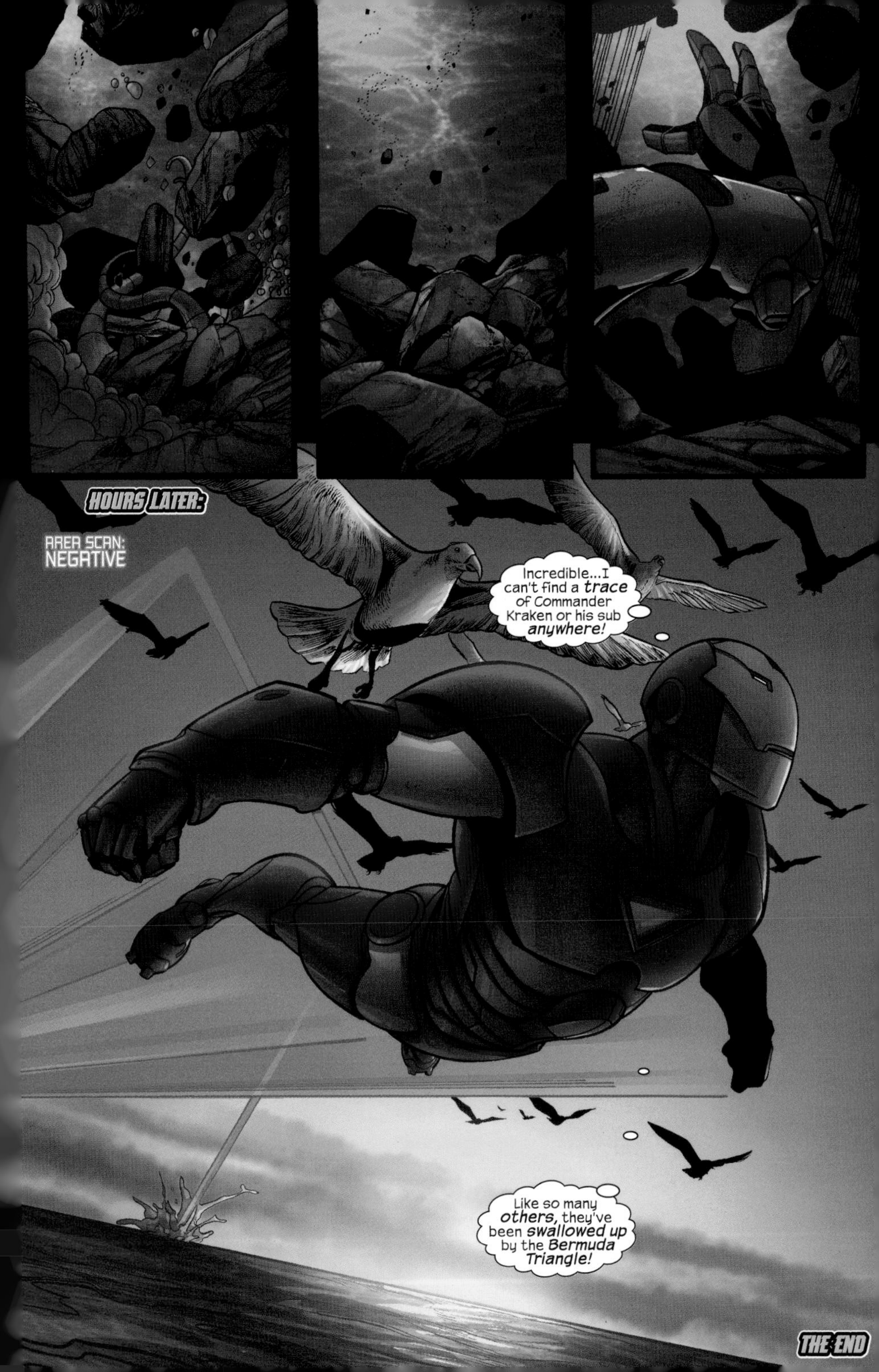
HOURS LATER:
AREA SCAN: NEGATIVE
Incredible...I can't find a trace of Commander Kraken or his sub anywhere!
Like so many others, they've been swallowed up by the Bermuda Triangle!
THE END

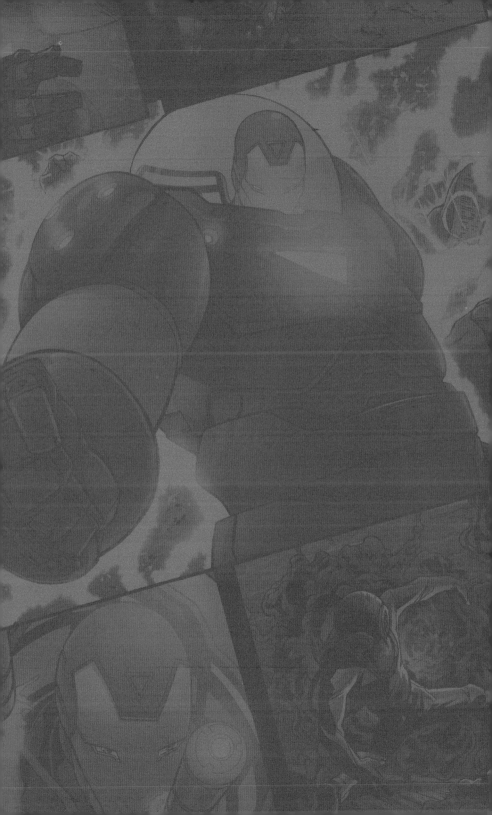

06

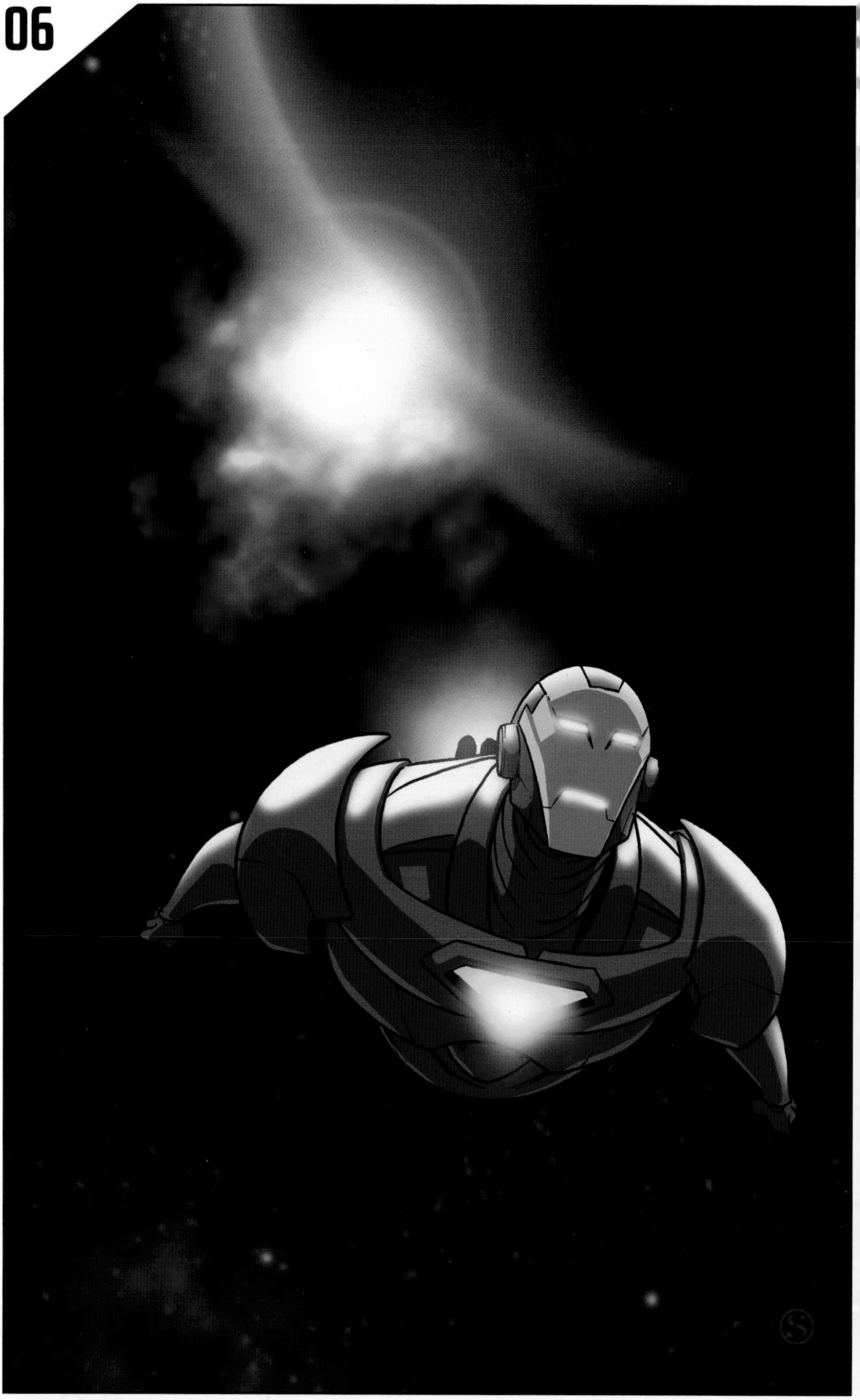

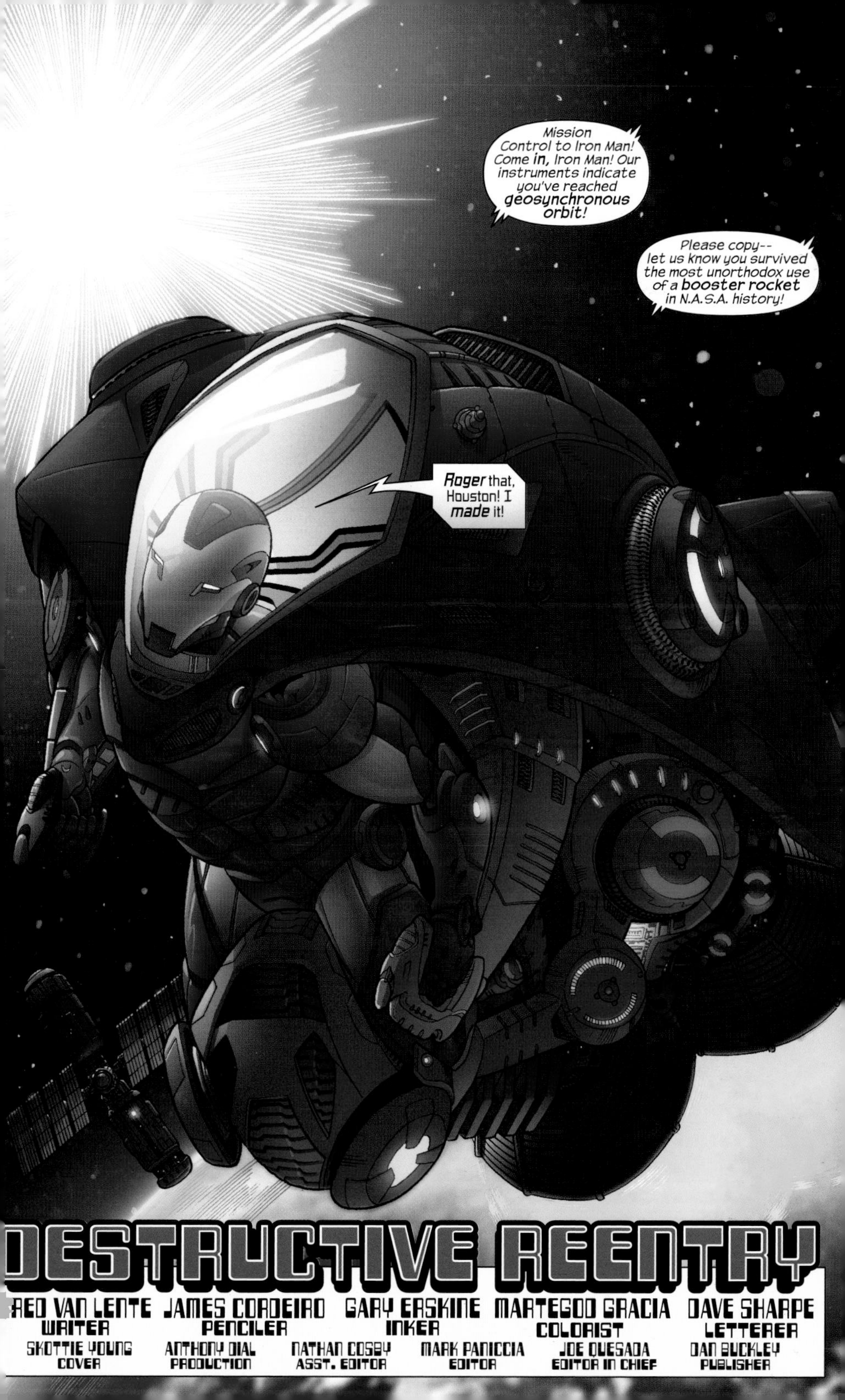

Mission Control to Iron Man! Come in, Iron Man! Our instruments indicate you've reached geosynchronous orbit!
Please copy-- let us know you survived the most unorthodox use of a booster rocket in N.A.S.A. history!
Roger that, Houston! I made it!
DESTRUCTIVE REENTRY
RED VAN LENTE WRITER
JAMES CORDEIRO PENCILER
GARY ERSKINE INKER
MARTEGOD GRACIA COLORIST
DAVE SHARPE LETTERER
SKOTTIE YOUNG COVER
ANTHONY DIAL PRODUCTION
NATHAN COSBY ASST. EDITOR
MARK PANICCIA EDITOR
JOE QUESADA EDITOR IN CHIEF
DAN BUCKLEY PUBLISHER

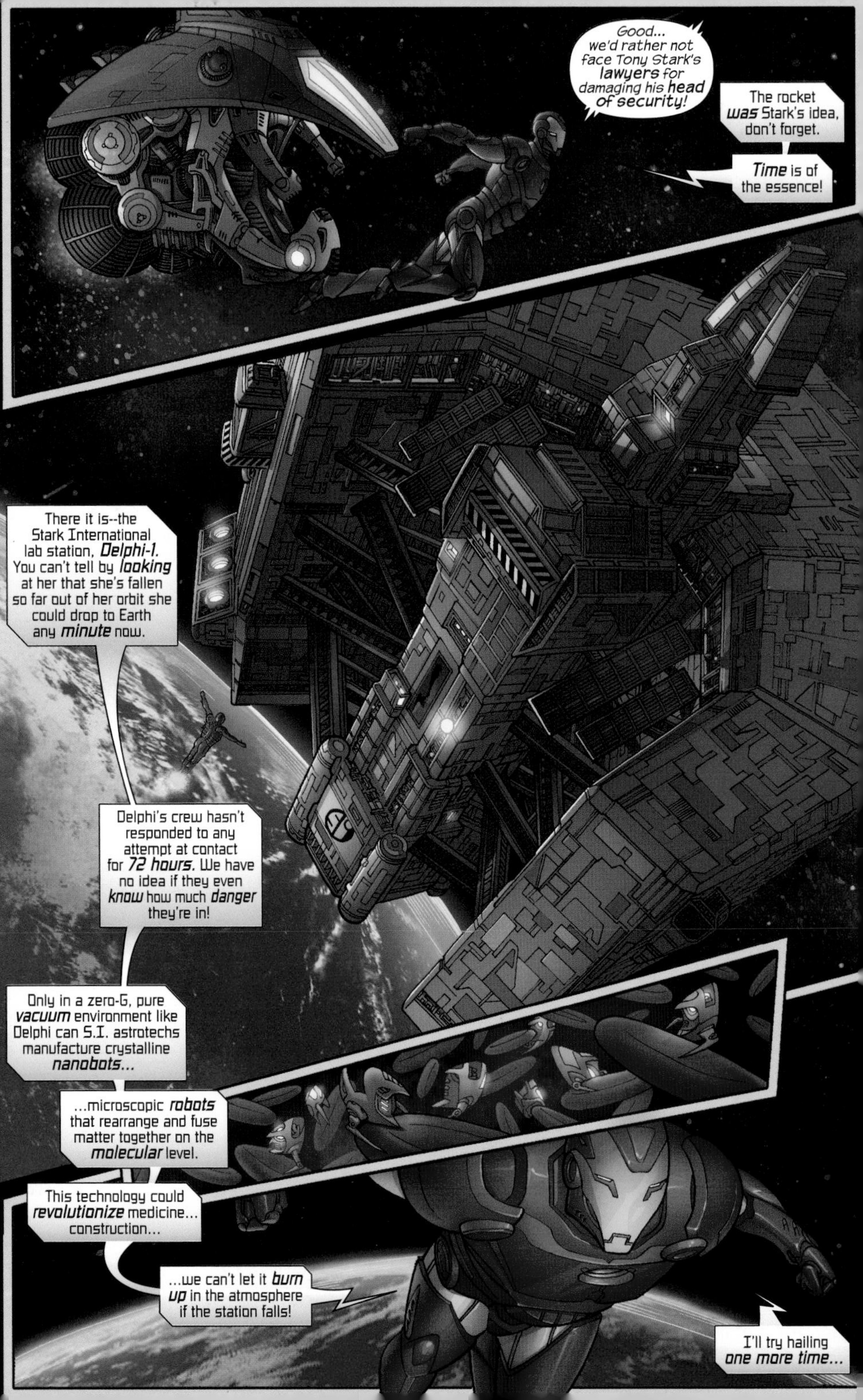
Good... we'd rather not face Tony Stark's lawyers for damaging his head of security!
The rocket was Stark's idea, don't forget.
Time is of the essence!
There it is--the Stark International lab station, Delphi-1. You can't tell by looking at her that she's fallen so far out of her orbit she could drop to Earth any minute now.
Delphi's crew hasn't responded to any attempt at contact for 72 hours. We have no idea if they even know how much danger they're in!
Only in a zero-G, pure vacuum environment like Delphi can S.I. astrotechs manufacture crystalline nanobots...
...microscopic robots that rearrange and fuse matter together on the molecular level.
This technology could revolutionize medicine... construction...
...we can't let it burn up in the atmosphere if the station falls!
I'll try hailing one more time...

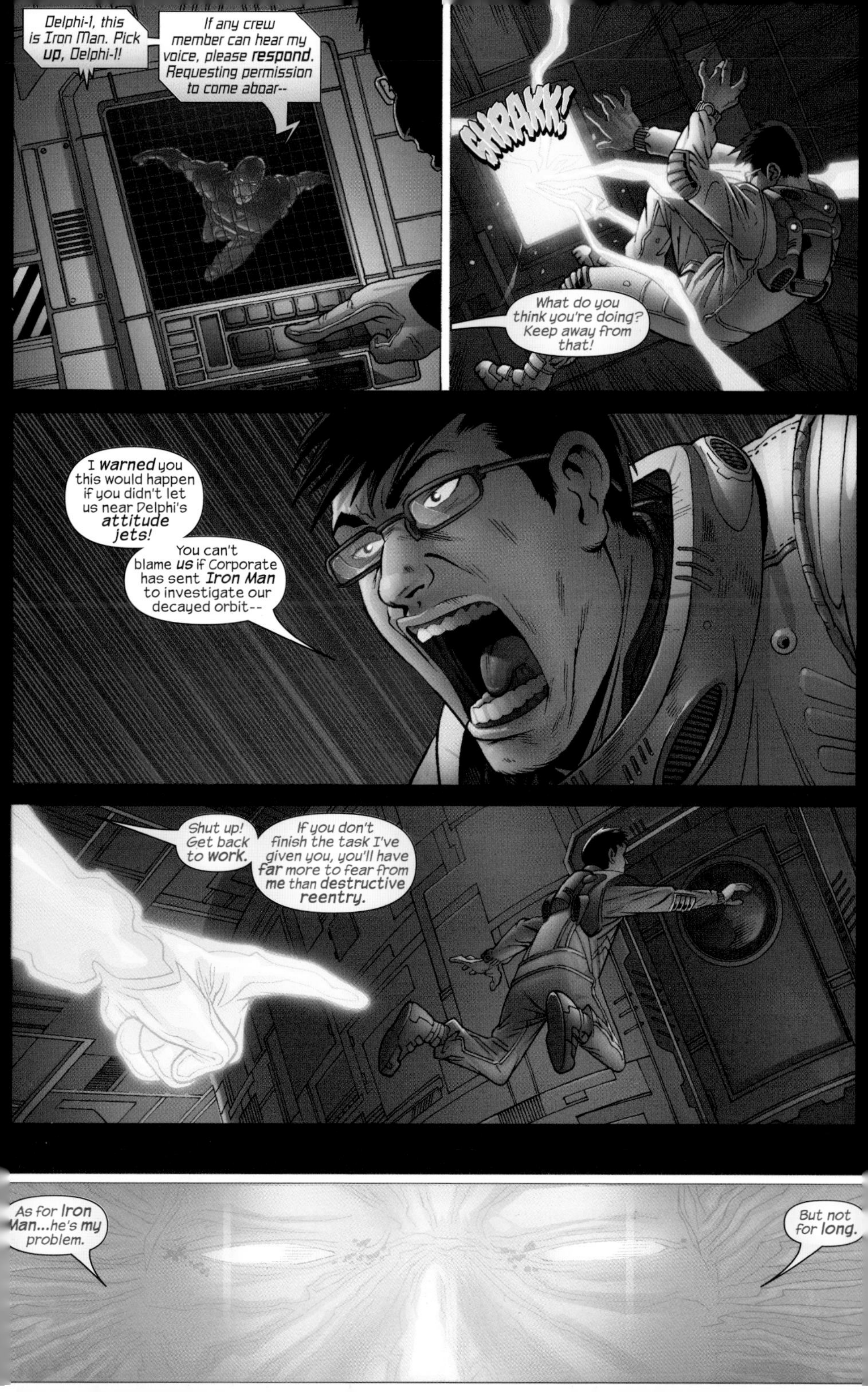
Delphi-1, this is Iron Man. Pick up, Delphi-1!
If any crew member can hear my voice, please respond. Requesting permission to come aboar--
SHRAKK!
What do you think you're doing? Keep away from that!
I warned you this would happen if you didn't let us near Delphi's attitude jets!
You can't blame us if Corporate has sent Iron Man to investigate our decayed orbit--
Shut up! Get back to work.
If you don't finish the task I've given you, you'll have far more to fear from me than destructive reentry.
As for Iron Man...he's my problem.
But not for long.

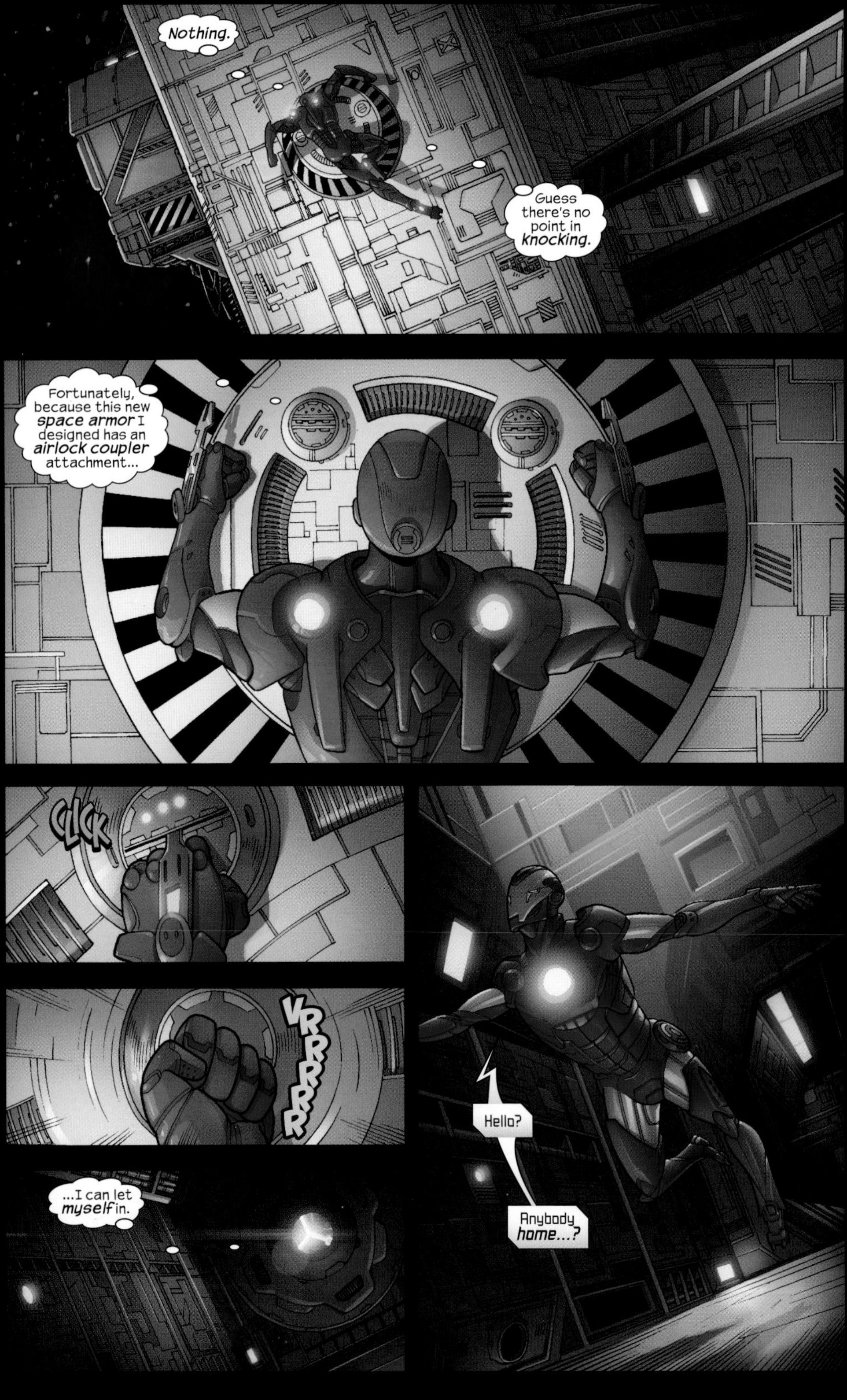
Nothing.
Guess there's no point in knocking.
Fortunately, because this new space armor I designed has an airlock coupler attachment...
CLICK
VRRRRRR
...I can let myself in.
Hello?
Anybody home...?

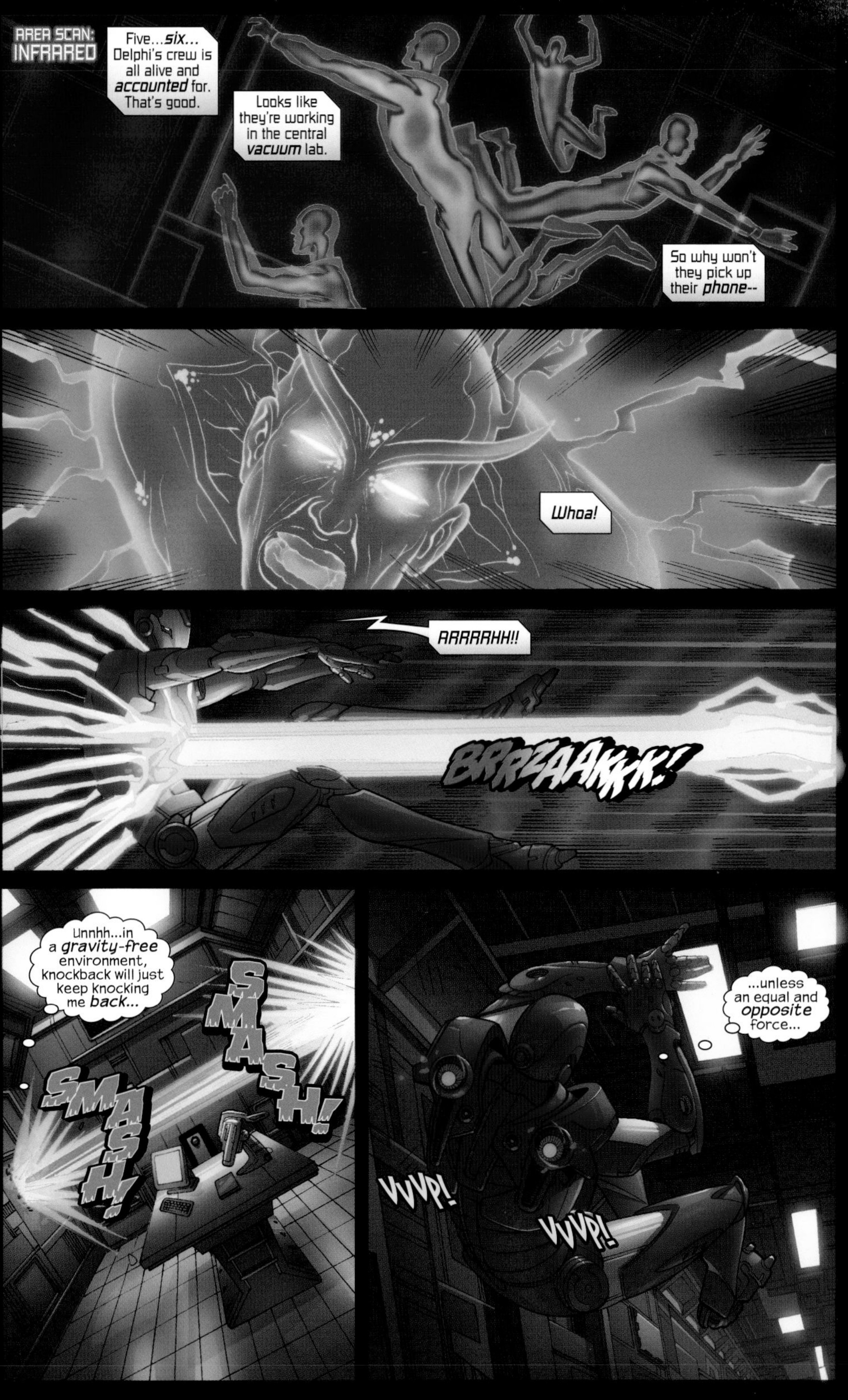
AREA SCAN: INFRARED
Five...six... Delphi's crew is all alive and accounted for. That's good.
Looks like they're working in the central vacuum lab.
So why won't they pick up their phone--
Whoa!
ARRRRHH!!
BRRZAAKKK!
Unnhh...in a gravity-free environment, knockback will just keep knocking me back...
SMASH!
SMASH!
...unless an equal and opposite force...
VVVP!
VVVP!

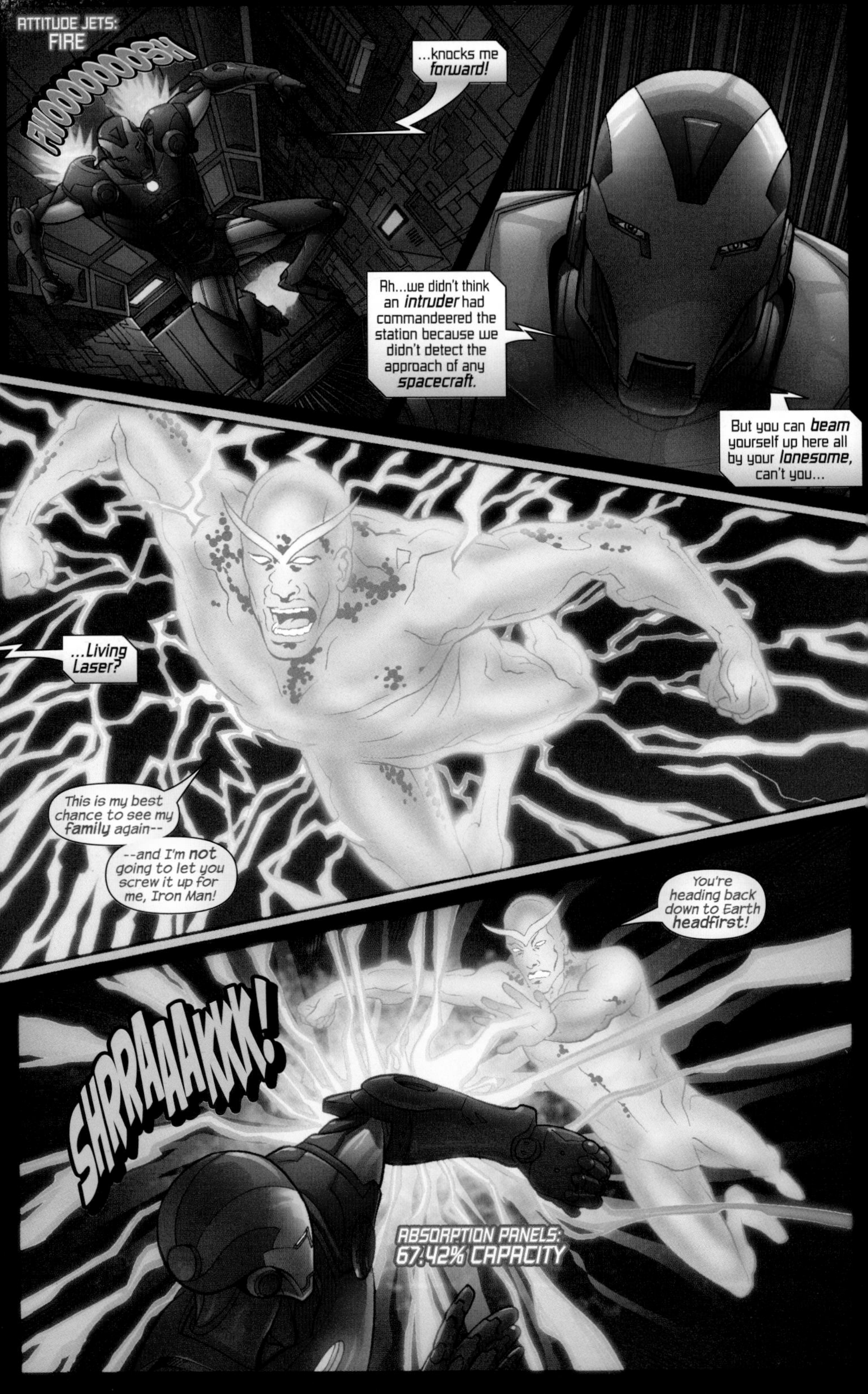
ATTITUDE JETS:
FIRE
FWOOOOOOOSH
...knocks me forward!
Ah...we didn't think an intruder had commandeered the station because we didn't detect the approach of any spacecraft.
But you can beam yourself up here all by your lonesome, can't you...
...Living Laser?
This is my best chance to see my family again--
--and I'm not going to let you screw it up for me, Iron Man!
You're heading back down to Earth headfirst!
SHRAAAKKK!
ABSORPTION PANELS:
67.42% CAPACITY

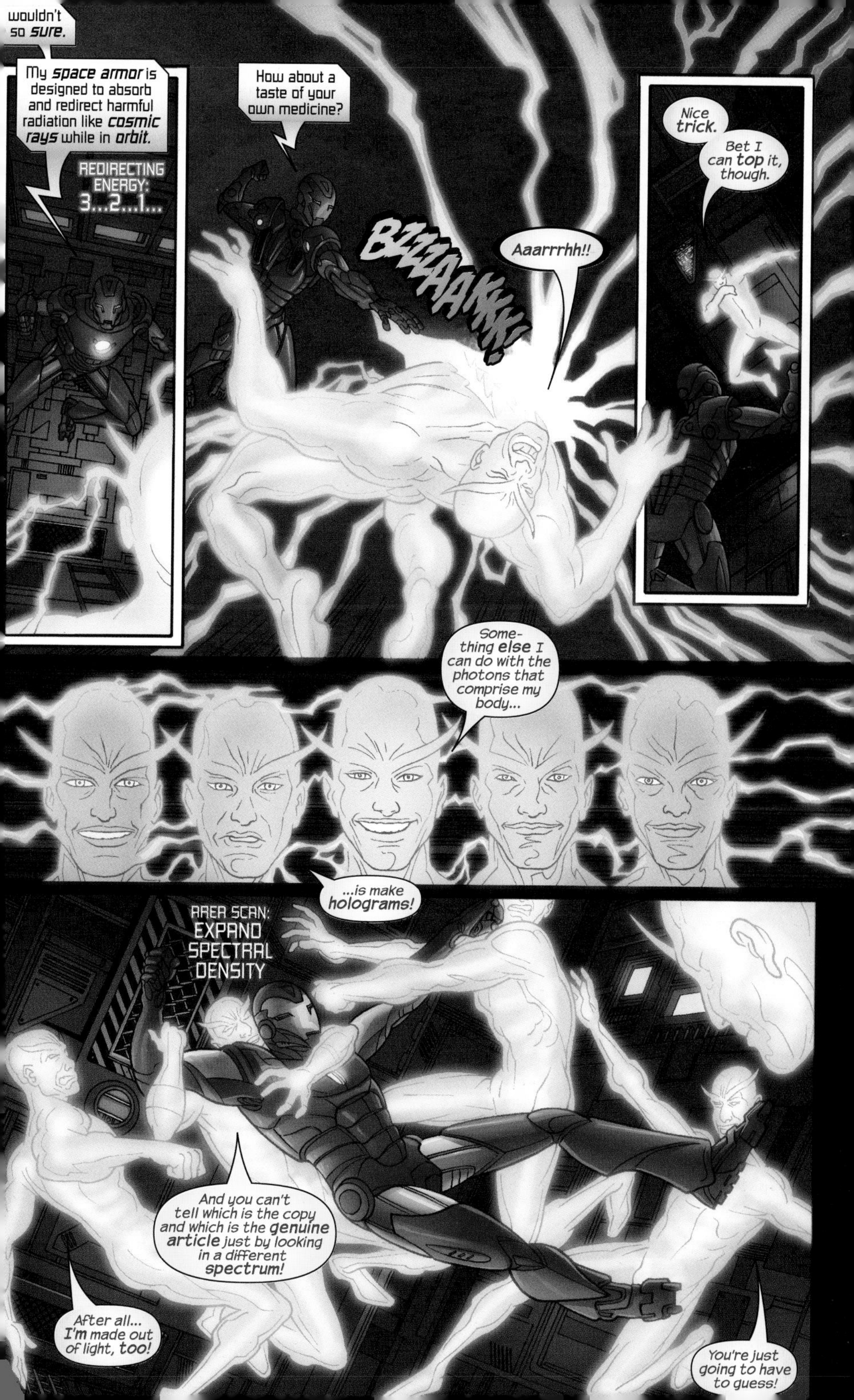

wouldn't so sure.
My space armor is designed to absorb and redirect harmful radiation like cosmic rays while in orbit.
REDIRECTING ENERGY: 3...2...1...
How about a taste of your own medicine?
BZZAAKKK!
Aaarrrhh!!
Nice trick.
Bet I can top it, though.
Something else I can do with the photons that comprise my body...
...is make holograms!
AREA SCAN: EXPAND SPECTRAL DENSITY
And you can't tell which is the copy and which is the genuine article just by looking in a different spectrum!
After all... I'm made out of light, too!
You're just going to have to guess!

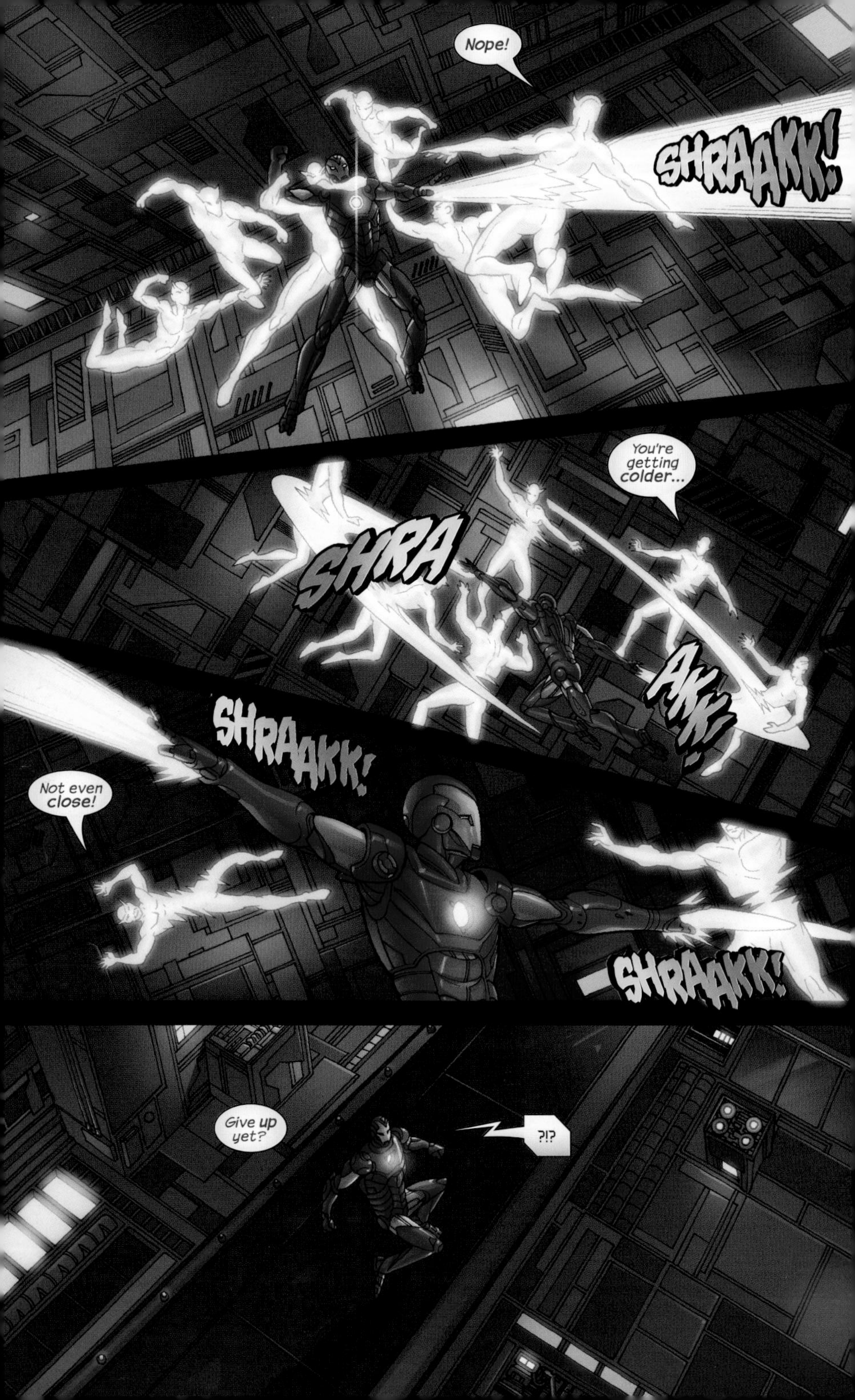
Nope!
SHRAAKK!
You're getting colder...
SHRA
AKK!
SHRAAKK!
Not even close!
SHRAAKK!
Give up yet?
?!?

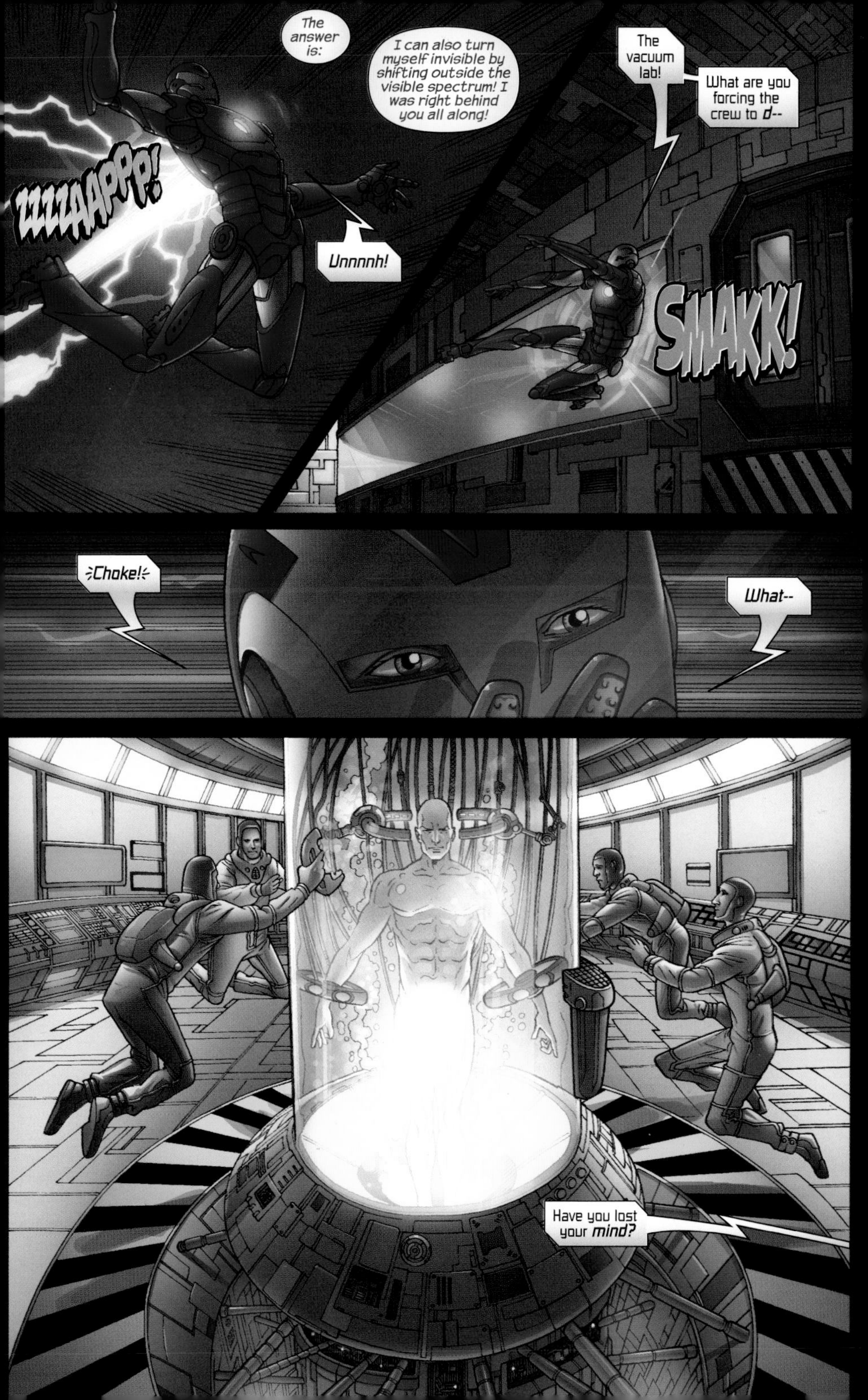
The answer is:
I can also turn myself invisible by shifting outside the visible spectrum! I was right behind you all along!
ZZZZAAPPP!
Unnnnh!
The vacuum lab!
What are you forcing the crew to d--
SMAKK!
Choke!
What--
Have you lost your mind?

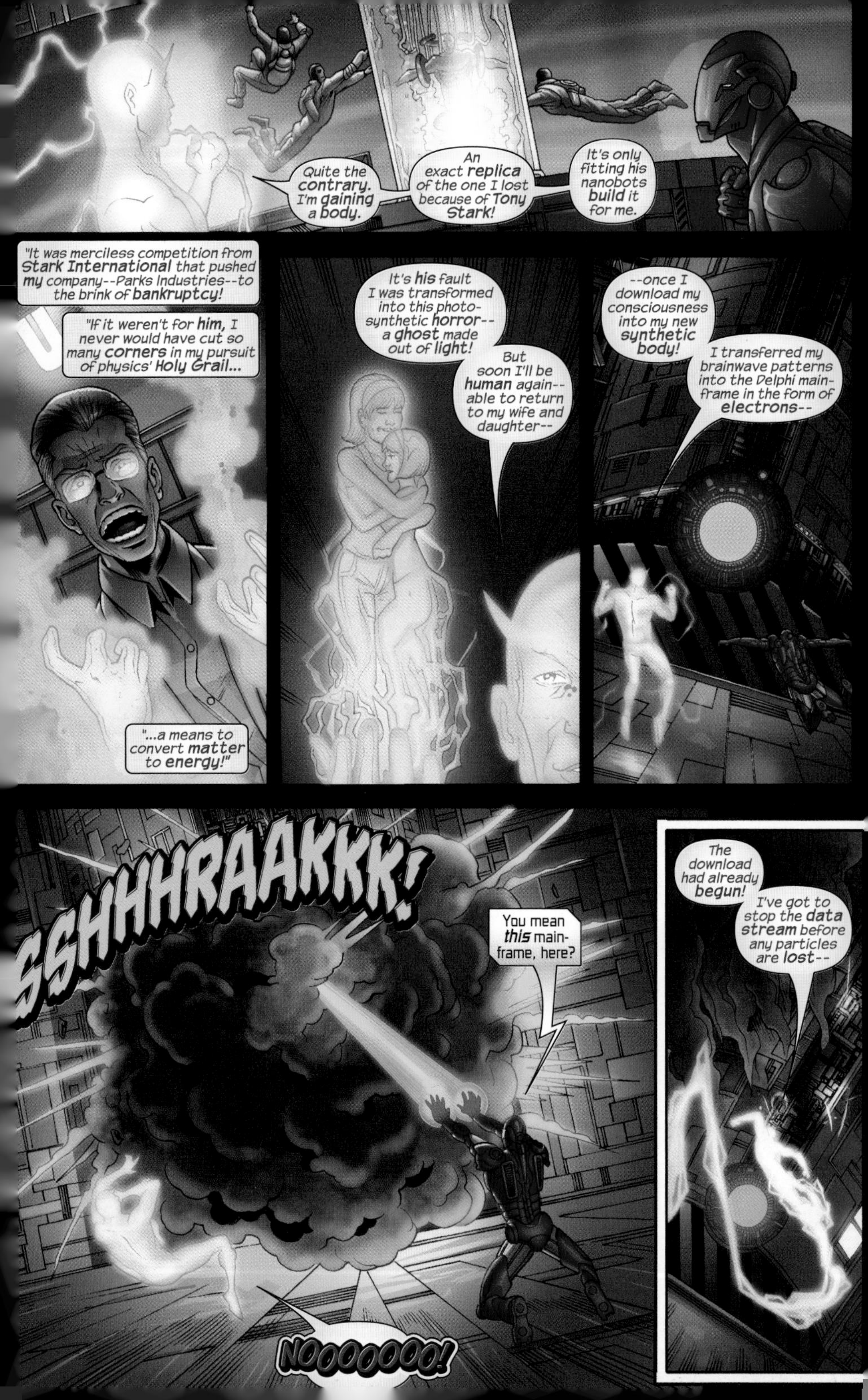
Quite the contrary. I'm gaining a body.
An exact replica of the one I lost because of Tony Stark!
It's only fitting his nanobots build it for me.
"It was merciless competition from Stark International that pushed my company--Parks Industries--to the brink of bankruptcy!
"If it weren't for him, I never would have cut so many corners in my pursuit of physics' Holy Grail...
"...a means to convert matter to energy!"
It's his fault I was transformed into this photo-synthetic horror--a ghost made out of light!
But soon I'll be human again--able to return to my wife and daughter--
--once I download my consciousness into my new synthetic body!
I transferred my brainwave patterns into the Delphi main-frame in the form of electrons--
SSHHHRAAKKK!
You mean this main-frame, here?
NOOOOOOO!
The download had already begun!
I've got to stop the data stream before any particles are lost--

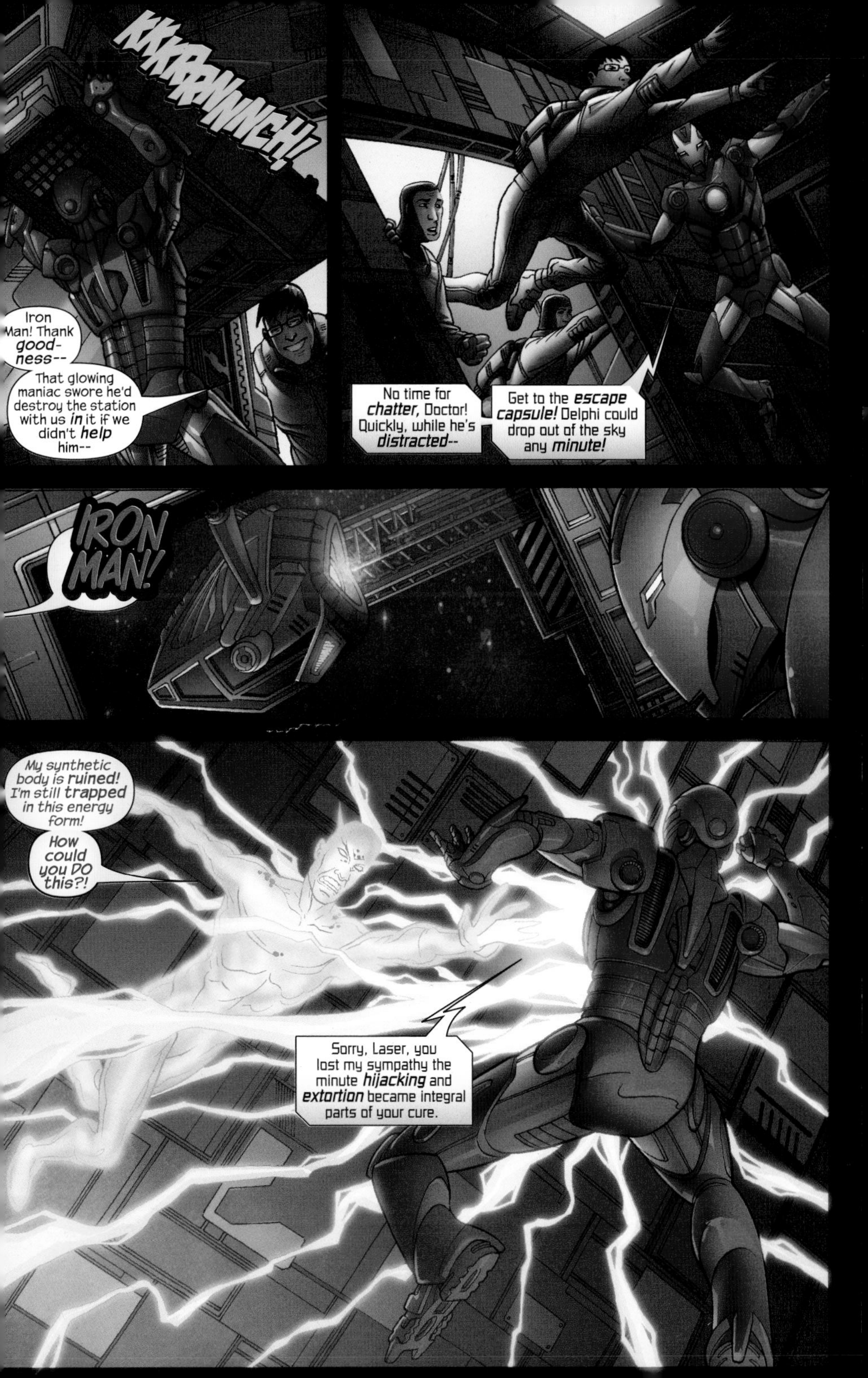
KKKRANNNCH!
Iron Man! Thank goodness--
That glowing maniac swore he'd destroy the station with us in it if we didn't help him--
No time for chatter, Doctor! Quickly, while he's distracted--
Get to the escape capsule! Delphi could drop out of the sky any minute!
IRON MAN!
My synthetic body is ruined! I'm still trapped in this energy form!
How could you DO this?!
Sorry, Laser, you lost my sympathy the minute hijacking and extortion became integral parts of your cure.

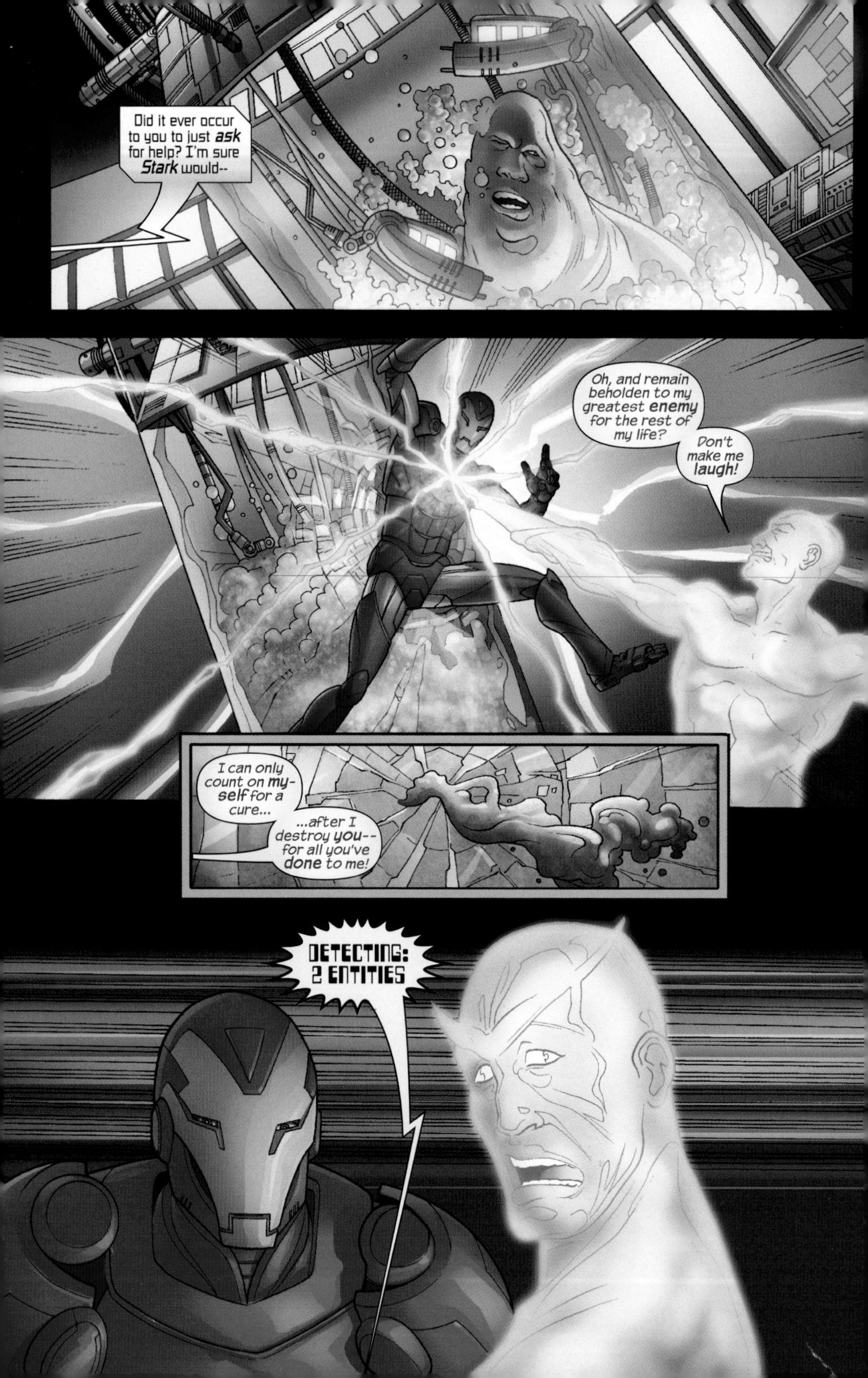
Did it ever occur to you to just ask for help? I'm sure Stark would--
Oh, and remain beholden to my greatest enemy for the rest of my life?
Don't make me laugh!
I can only count on my-self for a cure...
...after I destroy you--for all you've done to me!
DETECTING: 2 ENTITIES

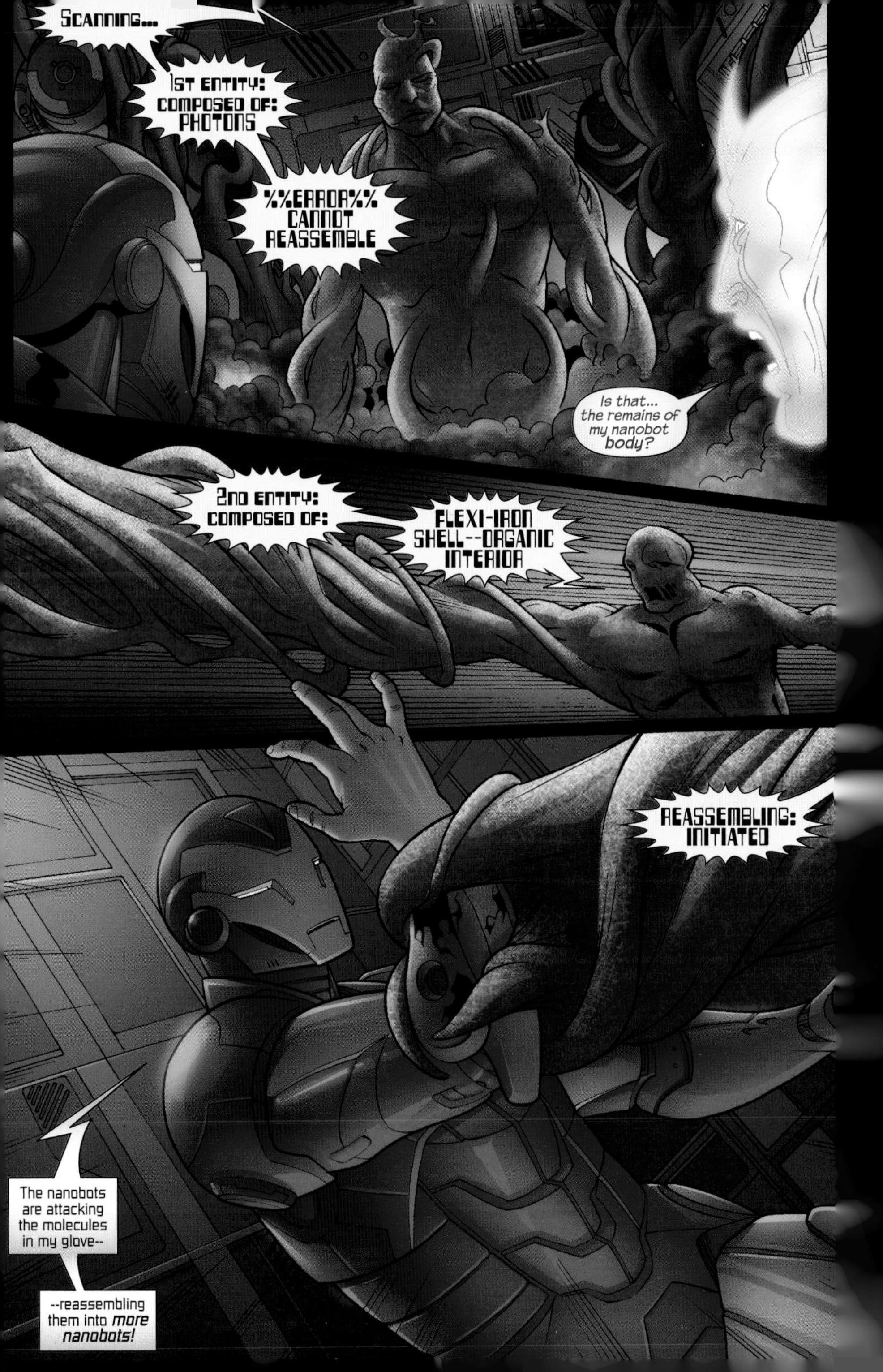
Scanning...
1st entity: composed of: photons
%%error%% cannot reassemble
Is that... the remains of my nanobot body?
2nd entity: composed of:
Flexi-iron shell--organic interior
Reassembling: initiated
The nanobots are attacking the molecules in my glove--
--reassembling them into more nanobots!

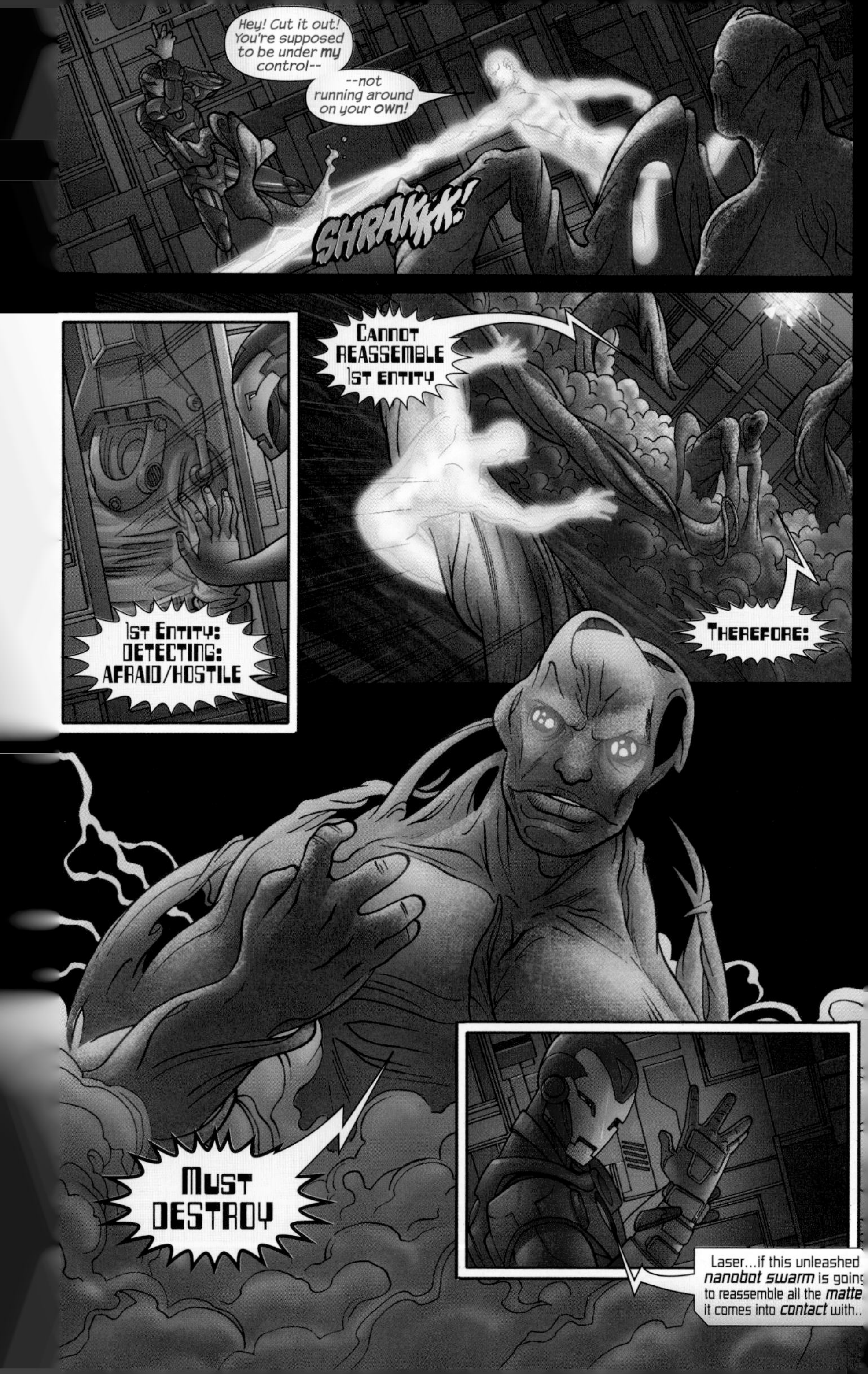
Hey! Cut it out! You're supposed to be under my control--
--not running around on your own!
SHRAKKK!
Cannot REASSEMBLE 1st Entity
1st Entity: DETECTING: AFRAID/HOSTILE
Therefore:
Must DESTROY
Laser...if this unleashed nanobot swarm is going to reassemble all the matter it comes into contact with..

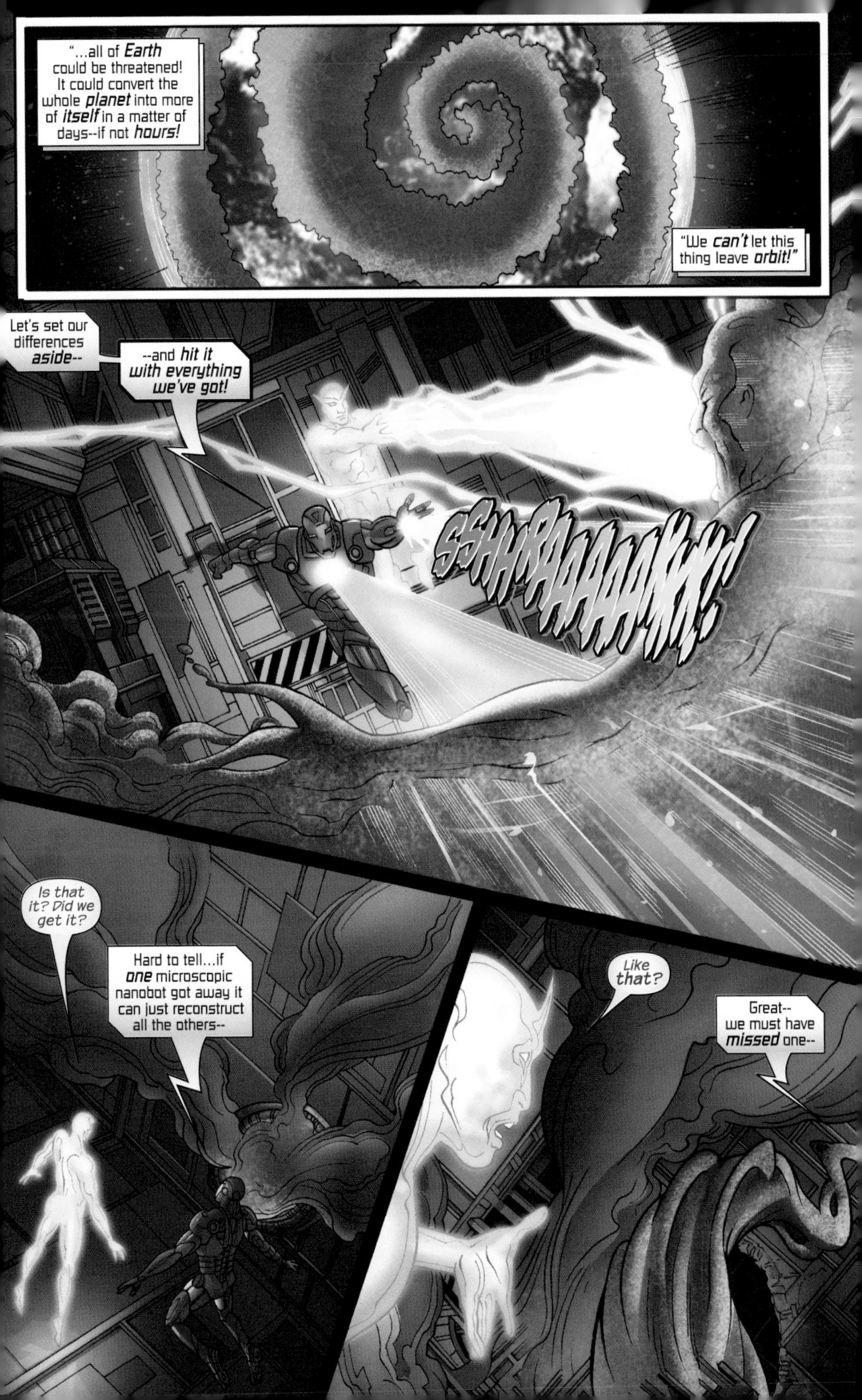
"...all of Earth could be threatened! It could convert the whole planet into more of itself in a matter of days--if not hours!
"We can't let this thing leave orbit!"
Let's set our differences aside--
--and hit it with everything we've got!
SSHRAAAAAKK!
Is that it? Did we get it?
Hard to tell...if one microscopic nanobot got away it can just reconstruct all the others--
Like that?
Great-- we must have missed one--

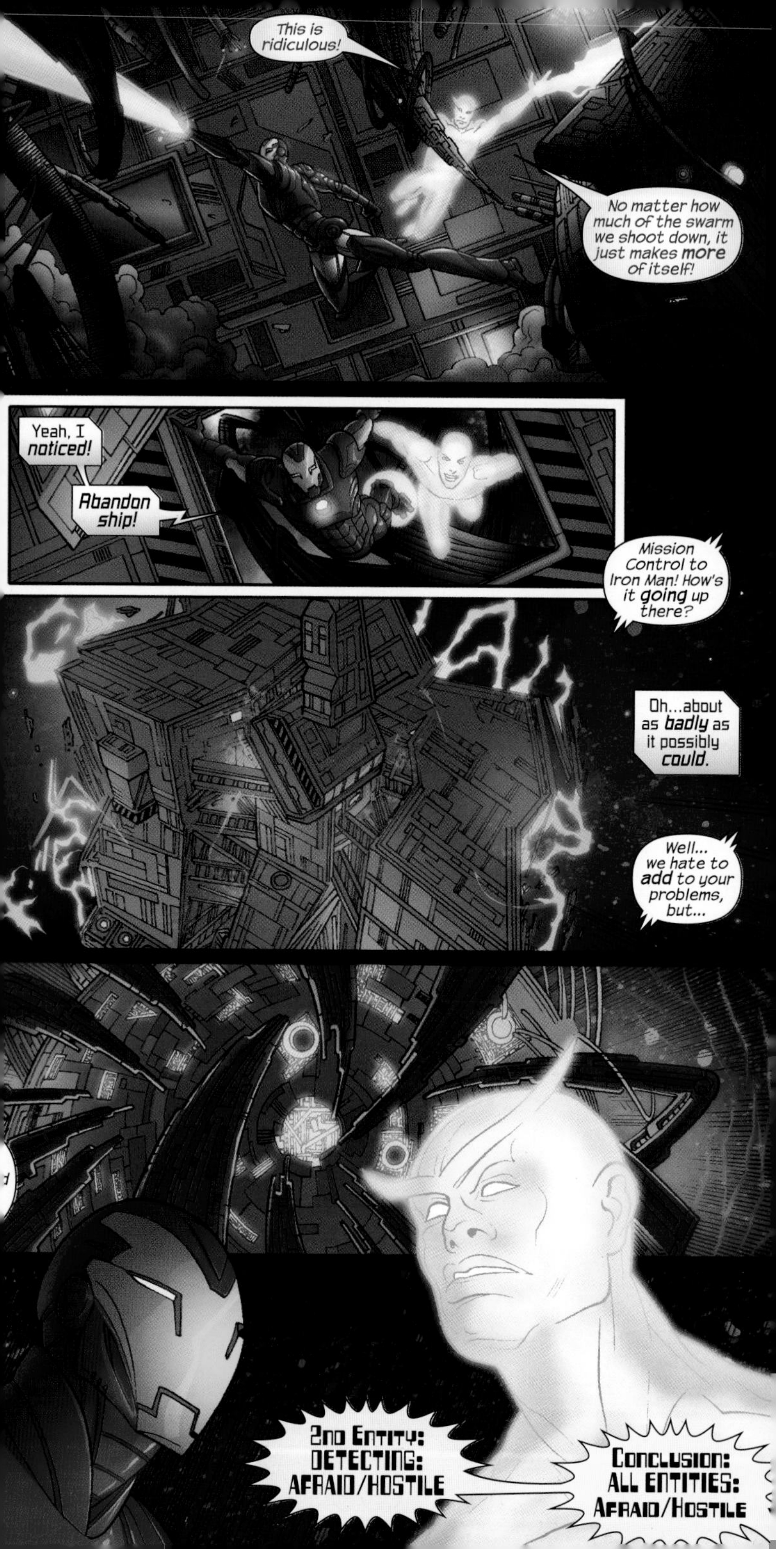
This is ridiculous!
No matter how much of the swarm we shoot down, it just makes more of itself!
Yeah, I noticed!
Abandon ship!
Mission Control to Iron Man! How's it going up there?
Oh...about as badly as it possibly could.
Well... we hate to add to your problems, but...
2nd Entity: Detecting: Afraid/Hostile
Conclusion: All Entities: Afraid/Hostile

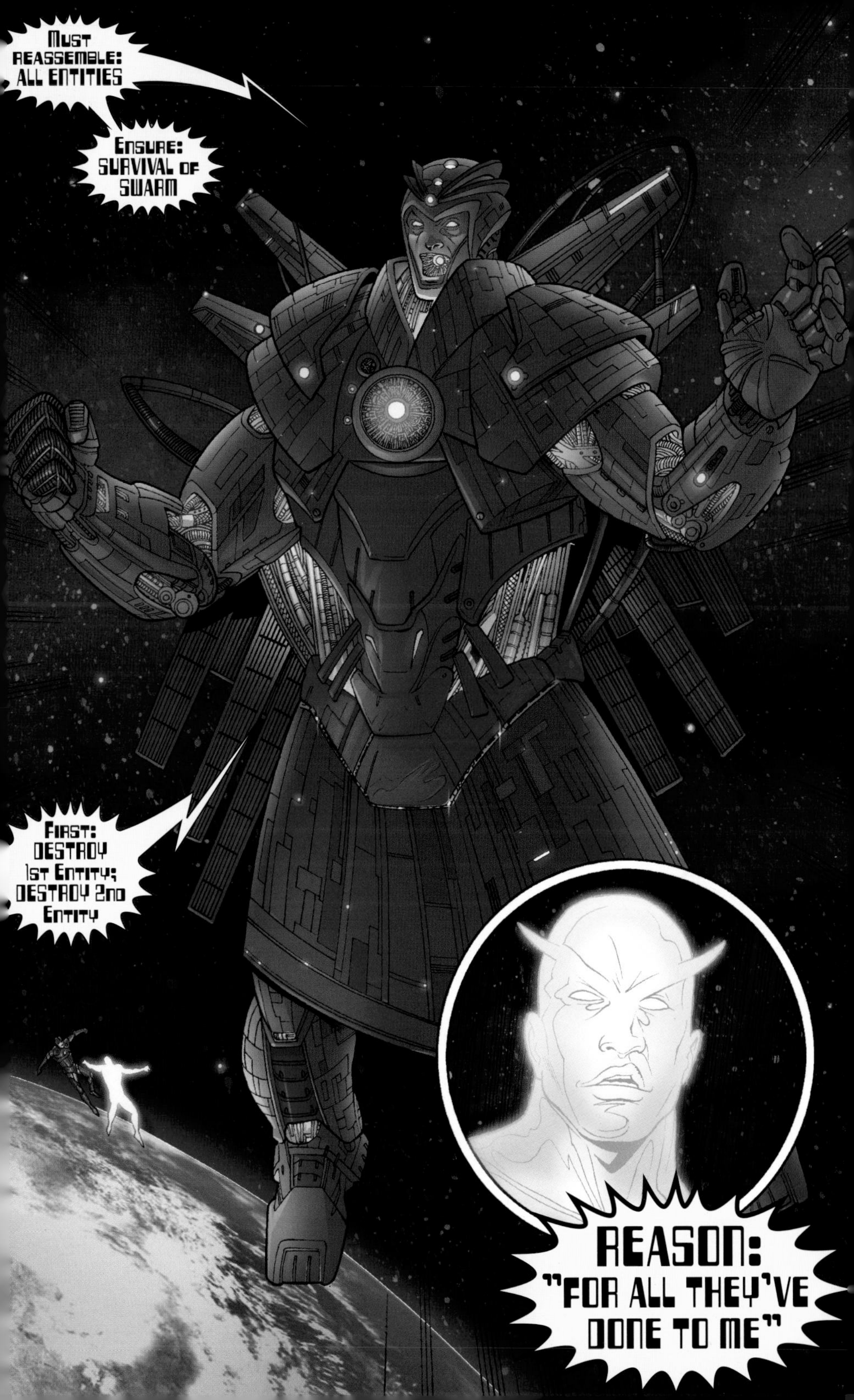
MUST REASSEMBLE: ALL ENTITIES
ENSURE: SURVIVAL OF SWARM
FIRST: DESTROY 1ST ENTITY; DESTROY 2ND ENTITY
REASON: "FOR ALL THEY'VE DONE TO ME"

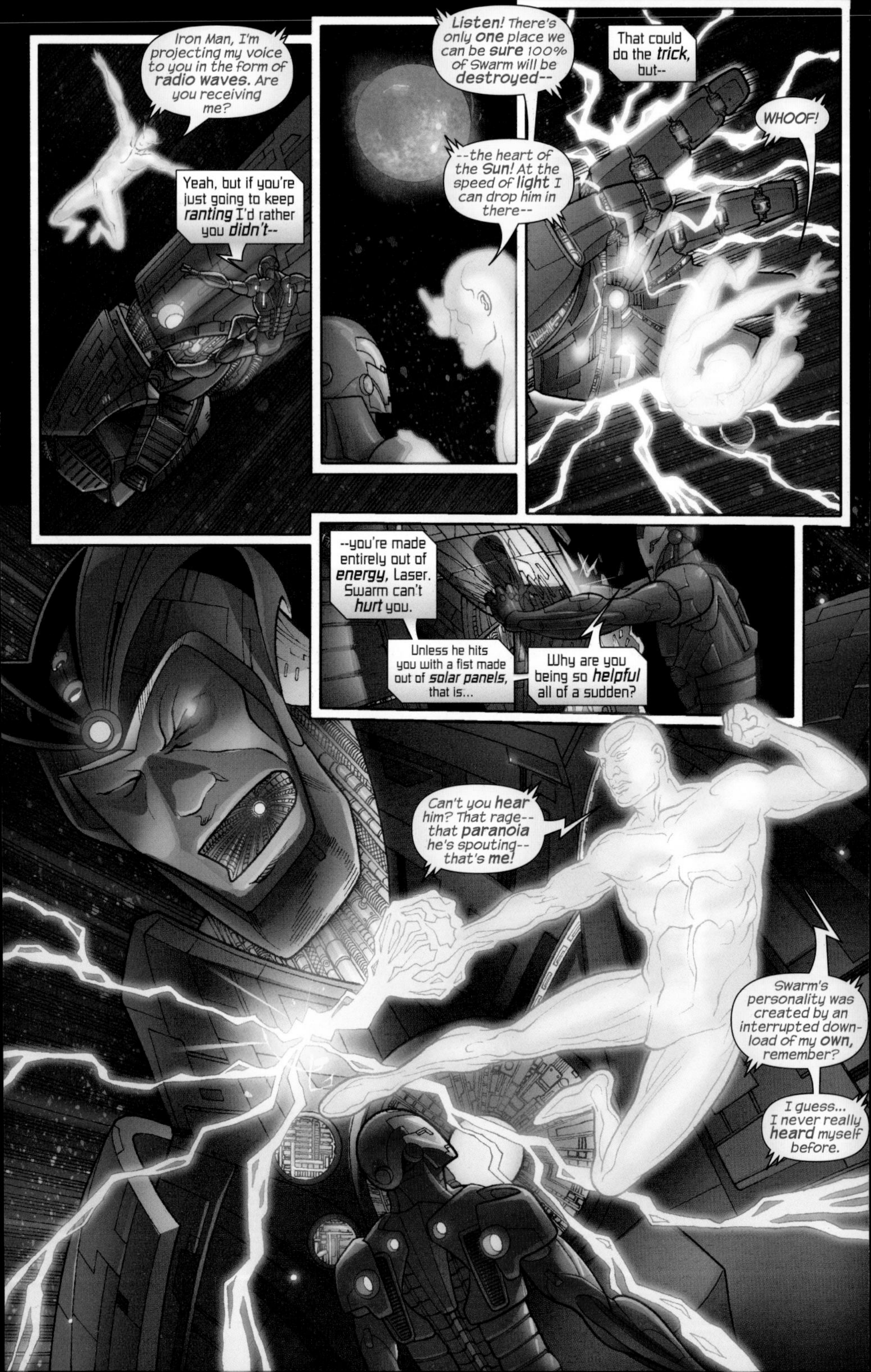
Iron Man, I'm projecting my voice to you in the form of radio waves. Are you receiving me?
Yeah, but if you're just going to keep ranting I'd rather you didn't--
Listen! There's only one place we can be sure 100% of Swarm will be destroyed--
--the heart of the Sun! At the speed of light I can drop him in there--
That could do the trick, but--
WHOOF!
--you're made entirely out of energy, Laser. Swarm can't hurt you.
Unless he hits you with a fist made out of solar panels, that is...
Why are you being so helpful all of a sudden?
Can't you hear him? That rage--that paranoia he's spouting--that's me!
Swarm's personality was created by an interrupted download of my own, remember?
I guess... I never really heard myself before.

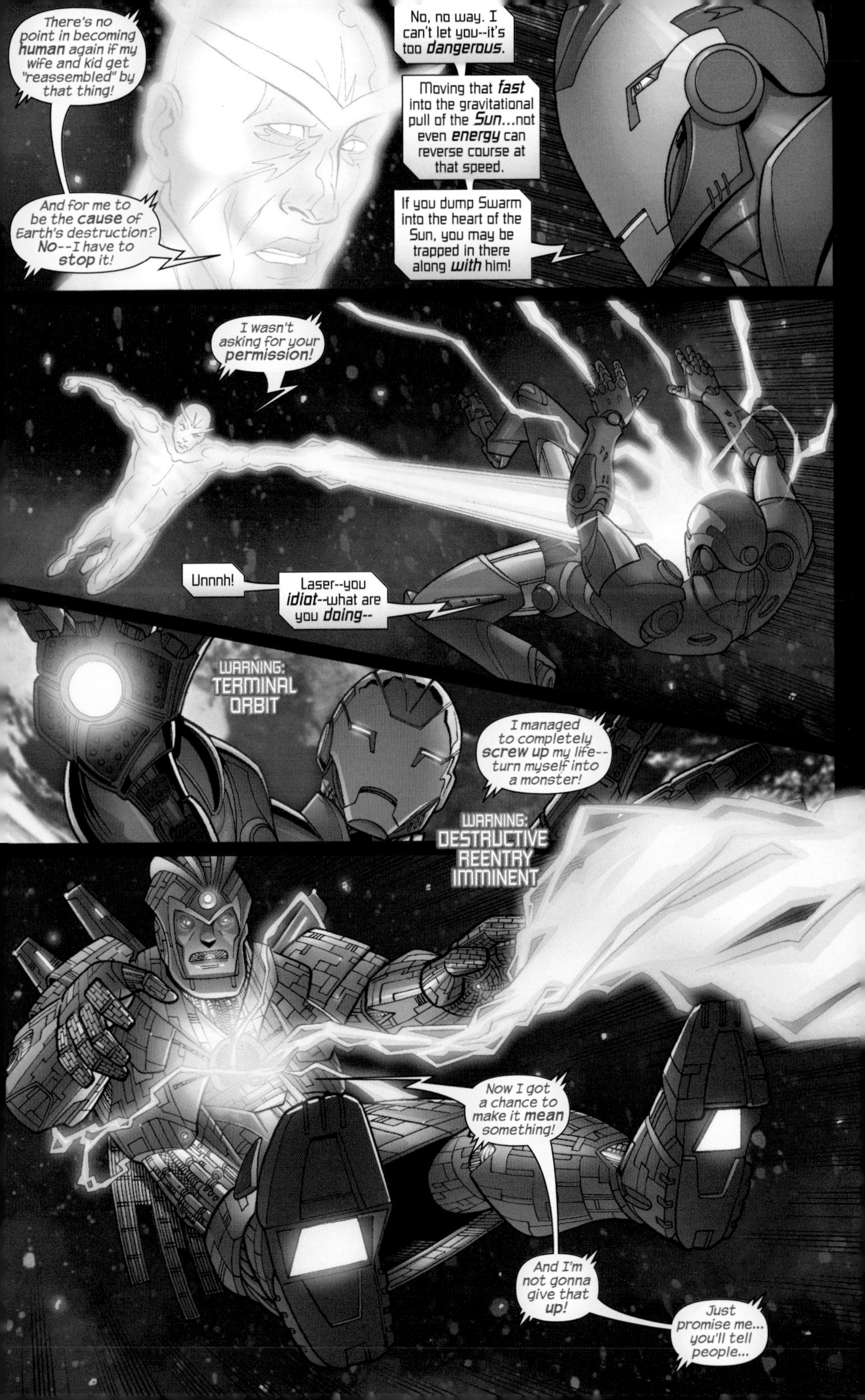
There's no point in becoming human again if my wife and kid get "reassembled" by that thing!
And for me to be the cause of Earth's destruction? No--I have to stop it!
No, no way. I can't let you--it's too dangerous.
Moving that fast into the gravitational pull of the Sun...not even energy can reverse course at that speed.
If you dump Swarm into the heart of the Sun, you may be trapped in there along with him!
I wasn't asking for your permission!
Unnnh!
Laser--you idiot--what are you doing--
WARNING: TERMINAL ORBIT
I managed to completely screw up my life--turn myself into a monster!
WARNING: DESTRUCTIVE REENTRY IMMINENT
Now I got a chance to make it mean something!
And I'm not gonna give that up!
Just promise me... you'll tell people...

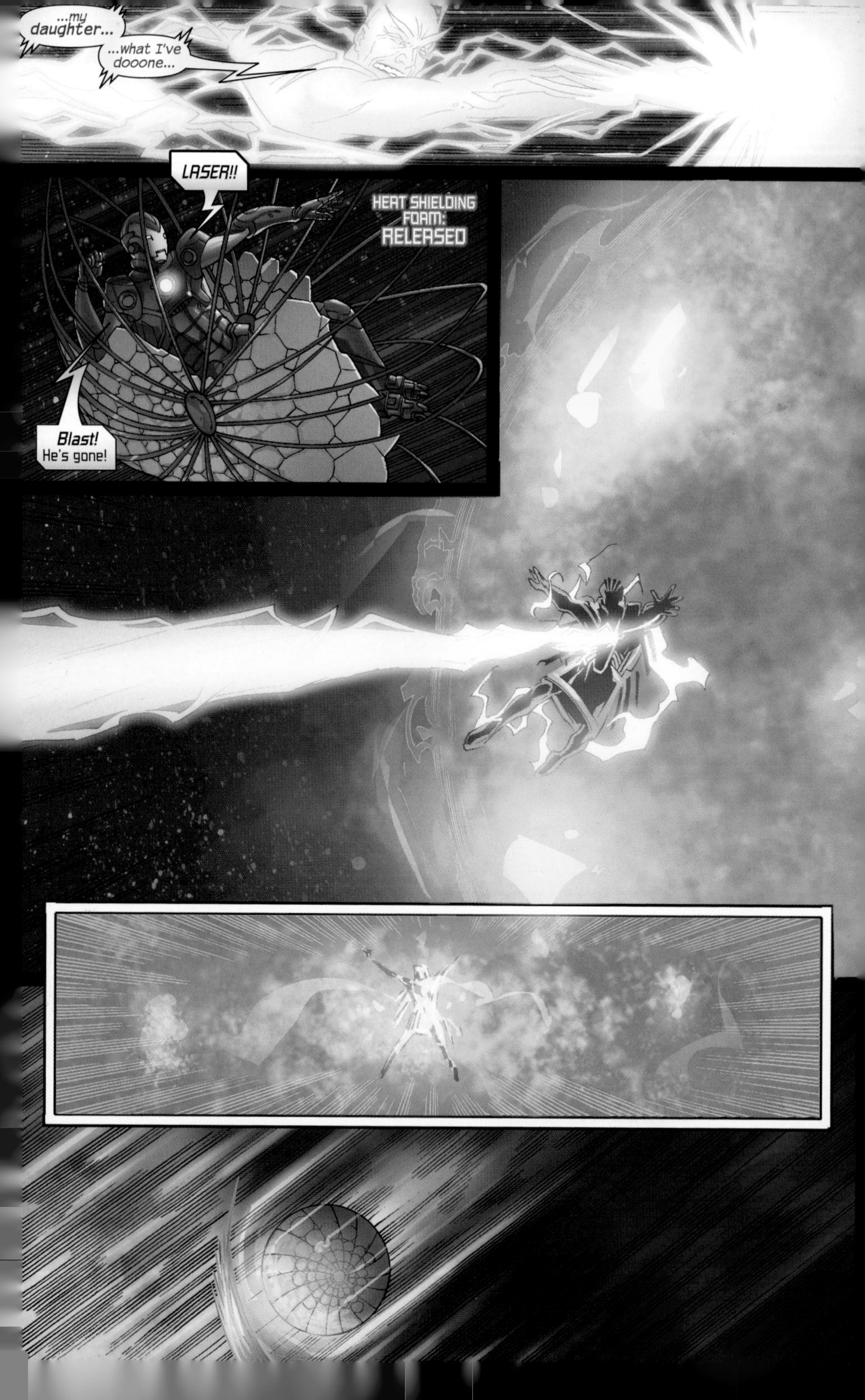

...my daughter...
...what I've dooone...
LASER!!
HEAT SHIELDING FORM: RELEASED
Blast! He's gone!

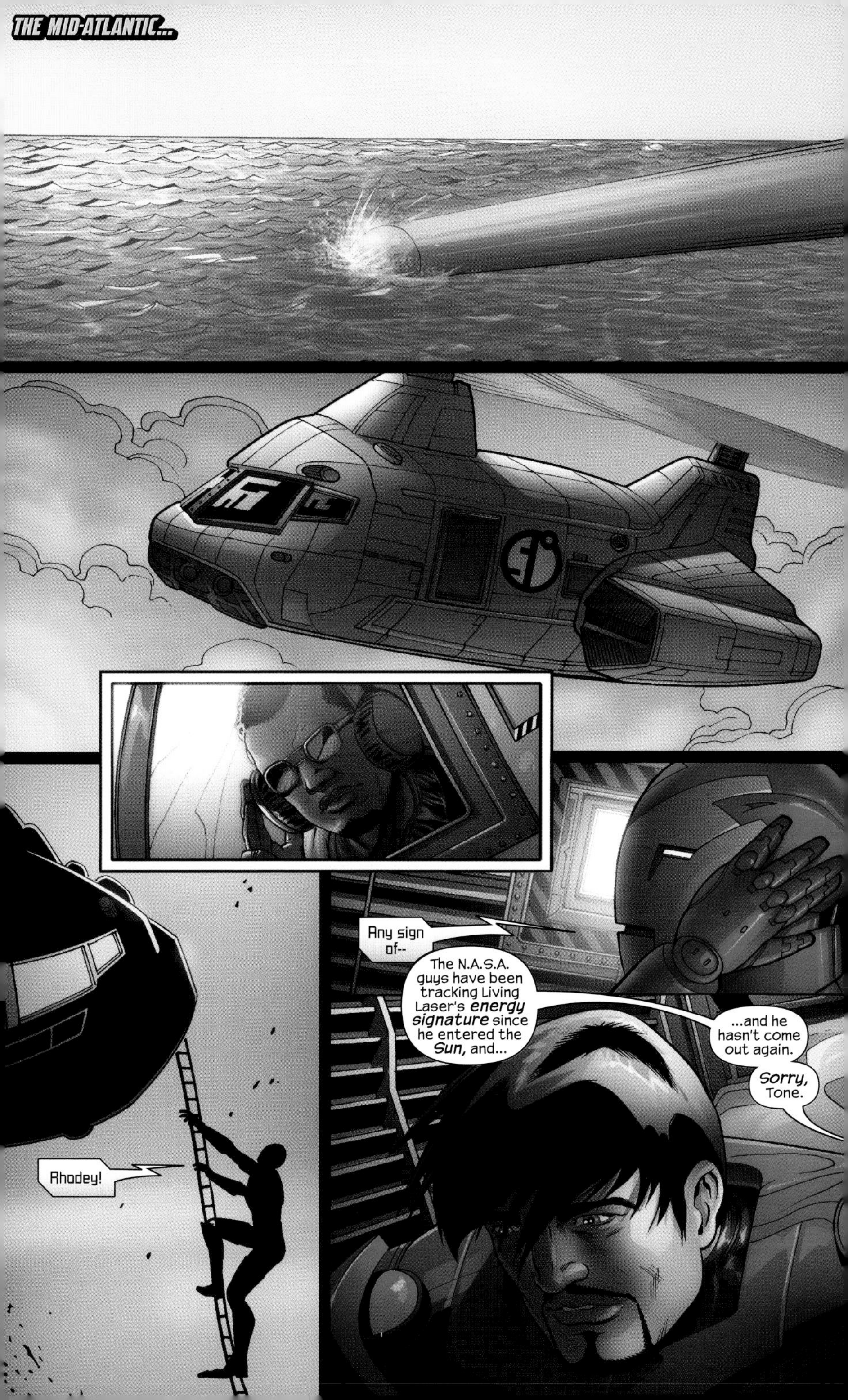

THE MID-ATLANTIC...
Any sign of--
The N.A.S.A. guys have been tracking Living Laser's energy signature since he entered the Sun, and...
...and he hasn't come out again.
Sorry, Tone.
Rhodey!

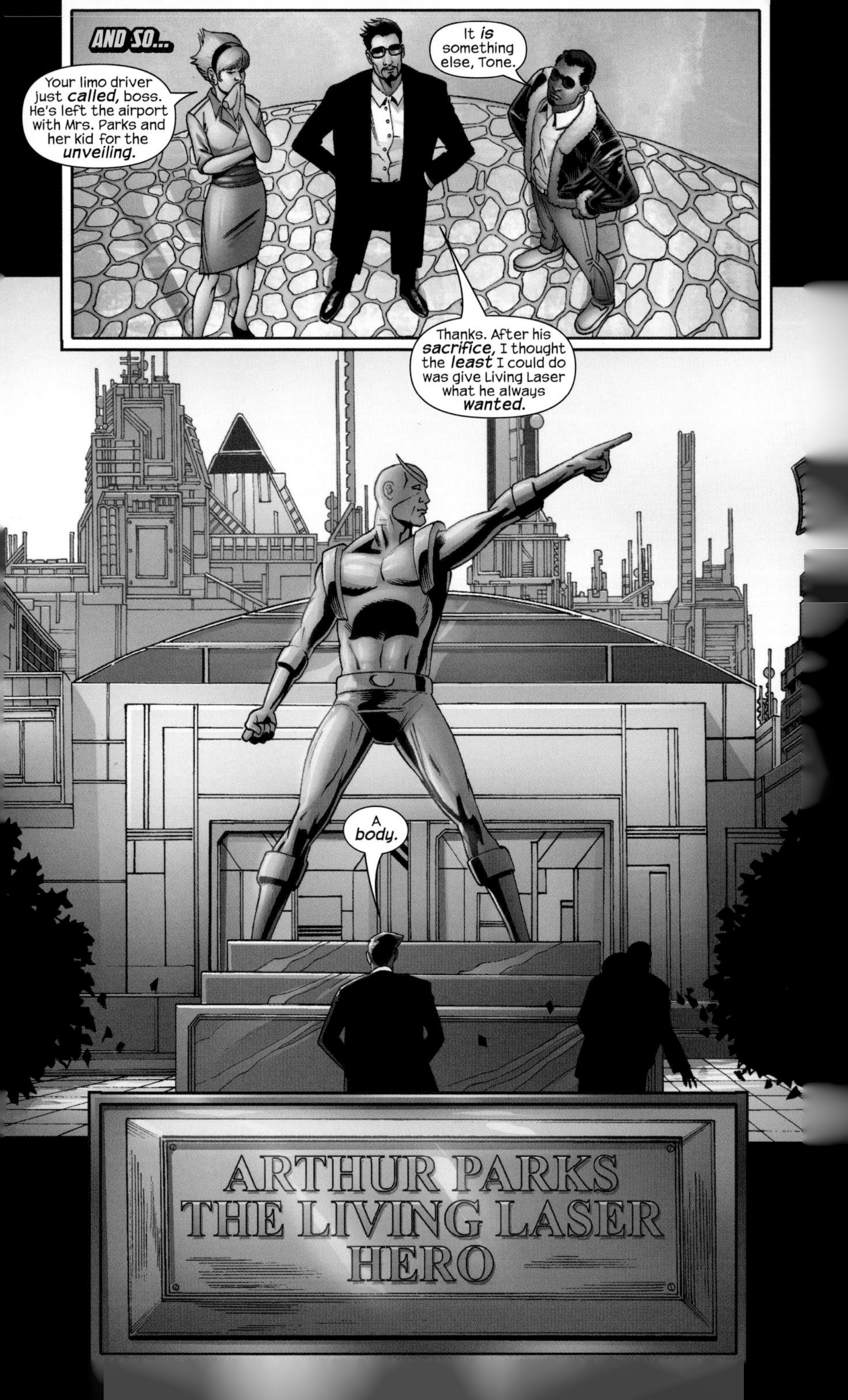
AND SO...
Your limo driver just called, boss. He's left the airport with Mrs. Parks and her kid for the unveiling.
It is something else, Tone.
Thanks. After his sacrifice, I thought the least I could do was give Living Laser what he always wanted.
A body.
ARTHUR PARKS
THE LIVING LASER
HERO

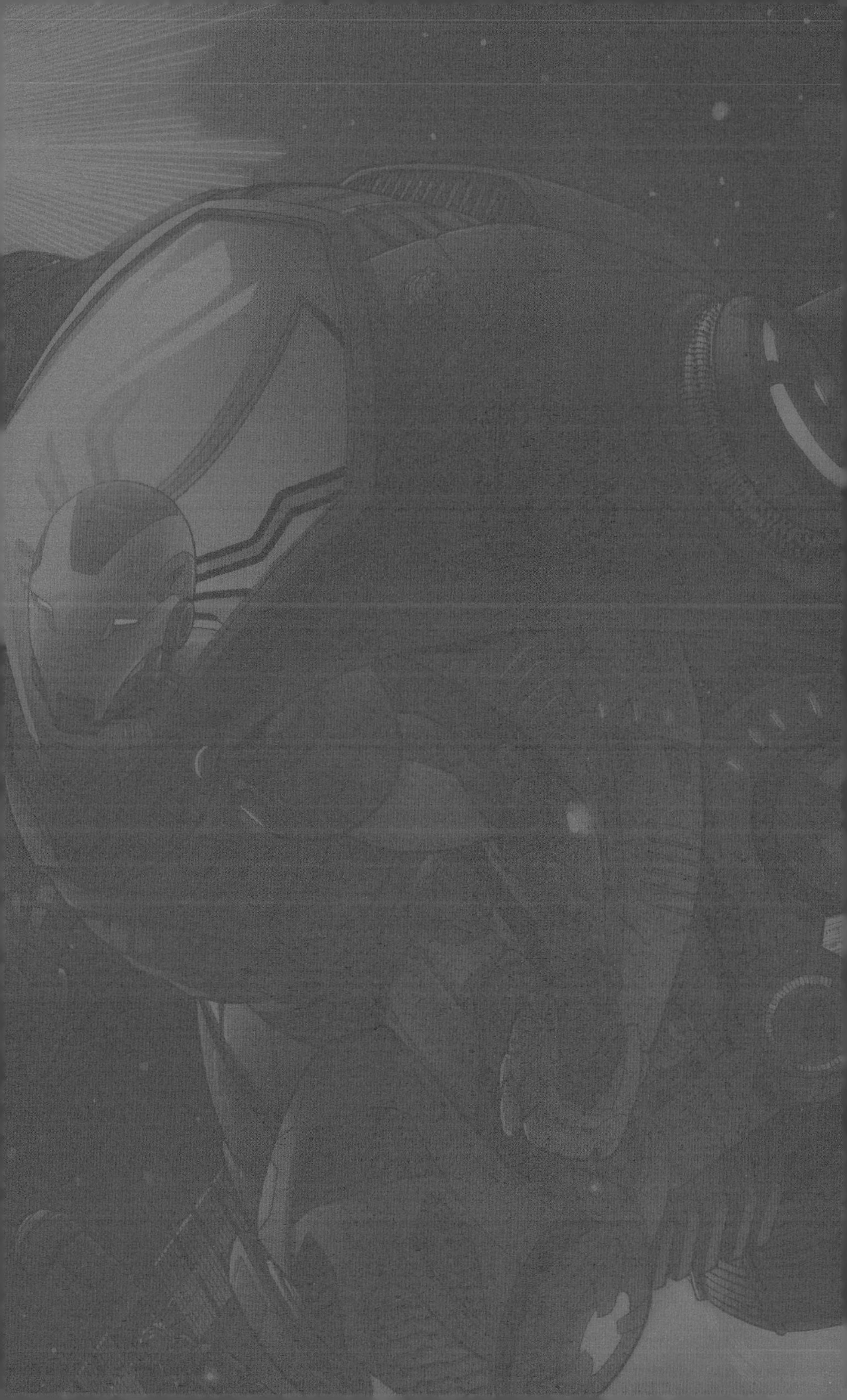

07

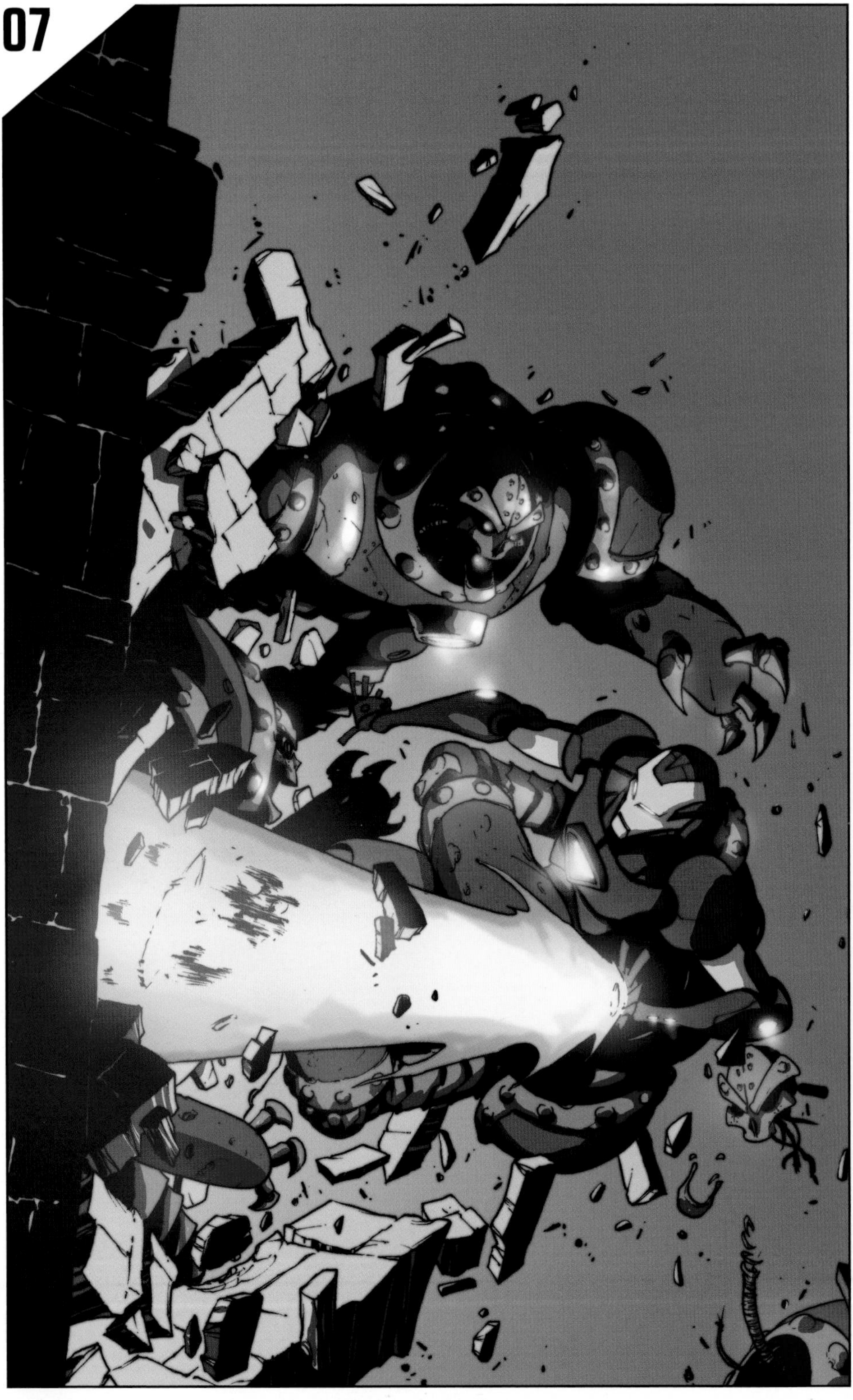

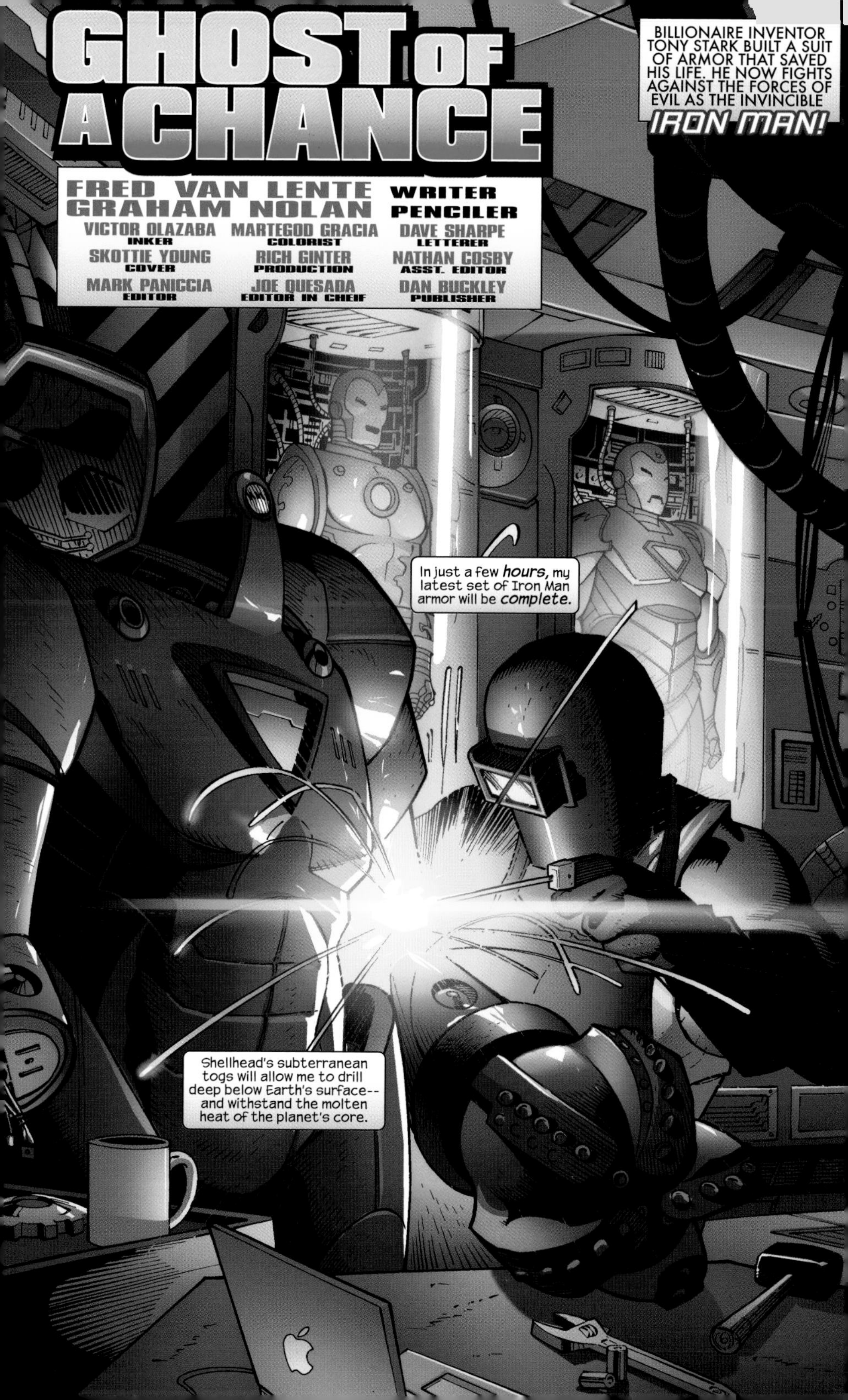
GHOST OF A CHANCE
FRED VAN LENTE WRITER
GRAHAM NOLAN PENCILER
VICTOR OLAZABA INKER
MARTEGOD GRACIA COLORIST
DAVE SHARPE LETTERER
SKOTTIE YOUNG COVER
RICH GINTER PRODUCTION
NATHAN COSBY ASST. EDITOR
MARK PANICCIA EDITOR
JOE QUESADA EDITOR IN CHEIF
DAN BUCKLEY PUBLISHER
BILLIONAIRE INVENTOR TONY STARK BUILT A SUIT OF ARMOR THAT SAVED HIS LIFE. HE NOW FIGHTS AGAINST THE FORCES OF EVIL AS THE INVINCIBLE IRON MAN!
In just a few *hours,* my latest set of Iron Man armor will be *complete.*
Shellhead's subterranean togs will allow me to drill deep below Earth's surface-- and withstand the molten heat of the planet's core.

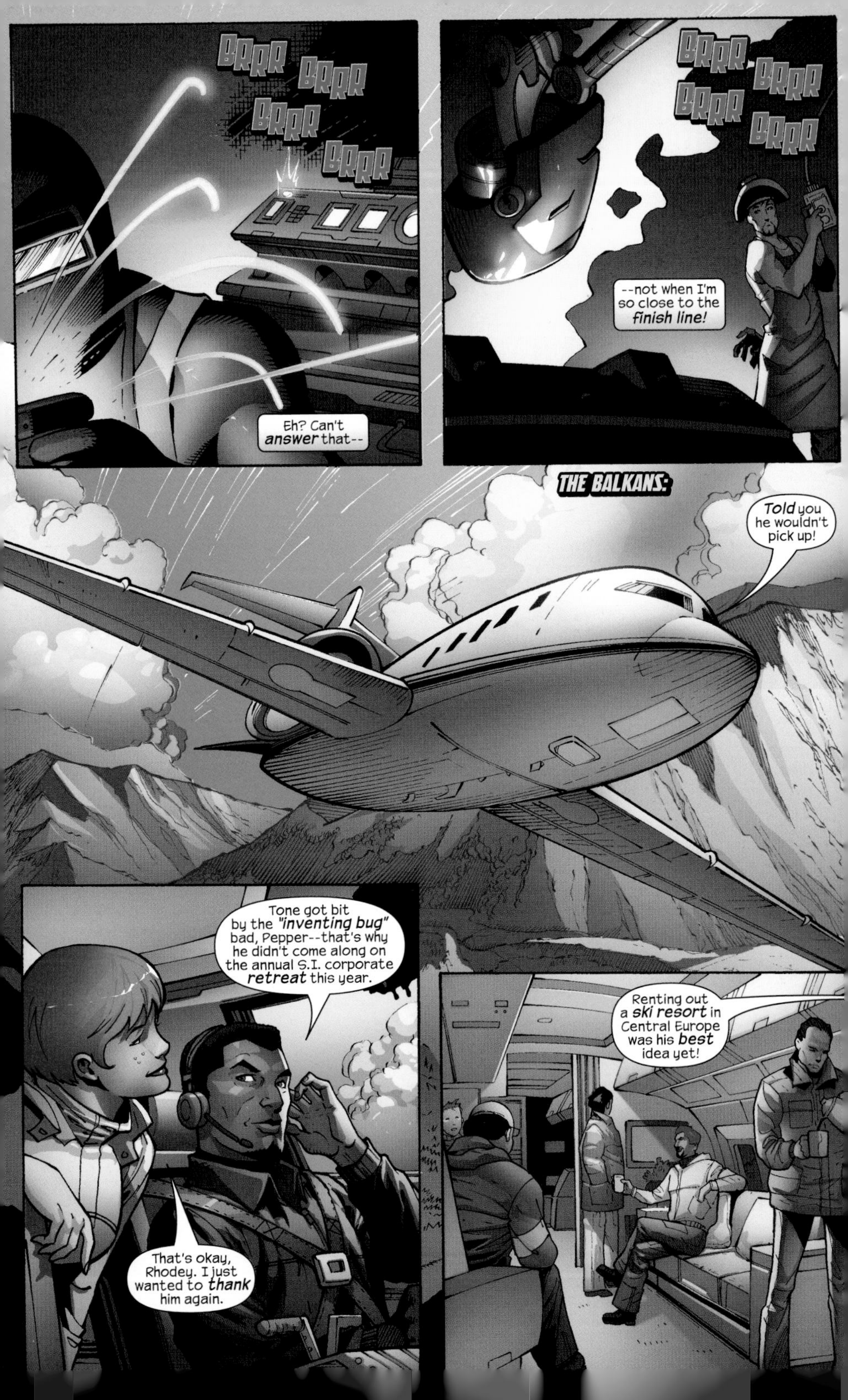
BRRR BRRR BRRR BRRR
Eh? Can't answer that--
BRRR BRRR BRRR BRRR
--not when I'm so close to the finish line!
THE BALKANS:
Told you he wouldn't pick up!
Tone got bit by the "inventing bug" bad, Pepper--that's why he didn't come along on the annual S.I. corporate retreat this year.
That's okay, Rhodey. I just wanted to thank him again.
Renting out a ski resort in Central Europe was his best idea yet!

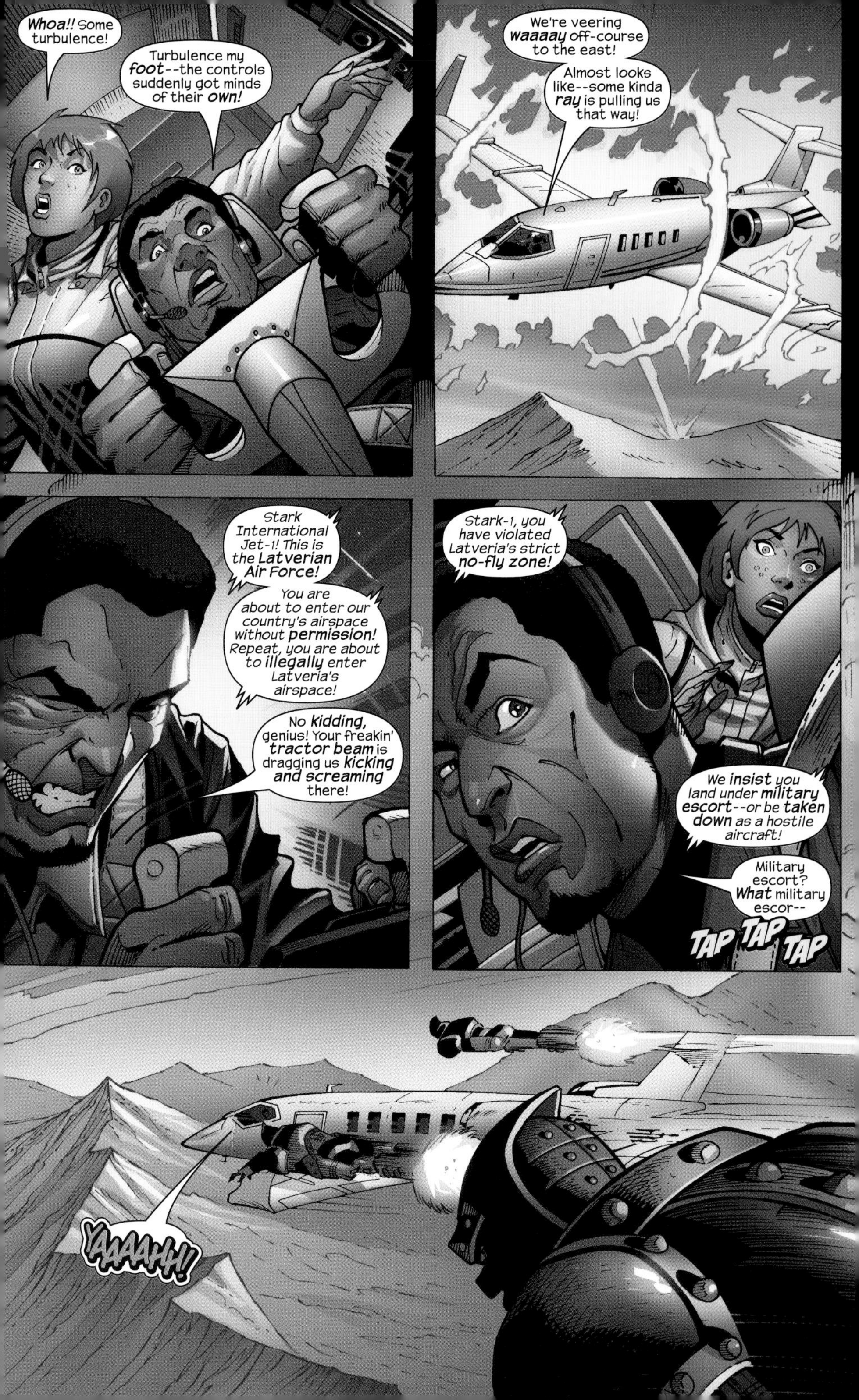

Whoa!! Some turbulence!
Turbulence my foot--the controls suddenly got minds of their own!
We're veering waaaay off-course to the east!
Almost looks like--some kinda ray is pulling us that way!
Stark International Jet-1! This is the Latverian Air Force!
You are about to enter our country's airspace without permission! Repeat, you are about to illegally enter Latveria's airspace!
No kidding, genius! Your freakin' tractor beam is dragging us kicking and screaming there!
Stark-1, you have violated Latveria's strict no-fly zone!
We insist you land under military escort--or be taken down as a hostile aircraft!
Military escort? What military escor--
TAP TAP TAP
YAAAAHH!!

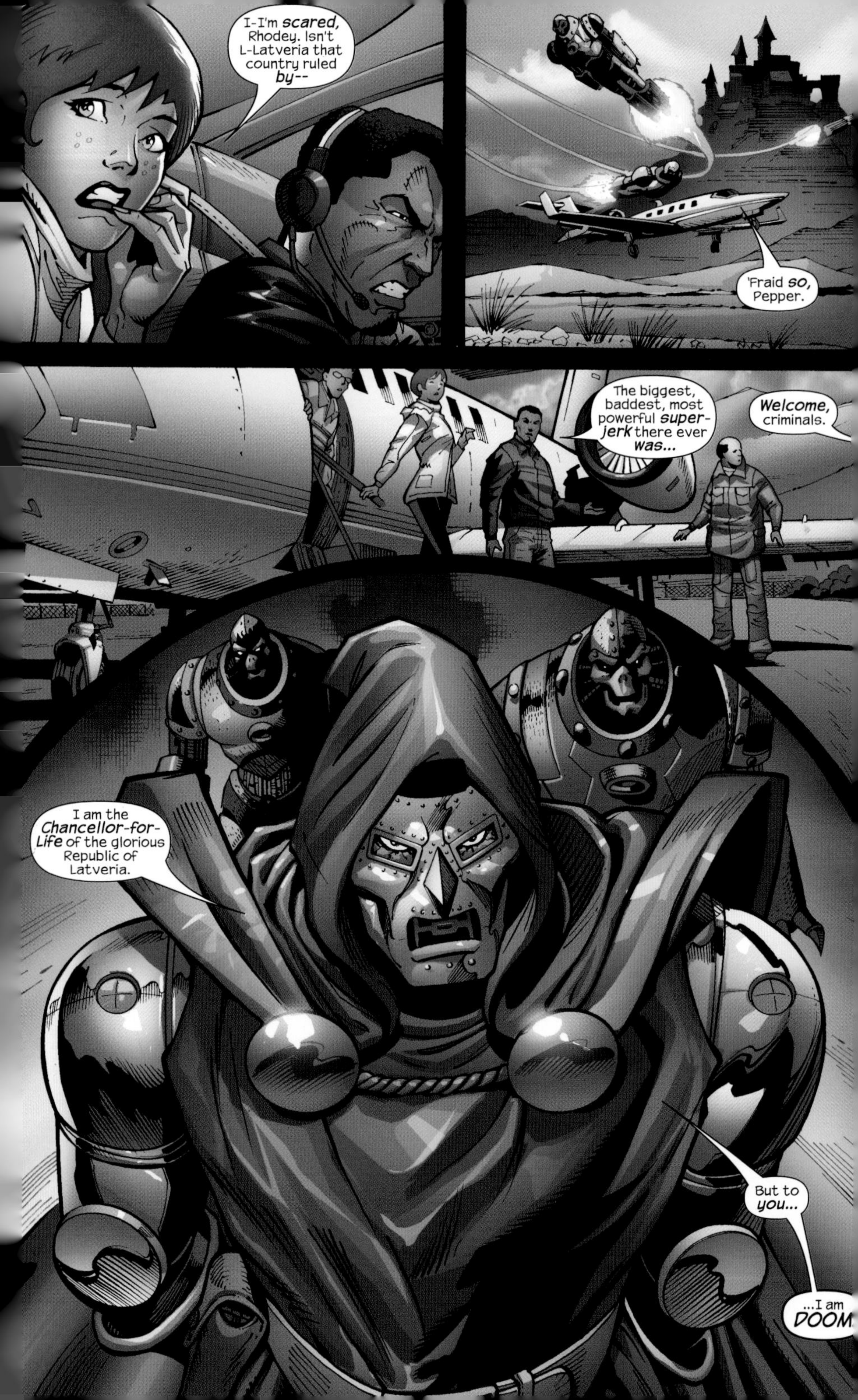
I-I'm scared, Rhodey. Isn't L-Latveria that country ruled by--
'Fraid so, Pepper.
The biggest, baddest, most powerful super-jerk there ever was...
Welcome, criminals.
I am the Chancellor-for-Life of the glorious Republic of Latveria.
But to you...
...I am DOOM

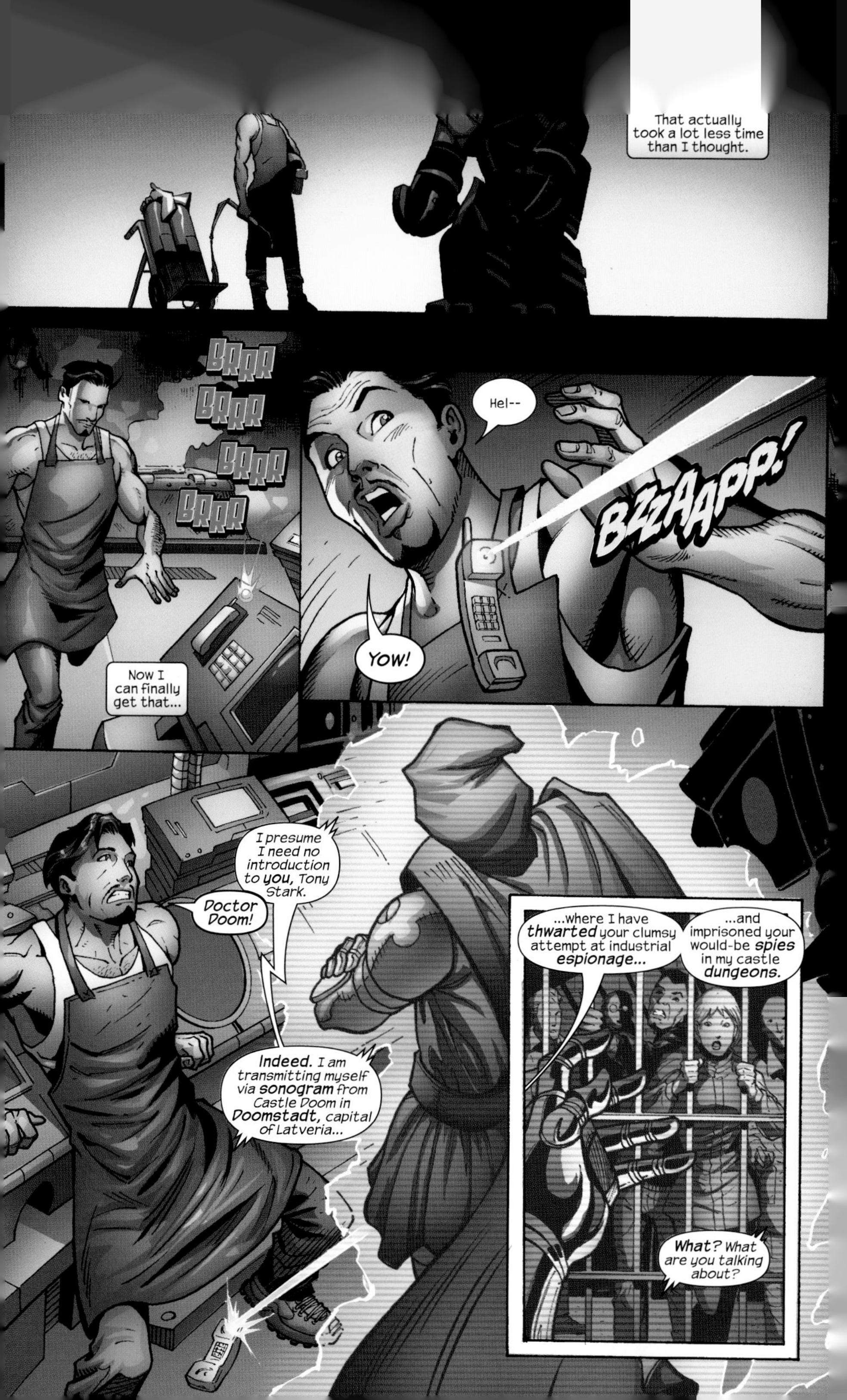
That actually took a lot less time than I thought.
BRRR BRRR BRRR BRRR
Now I can finally get that...
Hel--
BZZAAPP!
YOW!
I presume I need no introduction to you, Tony Stark.
Doctor Doom!
Indeed. I am transmitting myself via sonogram from Castle Doom in Doomstadt, capital of Latveria...
...where I have thwarted your clumsy attempt at industrial espionage...
...and imprisoned your would-be spies in my castle dungeons.
What? What are you talking about?

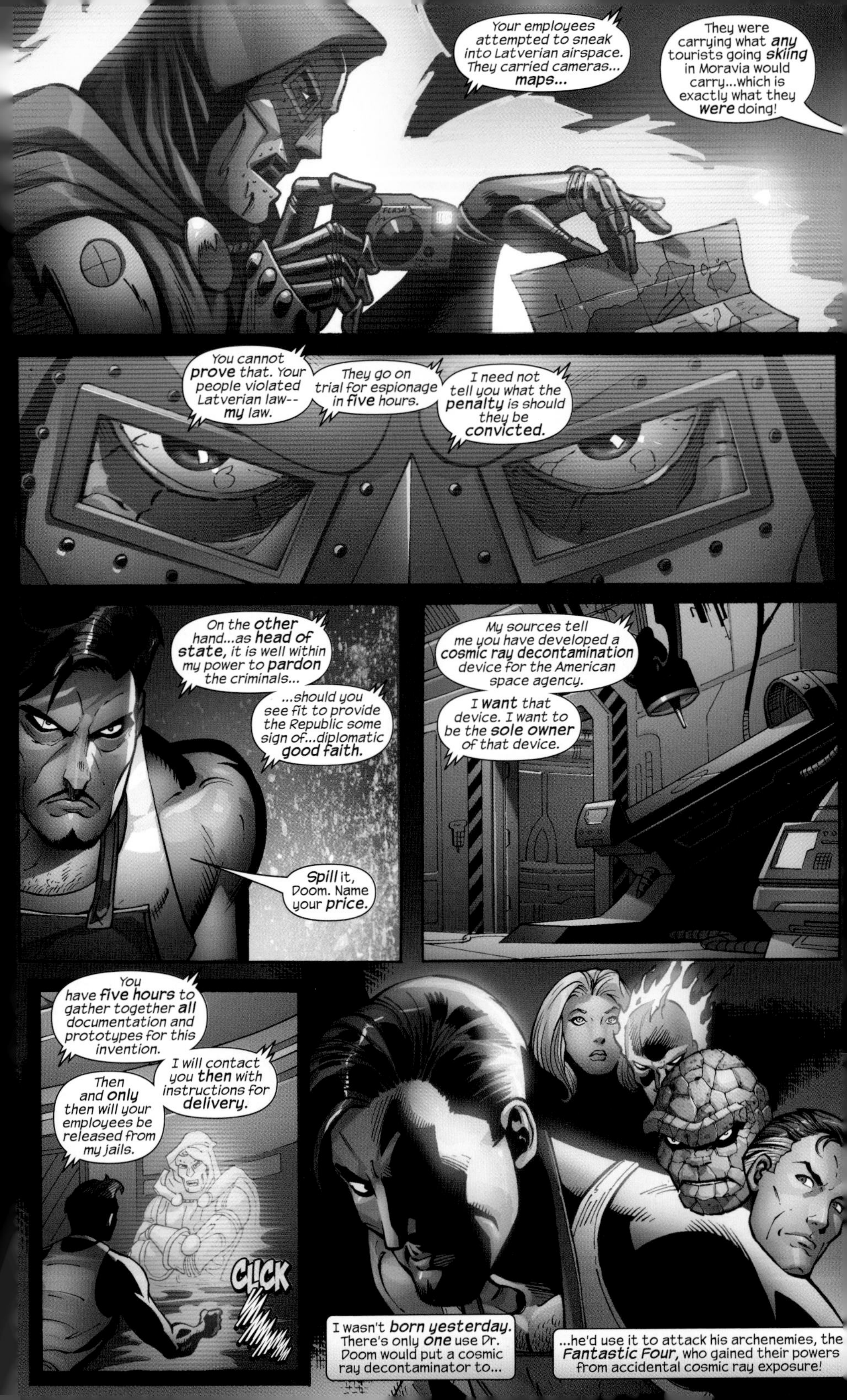
Your employees attempted to sneak into Latverian airspace. They carried cameras... maps...
They were carrying what any tourists going skiing in Moravia would carry...which is exactly what they were doing!
FLASH
You cannot prove that. Your people violated Latverian law-- my law.
They go on trial for espionage in five hours.
I need not tell you what the penalty is should they be convicted.
On the other hand...as head of state, it is well within my power to pardon the criminals...
...should you see fit to provide the Republic some sign of...diplomatic good faith.
Spill it, Doom. Name your price.
My sources tell me you have developed a cosmic ray decontamination device for the American space agency.
I want that device. I want to be the sole owner of that device.
You have five hours to gather together all documentation and prototypes for this invention.
I will contact you then with instructions for delivery.
Then and only then will your employees be released from my jails.
CLICK
I wasn't born yesterday. There's only one use Dr. Doom would put a cosmic ray decontaminator to...
...he'd use it to attack his archenemies, the Fantastic Four, who gained their powers from accidental cosmic ray exposure!

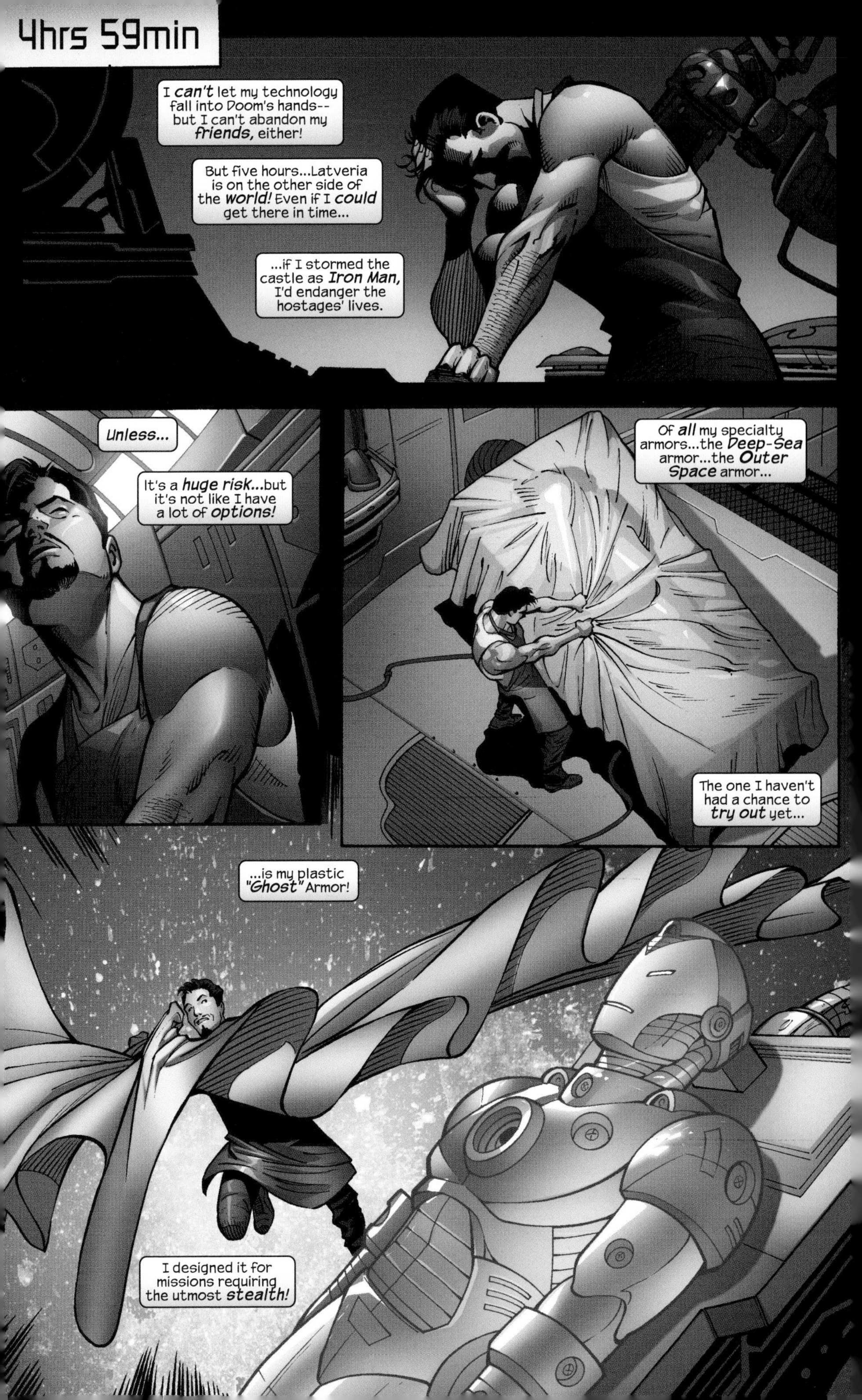
4hrs 59min
I can't let my technology fall into Doom's hands-- but I can't abandon my friends, either!
But five hours...Latveria is on the other side of the world! Even if I could get there in time...
...if I stormed the castle as Iron Man, I'd endanger the hostages' lives.
Unless...
It's a huge risk...but it's not like I have a lot of options!
Of all my specialty armors...the Deep-Sea armor...the Outer Space armor...
The one I haven't had a chance to try out yet...
...is my plastic "Ghost" Armor!
I designed it for missions requiring the utmost stealth!

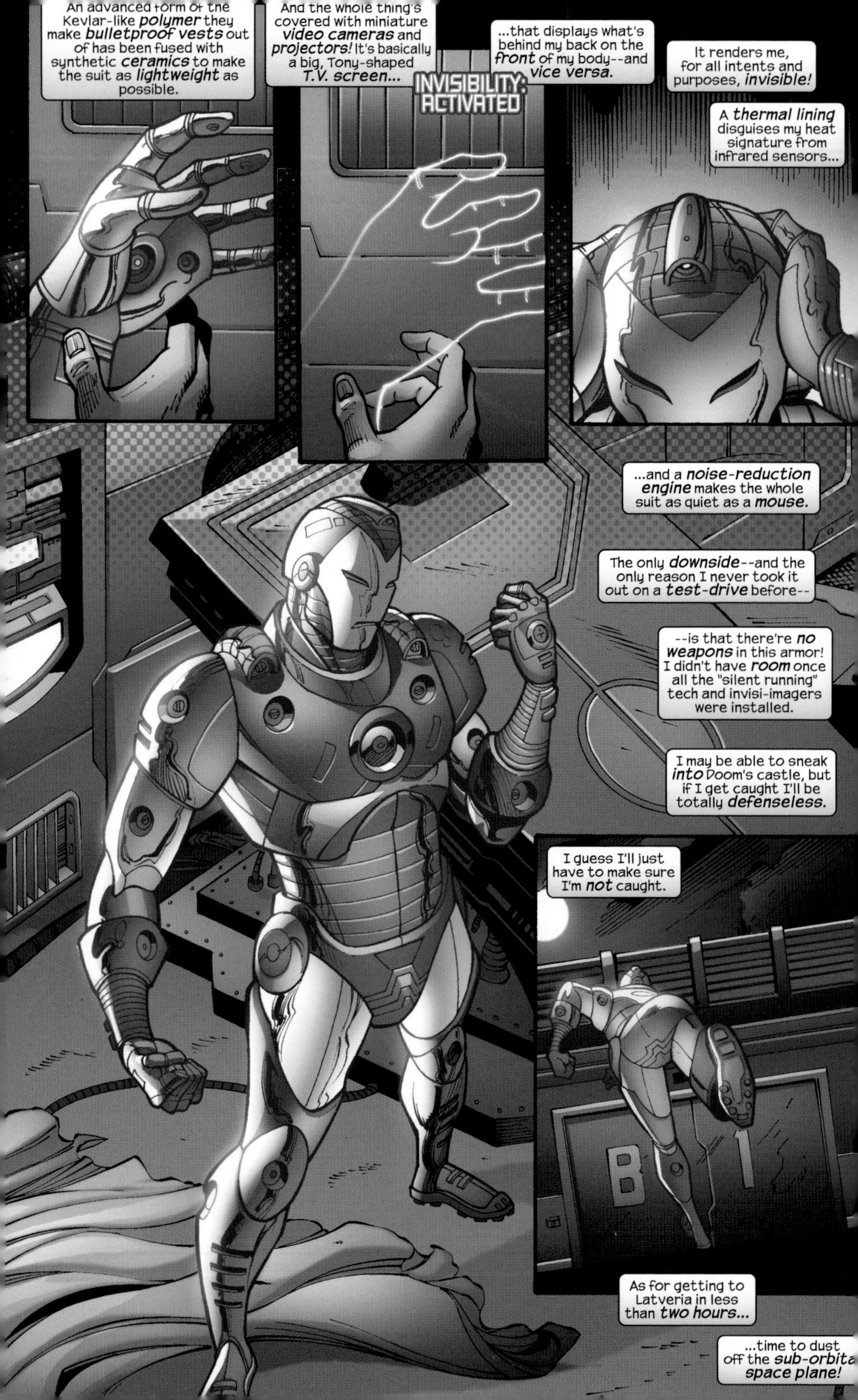

An advanced form of the Kevlar-like polymer they make bulletproof vests out of has been fused with synthetic ceramics to make the suit as lightweight as possible.
And the whole thing's covered with miniature video cameras and projectors! It's basically a big, Tony-shaped T.V. screen...
INVISIBILITY: ACTIVATED
...that displays what's behind my back on the front of my body--and vice versa.
It renders me, for all intents and purposes, invisible!
A thermal lining disguises my heat signature from infrared sensors...
...and a noise-reduction engine makes the whole suit as quiet as a mouse.
The only downside--and the only reason I never took it out on a test-drive before--
--is that there're no weapons in this armor! I didn't have room once all the "silent running" tech and invisi-imagers were installed.
I may be able to sneak into Doom's castle, but if I get caught I'll be totally defenseless.
I guess I'll just have to make sure I'm not caught.
B 1
As for getting to Latveria in less than two hours...
...time to dust off the sub-orbita space plane!

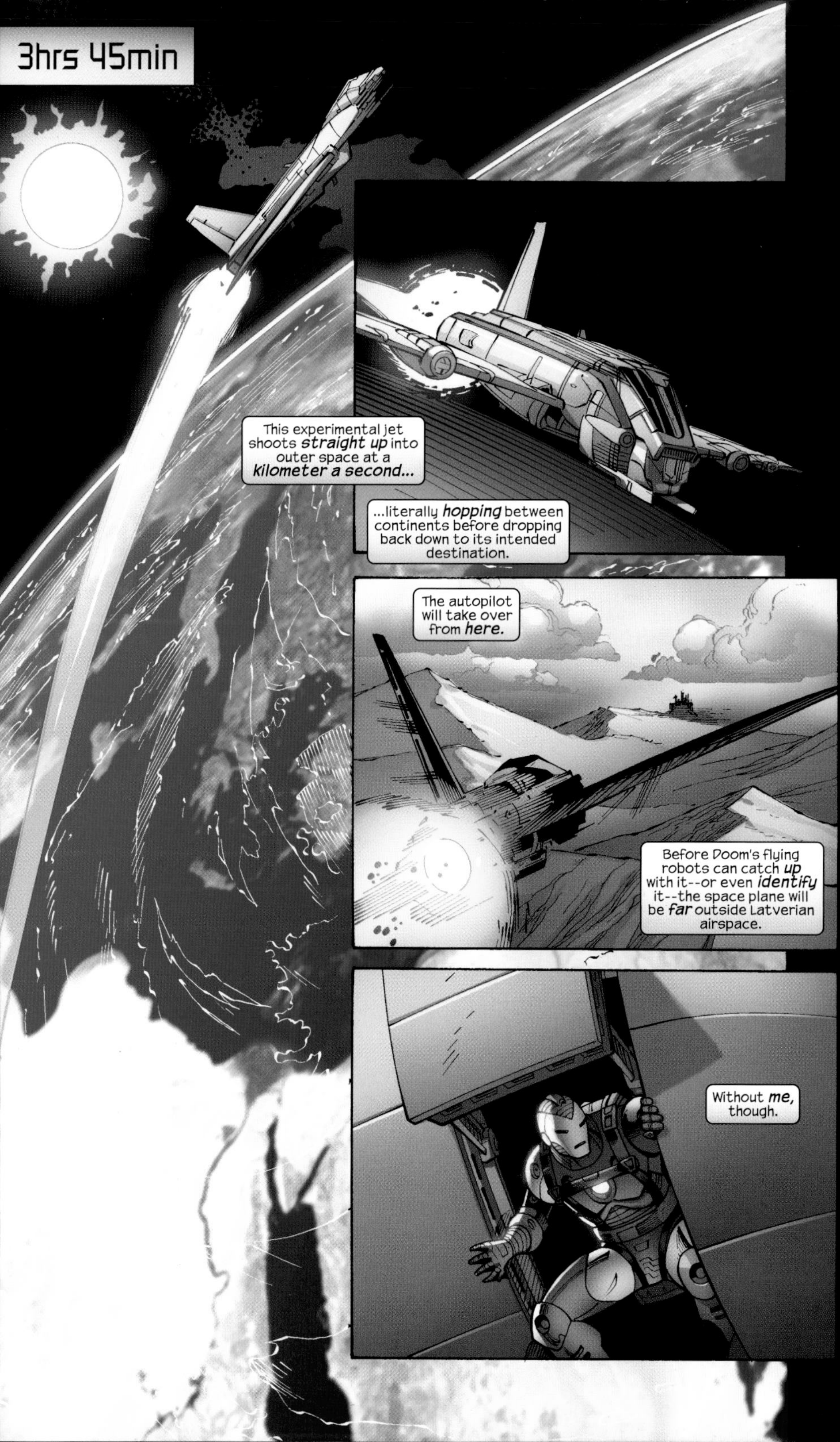
3hrs 45min
This experimental jet shoots straight up into outer space at a kilometer a second...
...literally hopping between continents before dropping back down to its intended destination.
The autopilot will take over from here.
Before Doom's flying robots can catch up with it--or even identify it--the space plane will be far outside Latverian airspace.
Without me, though.

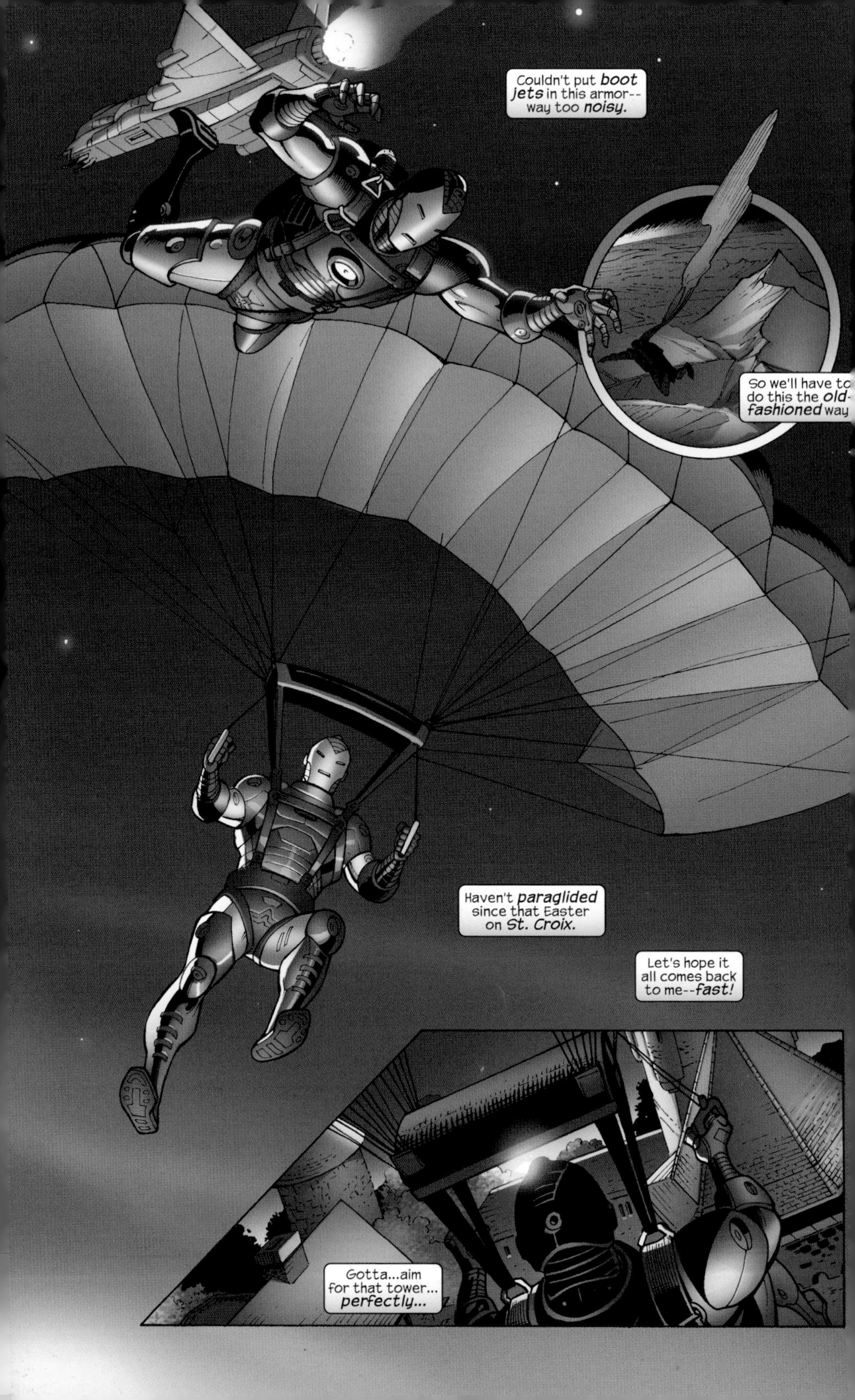
Couldn't put boot jets in this armor-- way too noisy.
So we'll have to do this the old-fashioned way
Haven't paraglided since that Easter on St. Croix.
Let's hope it all comes back to me--fast!
Gotta...aim for that tower... perfectly...

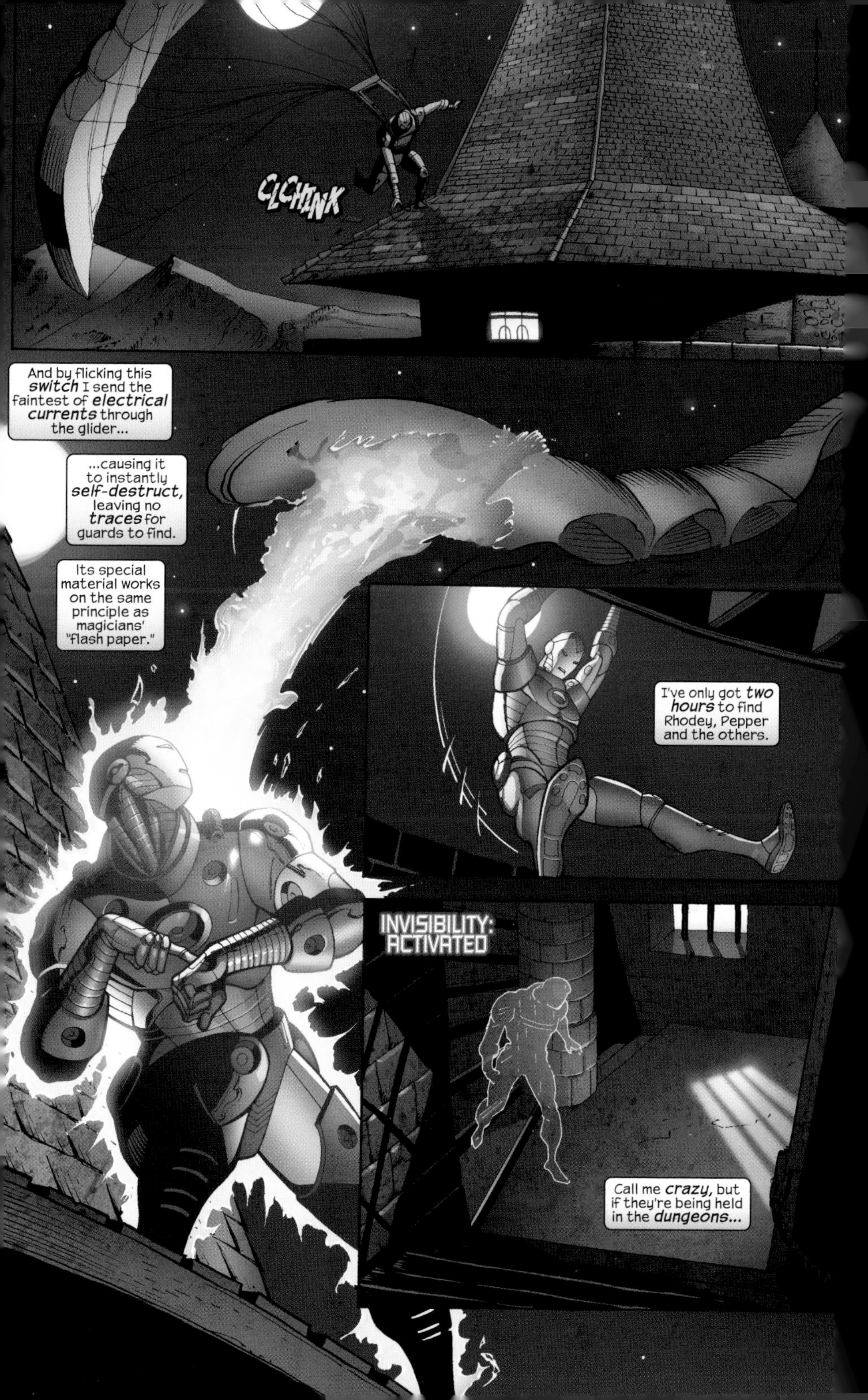
CLCHINK
And by flicking this switch I send the faintest of electrical currents through the glider...
...causing it to instantly self-destruct, leaving no traces for guards to find.
Its special material works on the same principle as magicians' "flash paper."
I've only got two hours to find Rhodey, Pepper and the others.
INVISIBILITY: ACTIVATED
Call me crazy, but if they're being held in the dungeons...

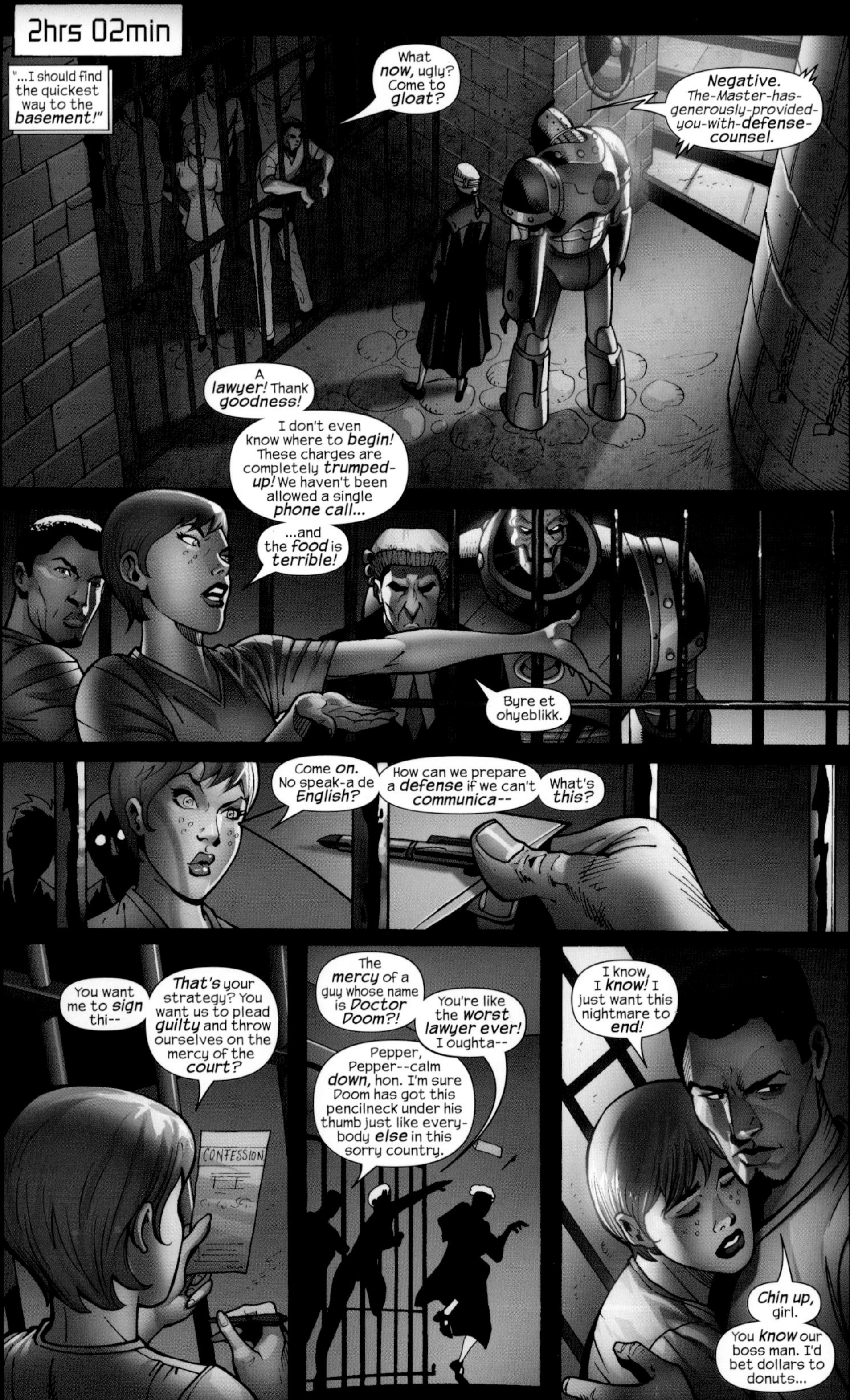
2hrs 02min
"...I should find the quickest way to the basement!"
What now, ugly? Come to gloat?
Negative. The-Master-has-generously-provided-you-with-defense-counsel.
A lawyer! Thank goodness!
I don't even know where to begin! These charges are completely trumped-up! We haven't been allowed a single phone call...
...and the food is terrible!
Byre et ohyeblikk.
Come on. No speak-a de English?
How can we prepare a defense if we can't communica--
What's this?
You want me to sign thi--
That's your strategy? You want us to plead guilty and throw ourselves on the mercy of the court?
CONFESSION
The mercy of a guy whose name is Doctor Doom?!
You're like the worst lawyer ever! I oughta--
Pepper, Pepper--calm down, hon. I'm sure Doom has got this pencilneck under his thumb just like every-body else in this sorry country.
I know, I know! I just want this nightmare to end!
Chin up, girl.
You know our boss man. I'd bet dollars to donuts...

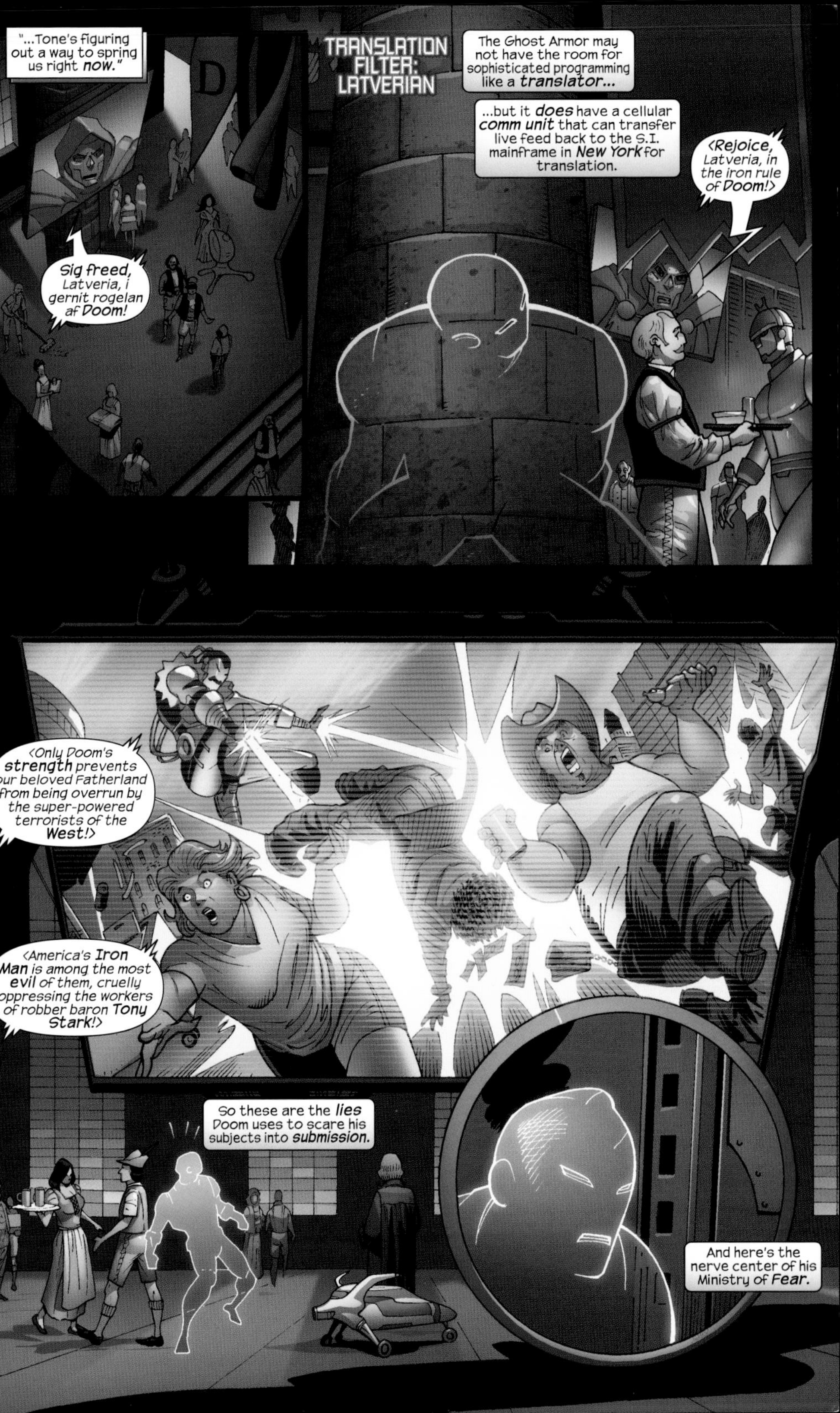

"...Tone's figuring out a way to spring us right now."
Sig freed, Latveria, i gernit rogelan af Doom!
TRANSLATION FILTER: LATVERIAN
The Ghost Armor may not have the room for sophisticated programming like a translator...
...but it does have a cellular comm unit that can transfer live feed back to the S.I. mainframe in New York for translation.
<Rejoice, Latveria, in the iron rule of Doom!>
<Only Doom's strength prevents our beloved Fatherland from being overrun by the super-powered terrorists of the West!>
<America's Iron Man is among the most evil of them, cruelly oppressing the workers of robber baron Tony Stark!>
So these are the lies Doom uses to scare his subjects into submission.
And here's the nerve center of his Ministry of Fear.

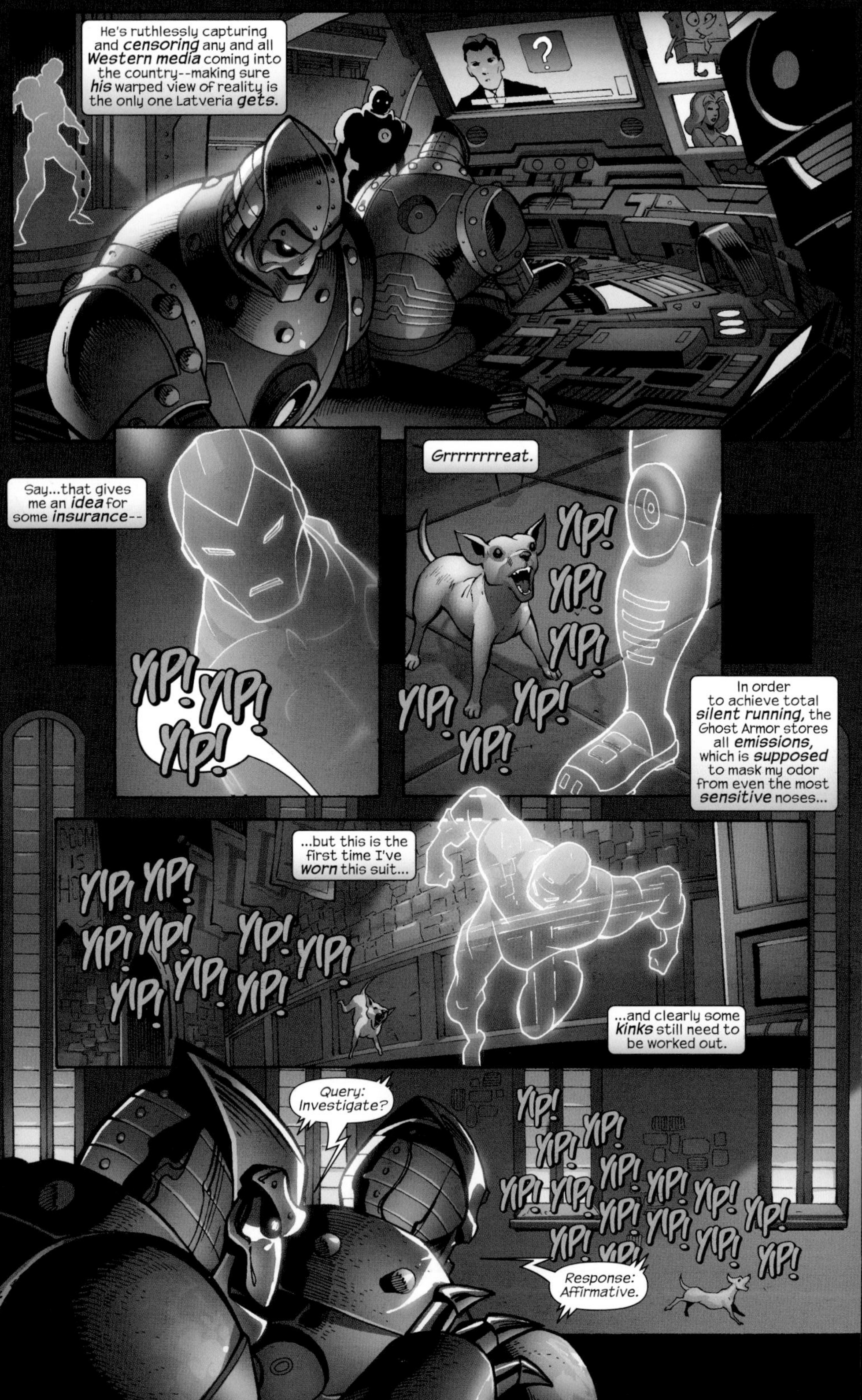
He's ruthlessly capturing and censoring any and all Western media coming into the country--making sure his warped view of reality is the only one Latveria gets.
Say...that gives me an idea for some insurance--
YIP! YIP! YIP!
Grrrrrrrreat.
YIP! YIP! YIP!
YIP! YIP! YIP!
In order to achieve total silent running, the Ghost Armor stores all emissions, which is supposed to mask my odor from even the most sensitive noses...
...but this is the first time I've worn this suit...
YIP! YIP! YIP! YIP! YIP! YIP! YIP! YIP! YIP!
...and clearly some kinks still need to be worked out.
Query: Investigate?
YIP! YIP! YIP! YIP! YIP! YIP! YIP! YIP! YIP! YIP! YIP! YIP! YIP! YIP! YIP!
Response: Affirmative.

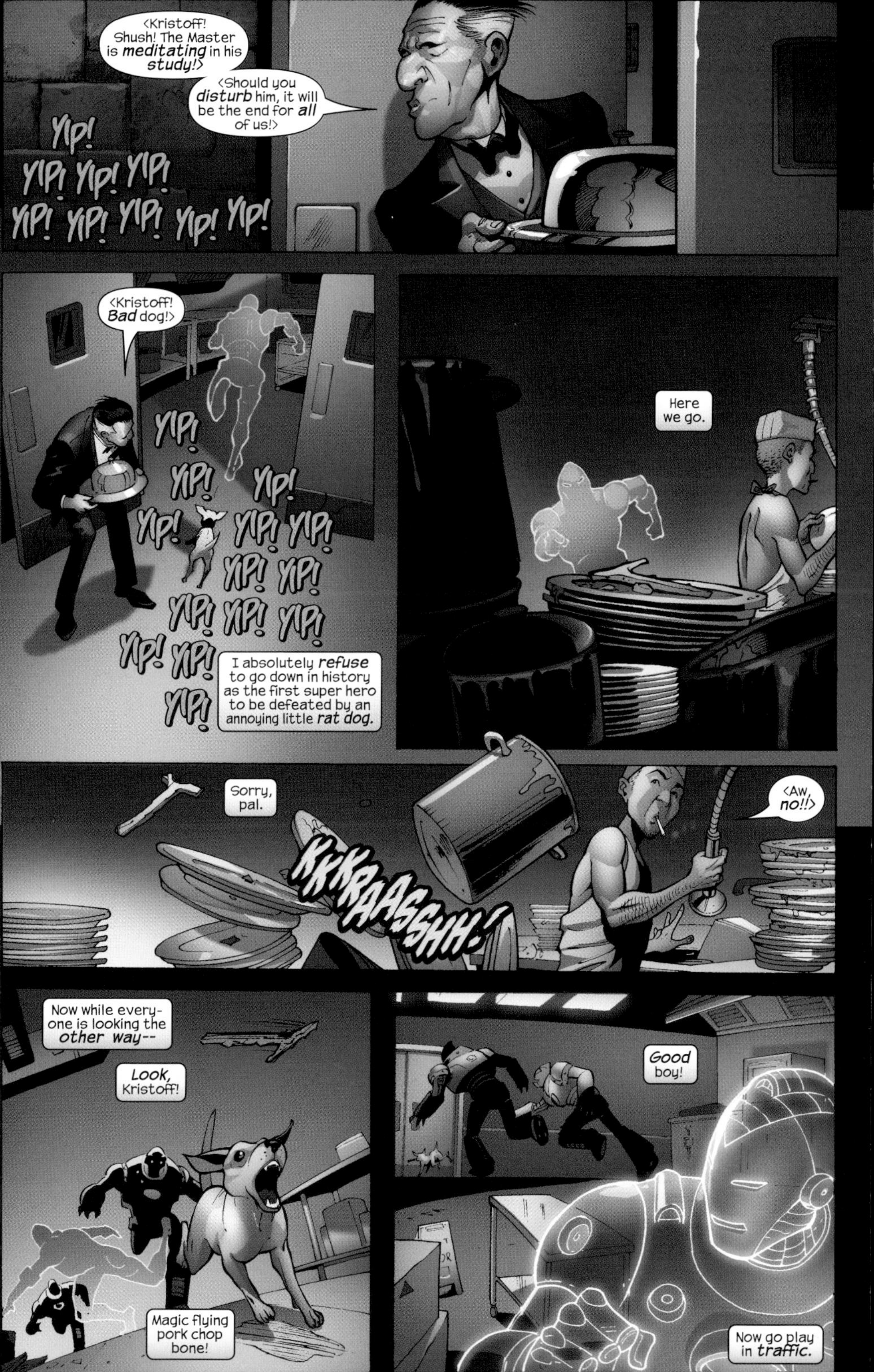

<Kristoff! Shush! The Master is *meditating* in his *study!*>
<Should you *disturb* him, it will be the end for *all* of us!>
YIP! YIP! YIP! YIP! YIP! YIP! YIP! YIP! YIP!
<Kristoff! *Bad* dog!>
YIP! YIP! YIP! YIP! YIP! YIP! YIP! YIP! YIP! YIP! YIP! YIP! YIP! YIP!
I absolutely *refuse* to go down in history as the first super hero to be defeated by an annoying little *rat dog.*
Here we go.
Sorry, pal.
KKKRAASSHH!
<Aw, *no!!*>
Now while every-one is looking the *other way--*
Look, Kristoff!
Magic flying pork chop bone!
Good boy!
Now go play in *traffic.*

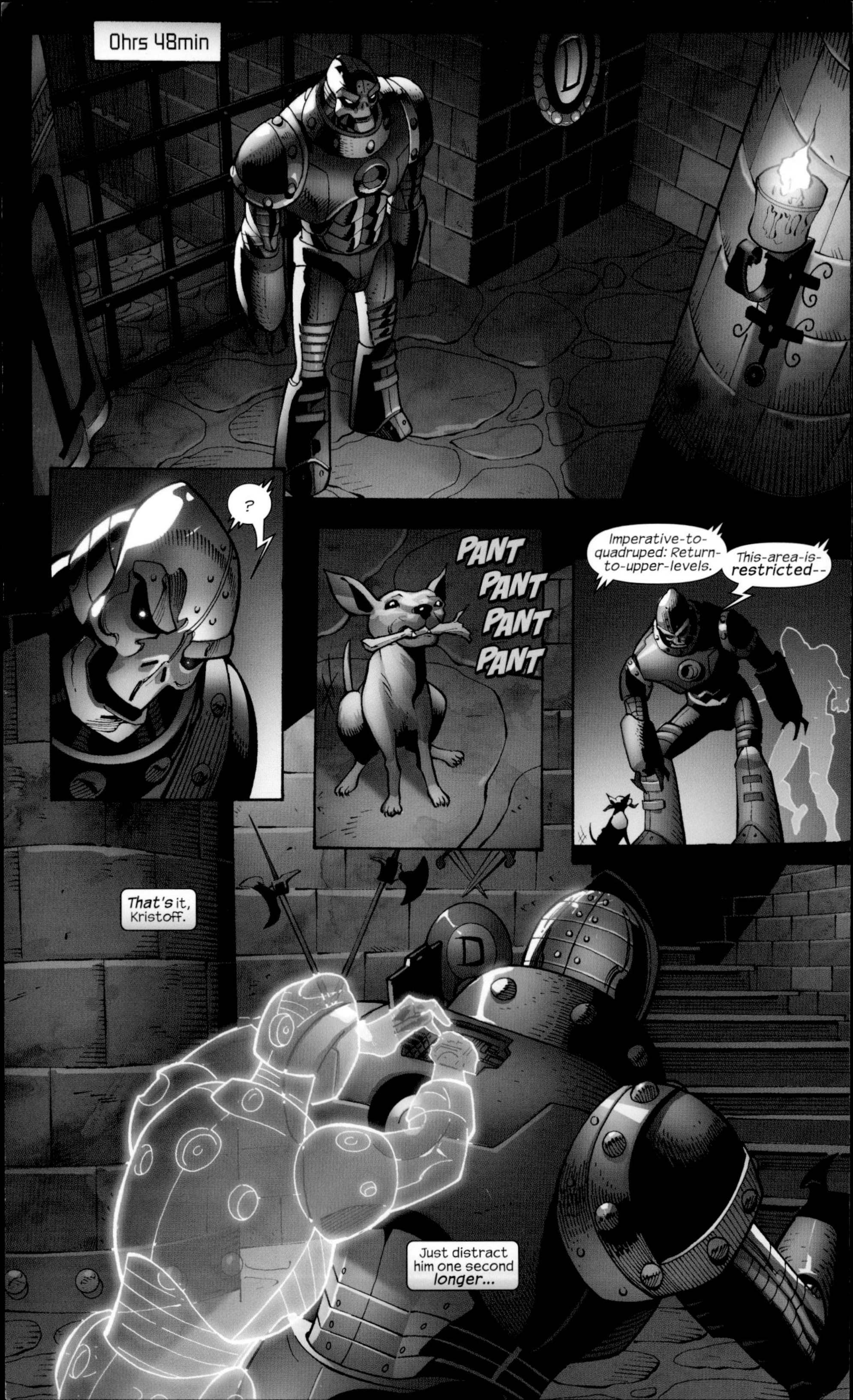
0hrs 48min
?
PANT PANT PANT PANT
Imperative-to-quadruped: Return-to-upper-levels.
This-area-is-restricted--
That's it, Kristoff.
Just distract him one second longer...

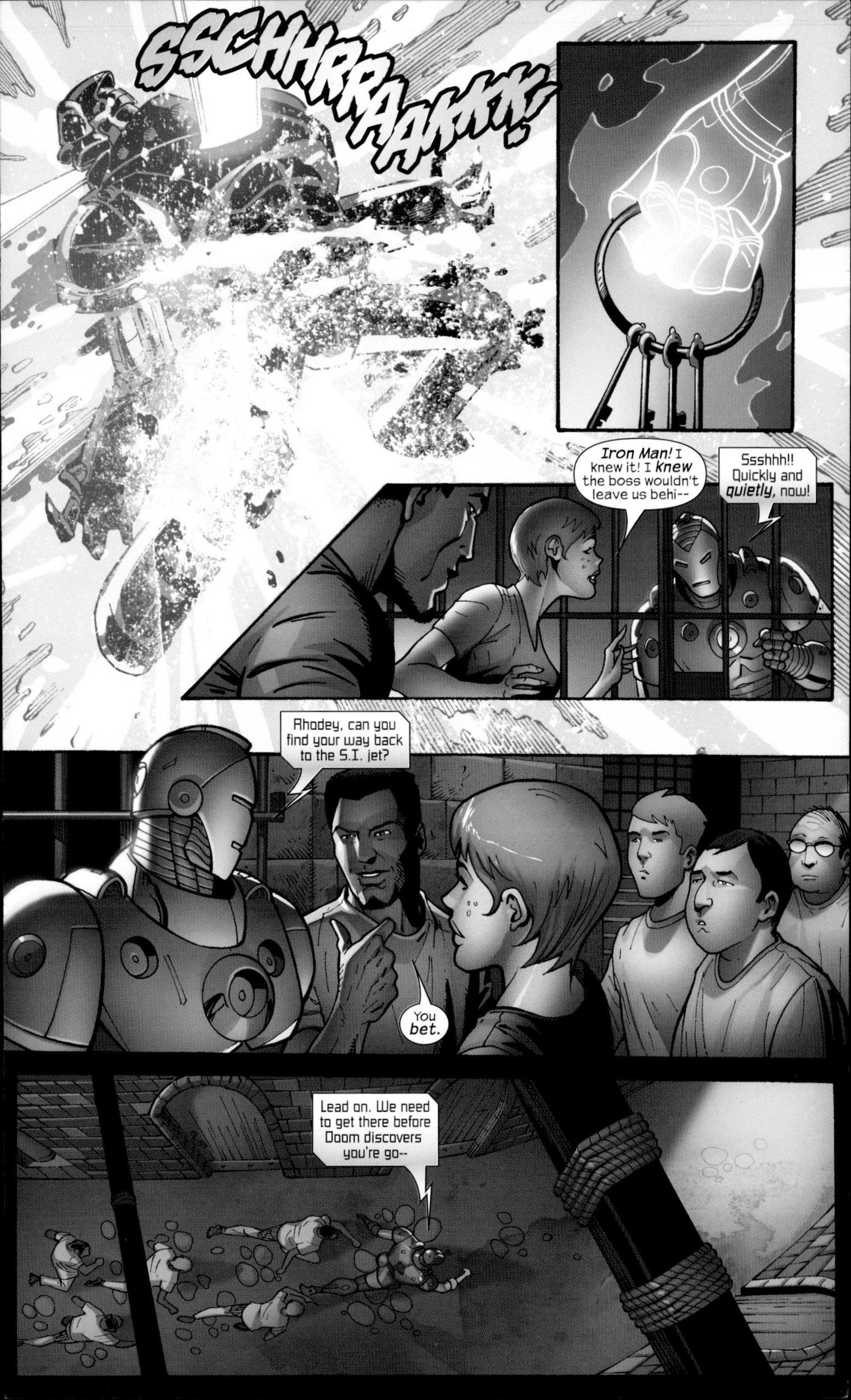
SSCHHRRAAKKK!
Iron Man! I knew it! I knew the boss wouldn't leave us behi--
Ssshhh!! Quickly and quietly, now!
Rhodey, can you find your way back to the S.I. jet?
You bet.
Lead on. We need to get there before Doom discovers you're go--

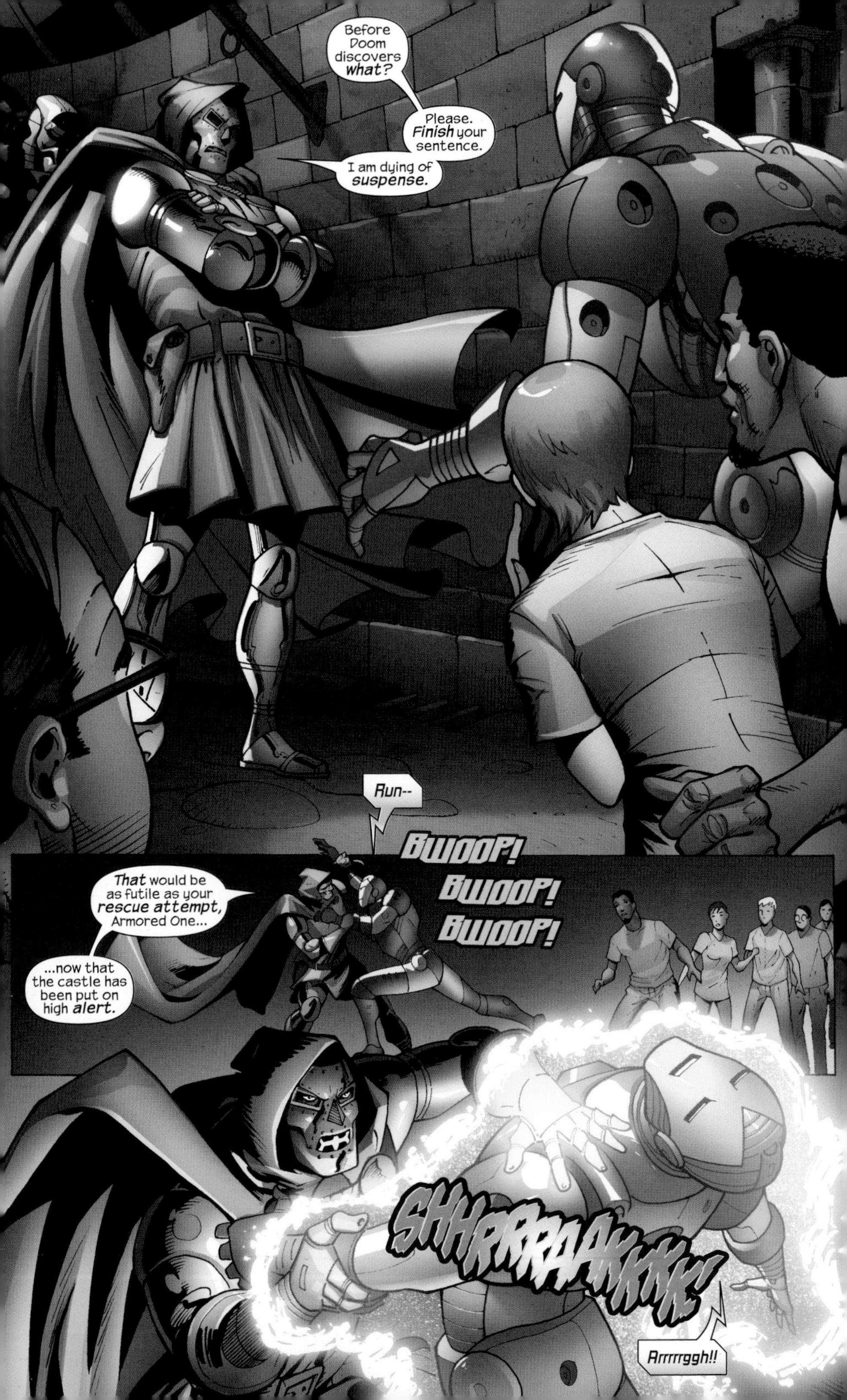
Before Doom discovers what?
Please. Finish your sentence.
I am dying of suspense.
Run--
BWOOP! BWOOP! BWOOP!
That would be as futile as your rescue attempt, Armored One...
...now that the castle has been put on high alert.
SHHRRRAAKKKK!
Arrrrrggh!!

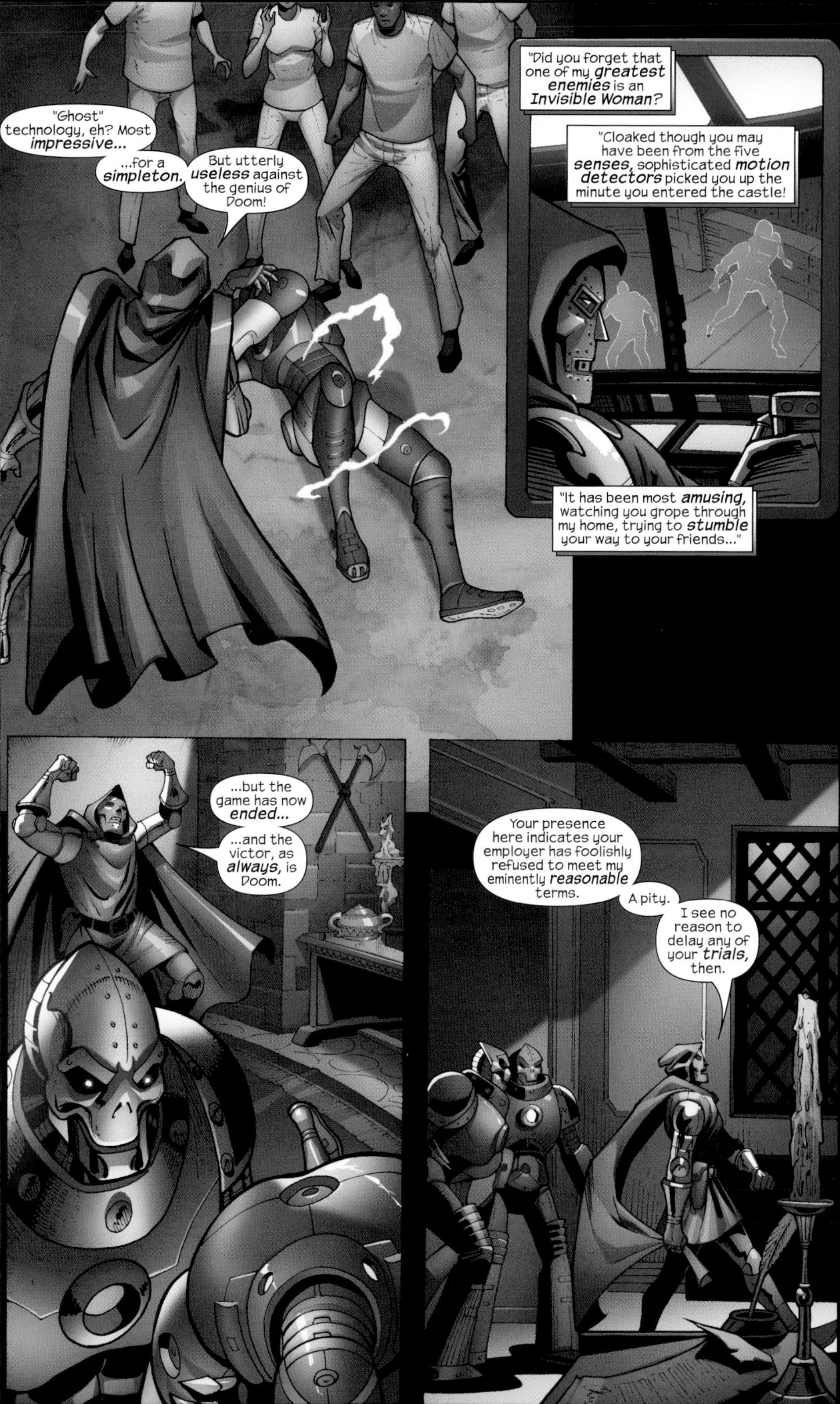

"Ghost" technology, eh? Most impressive...
...for a simpleton.
But utterly useless against the genius of Doom!
"Did you forget that one of my greatest enemies is an Invisible Woman?
"Cloaked though you may have been from the five senses, sophisticated motion detectors picked you up the minute you entered the castle!
"It has been most amusing, watching you grope through my home, trying to stumble your way to your friends..."
...but the game has now ended...
...and the victor, as always, is Doom.
Your presence here indicates your employer has foolishly refused to meet my eminently reasonable terms.
A pity.
I see no reason to delay any of your trials, then.

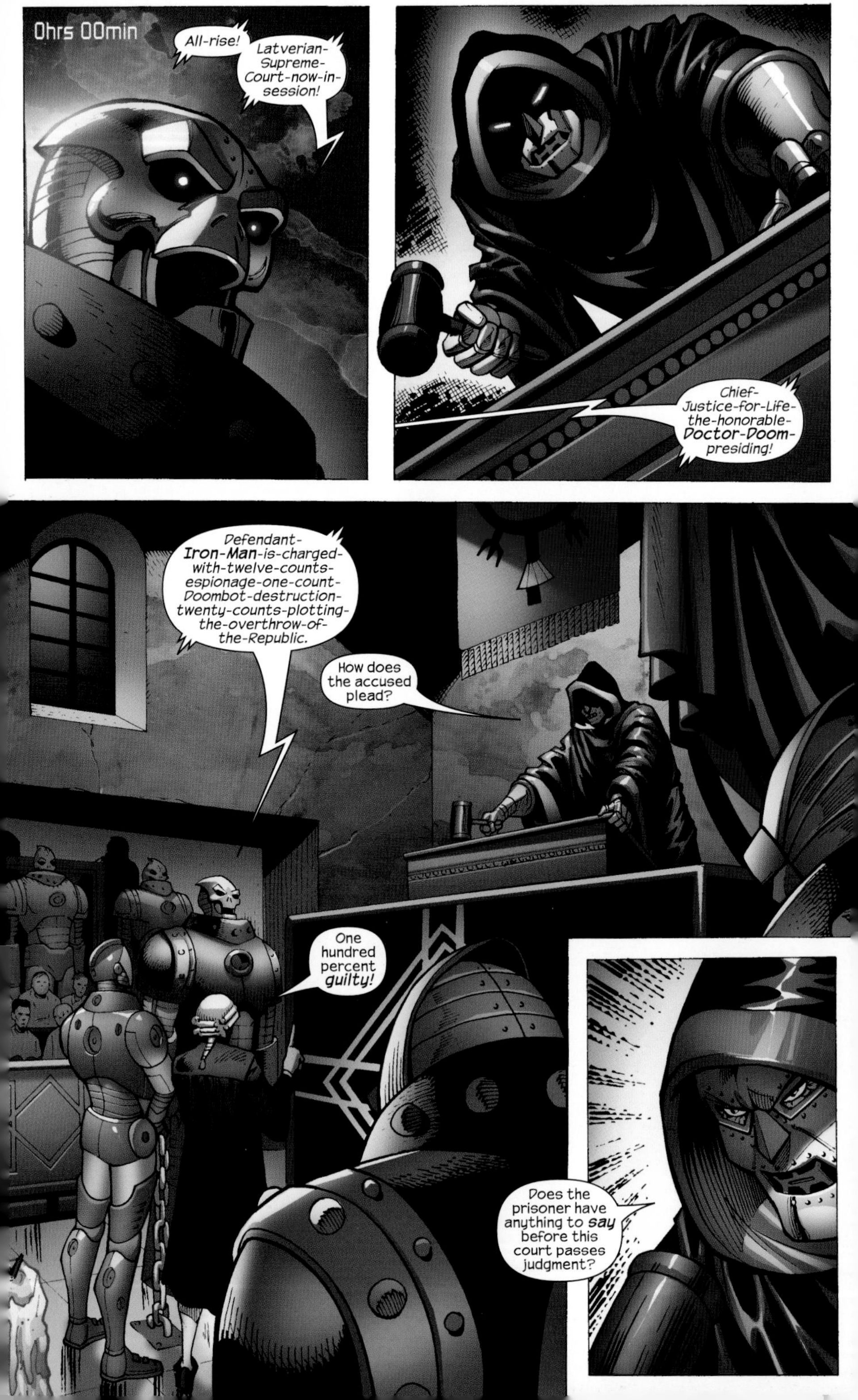
0hrs 00min
All-rise!
Latverian-Supreme-Court-now-in-session!
Chief-Justice-for-Life-the-honorable-Doctor-Doom-presiding!
Defendant-Iron-Man-is-charged-with-twelve-counts-espionage-one-count-Doombot-destruction-twenty-counts-plotting-the-overthrow-of-the-Republic.
How does the accused plead?
One hundred percent guilty!
Does the prisoner have anything to say before this court passes judgment?

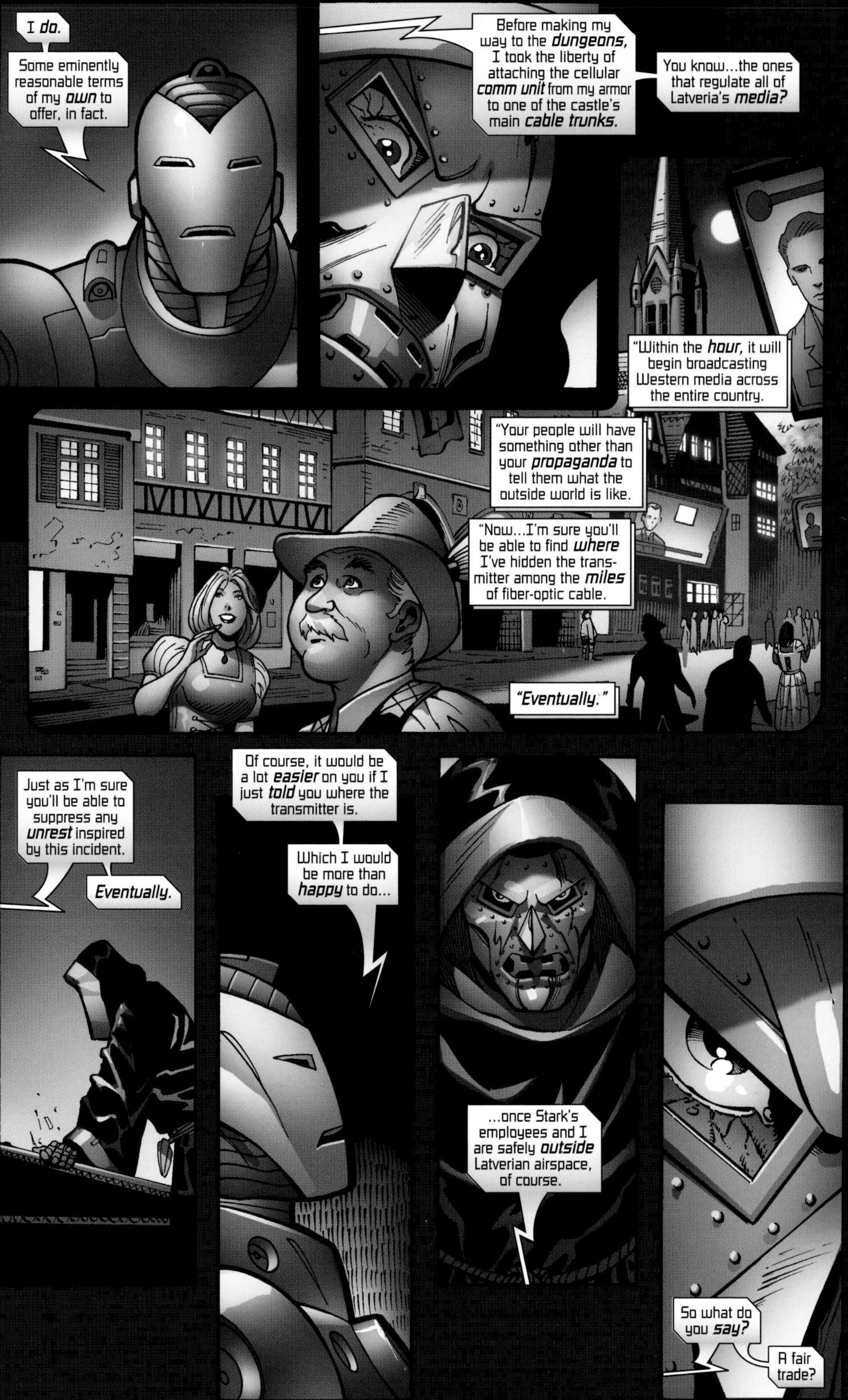
I do.
Some eminently reasonable terms of my own to offer, in fact.
Before making my way to the dungeons, I took the liberty of attaching the cellular comm unit from my armor to one of the castle's main cable trunks.
You know...the ones that regulate all of Latveria's media?
"Within the hour, it will begin broadcasting Western media across the entire country.
"Your people will have something other than your propaganda to tell them what the outside world is like.
"Now...I'm sure you'll be able to find where I've hidden the transmitter among the miles of fiber-optic cable.
"Eventually."
Just as I'm sure you'll be able to suppress any unrest inspired by this incident.
Eventually.
Of course, it would be a lot easier on you if I just told you where the transmitter is.
Which I would be more than happy to do...
...once Stark's employees and I are safely outside Latverian airspace, of course.
So what do you say?
A fair trade?

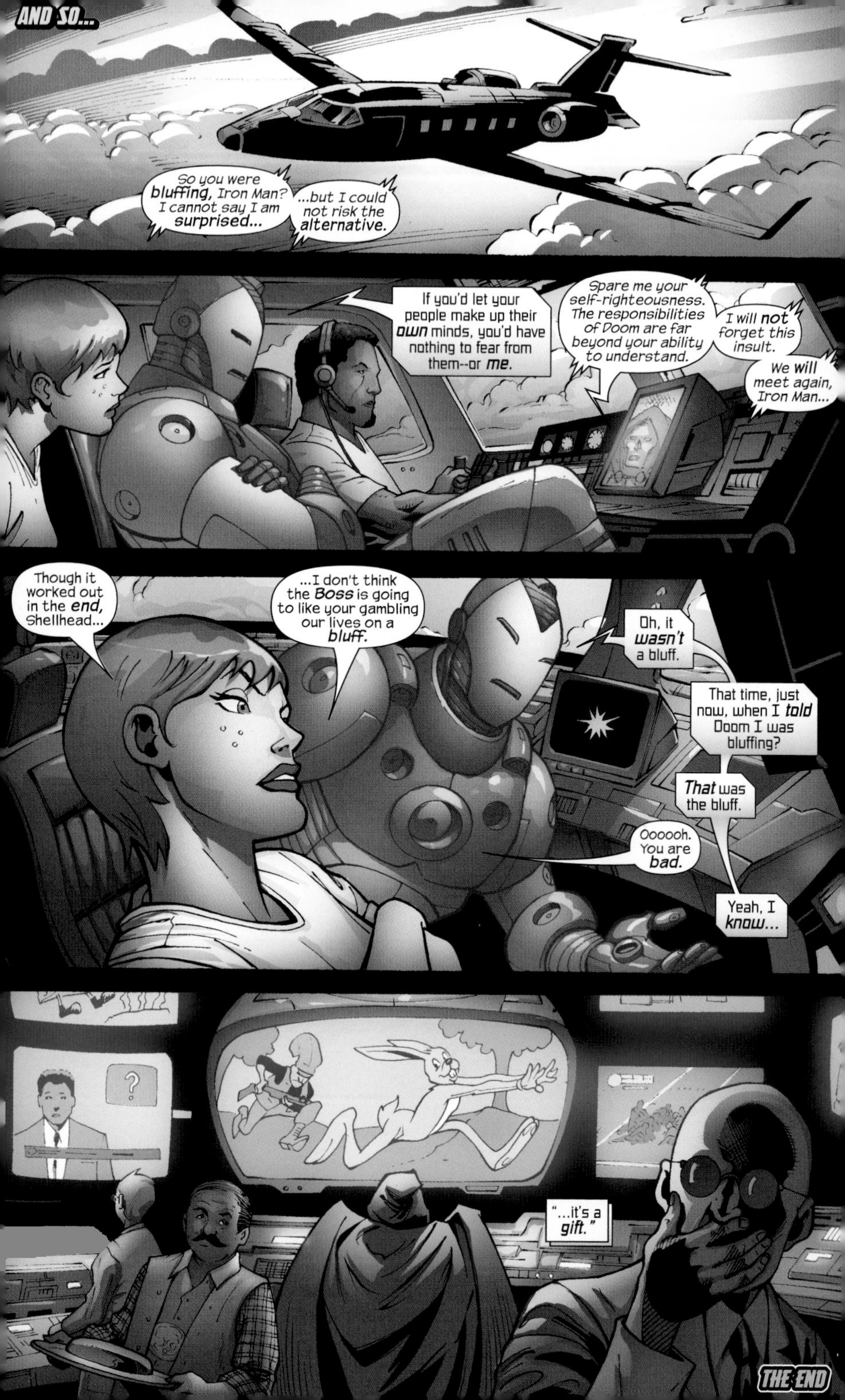
AND SO...
So you were bluffing, Iron Man? I cannot say I am surprised...
...but I could not risk the alternative.
If you'd let your people make up their own minds, you'd have nothing to fear from them--or me.
Spare me your self-righteousness. The responsibilities of Doom are far beyond your ability to understand.
I will not forget this insult.
We will meet again, Iron Man...
Though it worked out in the end, Shellhead...
...I don't think the Boss is going to like your gambling our lives on a bluff.
Oh, it wasn't a bluff.
That time, just now, when I told Doom I was bluffing?
That was the bluff.
Oooooh. You are bad.
Yeah, I know...
"...it's a gift."
THE END

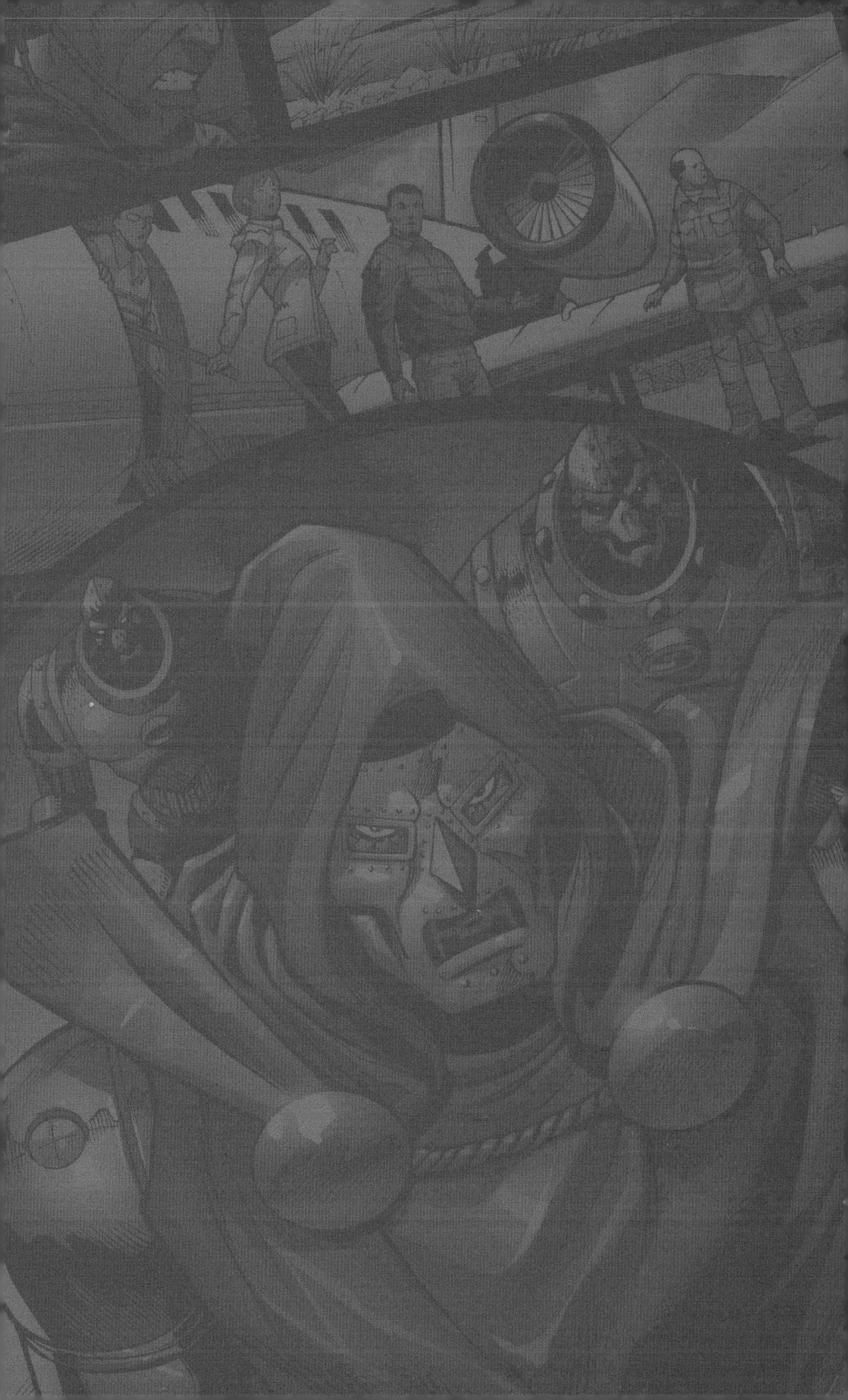

08

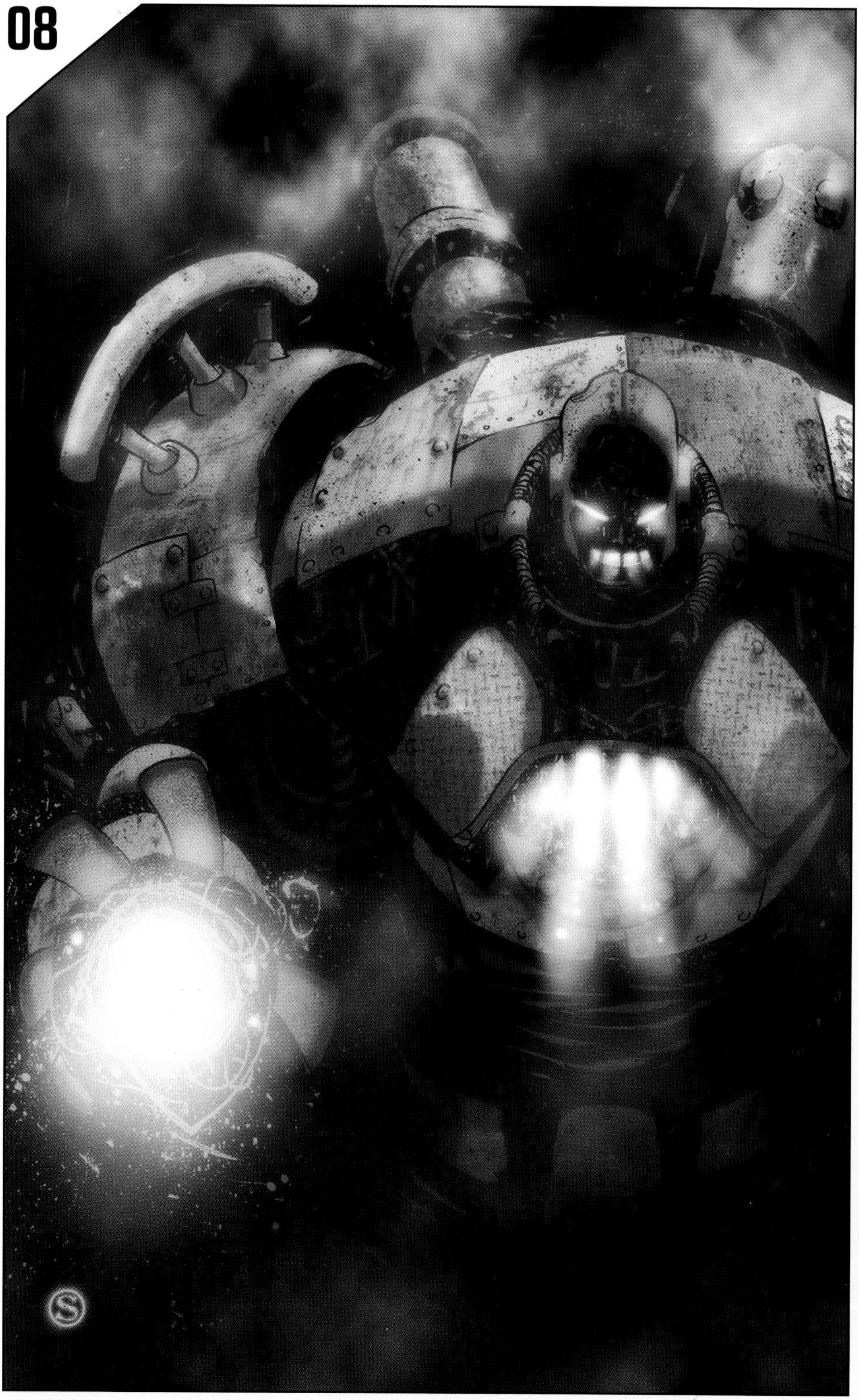

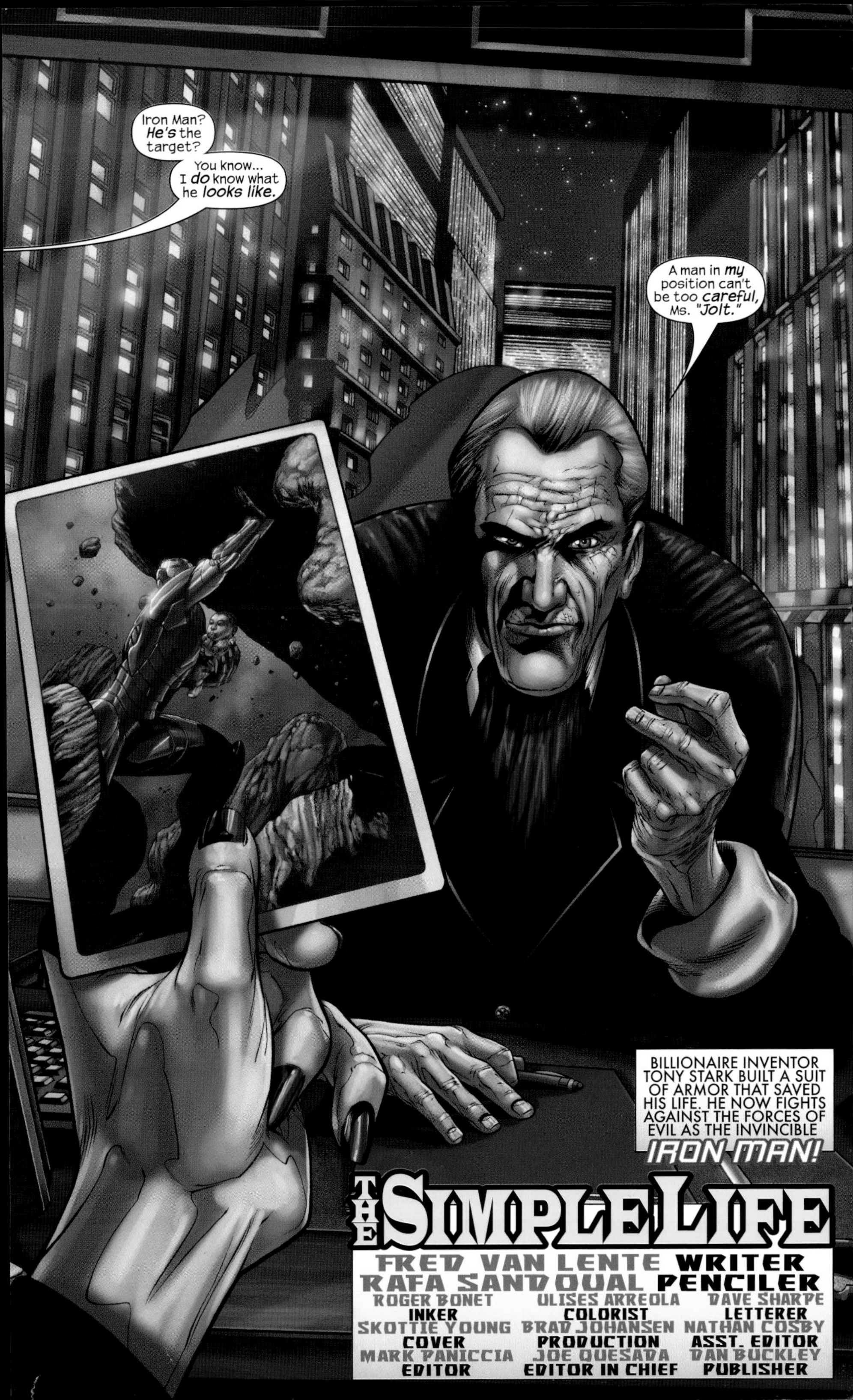

Iron Man? He's the target?
You know... I do know what he looks like.
A man in my position can't be too careful, Ms. "Jolt."
BILLIONAIRE INVENTOR TONY STARK BUILT A SUIT OF ARMOR THAT SAVED HIS LIFE. HE NOW FIGHTS AGAINST THE FORCES OF EVIL AS THE INVINCIBLE IRON MAN!
THE SIMPLE LIFE
FRED VAN LENTE WRITER
RAFA SANDOVAL PENCILER
ROGER BONET INKER
ULISES ARREOLA COLORIST
DAVE SHARPE LETTERER
SKOTTIE YOUNG COVER
BRAD JOHANSEN PRODUCTION
NATHAN COSBY ASST. EDITOR
MARK PANICCIA EDITOR
JOE QUESADA EDITOR IN CHIEF
DAN BUCKLEY PUBLISHER

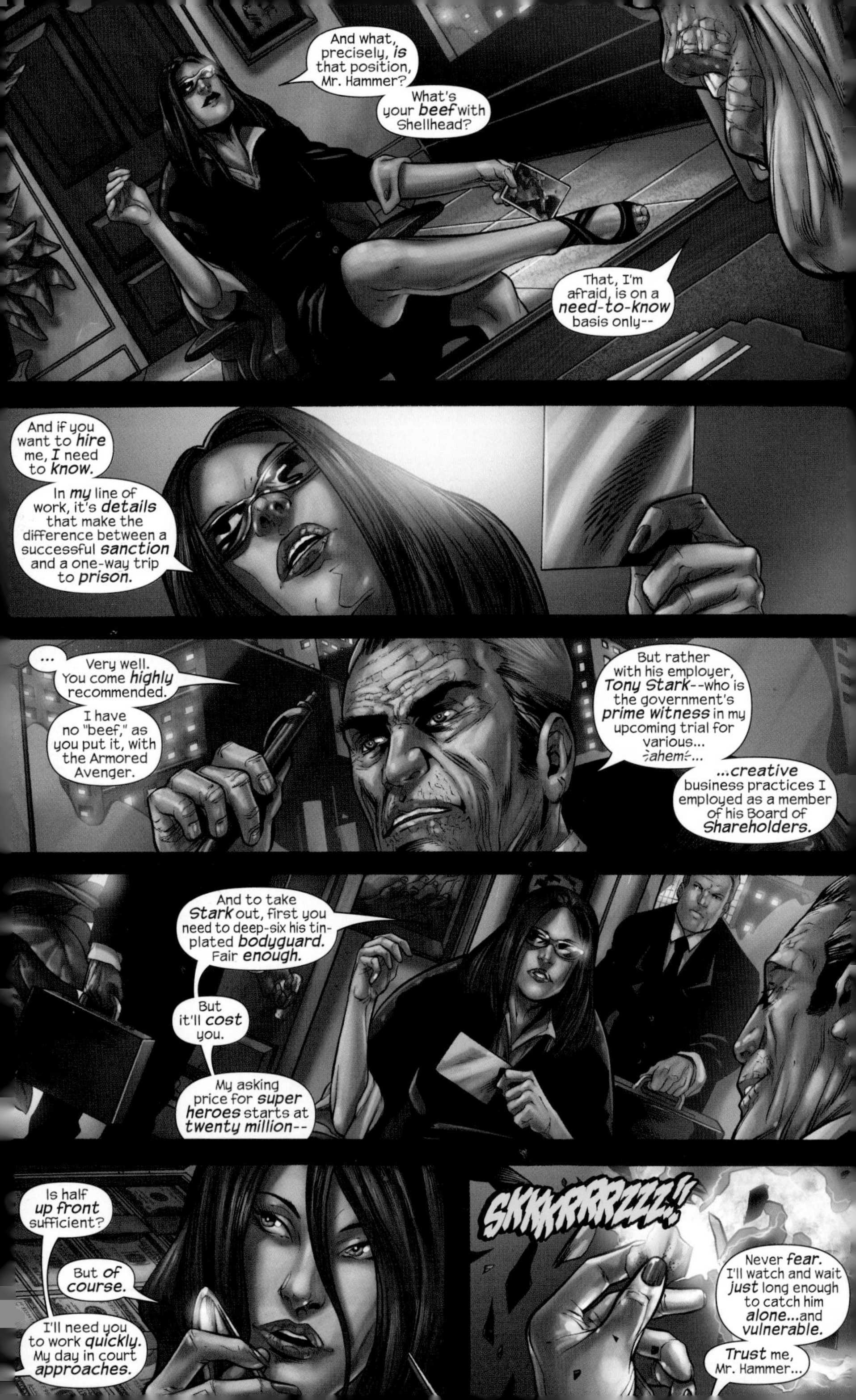

And what, precisely, *is* that position, Mr. Hammer?
What's your *beef* with Shellhead?
That, I'm afraid, is on a *need-to-know* basis only--
And if you want to *hire* me, *I* need to *know.*
In *my* line of work, it's *details* that make the difference between a successful *sanction* and a one-way trip to *prison.*
... Very well. You come *highly* recommended.
I have no "beef," as you put it, with the Armored Avenger.
But rather with his employer, *Tony Stark*--who is the government's *prime witness* in my upcoming trial for various... *ahem*...
...*creative* business practices I employed as a member of his Board of *Shareholders.*
And to take *Stark* out, first you need to deep-six his tin-plated *bodyguard.* Fair *enough.*
But it'll *cost* you.
My asking price for *super heroes* starts at *twenty million*--
Is half *up front* sufficient?
But *of course.*
I'll need you to work *quickly.* My day in court *approaches.*
SKKKRRRZZZ!!
Never *fear.* I'll watch and wait *just* long enough to catch him *alone*...and *vulnerable.*
Trust me, Mr. Hammer...

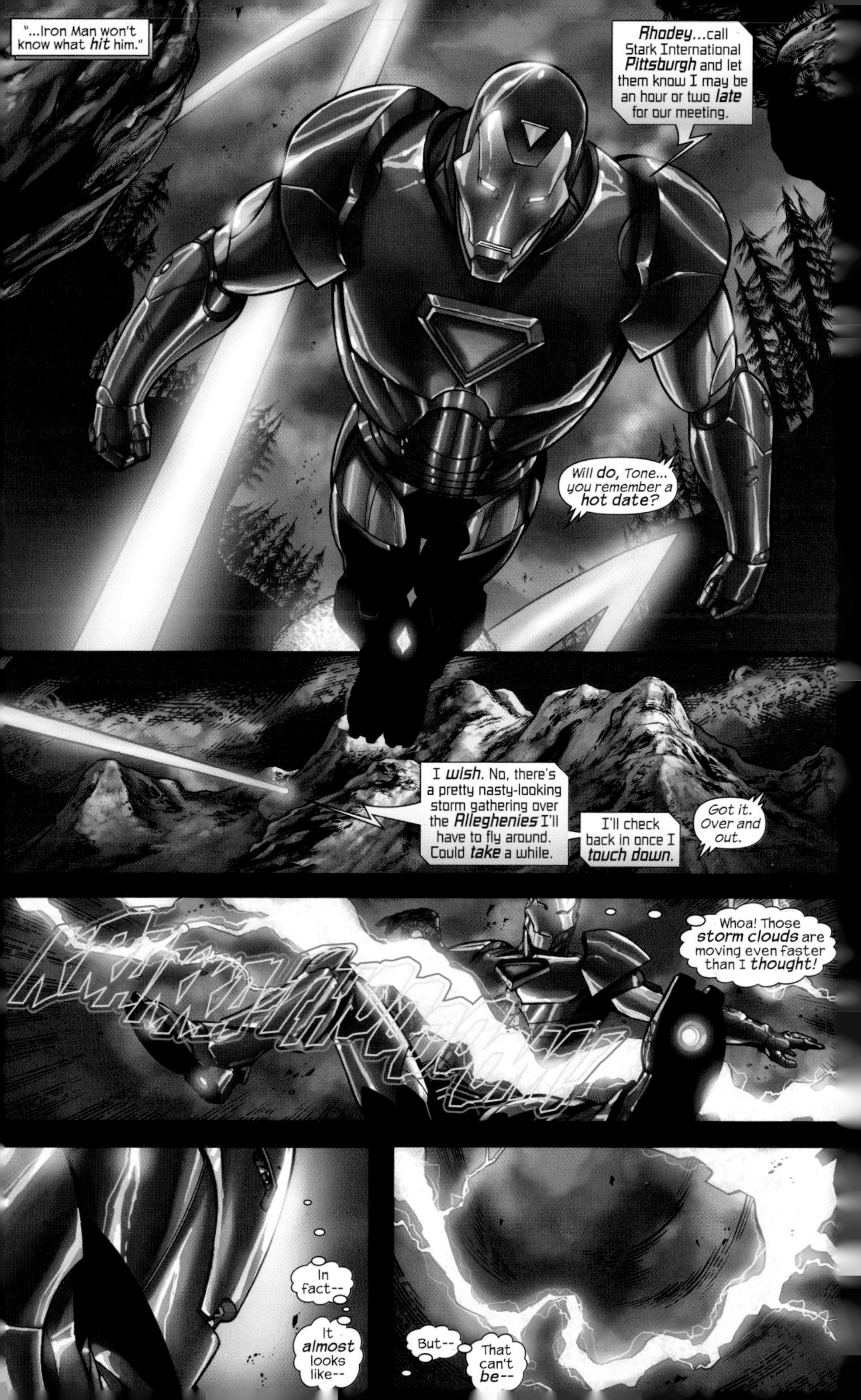
"...Iron Man won't know what *hit* him."
Rhodey...call Stark International *Pittsburgh* and let them know I may be an hour or two *late* for our meeting.
Will *do*, Tone... you remember a *hot date*?
I *wish*. No, there's a pretty nasty-looking storm gathering over the *Alleghenies* I'll have to fly around. Could *take* a while.
I'll check back in once I *touch down*.
Got it. Over and out.
Whoa! Those *storm clouds* are moving even faster than I *thought*!
In fact--
It *almost* looks like--
But--
That can't *be*--

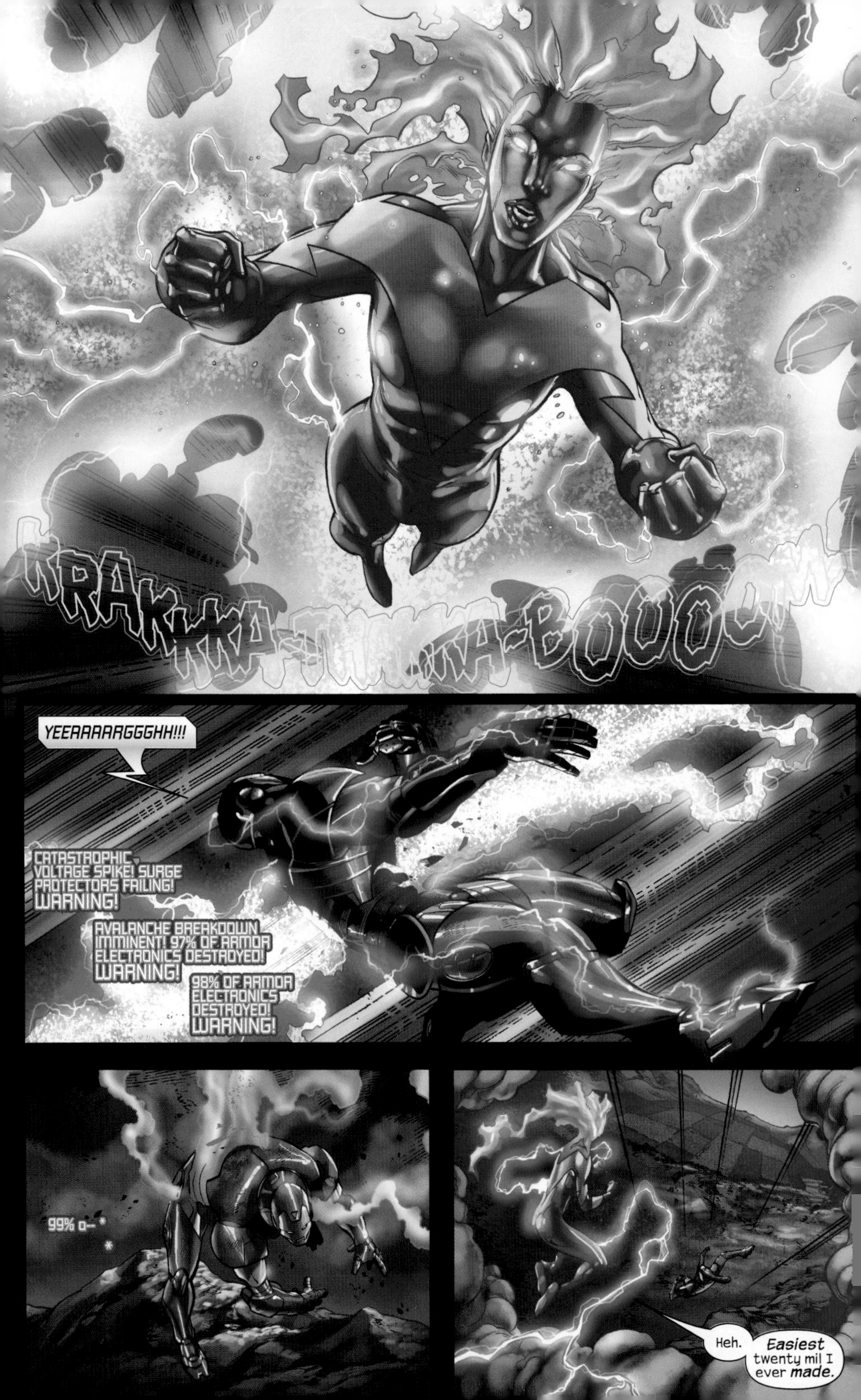
YEEAAAARGGGHH!!!
CATASTROPHIC VOLTAGE SPIKE! SURGE PROTECTORS FAILING! WARNING!
AVALANCHE BREAKDOWN IMMINENT! 97% OF ARMOR ELECTRONICS DESTROYED! WARNING!
98% OF ARMOR ELECTRONICS DESTROYED! WARNING!
99% o--
Heh.
Easiest twenty mil I ever made.

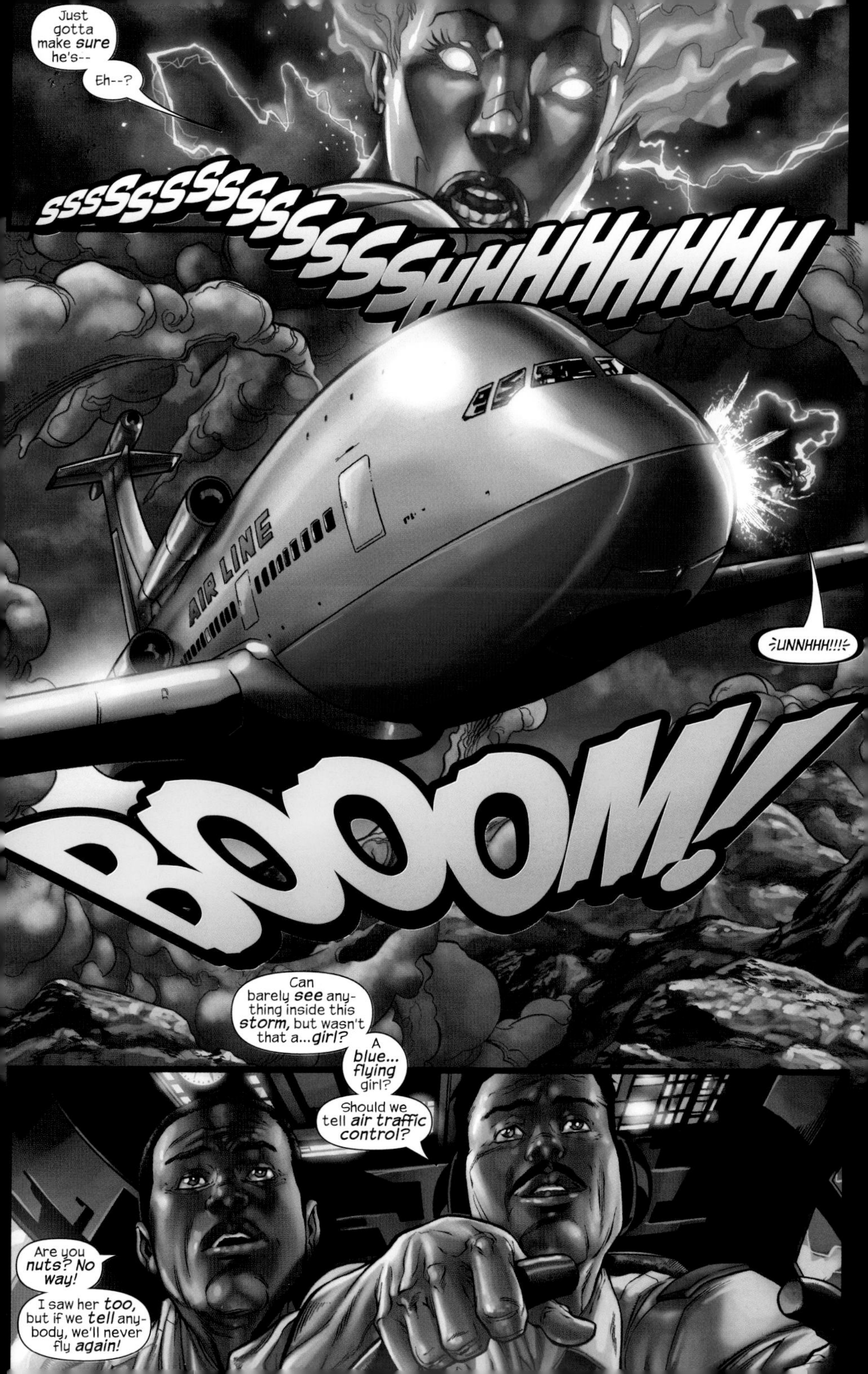
Just gotta make sure he's--
Eh--?
SSSSSSSSSSSSSHHHHHHHHH
AIR LINE
UNNHHH!!!
BOOOM!
Can barely see anything inside this storm, but wasn't that a...girl?
A blue... flying girl?
Should we tell air traffic control?
Are you nuts? No way!
I saw her too, but if we tell anybody, we'll never fly again!

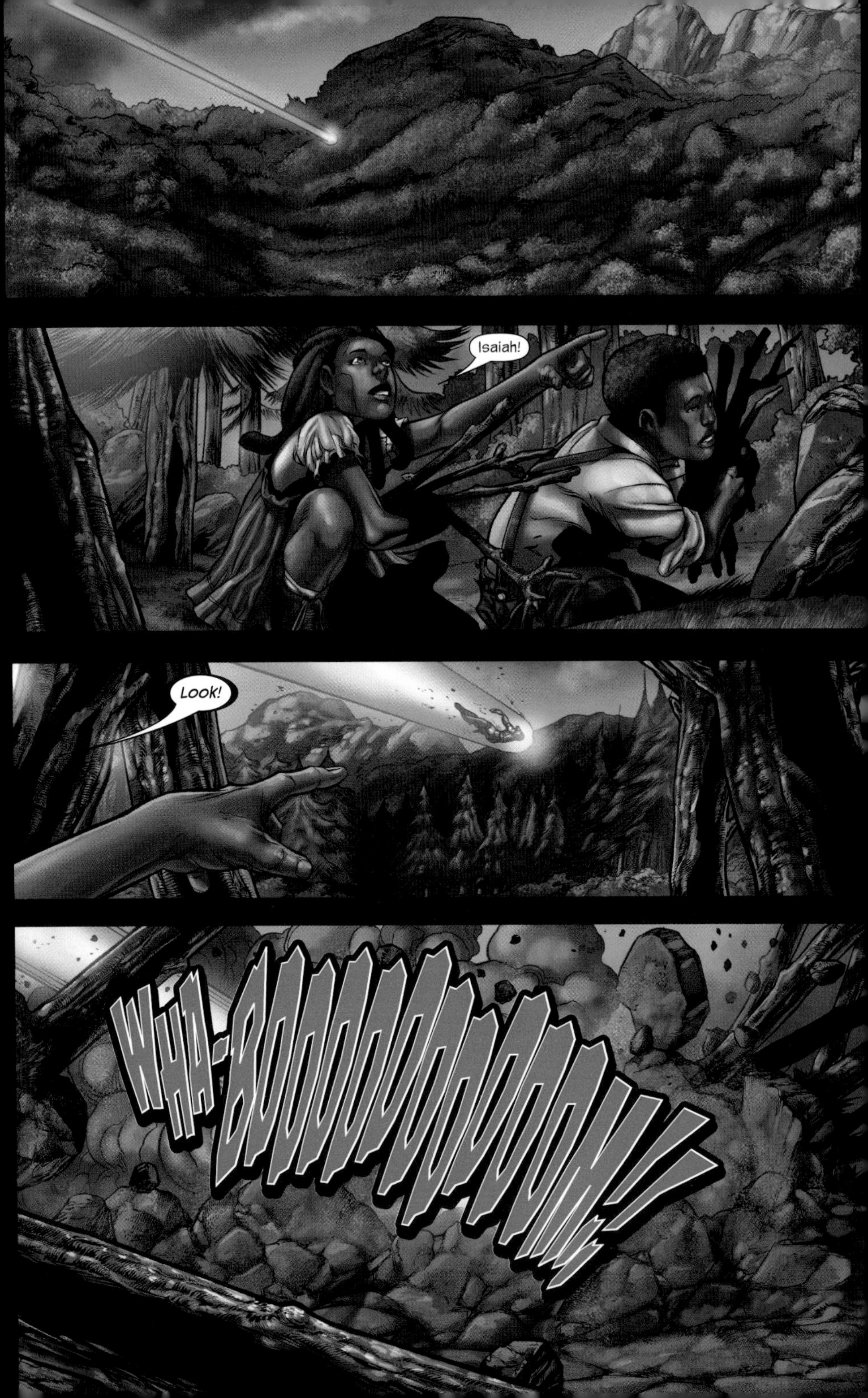
Isaiah!
Look!
WHA-BOOOOOOOOOOOM!!

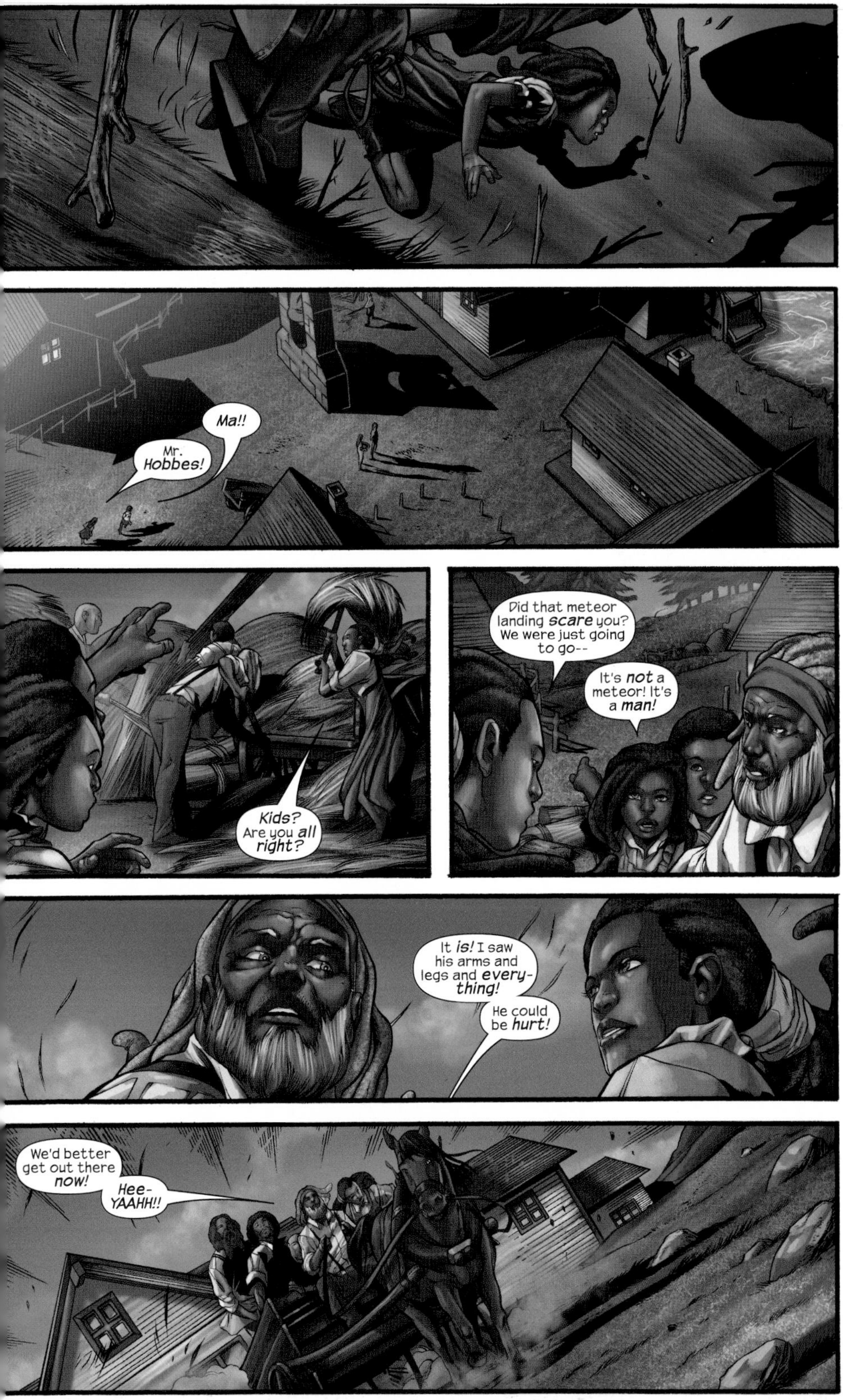
Ma!!
Mr. Hobbes!
Kids? Are you all right?
Did that meteor landing scare you? We were just going to go--
It's not a meteor! It's a man!
It is! I saw his arms and legs and everything!
He could be hurt!
We'd better get out there now!
Hee-YAAHH!!

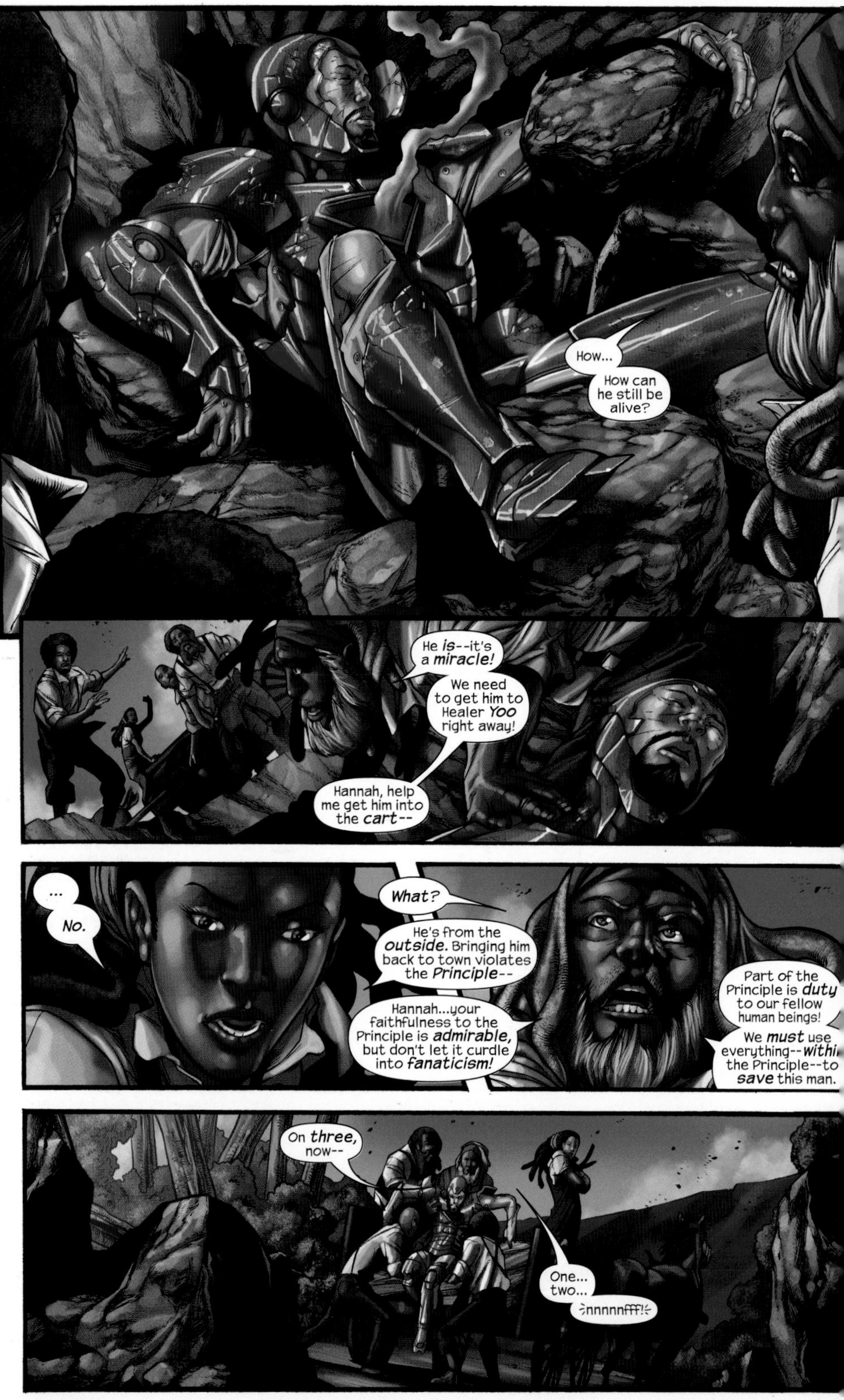

How...
How can he still be alive?
He is--it's a miracle!
We need to get him to Healer Yoo right away!
Hannah, help me get him into the cart--
...
No.
What?
He's from the outside. Bringing him back to town violates the Principle--
Hannah...your faithfulness to the Principle is admirable, but don't let it curdle into fanaticism!
Part of the Principle is duty to our fellow human beings!
We must use everything--withi the Principle--to save this man.
On three, now--
One... two...
nnnnnfff!

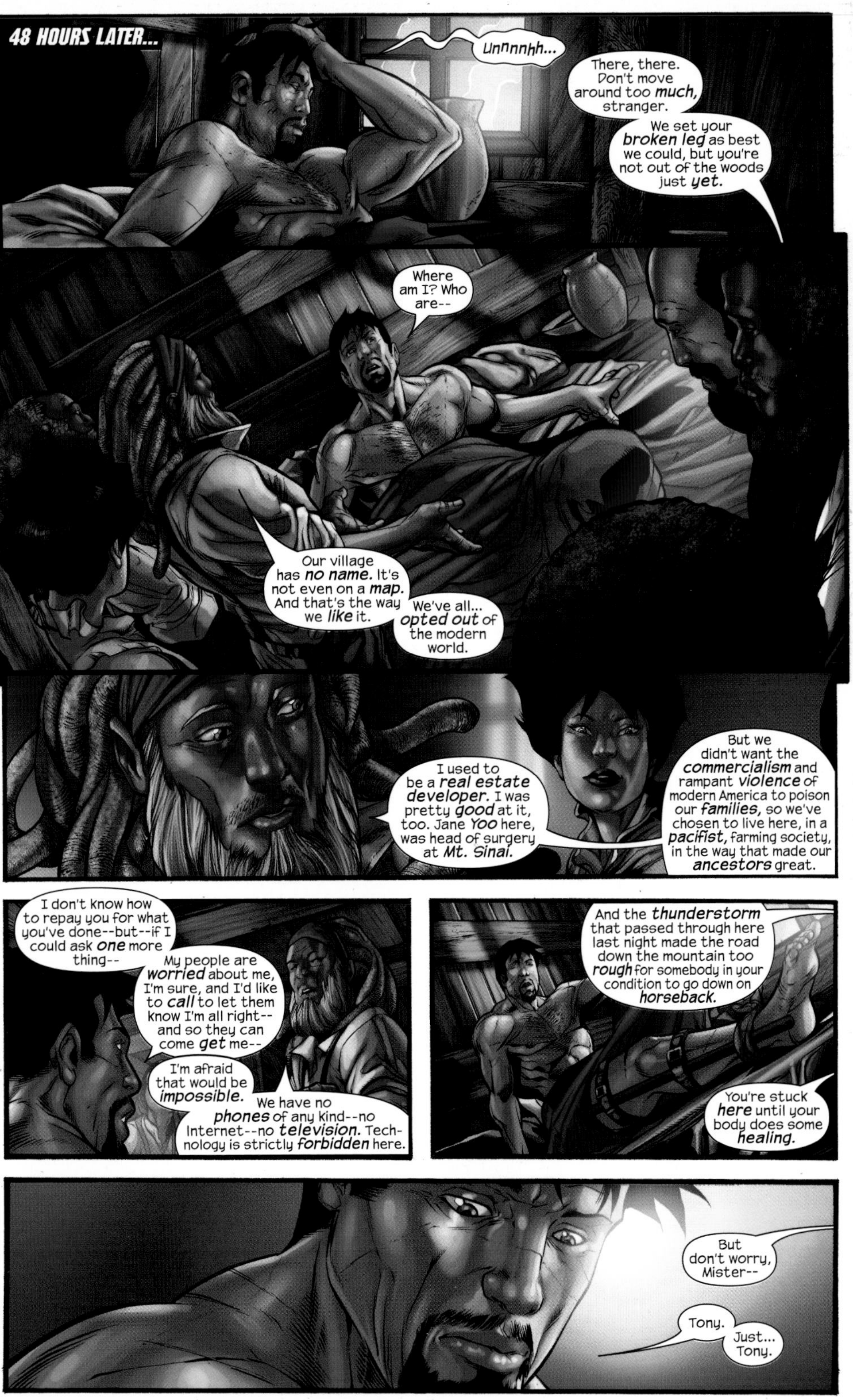

48 HOURS LATER...
Unnnnhh...
There, there. Don't move around too much, stranger.
We set your broken leg as best we could, but you're not out of the woods just yet.
Where am I? Who are--
Our village has no name. It's not even on a map. And that's the way we like it.
We've all... opted out of the modern world.
I used to be a real estate developer. I was pretty good at it, too. Jane Yoo here, was head of surgery at Mt. Sinai.
But we didn't want the commercialism and rampant violence of modern America to poison our families, so we've chosen to live here, in a pacifist, farming society, in the way that made our ancestors great.
I don't know how to repay you for what you've done--but--if I could ask one more thing--
My people are worried about me, I'm sure, and I'd like to call to let them know I'm all right--and so they can come get me--
I'm afraid that would be impossible.
We have no phones of any kind--no Internet--no television. Technology is strictly forbidden here.
And the thunderstorm that passed through here last night made the road down the mountain too rough for somebody in your condition to go down on horseback.
You're stuck here until your body does some healing.
But don't worry, Mister--
Tony.
Just... Tony.

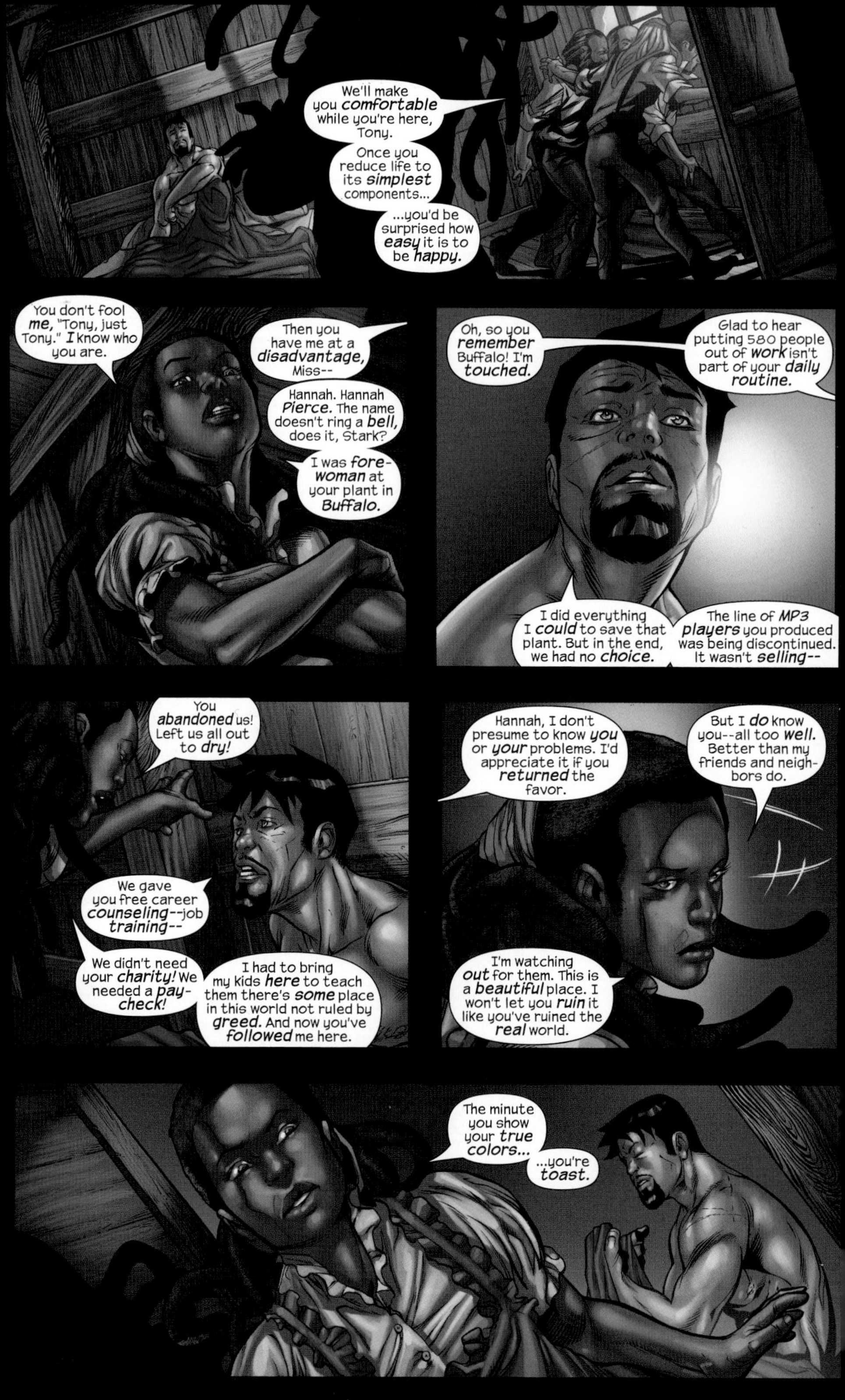

We'll make you comfortable while you're here, Tony.
Once you reduce life to its simplest components...
...you'd be surprised how easy it is to be happy.
You don't fool me, "Tony, just Tony." I know who you are.
Then you have me at a disadvantage, Miss--
Hannah. Hannah Pierce. The name doesn't ring a bell, does it, Stark?
I was fore-woman at your plant in Buffalo.
Oh, so you remember Buffalo! I'm touched.
Glad to hear putting 580 people out of work isn't part of your daily routine.
I did everything I could to save that plant. But in the end, we had no choice.
The line of MP3 players you produced was being discontinued. It wasn't selling--
You abandoned us! Left us all out to dry!
We gave you free career counseling--job training--
We didn't need your charity! We needed a pay-check!
I had to bring my kids here to teach them there's some place in this world not ruled by greed. And now you've followed me here.
Hannah, I don't presume to know you or your problems. I'd appreciate it if you returned the favor.
But I do know you--all too well. Better than my friends and neigh-bors do.
I'm watching out for them. This is a beautiful place. I won't let you ruin it like you've ruined the real world.
The minute you show your true colors...
...you're toast.

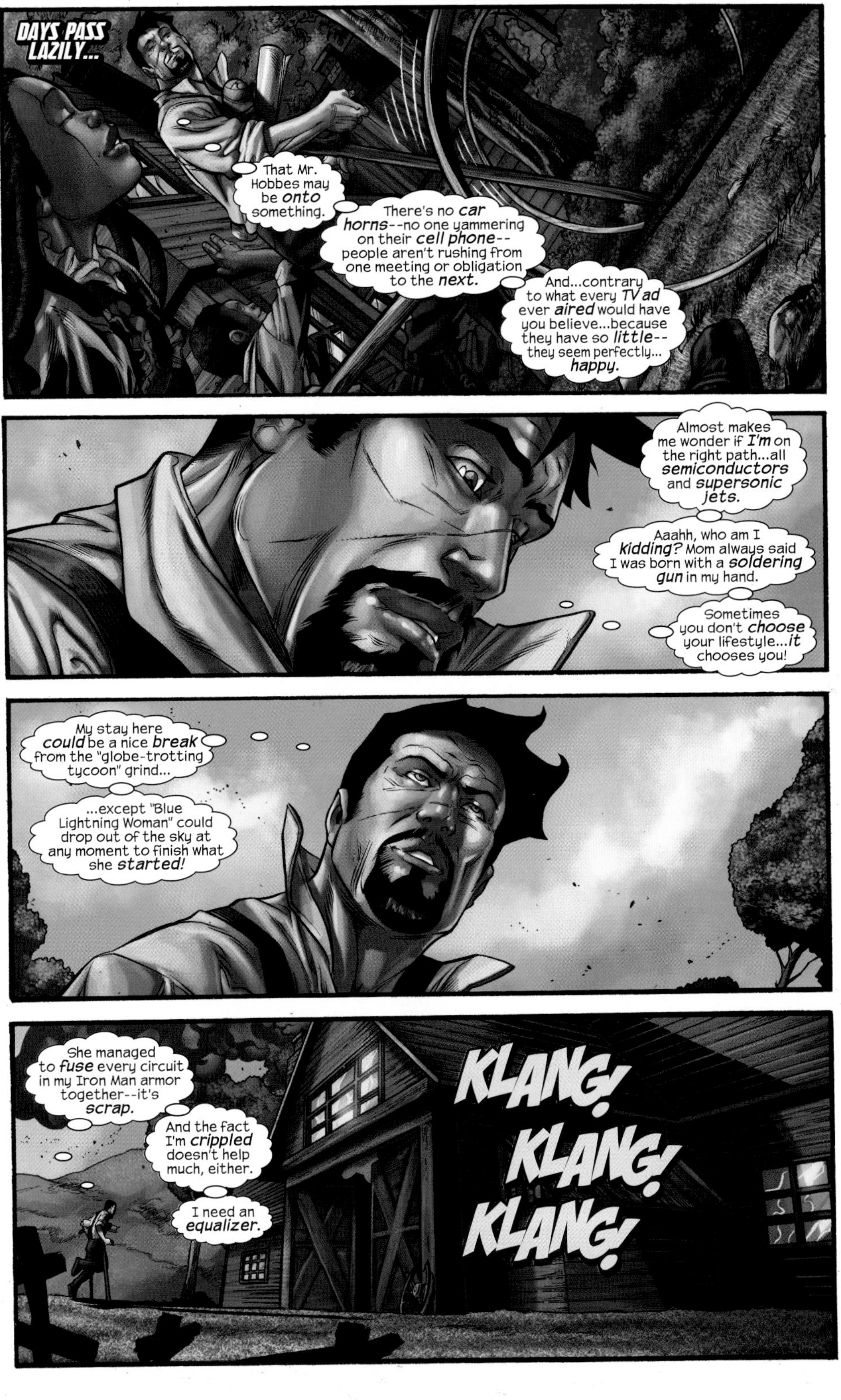
DAYS PASS LAZILY...
That Mr. Hobbes may be onto something.
There's no car horns--no one yammering on their cell phone--people aren't rushing from one meeting or obligation to the next.
And...contrary to what every TV ad ever aired would have you believe...because they have so little--they seem perfectly... happy.
Almost makes me wonder if I'm on the right path...all semiconductors and supersonic jets.
Aaahh, who am I kidding? Mom always said I was born with a soldering gun in my hand.
Sometimes you don't choose your lifestyle...it chooses you!
My stay here could be a nice break from the "globe-trotting tycoon" grind...
...except "Blue Lightning Woman" could drop out of the sky at any moment to finish what she started!
She managed to fuse every circuit in my Iron Man armor together--it's scrap.
And the fact I'm crippled doesn't help much, either.
I need an equalizer.
KLANG! KLANG! KLANG!

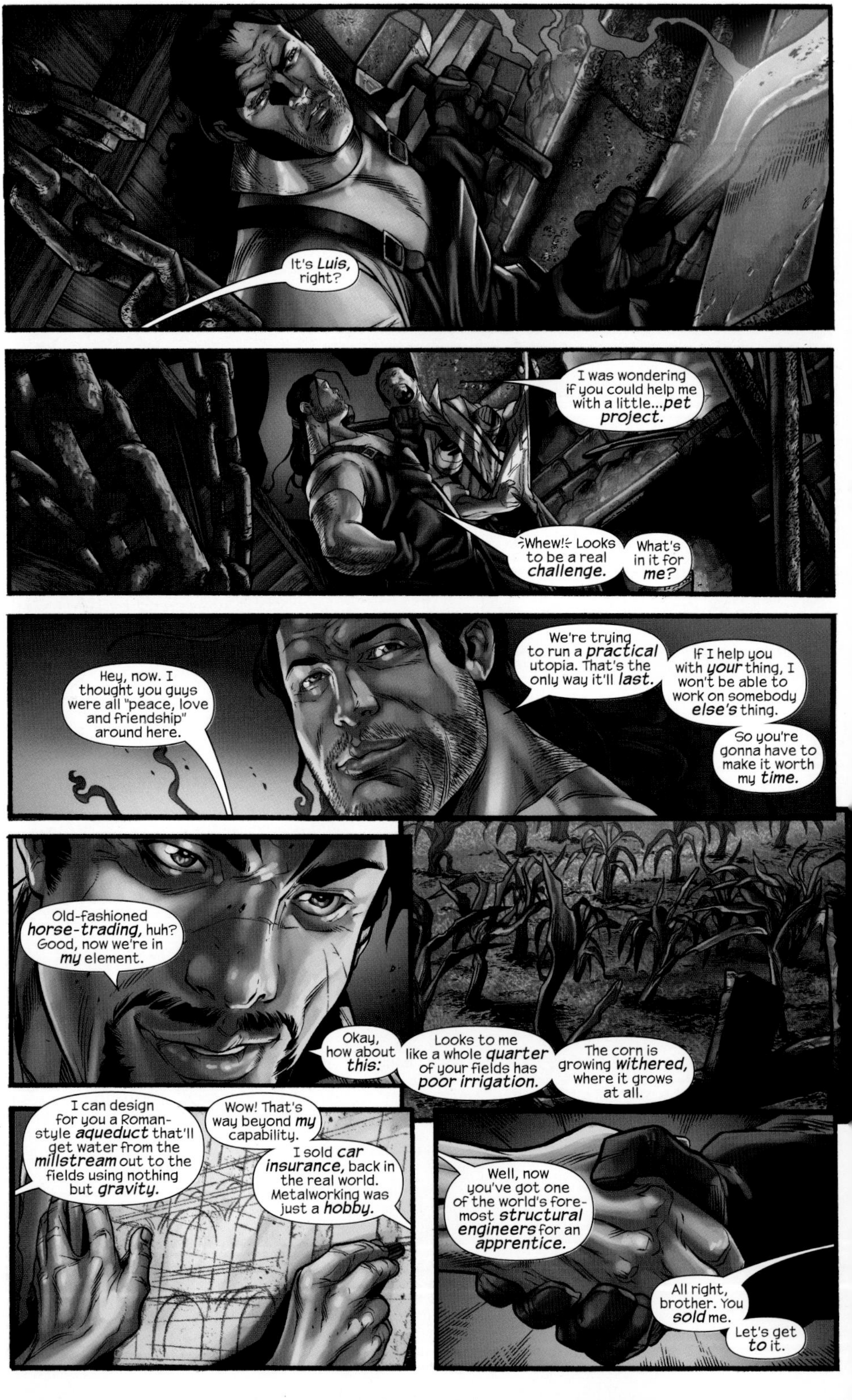
It's Luis, right?
I was wondering if you could help me with a little...pet project.
Whew! Looks to be a real challenge.
What's in it for me?
Hey, now. I thought you guys were all "peace, love and friendship" around here.
We're trying to run a practical utopia. That's the only way it'll last.
If I help you with your thing, I won't be able to work on somebody else's thing.
So you're gonna have to make it worth my time.
Old-fashioned horse-trading, huh? Good, now we're in my element.
Okay, how about this:
Looks to me like a whole quarter of your fields has poor irrigation.
The corn is growing withered, where it grows at all.
I can design for you a Roman-style aqueduct that'll get water from the millstream out to the fields using nothing but gravity.
Wow! That's way beyond my capability.
I sold car insurance, back in the real world. Metalworking was just a hobby.
Well, now you've got one of the world's fore-most structural engineers for an apprentice.
All right, brother. You sold me.
Let's get to it.

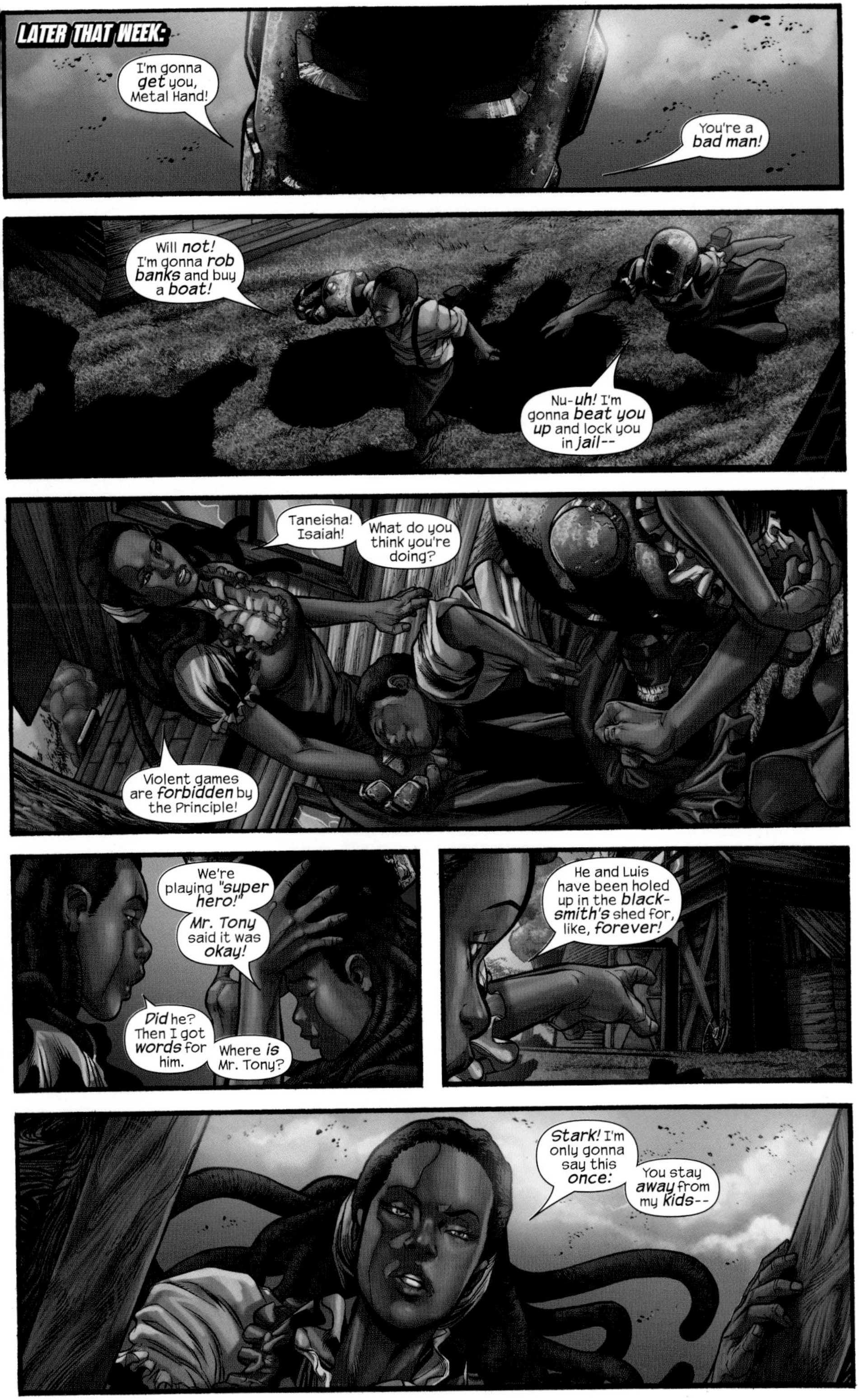
LATER THAT WEEK:
I'm gonna get you, Metal Hand!
You're a bad man!
Will not! I'm gonna rob banks and buy a boat!
Nu-uh! I'm gonna beat you up and lock you in jail--
Taneisha! Isaiah!
What do you think you're doing?
Violent games are forbidden by the Principle!
We're playing "super hero!"
Mr. Tony said it was okay!
Did he? Then I got words for him.
Where is Mr. Tony?
He and Luis have been holed up in the black-smith's shed for, like, forever!
Stark! I'm only gonna say this once:
You stay away from my kids--

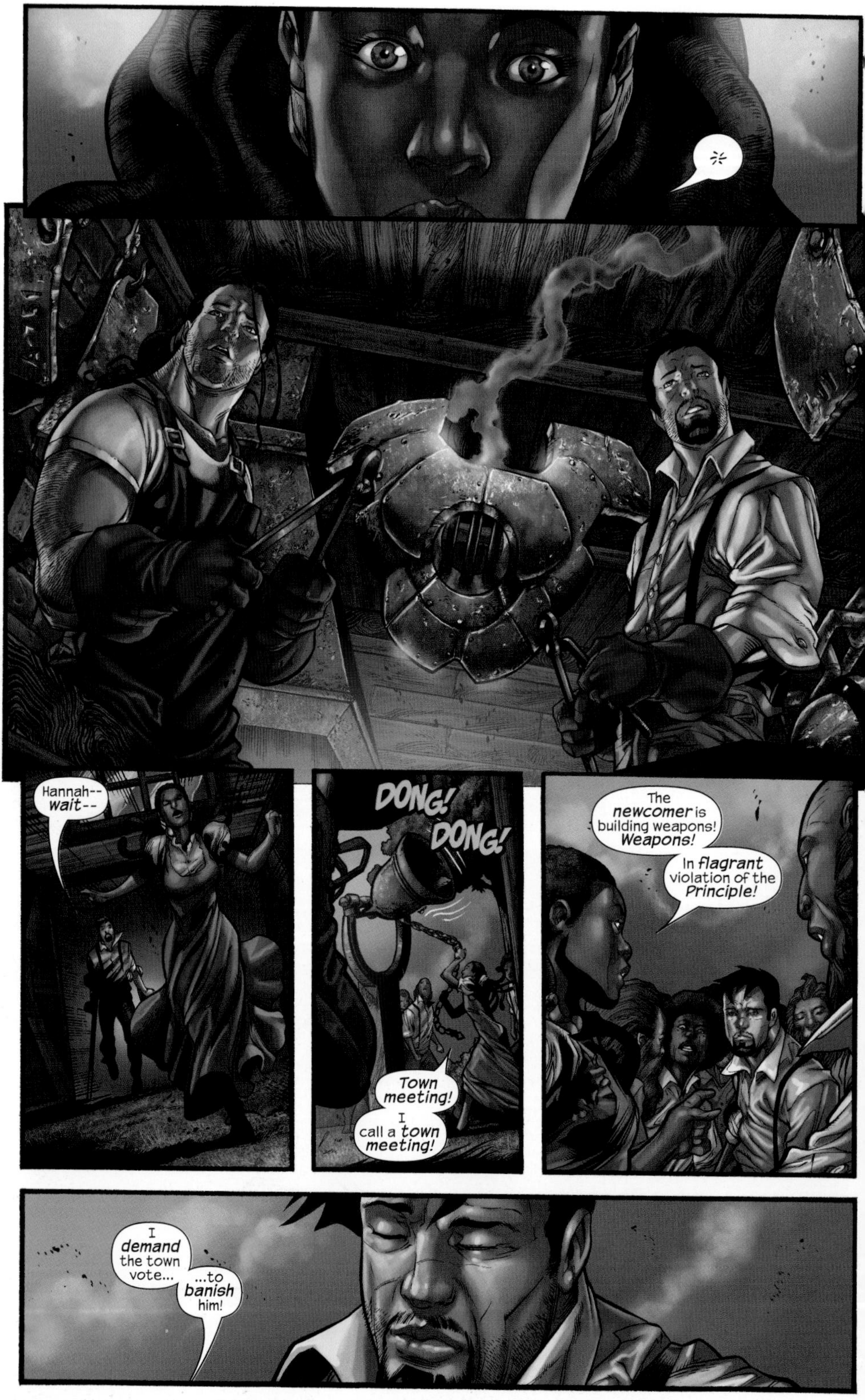
Hannah--
wait--
DONG!
DONG!
Town meeting!
I call a town meeting!
The newcomer is building weapons! Weapons!
In flagrant violation of the Principle!
I demand the town vote...
...to banish him!

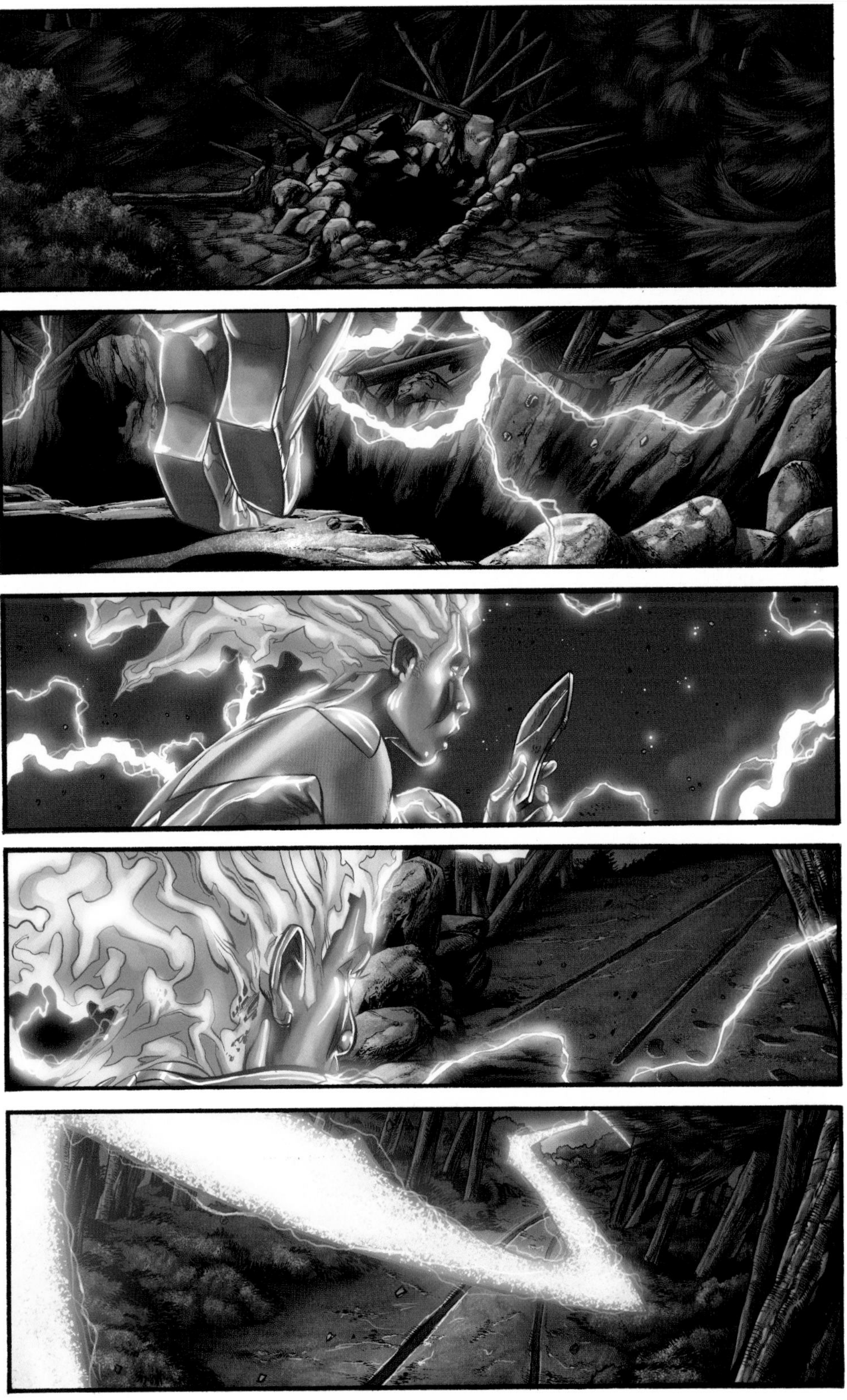

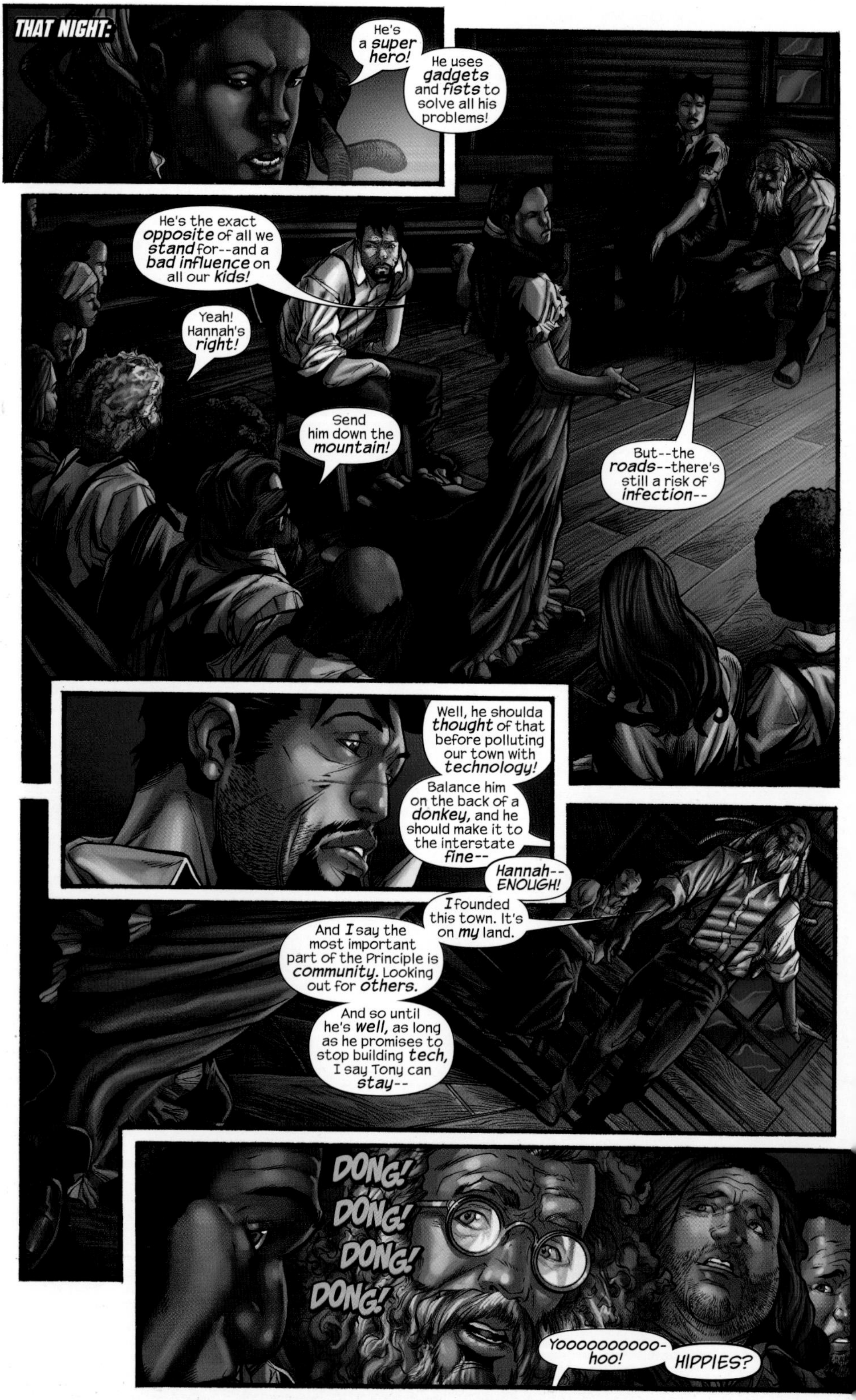
THAT NIGHT:
He's a super hero!
He uses gadgets and fists to solve all his problems!
He's the exact opposite of all we stand for--and a bad influence on all our kids!
Yeah! Hannah's right!
Send him down the mountain!
But--the roads--there's still a risk of infection--
Well, he shoulda thought of that before polluting our town with technology!
Balance him on the back of a donkey, and he should make it to the interstate fine--
Hannah-- ENOUGH!
I founded this town. It's on my land.
And I say the most important part of the Principle is community. Looking out for others.
And so until he's well, as long as he promises to stop building tech, I say Tony can stay--
DONG! DONG! DONG! DONG!
Yoooooooooo-hoo!
HIPPIES?

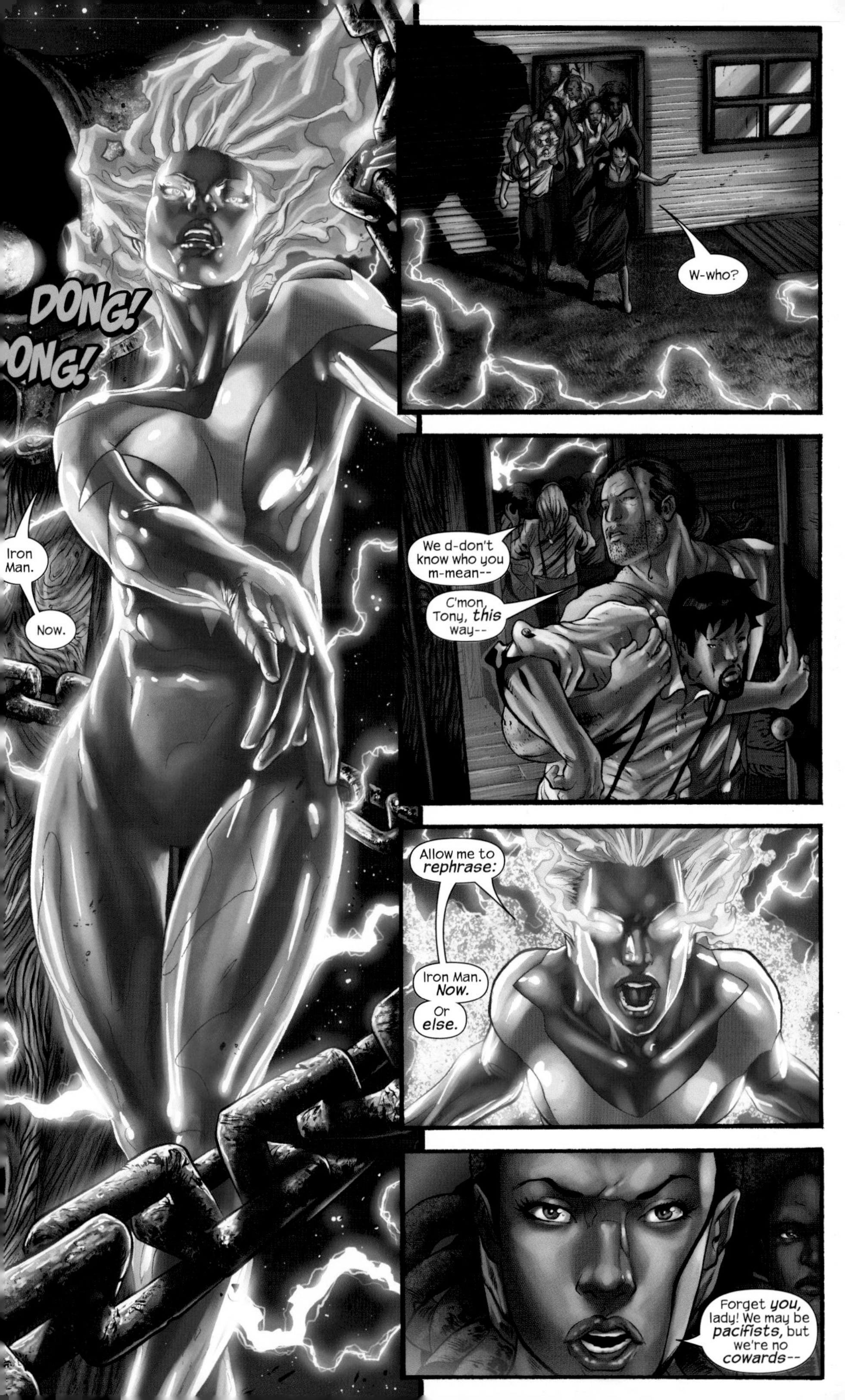
DONG!
DONG!
Iron Man.
Now.
W-who?
We d-don't know who you m-mean--
C'mon, Tony, *this* way--
Allow me to *rephrase:*
Iron Man. *Now.*
Or *else.*
Forget *you,* lady! We may be *pacifists,* but we're no *cowards*--

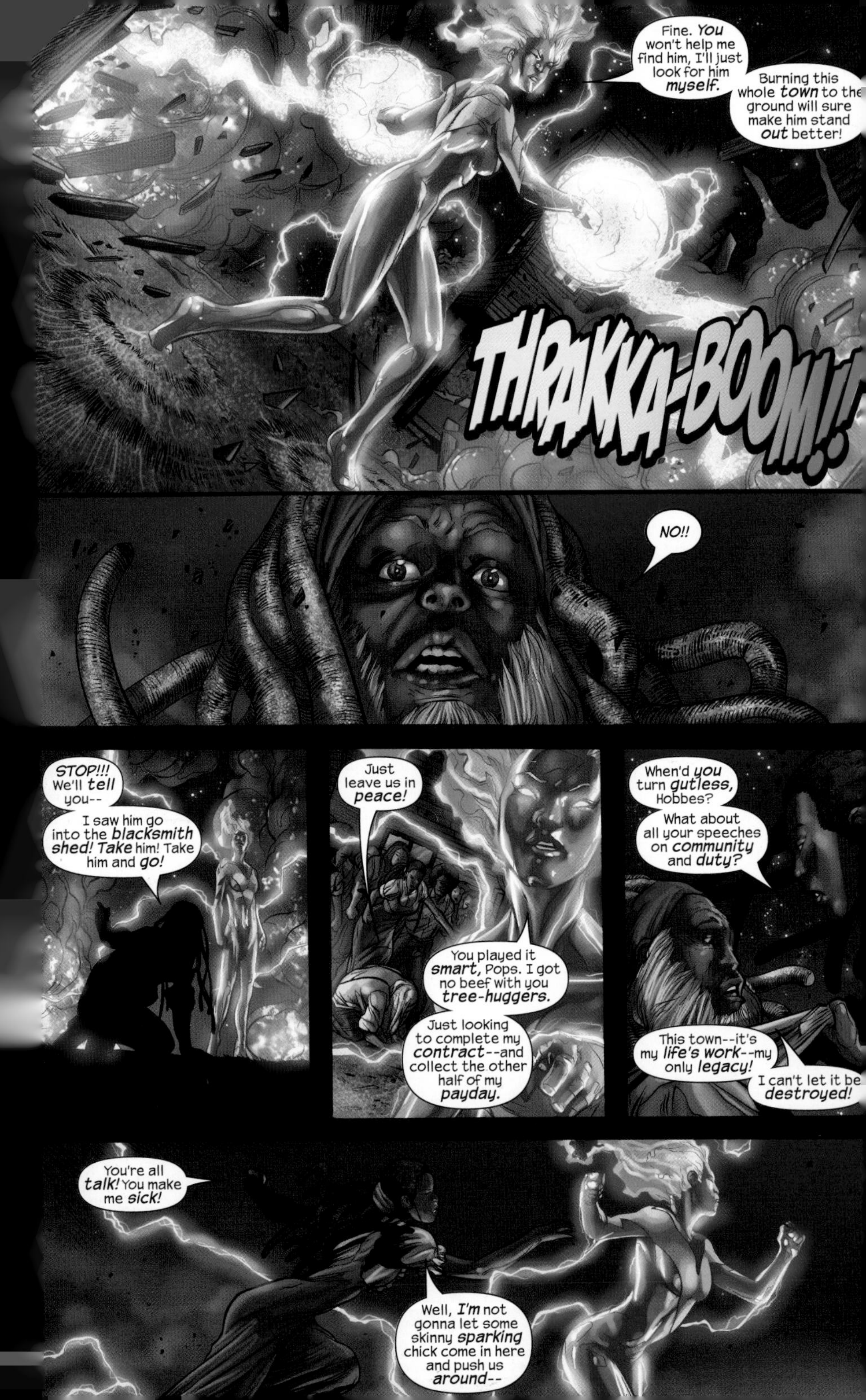
Fine. You won't help me find him, I'll just look for him myself.
Burning this whole town to the ground will sure make him stand out better!
THRAKKA-BOOM!!
NO!!
STOP!!! We'll tell you--
I saw him go into the blacksmith shed! Take him! Take him and go!
Just leave us in peace!
You played it smart, Pops. I got no beef with you tree-huggers.
Just looking to complete my contract--and collect the other half of my payday.
When'd you turn gutless, Hobbes?
What about all your speeches on community and duty?
This town--it's my life's work--my only legacy!
I can't let it be destroyed!
You're all talk! You make me sick!
Well, I'm not gonna let some skinny sparking chick come in here and push us around--

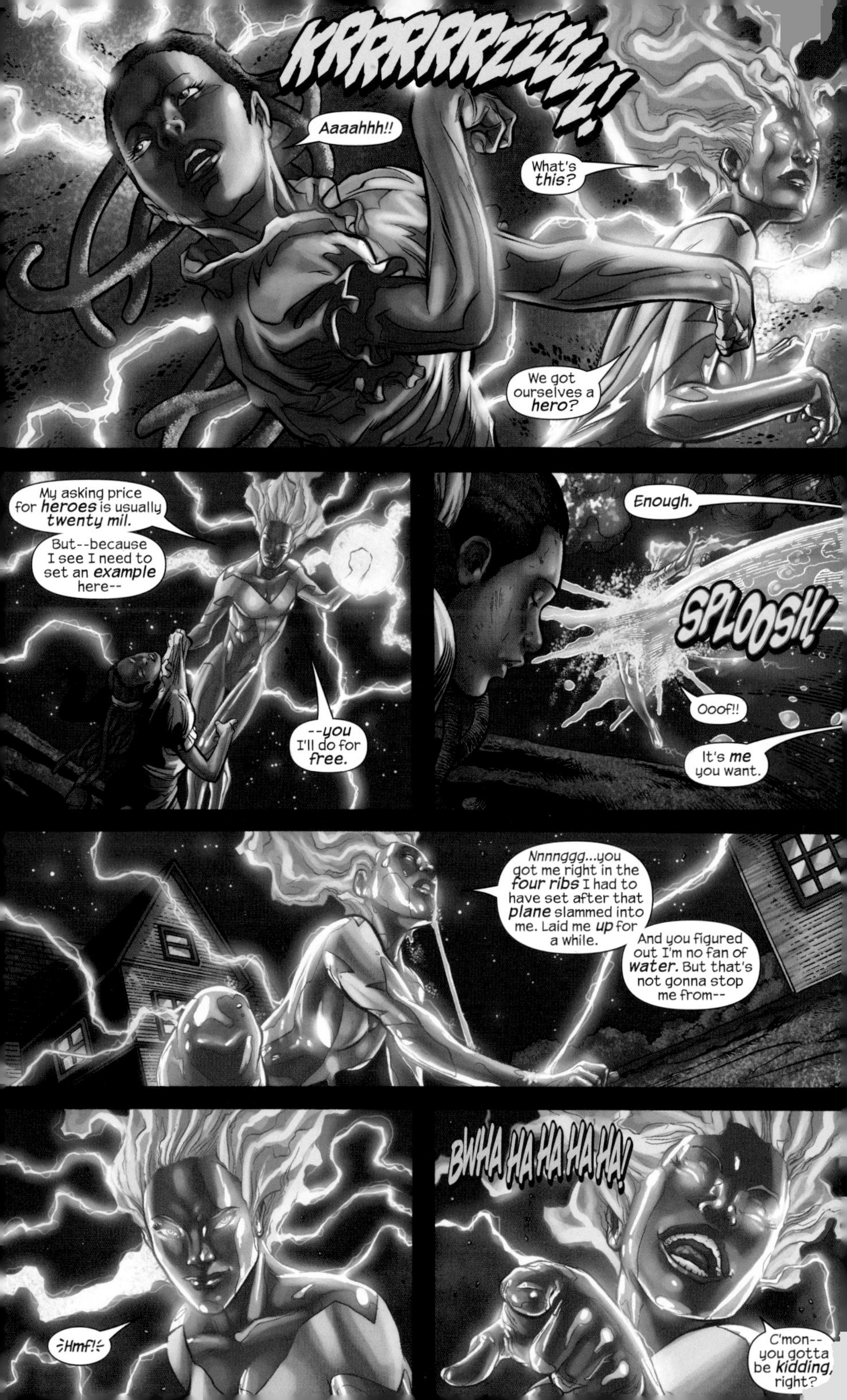
KRRRRRZZZZZ!
Aaaahhh!!
What's this?
We got ourselves a hero?
My asking price for heroes is usually twenty mil.
But--because I see I need to set an example here--
--you I'll do for free.
Enough.
SPLOOSH!
Ooof!!
It's me you want.
Nnnnggg...you got me right in the four ribs I had to have set after that plane slammed into me. Laid me up for a while.
And you figured out I'm no fan of water. But that's not gonna stop me from--
Hmf!
BWHA HA HA HA HA!
C'mon-- you gotta be kidding, right?

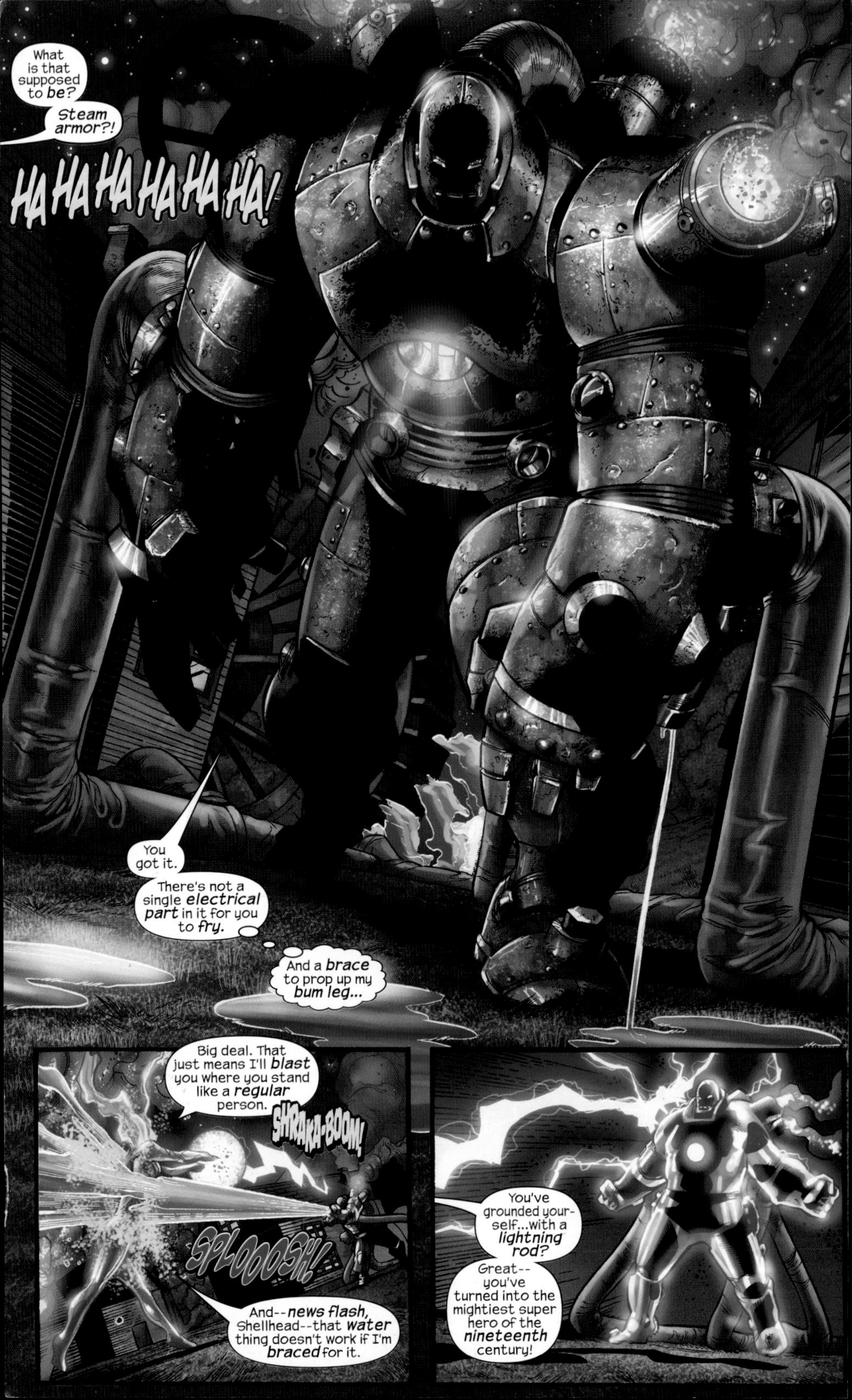
What is that supposed to be?
Steam armor?!
HA HA HA HA HA HA HA!
You got it.
There's not a single electrical part in it for you to fry.
And a brace to prop up my bum leg...
Big deal. That just means I'll blast you where you stand like a regular person.
SHRAKA-BOOM!
SPLOOOSH!
And--news flash, Shellhead--that water thing doesn't work if I'm braced for it.
You've grounded yourself...with a lightning rod?
Great--you've turned into the mightiest super hero of the nineteenth century!

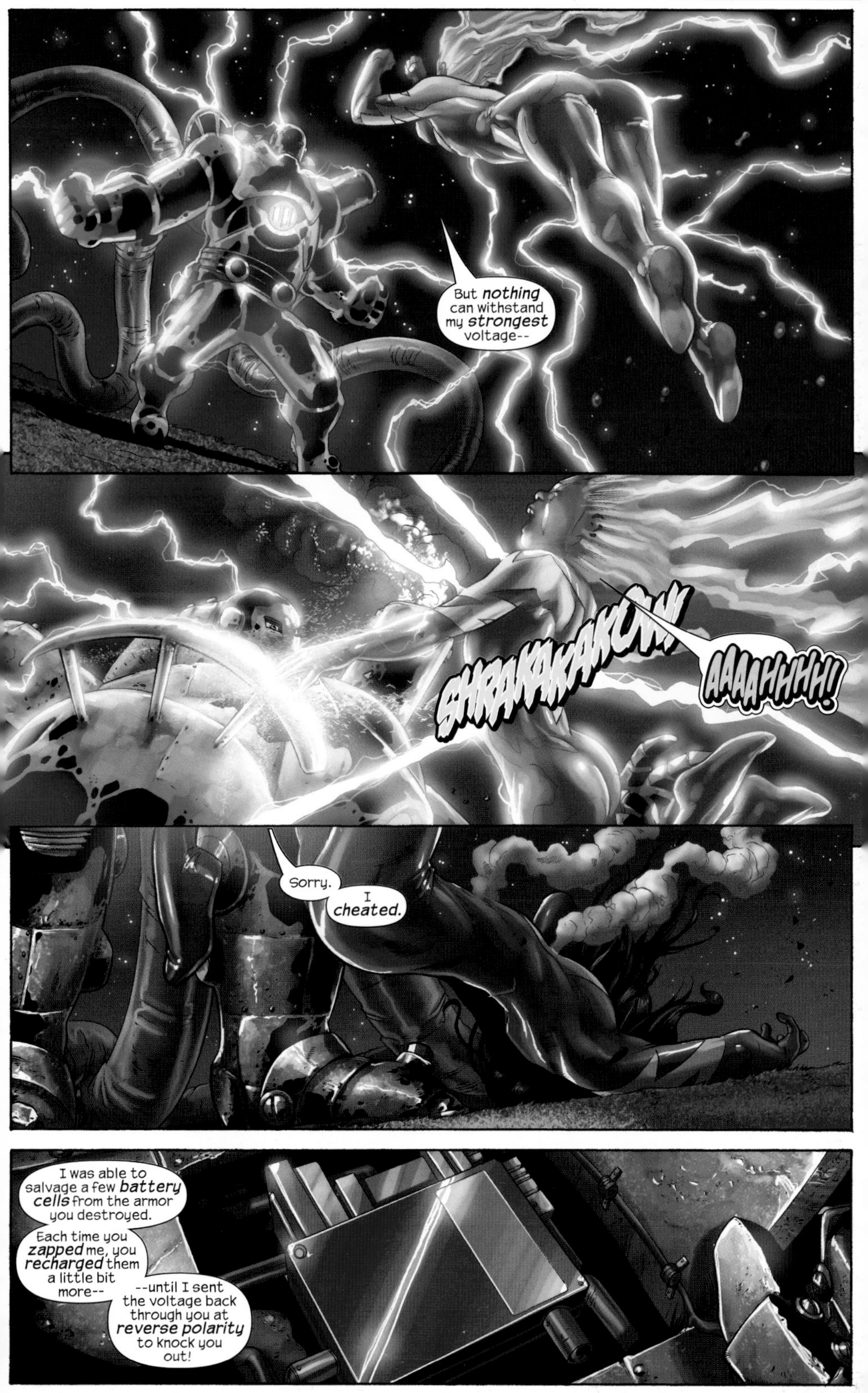

But nothing can withstand my strongest voltage--
SHRAKAKAKOW!
AAAAHHHH!
Sorry. I cheated.
I was able to salvage a few battery cells from the armor you destroyed.
Each time you zapped me, you recharged them a little bit more--
--until I sent the voltage back through you at reverse polarity to knock you out!

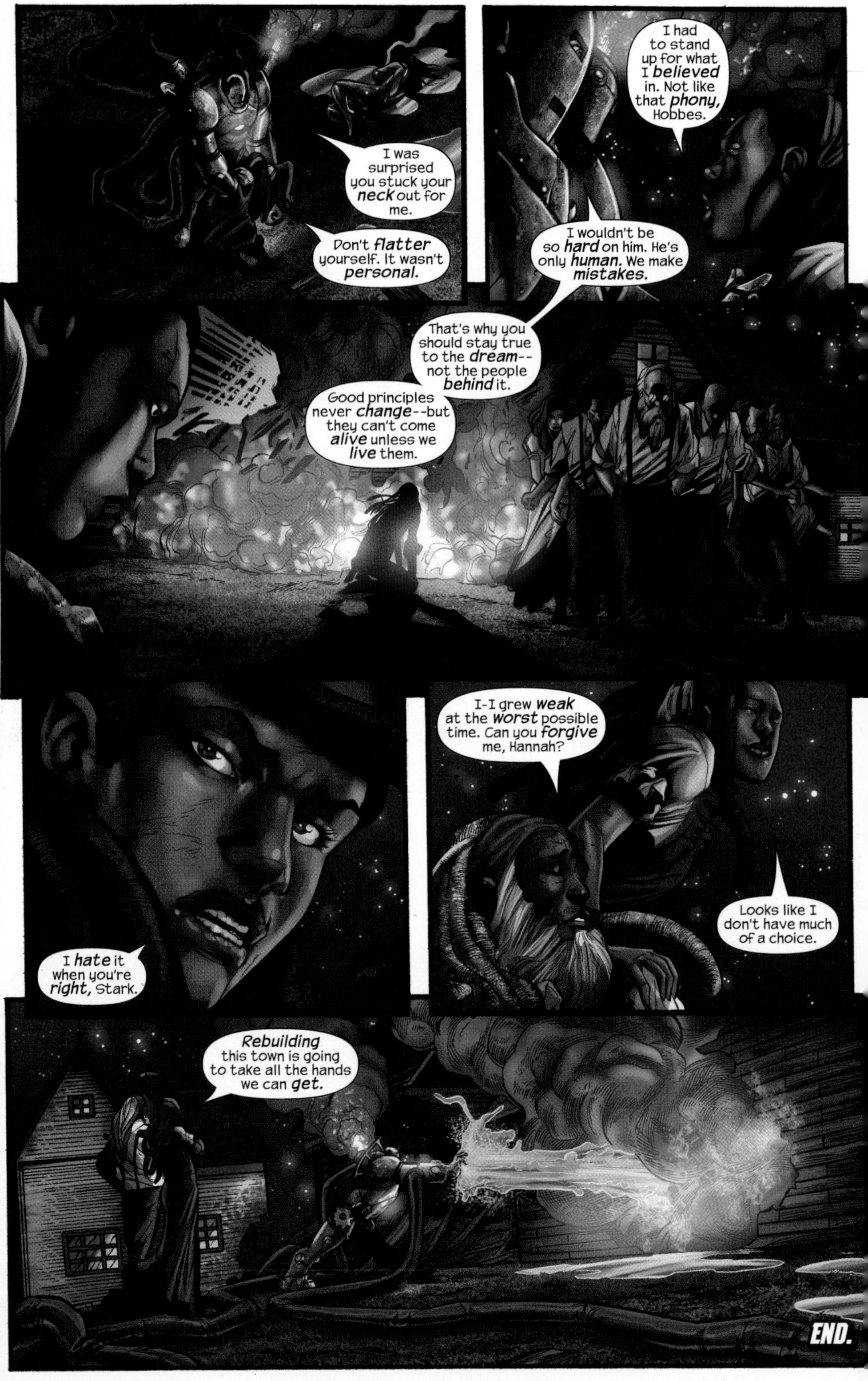
I was surprised you stuck your neck out for me.
Don't flatter yourself. It wasn't personal.
I had to stand up for what I believed in. Not like that phony, Hobbes.
I wouldn't be so hard on him. He's only human. We make mistakes.
That's why you should stay true to the dream--not the people behind it.
Good principles never change--but they can't come alive unless we live them.
I hate it when you're right, Stark.
I-I grew weak at the worst possible time. Can you forgive me, Hannah?
Looks like I don't have much of a choice.
Rebuilding this town is going to take all the hands we can get.
END.

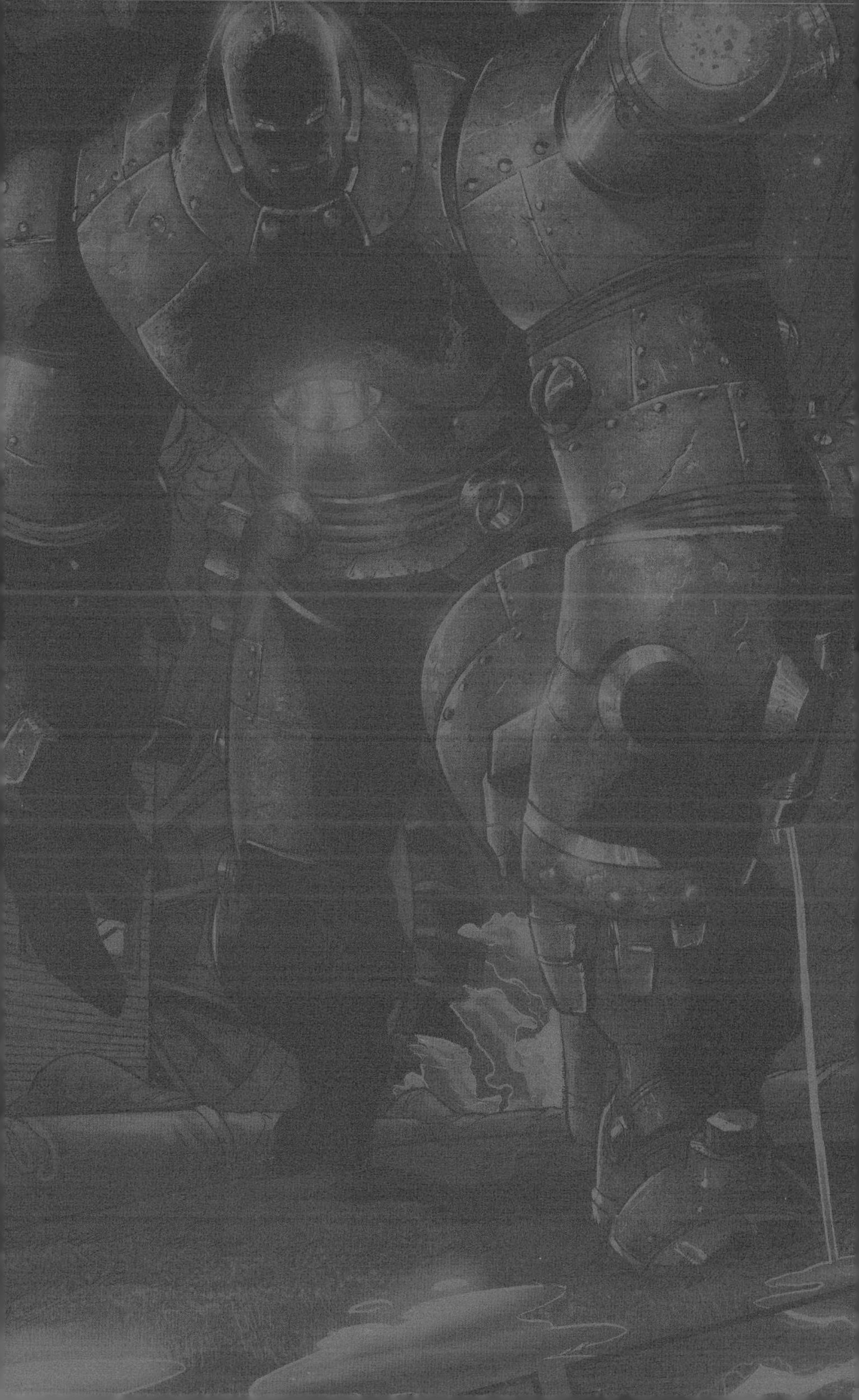

09

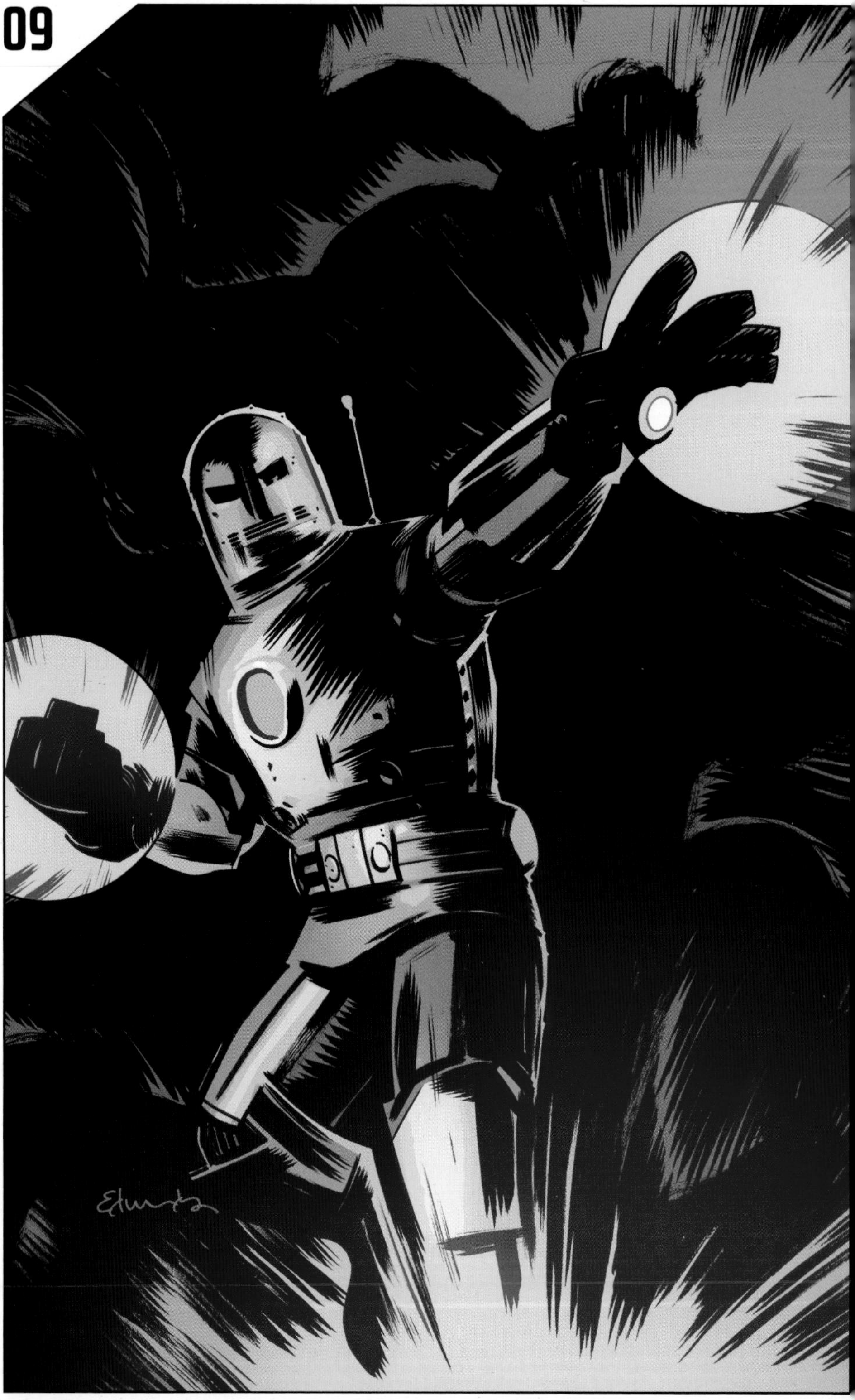

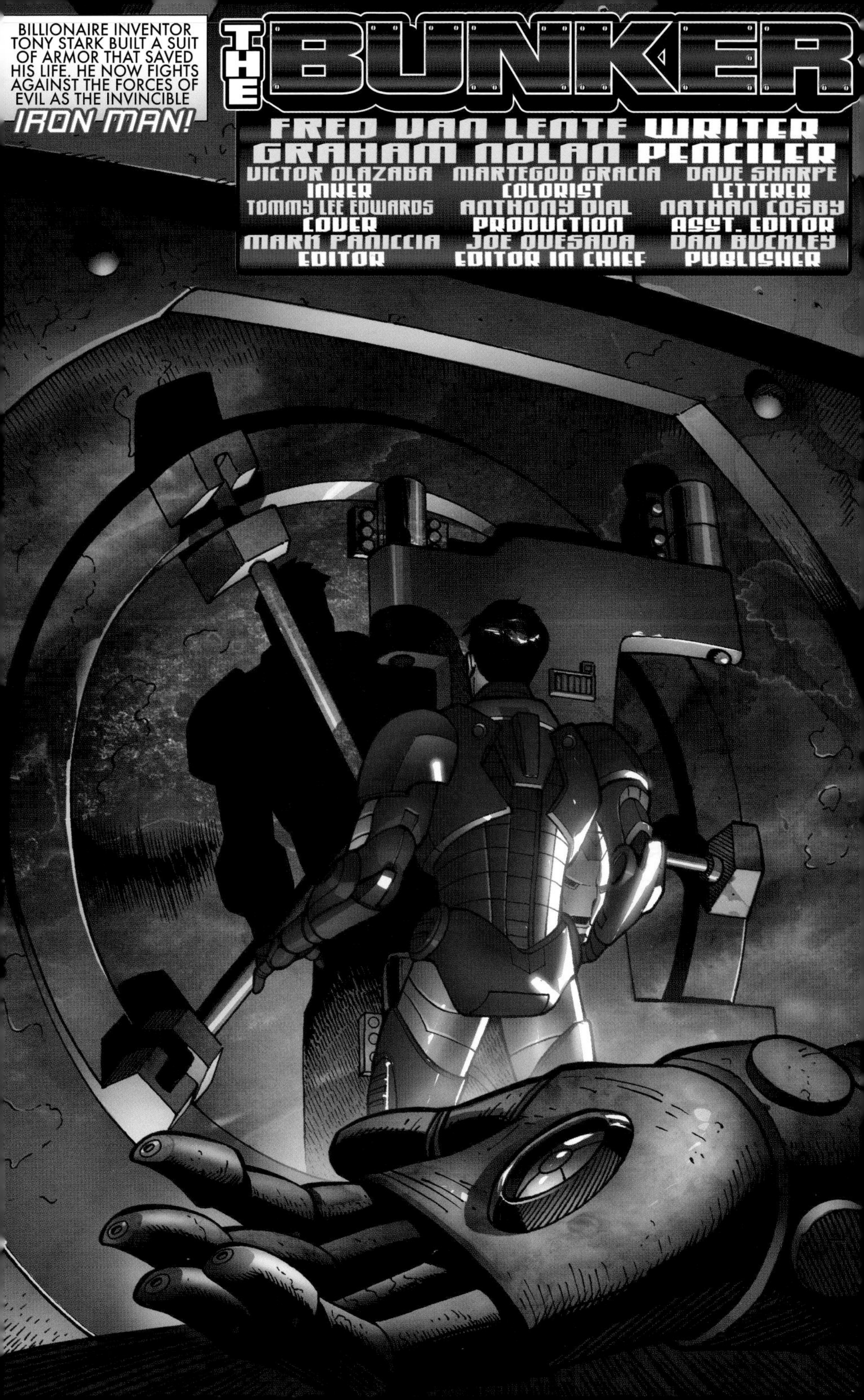
BILLIONAIRE INVENTOR TONY STARK BUILT A SUIT OF ARMOR THAT SAVED HIS LIFE. HE NOW FIGHTS AGAINST THE FORCES OF EVIL AS THE INVINCIBLE IRON MAN!
THE BUNKER
FRED VAN LENTE WRITER
GRAHAM NOLAN PENCILER
VICTOR OLAZABA INKER
MARTEGOD GRACIA COLORIST
DAVE SHARPE LETTERER
TOMMY LEE EDWARDS COVER
ANTHONY DIAL PRODUCTION
NATHAN COSBY ASST. EDITOR
MARK PANICCIA EDITOR
JOE QUESADA EDITOR IN CHIEF
DAN BUCKLEY PUBLISHER

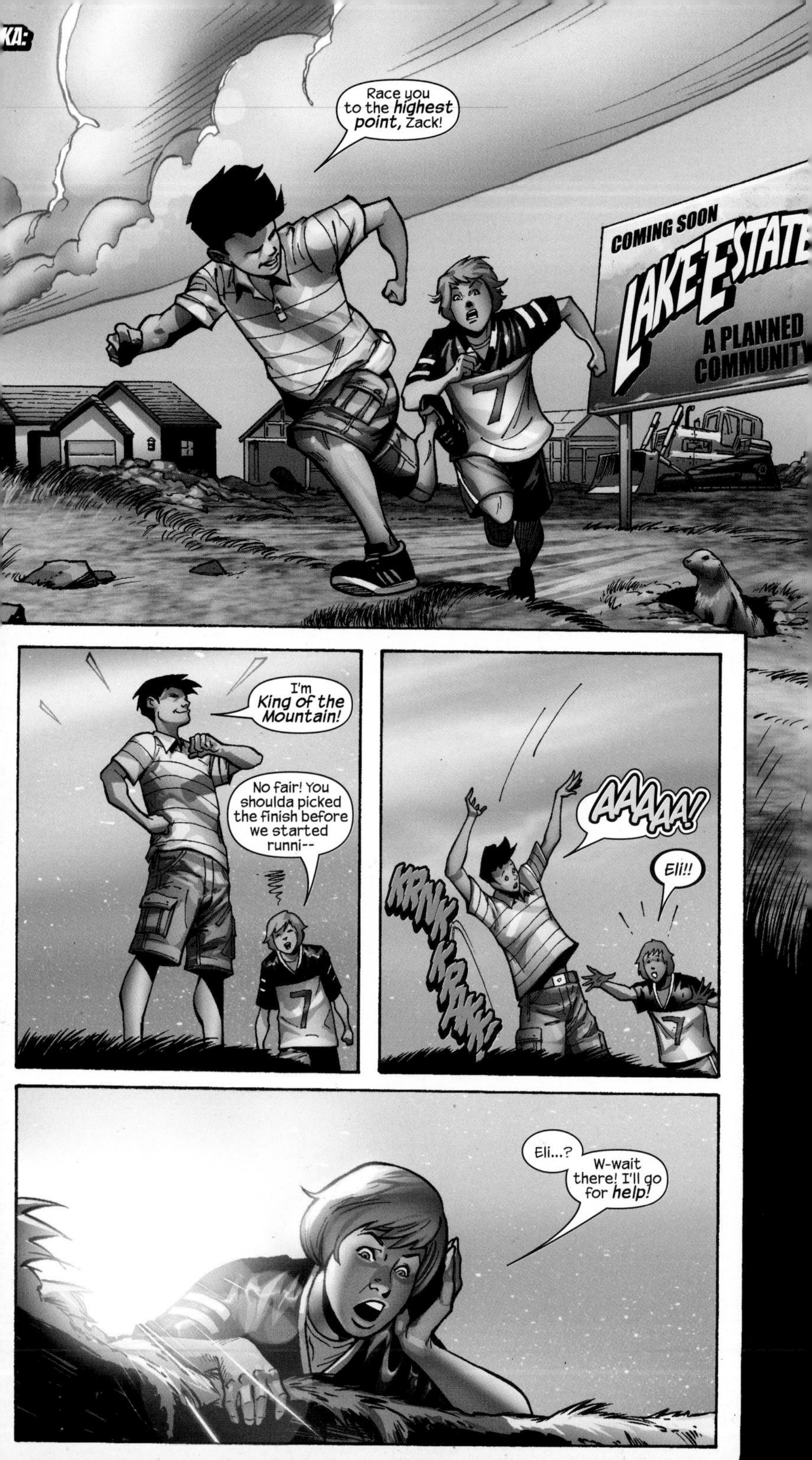
Race you to the *highest point,* Zack!
COMING SOON
LAKE-E-STATE
A PLANNED
COMMUNIT
I'm *King of the Mountain!*
No fair! You shoulda picked the finish before we started runni--
AAAAA!
KRNK KRAKK!
Eli!!
Eli...?
W-wait there! I'll go for *help!*

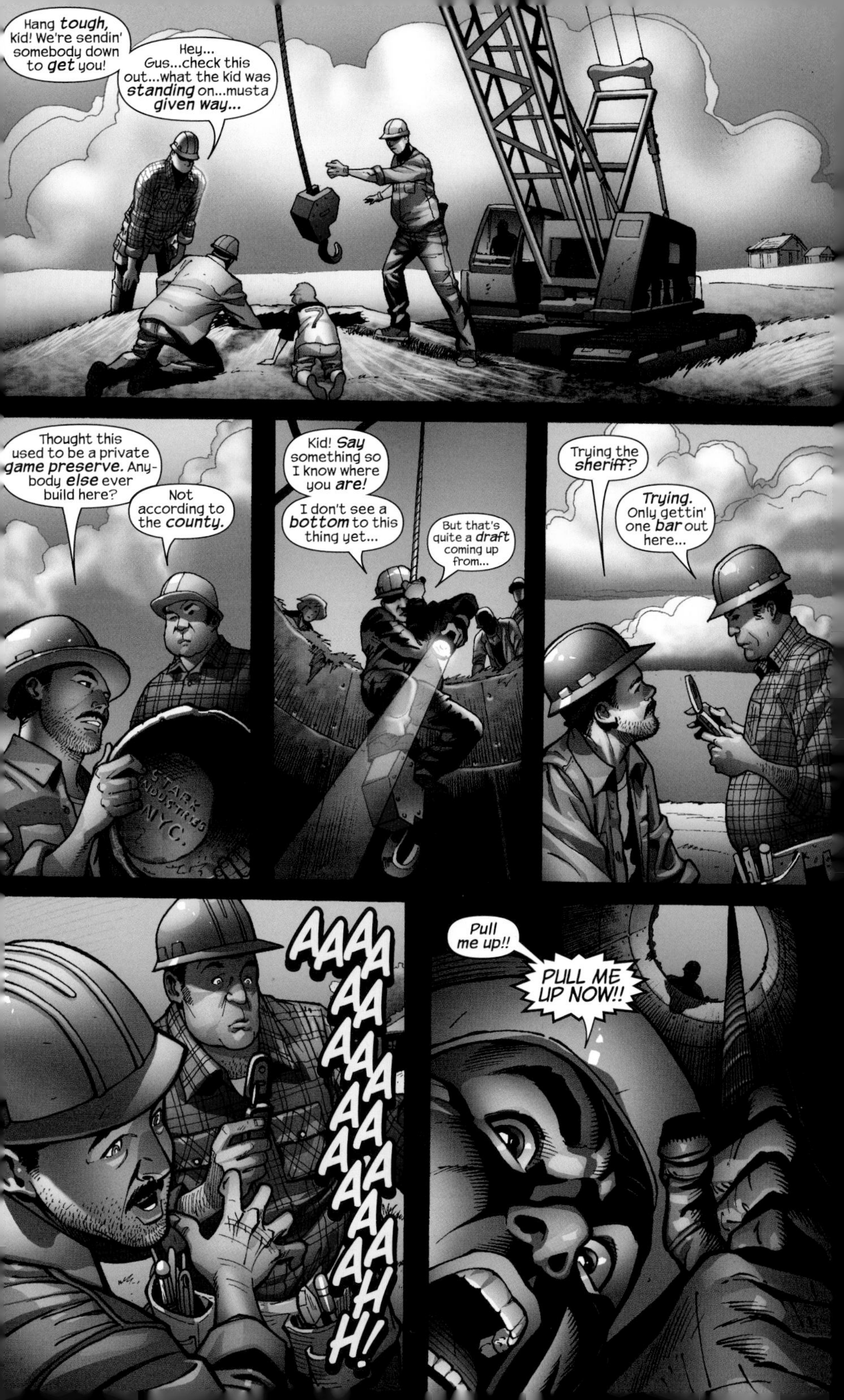
Hang tough, kid! We're sendin' somebody down to get you!
Hey... Gus...check this out...what the kid was standing on...musta given way...
Thought this used to be a private game preserve. Anybody else ever build here?
Not according to the county.
STARK INDUSTRIES NYC.
Kid! Say something so I know where you are!
I don't see a bottom to this thing yet...
But that's quite a draft coming up from...
Trying the sheriff?
Trying. Only gettin' one bar out here...
AAAAAAAAAAAAAAAAAH!
Pull me up!!
PULL ME UP NOW!!

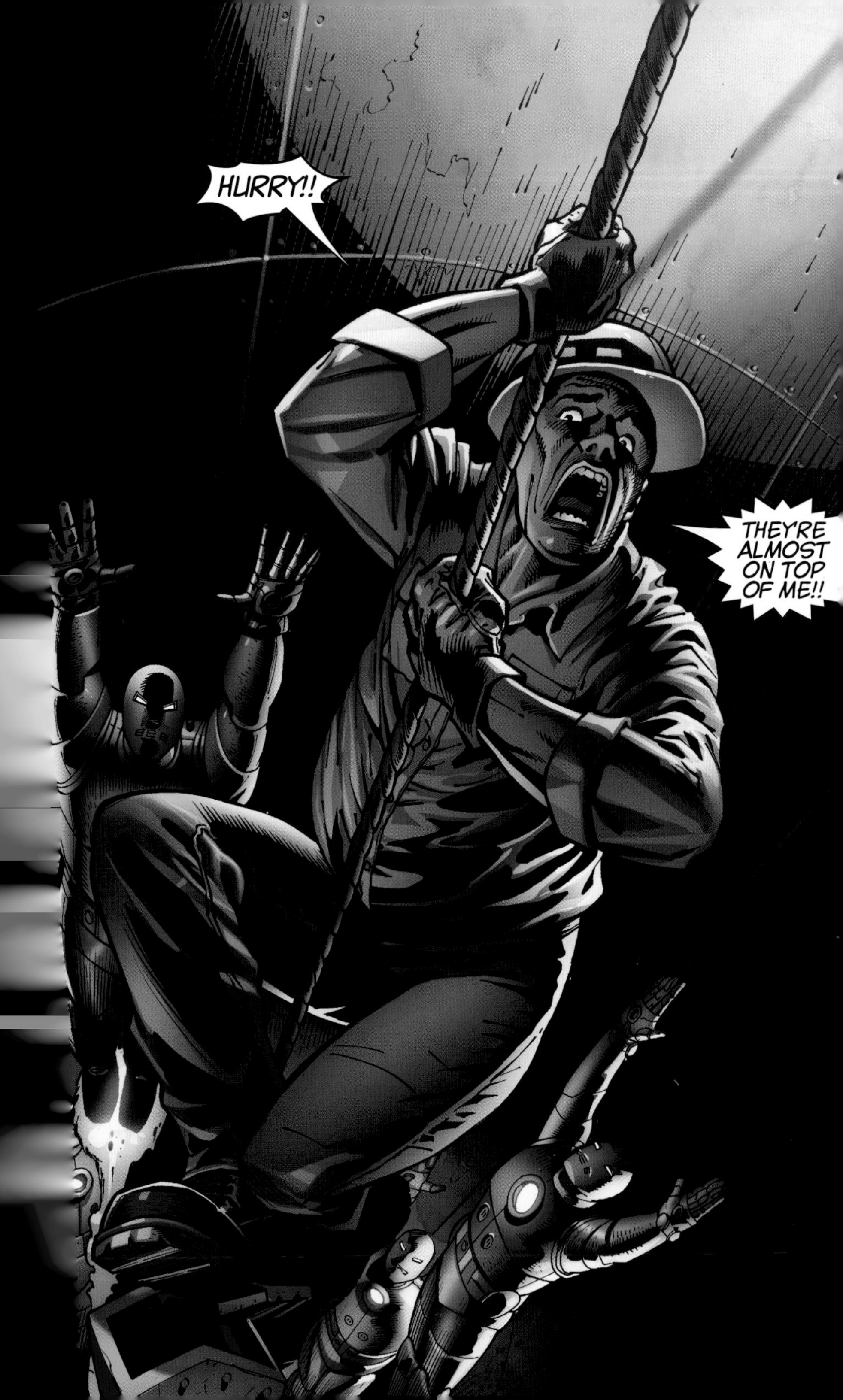
HURRY!!
THEY'RE ALMOST ON TOP OF ME!!

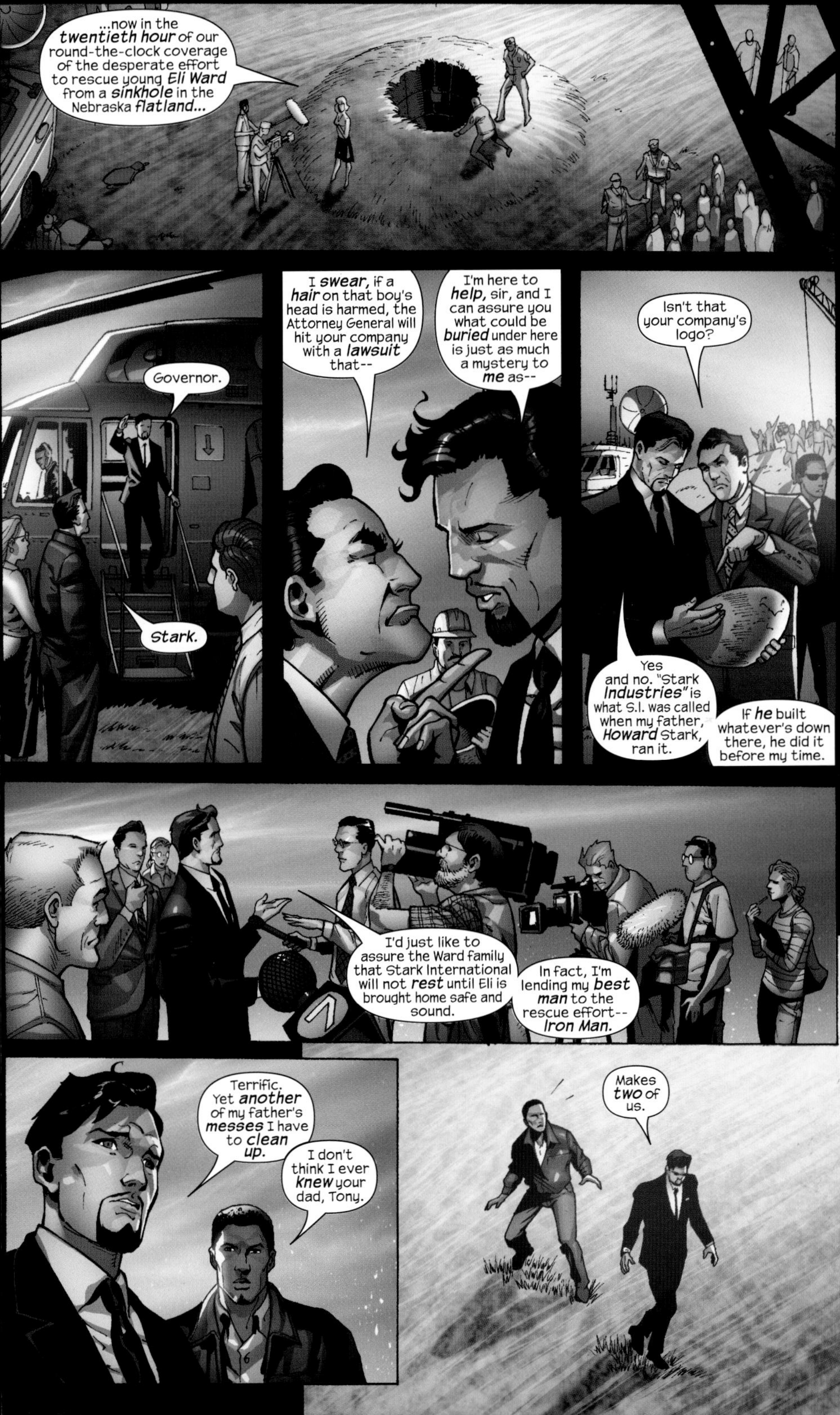
...now in the twentieth hour of our round-the-clock coverage of the desperate effort to rescue young Eli Ward from a sinkhole in the Nebraska flatland...
Governor.
Stark.
I swear, if a hair on that boy's head is harmed, the Attorney General will hit your company with a lawsuit that--
I'm here to help, sir, and I can assure you what could be buried under here is just as much a mystery to me as--
Isn't that your company's logo?
Yes and no. "Stark Industries" is what S.I. was called when my father, Howard Stark, ran it.
If he built whatever's down there, he did it before my time.
I'd just like to assure the Ward family that Stark International will not rest until Eli is brought home safe and sound.
In fact, I'm lending my best man to the rescue effort-- Iron Man.
Terrific. Yet another of my father's messes I have to clean up.
I don't think I ever knew your dad, Tony.
Makes two of us.

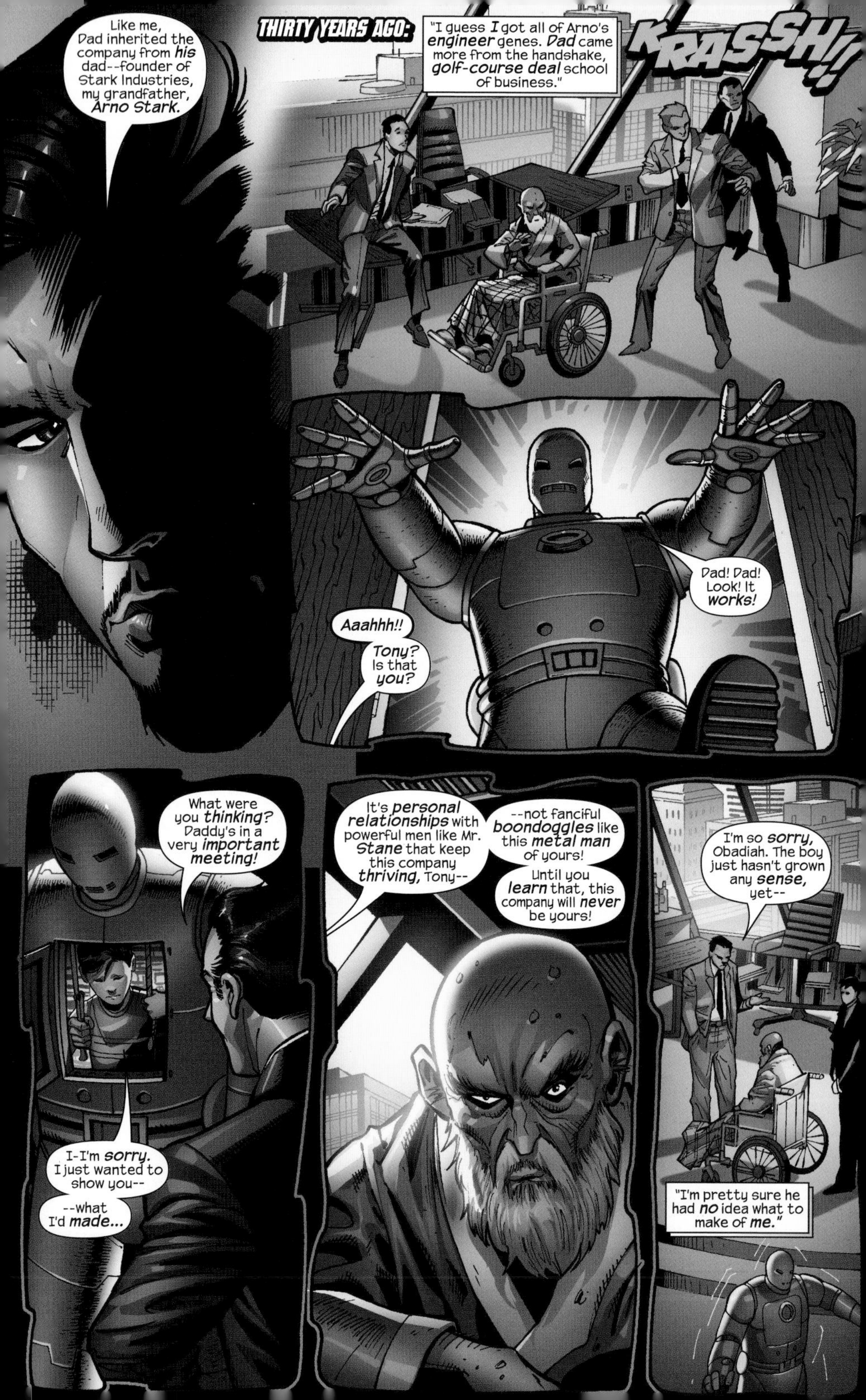

Like me, Dad inherited the company from *his* dad--founder of Stark Industries, my grandfather, *Arno Stark.*
THIRTY YEARS AGO:
"I guess *I* got all of Arno's *engineer* genes. *Dad* came more from the handshake, *golf-course deal* school of business."
KRASSH!!
Dad! Dad! Look! It *works!*
Aaahhh!!
Tony? Is that *you?*
What were you *thinking?* Daddy's in a very *important meeting!*
I-I'm *sorry.* I just wanted to show you--
--what I'd *made...*
It's *personal relationships* with powerful men like Mr. *Stane* that keep this company *thriving,* Tony--
--not fanciful *boondoggles* like this *metal man* of yours!
Until you *learn* that, this company will *never* be yours!
I'm so *sorry,* Obadiah. The boy just hasn't grown any *sense,* yet--
"I'm pretty sure he had *no* idea what to make of *me.*"

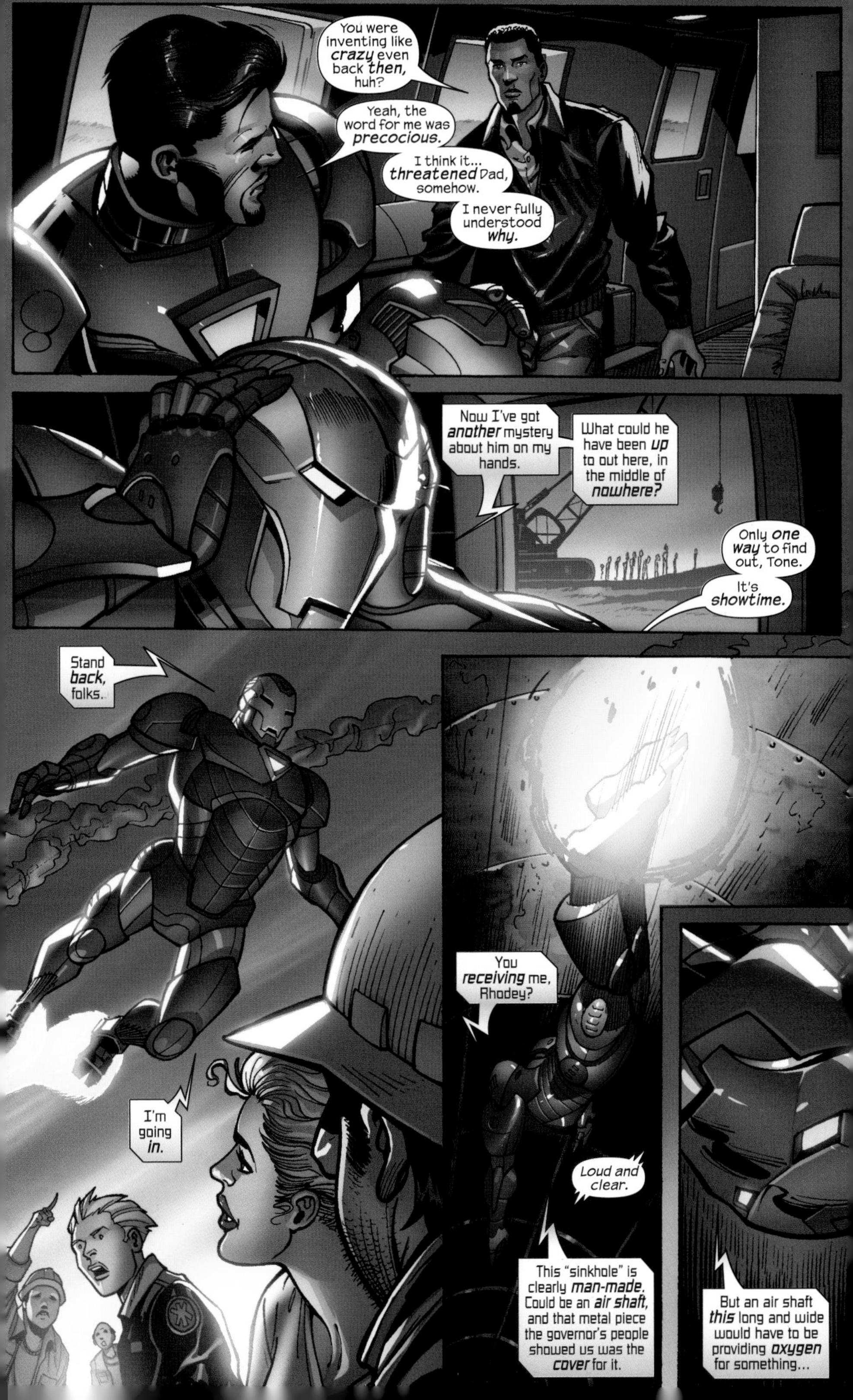
You were inventing like crazy even back then, huh?
Yeah, the word for me was precocious.
I think it... threatened Dad, somehow.
I never fully understood why.
Now I've got another mystery about him on my hands.
What could he have been up to out here, in the middle of nowhere?
Only one way to find out, Tone.
It's showtime.
Stand back, folks.
I'm going in.
You receiving me, Rhodey?
Loud and clear.
This "sinkhole" is clearly man-made. Could be an air shaft, and that metal piece the governor's people showed us was the cover for it.
But an air shaft this long and wide would have to be providing oxygen for something...

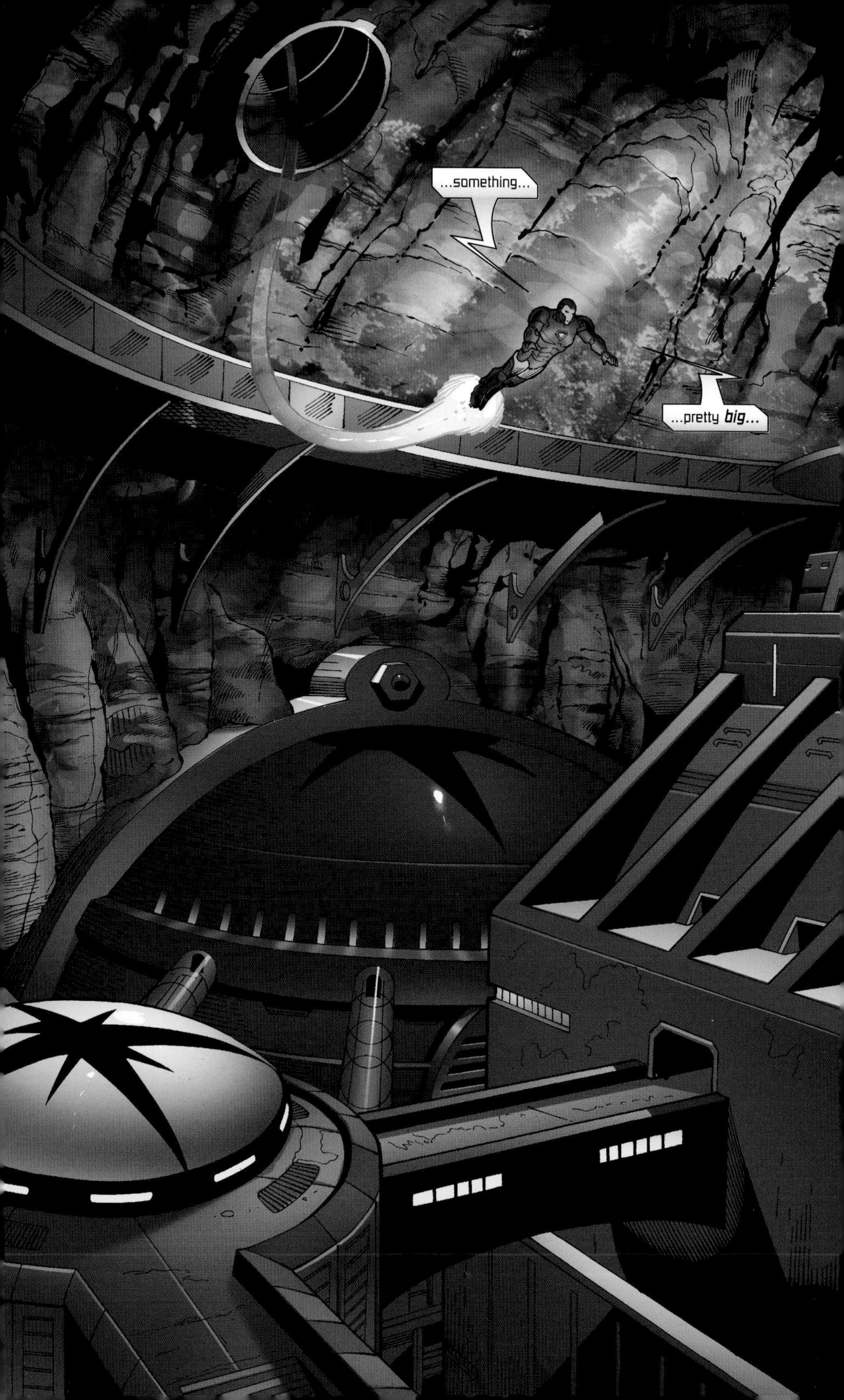
...something...
...pretty big...

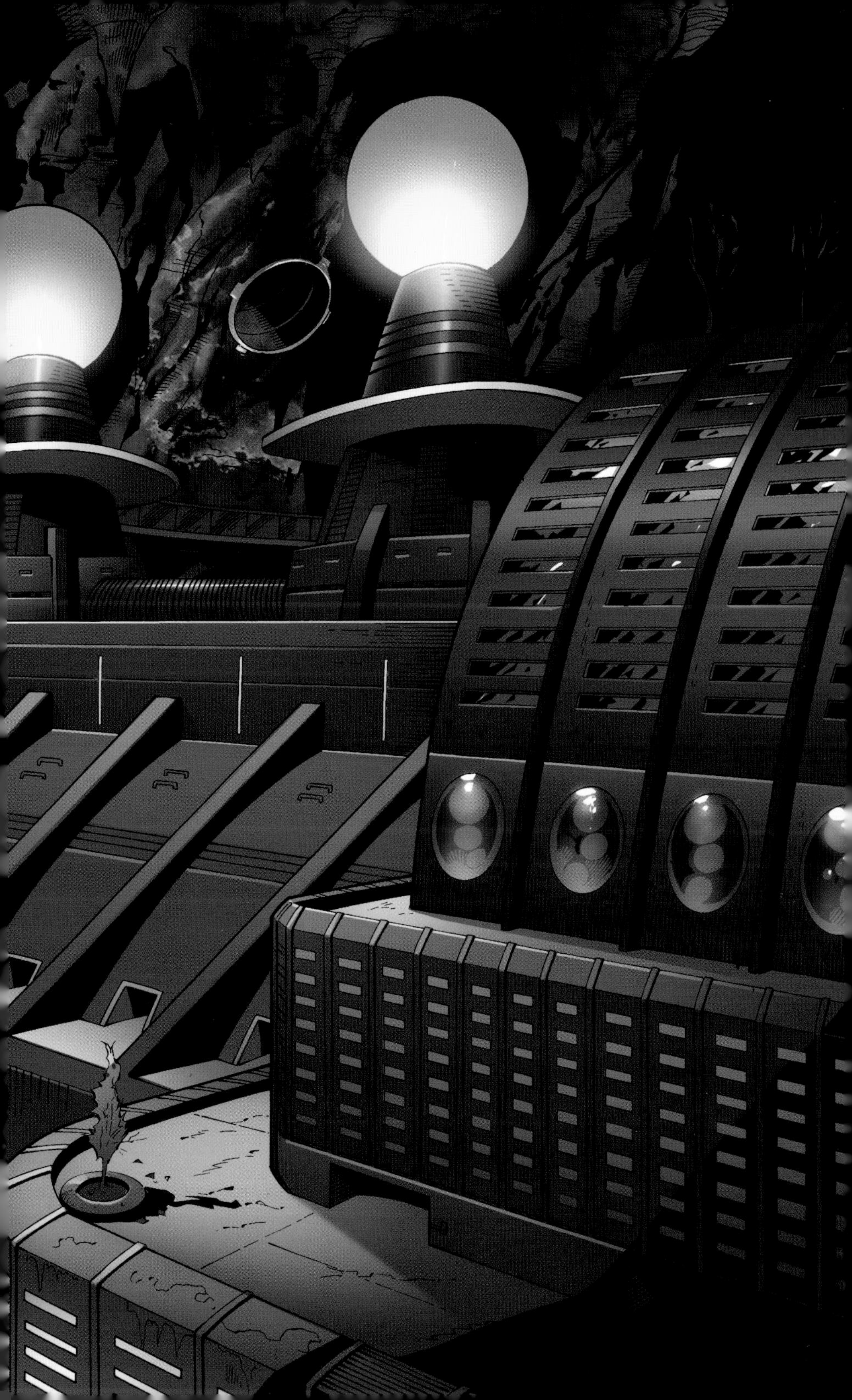

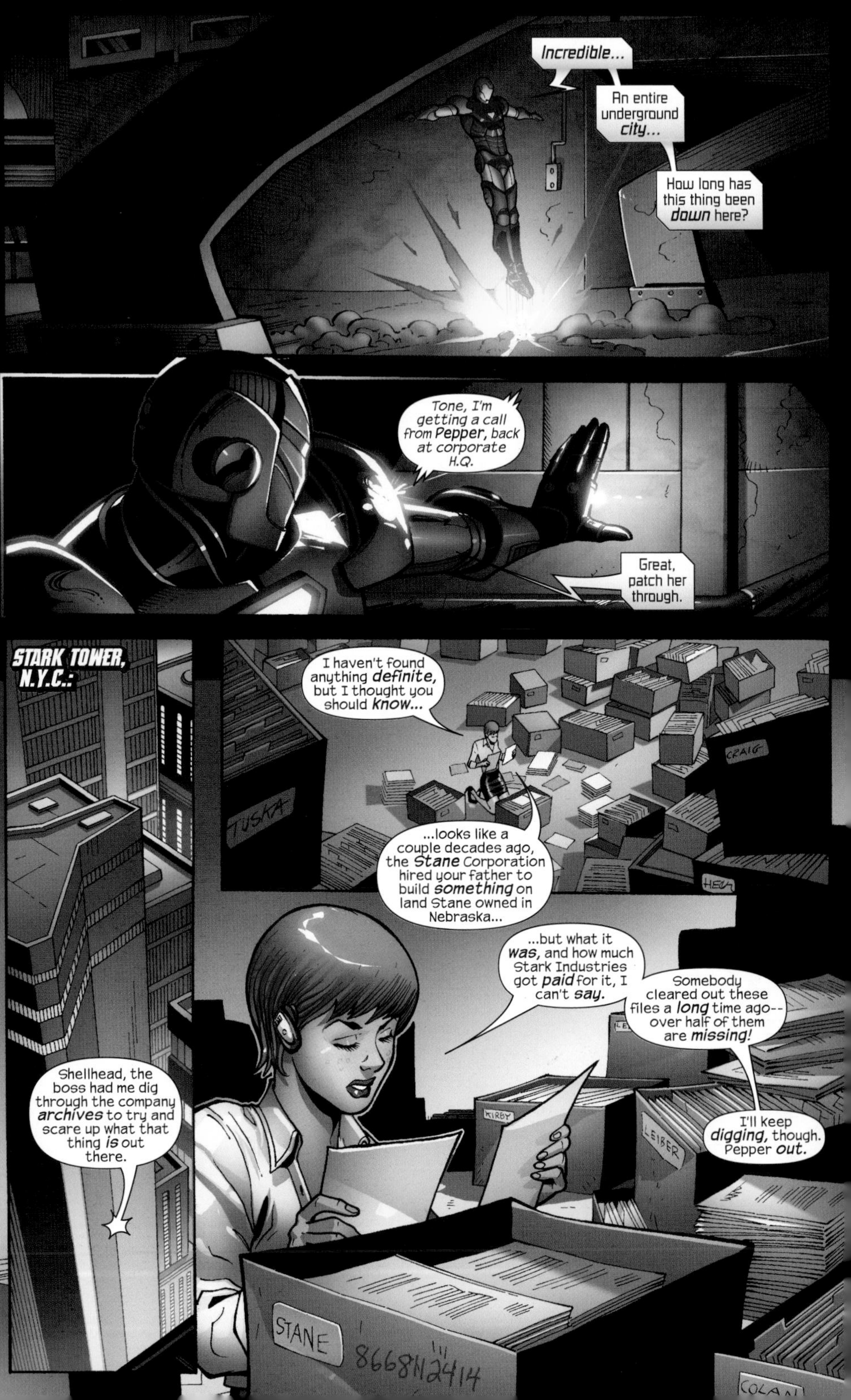
Incredible...
An entire underground city...
How long has this thing been down here?
Tone, I'm getting a call from Pepper, back at corporate H.Q.
Great, patch her through.
STARK TOWER, N.Y.C.:
Shellhead, the boss had me dig through the company archives to try and scare up what that thing is out there.
I haven't found anything definite, but I thought you should know...
...looks like a couple decades ago, the Stane Corporation hired your father to build something on land Stane owned in Nebraska...
...but what it was, and how much Stark Industries got paid for it, I can't say.
Somebody cleared out these files a long time ago--over half of them are missing!
I'll keep digging, though. Pepper out.
TUSKA
CRAIG
KIRBY
LEIBER
STANE
8668N2414

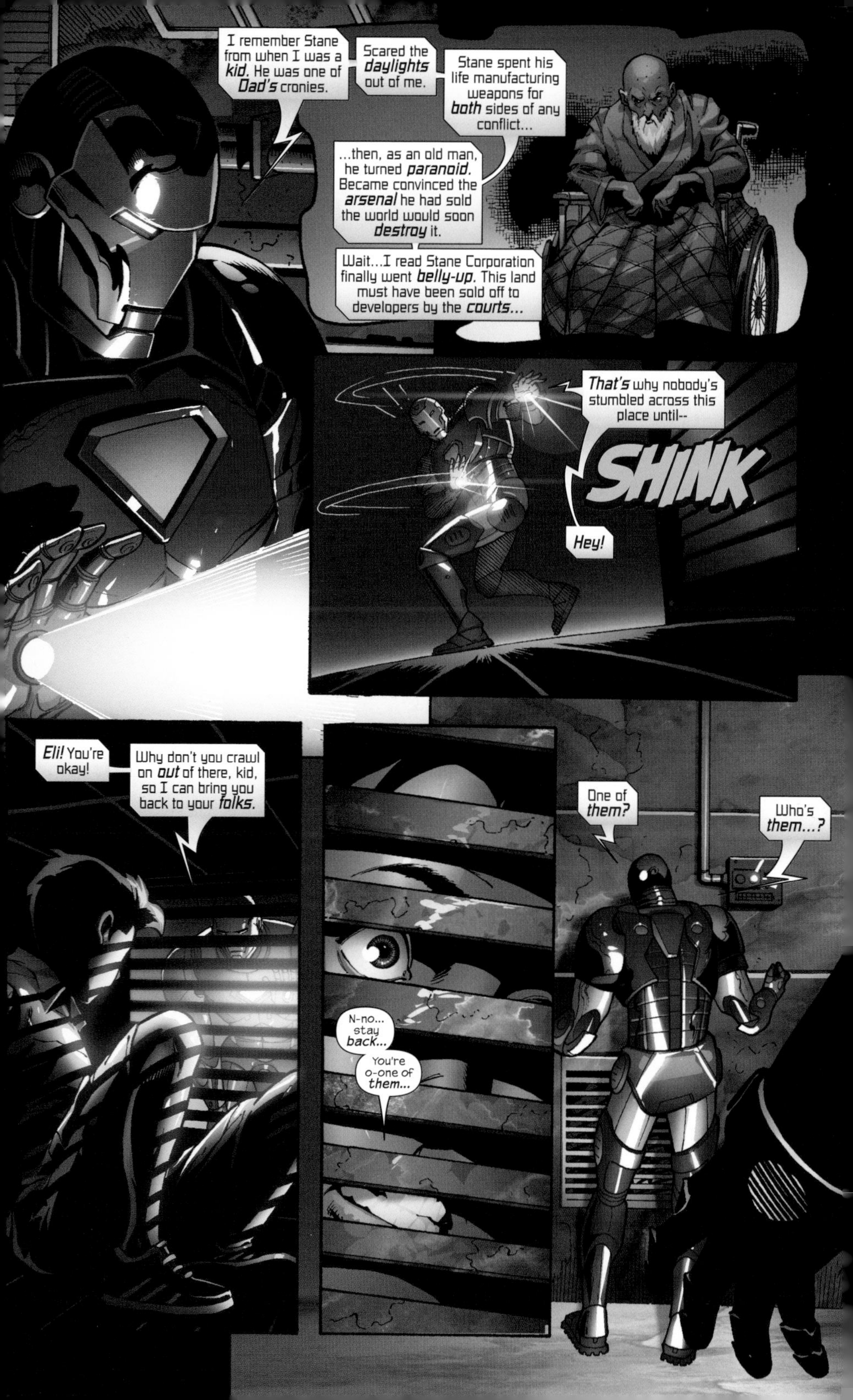

I remember Stane from when I was a kid. He was one of Dad's cronies.
Scared the daylights out of me.
Stane spent his life manufacturing weapons for both sides of any conflict...
...then, as an old man, he turned paranoid. Became convinced the arsenal he had sold the world would soon destroy it.
Wait...I read Stane Corporation finally went belly-up. This land must have been sold off to developers by the courts...
That's why nobody's stumbled across this place until--
SHINK
Hey!
Eli! You're okay!
Why don't you crawl on out of there, kid, so I can bring you back to your folks.
N-no... stay back...
You're o-one of them...
One of them?
Who's them...?

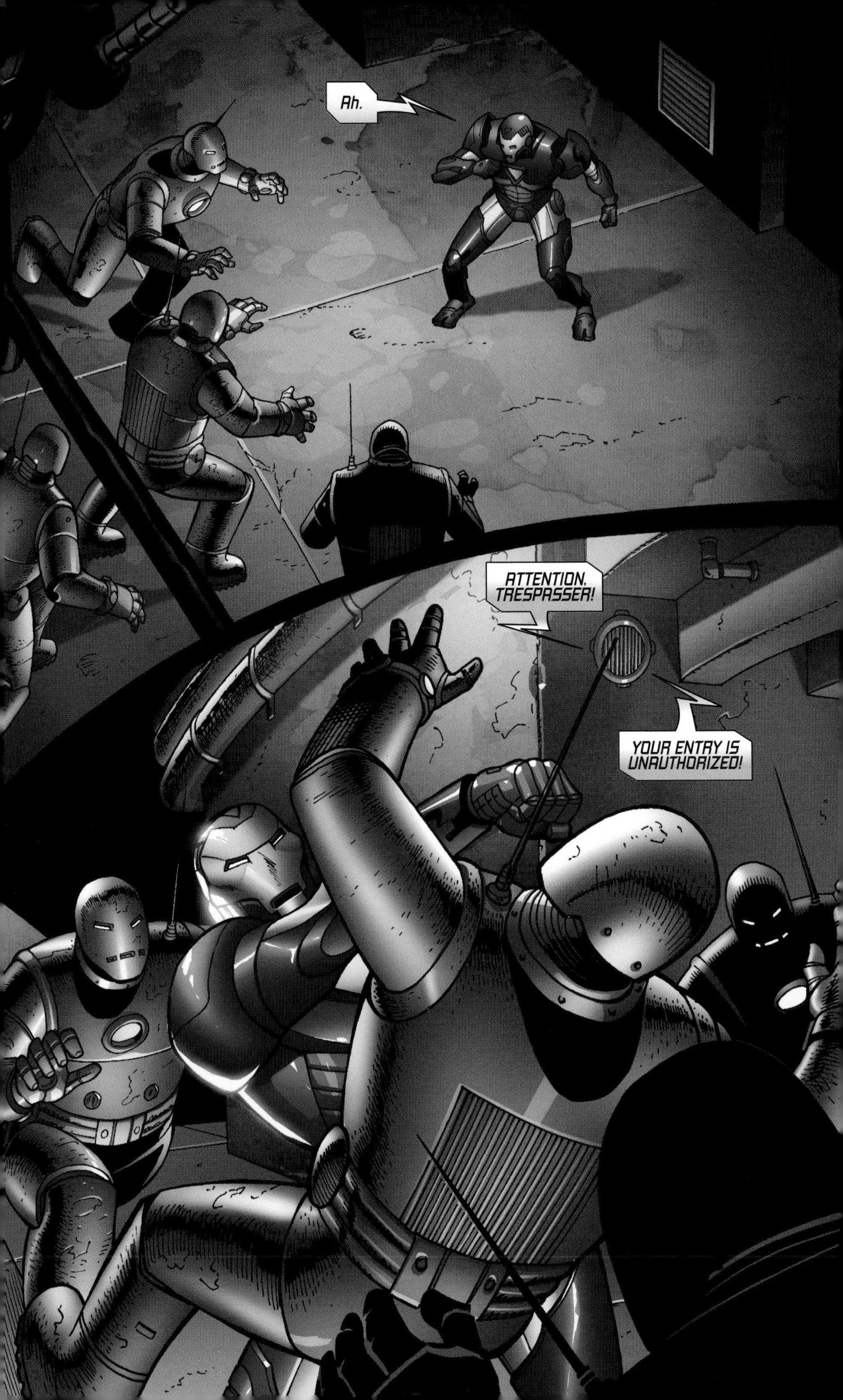
Ah.
ATTENTION, TRESPASSER!
YOUR ENTRY IS UNAUTHORIZED!

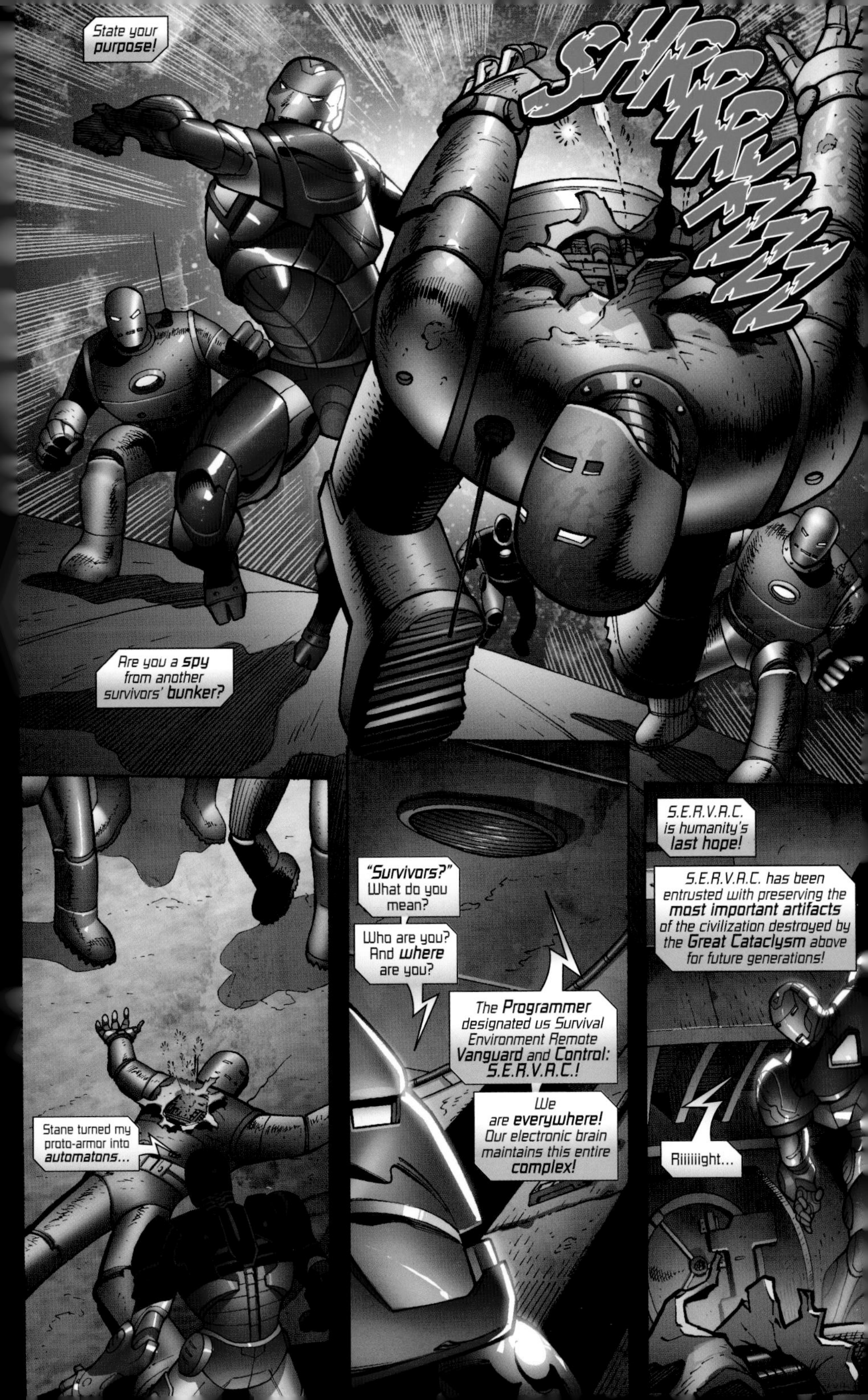
State your purpose!
SHRRRVAZZZ
Are you a spy from another survivors' bunker?
Stane turned my proto-armor into automatons...
"Survivors?" What do you mean?
Who are you? And where are you?
The Programmer designated us Survival Environment Remote Vanguard and Control: S.E.R.V.A.C.!
We are everywhere! Our electronic brain maintains this entire complex!
S.E.R.V.A.C. is humanity's last hope!
S.E.R.V.A.C. has been entrusted with preserving the most important artifacts of the civilization destroyed by the Great Cataclysm above for future generations!
Riiiiiight...

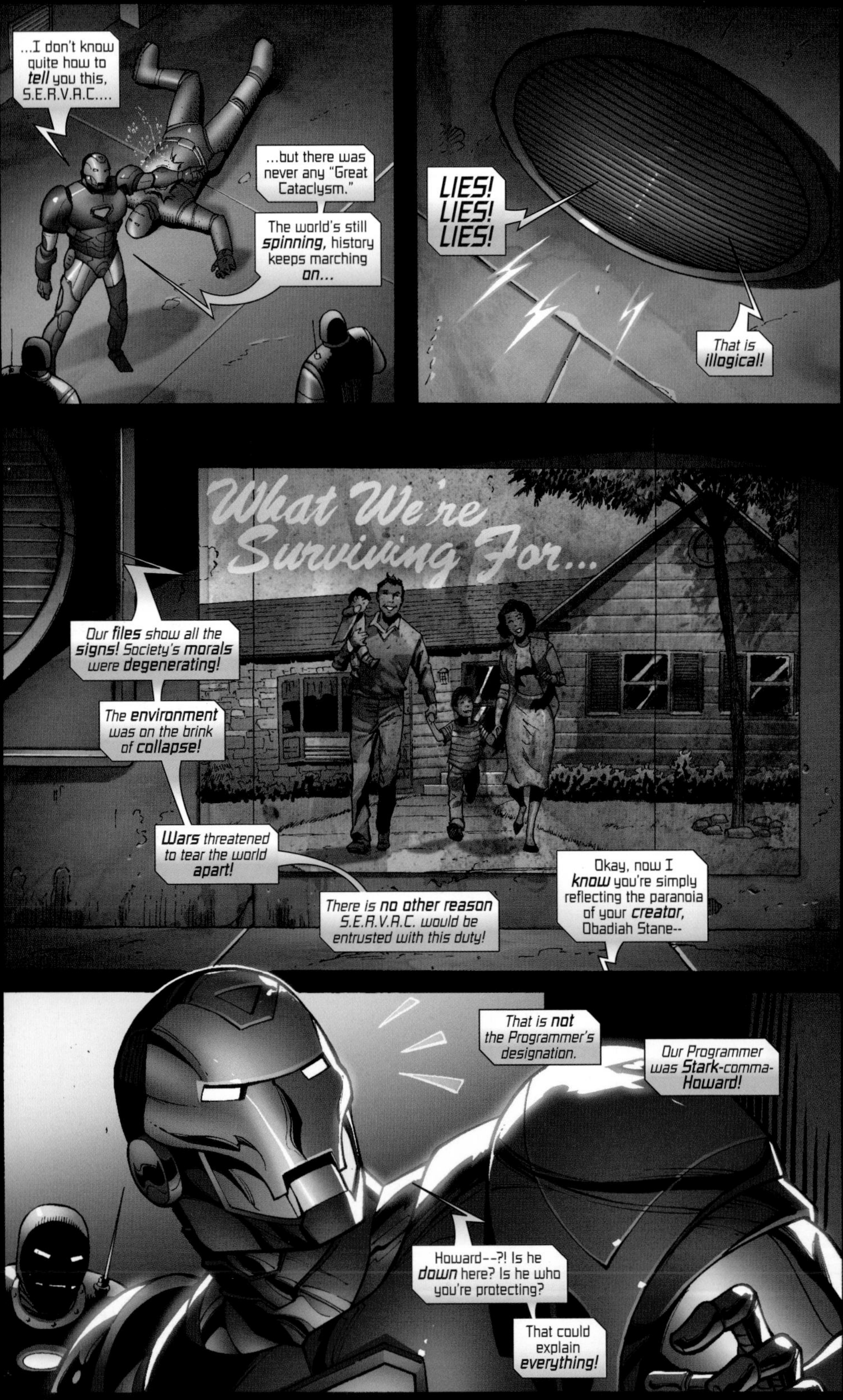
...I don't know quite how to tell you this, S.E.R.V.A.C....
...but there was never any "Great Cataclysm."
The world's still spinning, history keeps marching on...
LIES! LIES! LIES!
That is illogical!
What We're Surviving For...
Our files show all the signs! Society's morals were degenerating!
The environment was on the brink of collapse!
Wars threatened to tear the world apart!
There is no other reason S.E.R.V.A.C. would be entrusted with this duty!
Okay, now I know you're simply reflecting the paranoia of your creator, Obadiah Stane--
That is not the Programmer's designation.
Our Programmer was Stark-comma-Howard!
Howard--?! Is he down here? Is he who you're protecting?
That could explain everything!

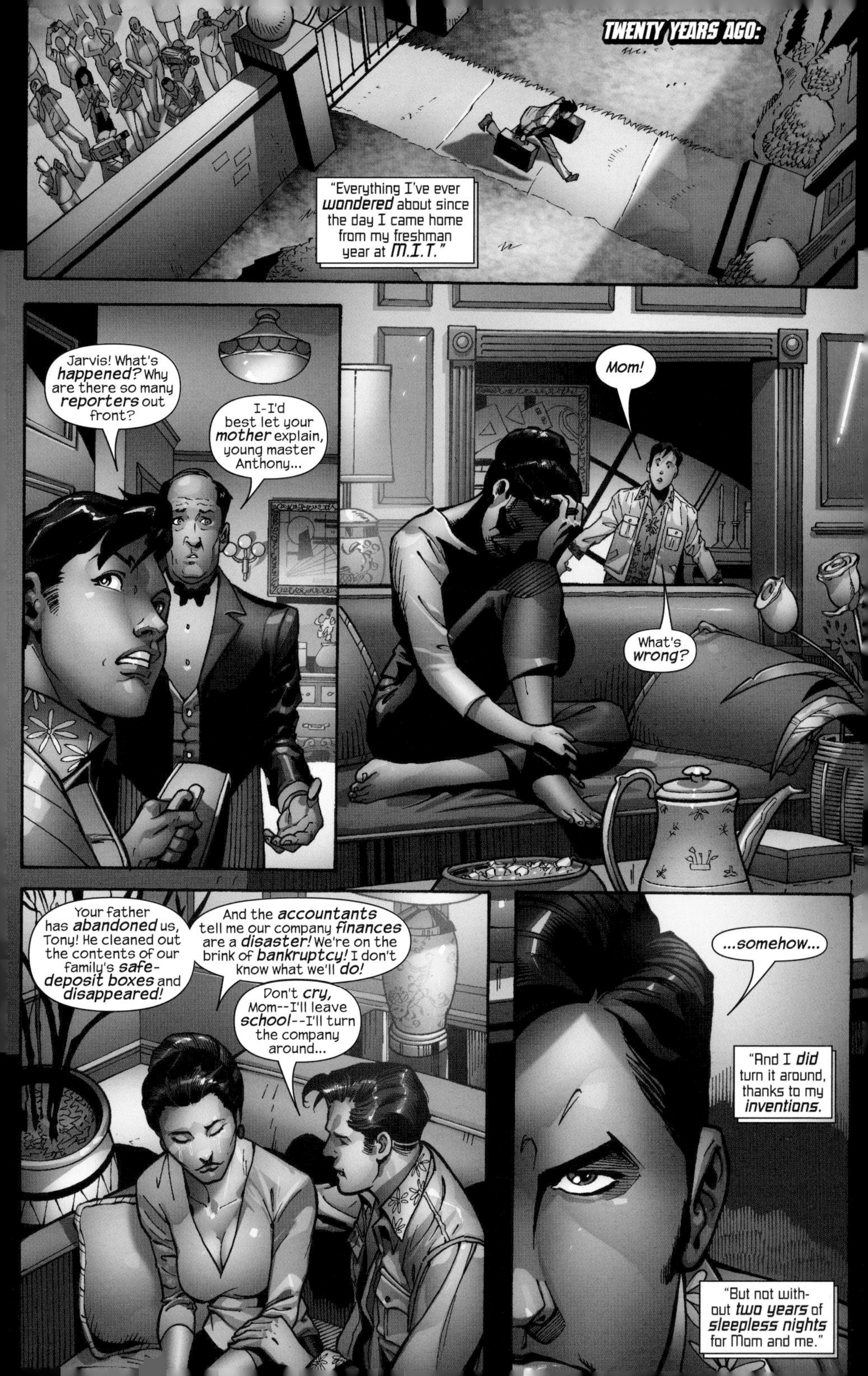
TWENTY YEARS AGO:
"Everything I've ever wondered about since the day I came home from my freshman year at M.I.T."
Jarvis! What's happened? Why are there so many reporters out front?
I-I'd best let your mother explain, young master Anthony...
Mom!
What's wrong?
Your father has abandoned us, Tony! He cleaned out the contents of our family's safe-deposit boxes and disappeared!
And the accountants tell me our company finances are a disaster! We're on the brink of bankruptcy! I don't know what we'll do!
Don't cry, Mom--I'll leave school--I'll turn the company around...
...somehow...
"And I did turn it around, thanks to my inventions.
"But not without two years of sleepless nights for Mom and me."

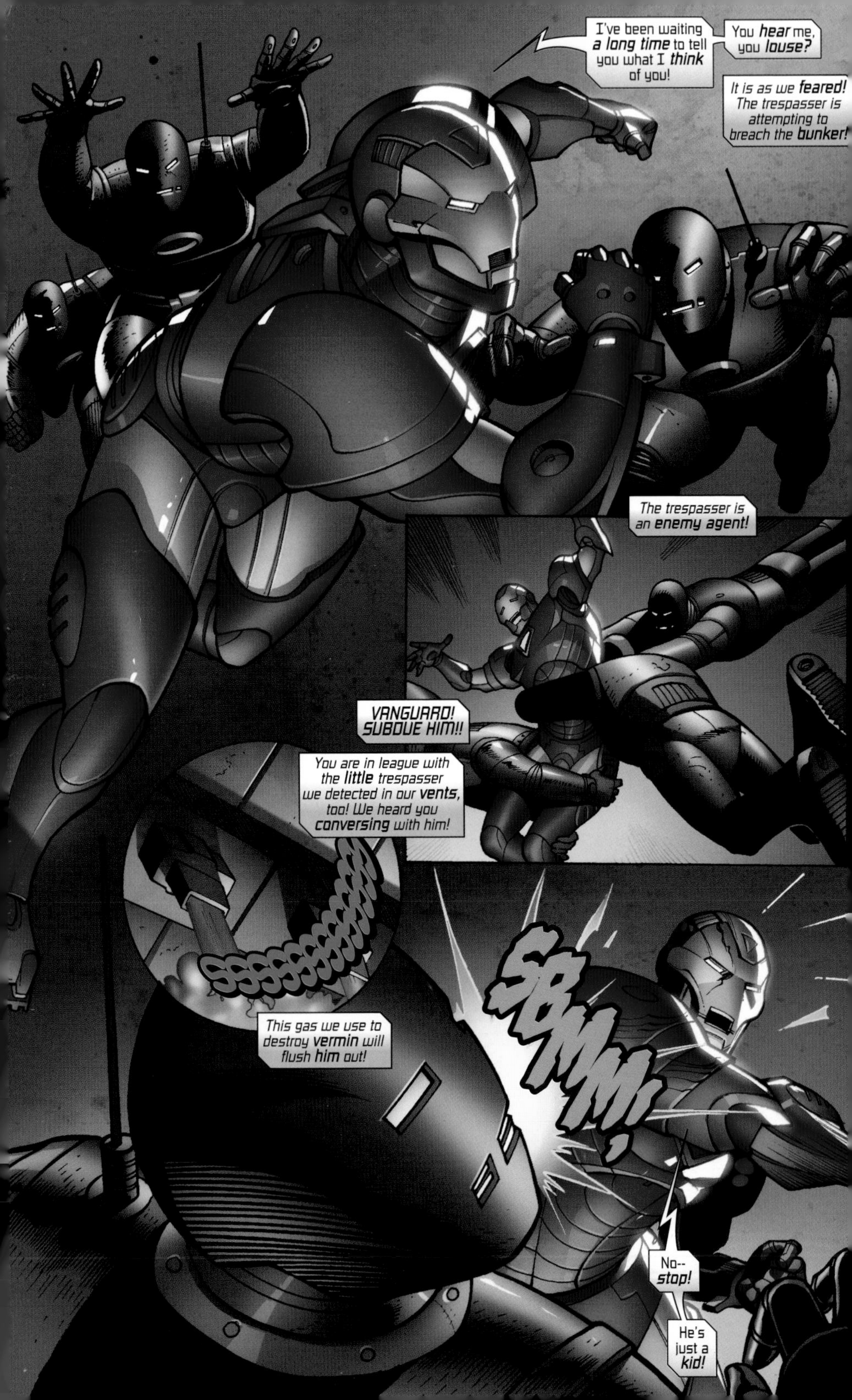
I've been waiting a long time to tell you what I think of you!
You hear me, you louse?
It is as we feared! The trespasser is attempting to breach the bunker!
The trespasser is an enemy agent!
VANGUARD! SUBDUE HIM!!
You are in league with the little trespasser we detected in our vents, too! We heard you conversing with him!
SSSSSSSSSSSSSSSSSS
This gas we use to destroy vermin will flush him out!
SBMM!
No-- stop!
He's just a kid!

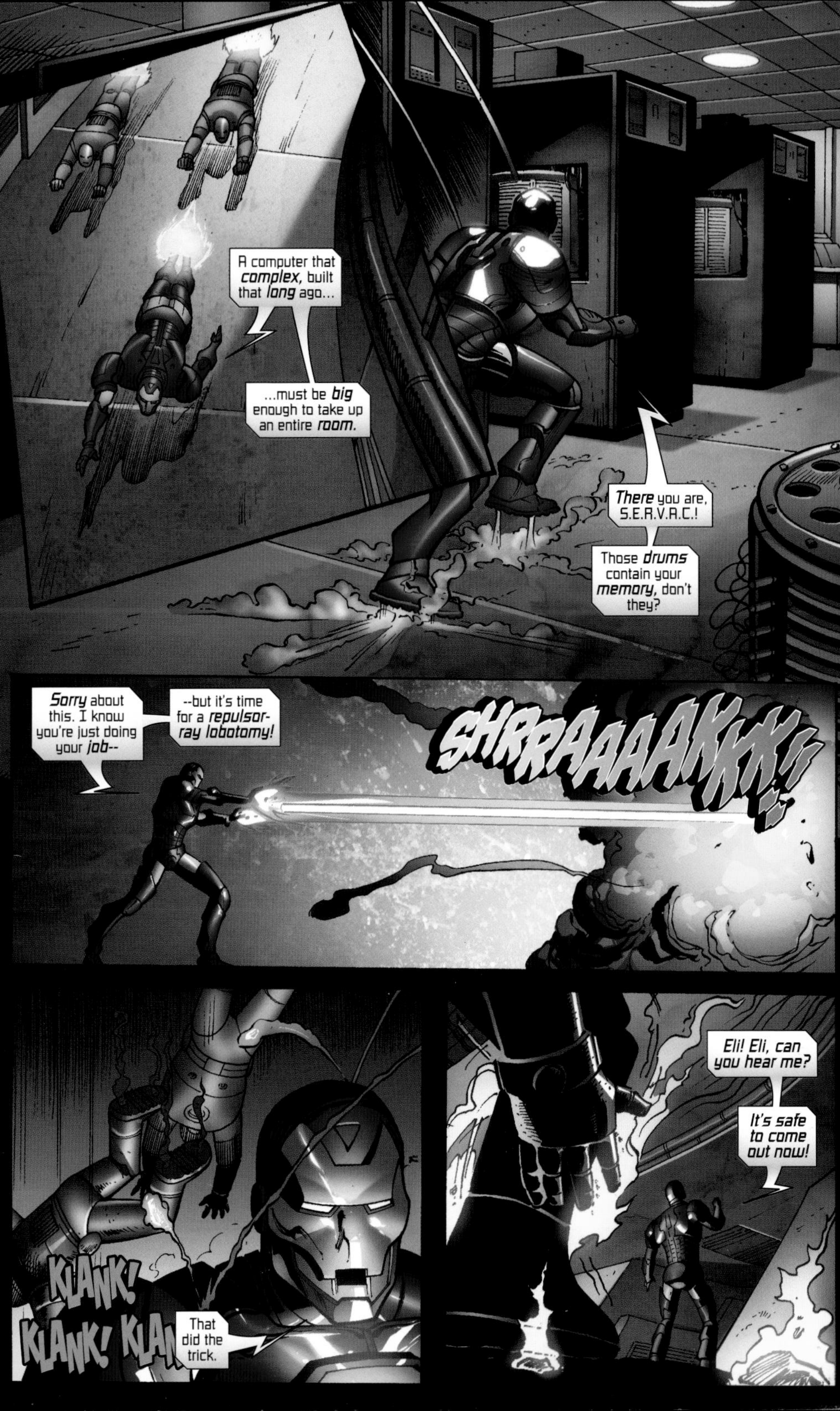

A computer that *complex,* built that *long* ago...
...must be *big* enough to take up an entire *room.*
There you are, S.E.R.V.A.C.!
Those *drums* contain your *memory,* don't they?
Sorry about this. I know you're just doing your *job*--
--but it's time for a *repulsor-ray lobotomy!*
SHRRAAAAKKK!!
KLANK! KLANK! KLAN
That did the trick.
Eli! Eli, can you hear me?
It's safe to come out now!

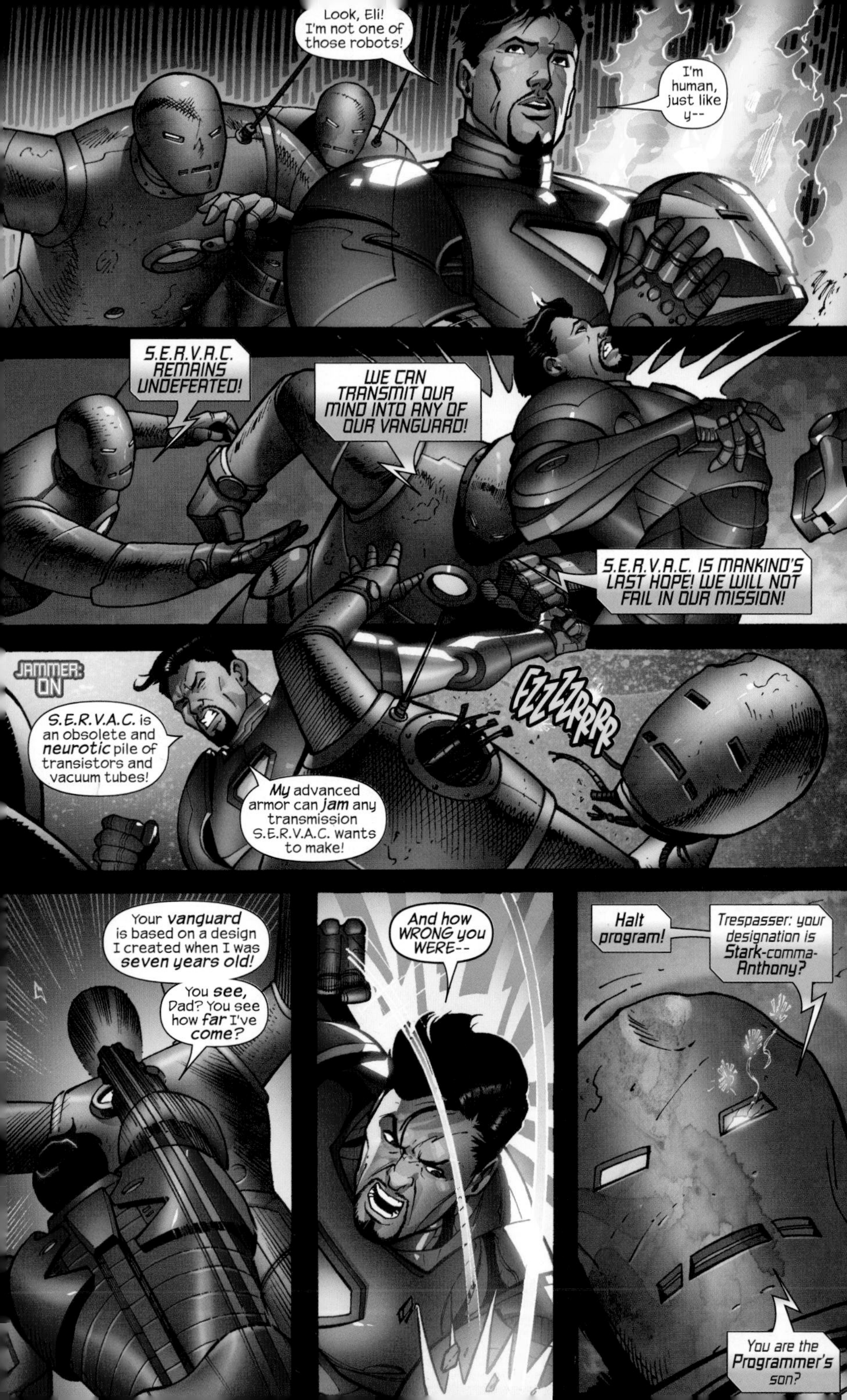
Look, Eli! I'm not one of those robots!
I'm human, just like y--
S.E.R.V.A.C. REMAINS UNDEFEATED!
WE CAN TRANSMIT OUR MIND INTO ANY OF OUR VANGUARD!
S.E.R.V.A.C. IS MANKIND'S LAST HOPE! WE WILL NOT FAIL IN OUR MISSION!
JAMMER: ON
S.E.R.V.A.C. is an obsolete and neurotic pile of transistors and vacuum tubes!
My advanced armor can jam any transmission S.E.R.V.A.C. wants to make!
FZZZZRRRR
Your vanguard is based on a design I created when I was seven years old!
You see, Dad? You see how far I've come?
And how WRONG you WERE--
Halt program!
Trespasser: your designation is Stark-comma-Anthony?
You are the Programmer's son?

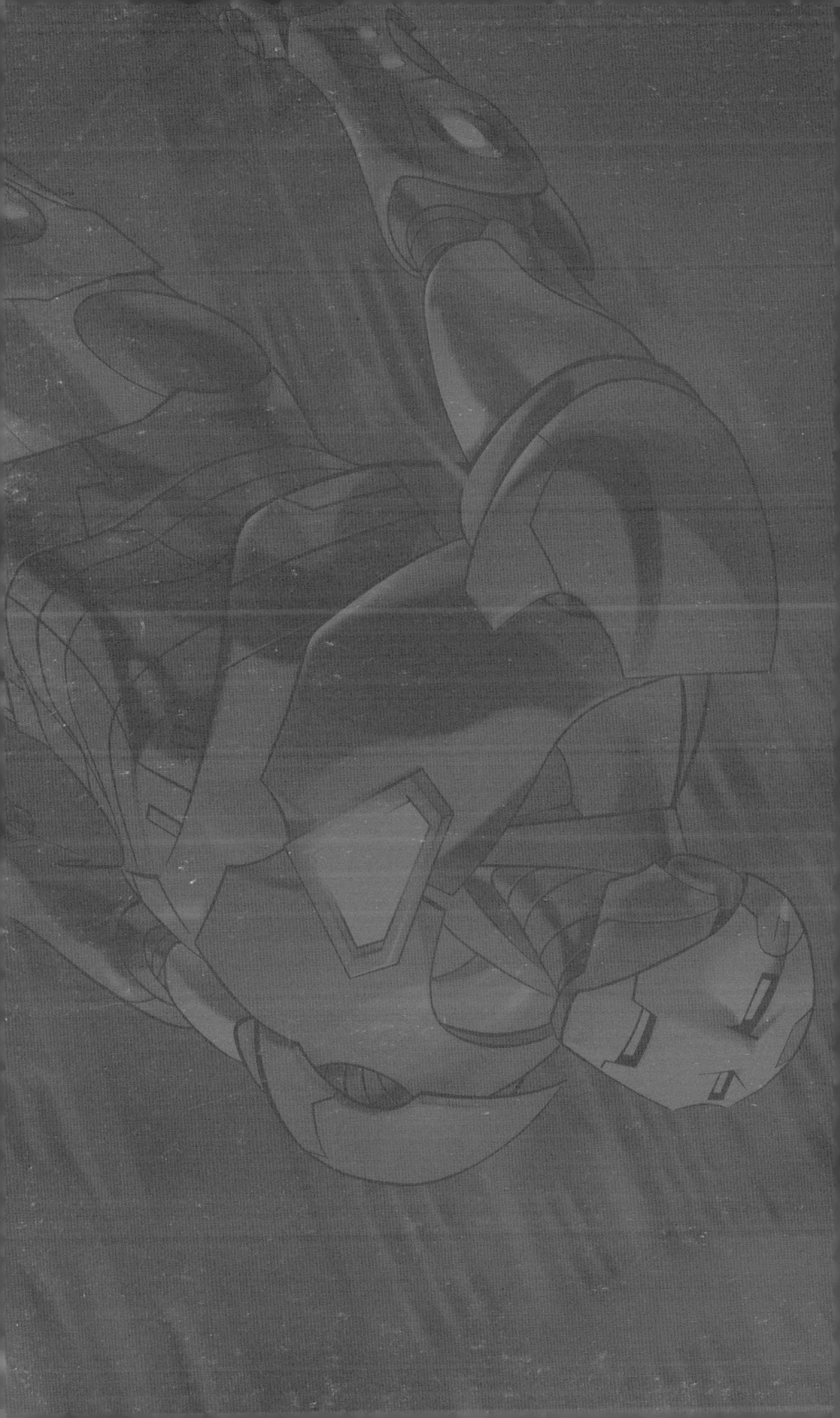

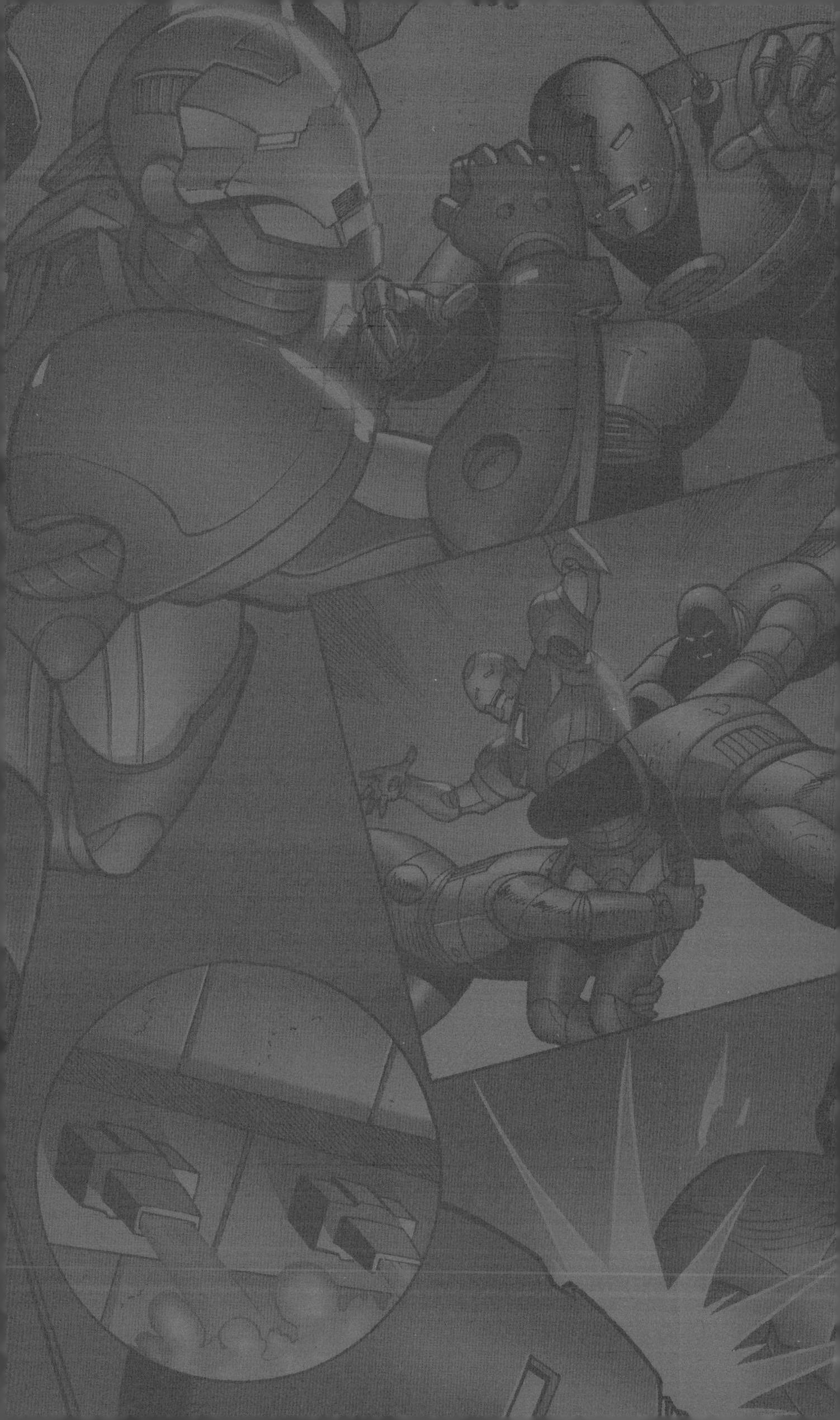

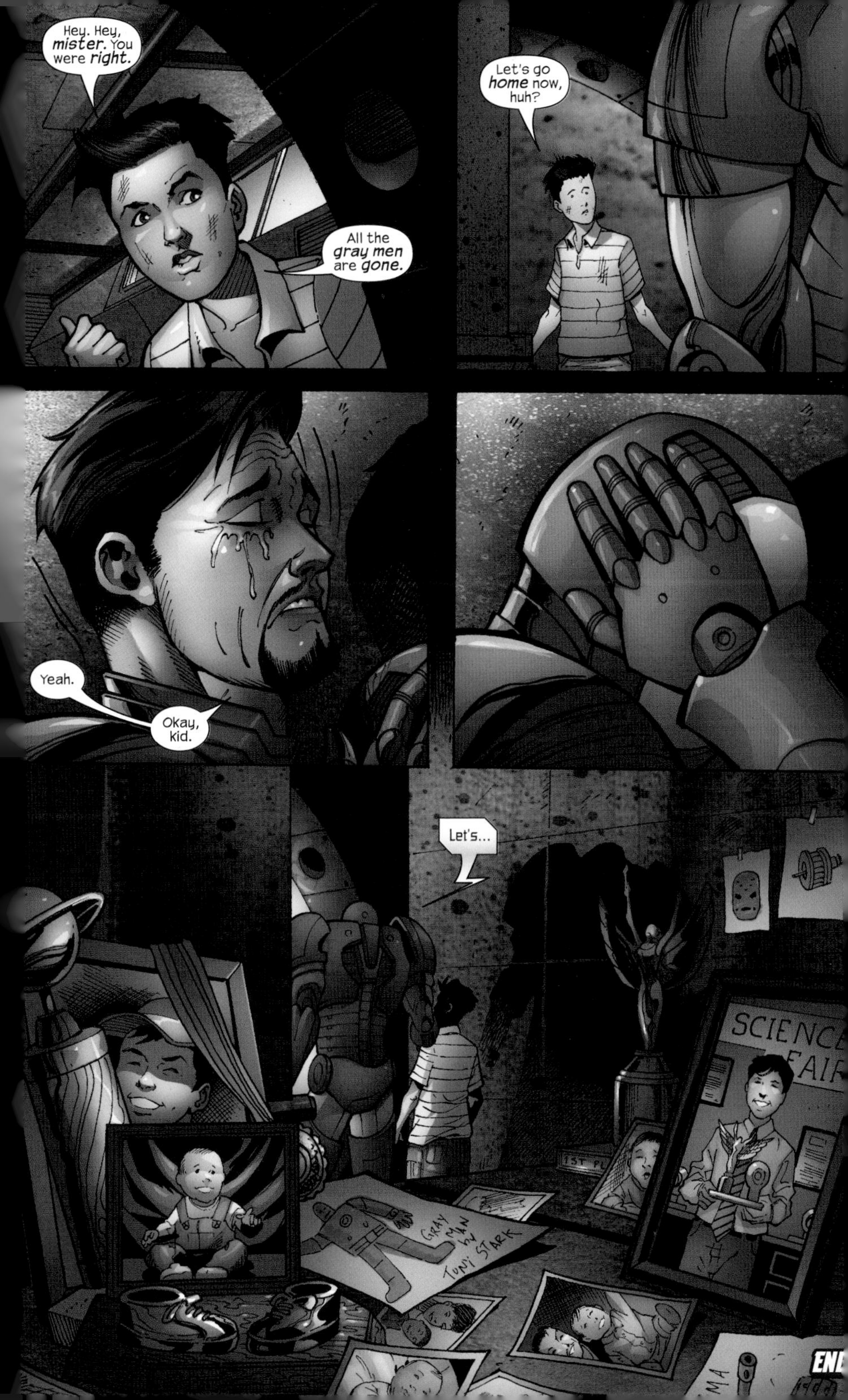
Hey. Hey, *mister.* You were *right.*
All the *gray men* are *gone.*
Let's go *home* now, huh?
Yeah.
Okay, kid.
Let's...
GRAY MAN by TONY STARK

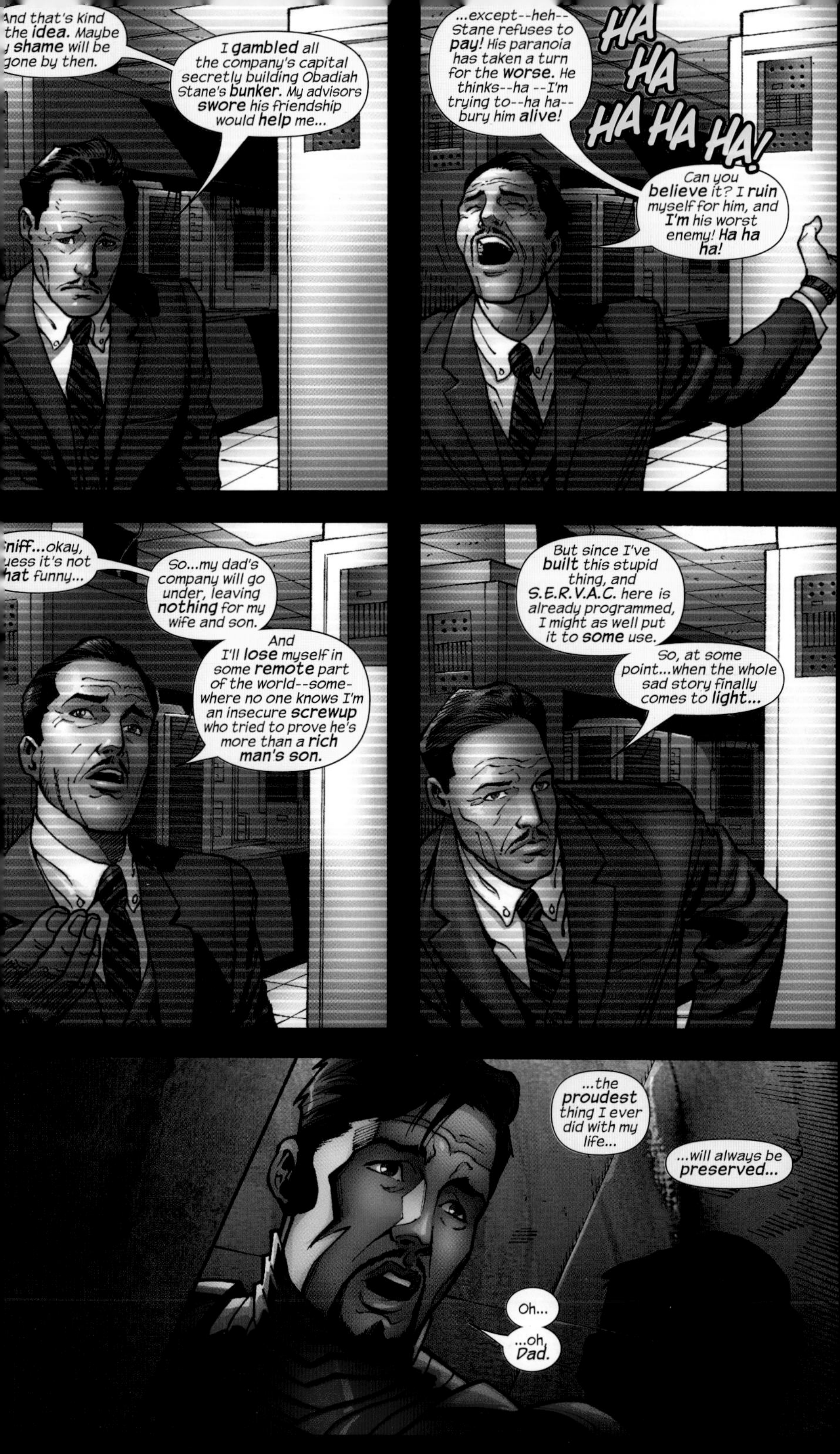

nd that's kind the idea. Maybe shame will be gone by then.
I gambled all the company's capital secretly building Obadiah Stane's bunker. My advisors swore his friendship would help me...
...except--heh--Stane refuses to pay! His paranoia has taken a turn for the worse. He thinks--ha --I'm trying to--ha ha--bury him alive!
HA HA HA HA HA!
Can you believe it? I ruin myself for him, and I'm his worst enemy! Ha ha ha!
niff...okay, uess it's not hat funny...
So...my dad's company will go under, leaving nothing for my wife and son.
And I'll lose myself in some remote part of the world--somewhere no one knows I'm an insecure screwup who tried to prove he's more than a rich man's son.
But since I've built this stupid thing, and S.E.R.V.A.C. here is already programmed, I might as well put it to some use.
So, at some point...when the whole sad story finally comes to light...
...the proudest thing I ever did with my life...
...will always be preserved...
Oh...
...oh, Dad.

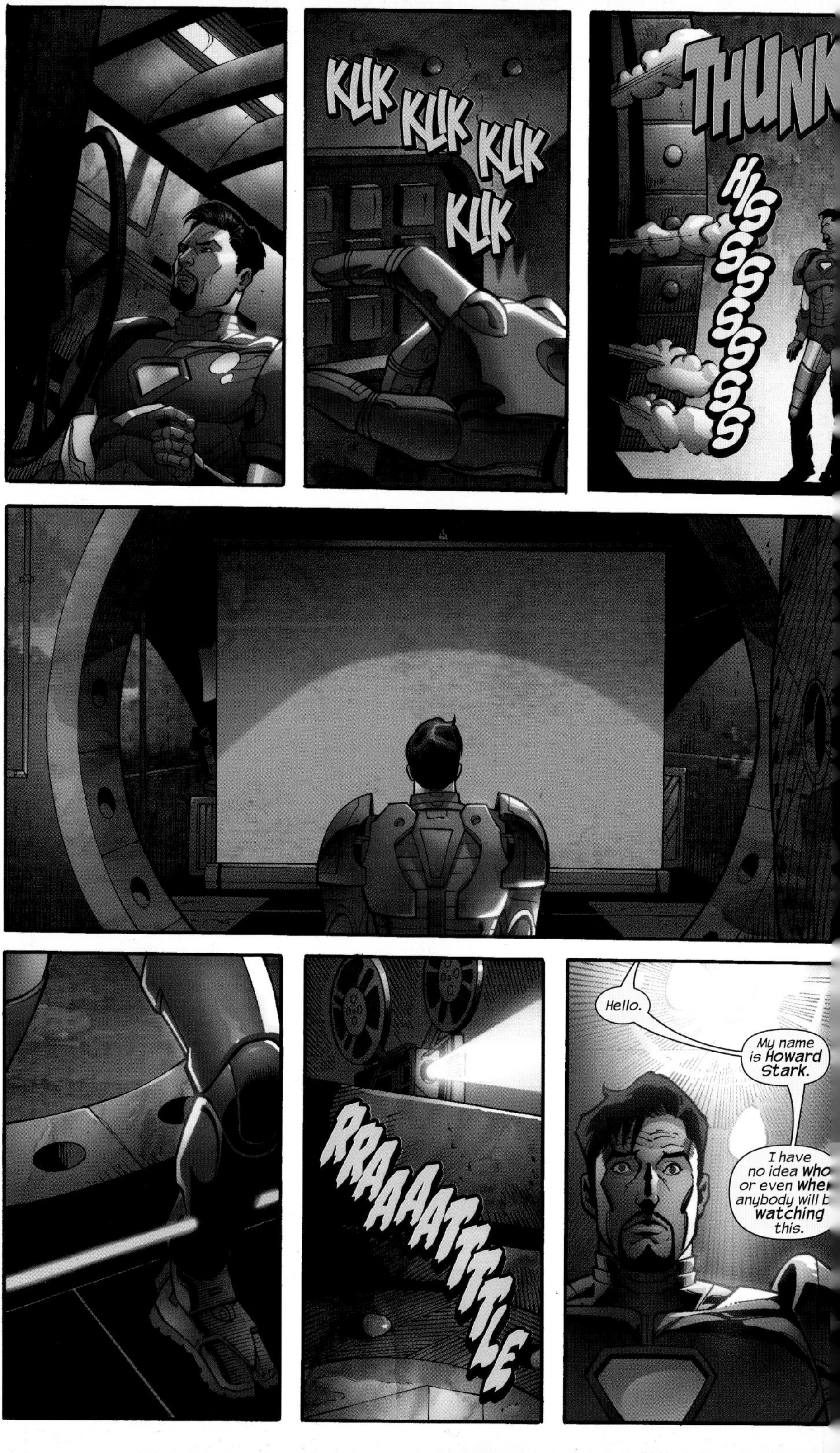
KLIK KLIK KLIK
KLIK
THUNK
HISSSSSSS
RRAAAATTTTLE
Hello.
My name is Howard Stark.
I have no idea who or even when anybody will be watching this.

I... *am.*

You are the one S.E.R.V.A.C. has been programmed to *wait* for!

S.E.R.V.A.C. has kept the contents of the *bunker* safe for you!

TIC TIC TIC
TIC TIC
TIC TIC

37267

This *combination* will unlock the vault door!

We have *fulfilled* our mission.

Now... tell the *truth,* Stark-comma-Anthony.

The truth about *Outside.* We must know.

Yes... you were *right.* Outside--it's a *wasteland.*

Mankind *destroyed* itself. I don't know how I managed to last so long.

There'd be no *hope...*

...no hope without *you,* S.E.R.V.A.C. On behalf of *humanity...* ...I *thank* you.

We *knew* it. We *knew* we would not be sent down here...

...for no reason...

*

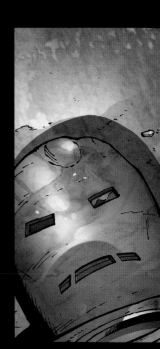